A Time
for
Everything

by

Mysti Parker

PUBLISHED BY:
Mysti Parker

A Time for Everything
Copyright © 2019 Mysti Parker
Second Printing
First Printing, 2015
Edited by: Kim Bowman
Cover design by: For the Muse Designs

Print Edition, License Notes

Dedication

To the men, women and children who suffered and died to knit our divided country back together.

$\mathcal{T}$able of $\mathcal{C}$ontents

Prologue

Brentwood, Tennessee — December 25, 1865

The angels are coming.

Portia lay on the frozen ground between her husband and daughter. Snow fluttered softly toward the earth in delicate flakes, each one melting on her face with a pleasant sting. She wouldn't have to wait much longer.

The sunrise, hidden by snow-laden clouds, gradually lit the gray sky. With numb fingers, she traced her husband's name, carved into the stoic slate. *Jake McAllister*, but let her hand drop to the ground before she touched that wretched date. *December 16, 1864* — the day her whole world began to fall apart.

It had been a day as cold as this one when Jake returned. Portia had stood on their porch, holding Abigail, both of them wrapped in shawls and a quilt. Yet the cold had managed to seep inside, wrapping icy fingers around her heart. Her husband lay lifeless in the back of a wagon. His once-rosy face had turned ashen. Blood caked his Confederate jacket. His hands, large and strong, yet once so gentle, were posed across his belly. His fingers were stiff and claw-like, wrapped around a phantom gun. He did not look like Jake. It had to have been a mannequin with a wig the same dusty red shade of his hair.

"That's not him," she'd repeated to the men who'd so methodically carried him into the house. Jake would pop out from somewhere, still the jokester he had always been, and she would slap him for playing such a cruel prank. Then she would laugh with him and hold him tight because he had finally returned to her and Abby.

But the longer her eyes absorbed the wretched sight, the more evidence she had discovered. Little freckles and scars she knew so well. The pea-sized patch on his jaw where his beard never grew. The missing end of his middle finger, taken by a vicious dog when they were children.

It wasn't a joke. Jake was dead.

She would never again feel the comfort of his arms around her, the warmth of his skin against hers, the precious nights only the two of them had shared. She would never again see him toss their giggling daughter into the air, hear his hearty laughter in return, or sit with him hand in hand on their front porch, listening to the katydids and tree frogs sing.

The December wind whistled across the ground and reminded her of the bitter truth. The only man she had ever loved now lay cold and dead under six feet of dirt.

Portia stared up at the swollen clouds rolling above the cemetery. Snow clung to her eyelashes. She blinked it away and touched Abby's stone. *Abigail E. McAllister — Born Feb 12, 1863 Died Aug 19, 1865.* The ground before it had not yet settled and still formed a small dome above her daughter's coffin. Brown winter grass and dirt peeked beneath the thickening layer of white.

Since that hot and hellish day in August, not a minute passed that she didn't recall every moment of her baby's death. Even now, as the cold pumped along her veins and turned her consciousness to ice, her final hours with Abby charged through her mind in vivid detail.

For weeks, Abby had deteriorated. Everything Portia had tried to feed her, typhoid had thrown back out. On that final day, her body had jerked with one spasm after another, each one more agonizing than the one before.

Portia rocked her baby and kissed her flushed, clammy cheeks. *"Please, please don't take her. You took my husband. Please don't take my baby. I'll do anything. Please, please, God..."*

Abby's eyes, when she could open them, begged for mercy. Within their hazel depths were supplications her two-year-old mouth couldn't speak.

Why is this happening to me?

Why won't you help me?

I'm scared...

She drew in a shallow breath, and whispered her last word. *"Mama."*

"I'm so sorry, Abby. Mama's so sorry!"

Her hazel eyes, once so bright and happy and curious, turned dull as her soul fled its broken vessel, dragging memories of her short life with it.

"Did you feel that, Jake? The baby kicked!"... "Just one more push. You can do it."... "It's a girl!"... "Abigail Ellen

9

McAllister — I think it has a nice ring to it, don't you?"…
"You, me, and our baby girl — we're a family now, Po."

And then she was gone, just like Jake.

Days and weeks had passed. Fall came and went. The sun rose and set, while the world kept spinning. Portia kept breathing somehow, kept going through the motions of life when she wanted no part of it.

Until this morning, when she woke with a plan.

The death angels had been surreptitious, plucking first Jake, then Abby from her life, ignoring her pleas to let her join them. They would not ignore her now. The burning cold had already rendered her numb through the thin barrier of her nightgown.

She no longer shivered but closed her eyes and smiled at the heavenly realms. Any time now, the angels would carry her home. On Christmas morning, no less. Every sound and sensation around her faded into peaceful silence… until she woke up, wrapped in a quilt, lying at the foot of a blazing, familiar hearth. Her best friend Ellen attacked the logs with an iron poker, sending orange sparks on a flight up the chimney.

Ellen's husband, Frank, leaned over her. "I promised my little brother I would take care of you. I plan on keeping that promise."

Tears stung her cold-burned cheeks. The angels would have to wait.

Chapter One

April 6, 1866

Worn and wrinkled from her constant handling, Portia picked up the paper and read it for the hundredth time:

Feb. 15, 1866 — Housekeeper and Tutor Needed
Apply If Interested to Mr. Beauregard Stanford
101 Stanford Lane, Lebanon, Tennessee

Frank and Ellen would be there any moment to pick up the few belongings she was taking. The surveyors were out there now, with their compasses and chains, ready to turn her land into profit. Tobacco was all the rage. Those with the means were snatching up land as quick as they could from abandoned plantations and those who needed money. Some of that money was now tucked into an envelope, ready to be given to Frank and Ellen, minus a little Portia had kept for herself. It was the least she could do for them so they could stay where they belonged. Whoever was now king of everything in Brentwood had demanded tribute from the Confederate sympathizers who wished to remain.

But she would *not* remain there, where memories lurked in the shadows and lingered on every surface. The emptiness — that horrible hollow ache within her chest — had not subsided since Jake and Abby died. Suicide sang a tempting song in her head every day, but she didn't want her death hanging over Frank's head. He had enough to worry about.

Since her conscience wouldn't let her end her own life, and since they needed the money more than she did, she had to say goodbye.

Frank came bursting in like he always did, along with a draft of fresh spring air that helped to dispel the gloom. He was a big bear of a man who reminded Portia a lot of Jake, though Jake had been scrawny compared to his older brother. She used to joke that Frank should stop putting his mule to work when he could just strap the plow to himself to work the fields.

"I guess you're ready," he said in that quick, gruff way he had when he wasn't particularly happy about something.

"Yes." Unexpected tears welled in her eyes, even though she had promised herself they wouldn't.

Not paying any heed to her emotional state, he spied her bag on the floor and yanked it up like it weighed nothing. Seven-year-old Jimmy stepped inside, and Frank tossed the bag to him. The boy was a spitting image of Jake at that age. He slumped under the bag's weight but managed to drag it out to the front porch. Frank grabbed the worn-out cedar chest and tucked it under his arm. He frowned and strode out, letting the screen door slam behind him.

Ellen came in next, holding little Louise on her left hip.

"It's not too late to change your mind, Po." Her eyes were puffy and red and had been in that state ever since Portia made her decision. She rubbed her pregnant belly and held a crumpled handkerchief in her fist.

"We've already talked about this." Portia couldn't keep from touching her own belly, now flat and plain as though Abigail had never thrived and tumbled in it at all. She hugged a small patchwork bag to her bosom. It held nothing practical, just things that mattered only to her, like Abby's baby spoon, some letters from Jake and one of his old shirts.

"Stay with us. We've got room."

Her imminent departure proved to be much harder than she had thought. But Portia reminded herself of this past winter, when Ellen had sacrificed her own supper just to keep her fed. She had to go — she wouldn't be a burden to them any longer.

"I can't. I just… can't."

Louise started crying, too. "Pwease, Aunt Po, don't weave us."

"I'm sorry, baby, but I have to." Portia swallowed past the stubborn knot in her throat and kissed Louise's chubby wet cheek.

Portia moved toward the door before she made a trio out of their crying duet. The morning sun haloed the gravestones across the road.

She tried to sound reassuring, but her voice fell flat and dull. "Lebanon's not that far. I'll visit soon as I can."

Ellen followed, taking Portia's hand in a strong, shaky grip. The freckles on her cheeks danced along with the quivering of her chin. "But you don't even know these people. How do you know you'll be all right?"

"I don't. But I need to get away. There's been enough sadness around here, and I've cried about all I can cry. It doesn't do Jake's or Abigail's memory justice to keep living like this."

"What about Samuel? We can try to find him."

"I don't expect we'll ever hear from my little brother again. If he's not dead, he's being held captive by some voodoo lady in New Orleans... according to his last letter."

"Po!"

"Well, it's true. He said he was going to marry that Creole woman and bring her back home. But he didn't. He missed my wedding and never saw his niece. I even wrote to him when Abby died and never got an answer. What would you suppose I do? Head to New Orleans and roam the streets, calling for him? He's either dead or... who knows? I'd rather take my chances in Lebanon."

Ellen dabbed her eyes. "You've never been farther than Nashville, Po. Aren't you scared?"

"Yes, I'm scared. But I can't live my whole life in fear. I'm twenty-five. If I want to start living again, I need to get to it."

She couldn't let fear and doubt keep her here in this stagnant place between emptiness and what might have been. So she hurried to the wagon, where Frank offered a hand to help her up. Settling into the seat, she tried to ignore Ellen's sobbing but feared her dear friend might lose her breath or drop Louise.

Portia reached down and rubbed Ellen's cheek. "I'll be fine. Don't you worry about me. Take care of Frank and the children and that little one who'll be here soon. I'll write, I promise."

"All right, just be careful. If they're the least bit ornery, you get back here!" Ellen attempted a smile and cleaned Louise's nose with a forceful swipe of her handkerchief.

Before another word could be said, Portia took the bulging envelope from her bag. She handed it to Ellen, who looked at it as though something might jump out and bite her.

"Take it," Portia said. "It's enough to pay your taxes and to buy some material and thread, maybe even some good coffee for a change."

Guilt and need sparred for dominance in Ellen's eyes, until she let out a sigh and took the envelope. She took a step back and looked toward the fields where a long-legged surveyor repositioned his tripod.

Frank climbed in the wagon and stared straight ahead. Portia didn't have to ask to know exactly what he was thinking. Though he would never say much about it, he felt responsible for his brother's widow and thought himself a failure because of her departure. Out of all of them, Frank's guilt weighed on her most. After Jake left to fight, he had worked twice as hard to keep them all fed, avoiding the call to duty only because he was blind in one eye. Every day since, the worry lines on his face dug deeper, while the hair on his head turned grayer.

All because he wanted to provide for his family and to take care of his little brother's wife, whom he loved like a sister.

He flicked the reins and the mules pulled them along. It was warm for early April, so Portia left the blanket folded up between them. The wagon rattled down the drive, but she couldn't help herself and took one last look at the house. It wasn't much more than an unpainted clapboard shack with sagging eaves and a crooked porch. But Jake had built it with his own two hands and it had been Portia's whole world for the past seven years. The most joyful days of her life had happened in and around that little house. She held no hope of ever finding such joy again and forced herself to focus on the road ahead.

They passed the small family graveyard where soft green grass covered Abby's plot. By the gate, a few crocuses poked their purple heads above the ground, blooming amidst the emerging yellow daffodils. Portia wished the lilies were in bloom so she could put some on the graves. She decided to come back this summer and do just that.

Frank broke the silence. "It ain't right. You ought to stay with your family."

She figured a remark like that was coming, but at least he was finally talking. "You don't need another mouth to feed."

"Po, you're skinny as a rail. It ain't like you eat much."

Uncertain how to answer him, she watched the fence posts go by and let her mind wander to Lebanon and the life awaiting her there. She'd answered the ad, not thinking she really had a chance at the position, but a letter had returned a month later, asking her to arrive as soon as possible. The Stanfords owned a horse farm, and the lady of the house had died, leaving a ten-year-old son in need of a tutor. She'd grown up with two brothers and taught school for a while before getting married, so she knew how to handle herself around boys. Hopefully, she and her new student would take to each other all right.

Miles passed along the dusty road toward Nashville. Rectangular plots topped with damp soil and new, tender grass filled every graveyard they passed. Frank remained silent until they pulled up to an inn just inside the city at dusk. He helped her down and carried her bag as they walked inside.

"Just tell 'em we're married, should they ask," he whispered.

Frank paid the innkeeper, and Portia was relieved when he didn't question their relationship. They both wore wedding rings, after all, though they were tarnished old things handed down from generations past.

He carried the bag to the room on the second floor, and Portia followed. Perching herself on the edge of the bed, she waited as he went back downstairs to retrieve the chest. She had never stayed at a hotel of any sort, but it wasn't as exotic as she had imagined. The small room was clean and warm, practically furnished like any bedroom in a modest home.

Mr. Stanford's business partner, Harry Franklin, was to fetch her at six in the morning to take her to Lebanon. They needed a good night's rest, though Portia figured sleep wouldn't come easy.

When Frank returned, he unwrapped some warm fried chicken and biscuits. The aroma set Portia's stomach rumbling.

"You didn't have to buy me supper," she said, thinking none too fondly about the cold hoecakes in her bag.

"It came with the room fee. Now eat up."

He was lying, of course, but she smiled and did as she was told.

After they ate, Frank made himself a pallet on the floor, while Portia took the bed. They both still wore the clothes they arrived in. She would have protested about sleeping in the same room, except the thought of being alone in a strange place drove her to near panic, and Frank had his pistol.

Portia awoke to Frank's gentle nudging. She'd barely slept, having tossed and turned most of the night on the strange mattress with its unfamiliar lumps and creaks. They took turns washing their hands and faces at the basin. Yawning, she arranged her hair into a loose bun and they headed downstairs. The dining room was mostly empty except for another couple at a corner table. She and Frank claimed a spot near the kitchen, where the smell of coffee and hotcakes made her mouth water.

Frank chuckled as she licked her lips.

"Told you I'm just another hungry mouth to feed," she said.

"I don't know where you put it, unless your legs are hollow. But you still oughta give us a chance."

"You're a good man, you know. Jake thought you hung the moon."

He held Portia's gaze for a moment before waving the innkeeper's wife over. He spent his last few coins on a big stack of hotcakes, bacon, and two cups of coffee. They didn't speak at all until they had eaten every last crumb from their plates.

She had just placed her napkin on the empty plate when a black man entered the room. He wore gray checked trousers, a white buttoned shirt, and black vest. A black felt hat, faded and ragged around the rim, sat cockeyed on his head. He looked around as if searching for someone else, but the other couple had already gone, leaving Frank and Portia as the only candidates for attention. He flashed them a broad white smile.

"Good mornin, good mornin." The man removed his hat and tucked it under his arm as he reached their table. Gray tinged his sideburns and wrinkles creased the corners of his eyes. "I'm Isaac Carter, and I'm lookin' for a Portia McAllister."

Portia wiped her mouth and stood. "I'm Portia. And this is my brother-in-law, Frank... but we were expecting—"

"Mr. Franklin," Isaac said, nodding. "He had to run an errand here in town, so he asked me to come in and fetch you."

Hand hovering near his belt, Frank stood too, eyeing the man like he might rob them at any moment. She cast him a glance he didn't notice.

"Sorry if I spooked ya," Isaac said, still smiling. "Good to meet ya, ma'am, and you too, sir."

Portia liked him immediately. "It's nice to meet you, Mr. Carter."

She nudged Frank, who relaxed a little and dropped his hand to his side.

"I think you's a bit younger than Mr. Beau expected, but that's all right. Can I carry your bags for ya?"

"You can carry the chest," Frank said.

"Yes, sir."

The men carried Portia's belongings outside to a black buggy hitched to two sleek horses that were so dark brown they were almost black. The closest thing to horses she and Jake had owned were mules, and they weren't nearly as pleasant to look at. While Frank helped her up to the rear seat, Isaac took his place ahead of her in the driver's seat. He took a rifle from the floorboard and set it on his lap.

Frank glanced at Isaac and motioned her to lean close so he could whisper in her ear. "I don't like this, Po, you ridin' off alone with this colored man and this Mr. Franklin fella."

"I'll be fine."

"Well, I don't know them enough to trust them. I don't know this Mr. Stanford, either, and you'll be living in his house. Keep this nearby."

He handed her his pistol. She started to protest that this would leave him without protection on the return journey to Brentwood, but his size alone was impressive enough to deter trouble. Besides, Frank knew she could shoot. He taught her himself.

She had just placed the gun into the carry bag at her feet when a white man with sandy brown hair and a brown leather vest came around the corner of the hotel. Jogging toward them, he waved with one hand, and had a paper-wrapped package tucked under the other arm. He was handsome in a Greek sort of way, his facial features prominent and symmetrical like the busts she'd seen once in a Nashville library. He ran up to Frank, extending one hand.

Frank simply stared at him until the stranger spoke.

"Harry Franklin. Sorry for the delay. You must be…"

"Frank McAllister." He finally took Mr. Franklin's outstretched hand and gave it a firm shake. "This is Portia, my sister-in-law."

Mr. Franklin's smile reminded Portia of a child who had looted a cookie jar — guilty and giddy at the same time. "Wonderful. Beau will definitely be, um, surprised. I think he expected a more grandmotherly type. Not that *I'm* complaining, mind you."

With the look Frank gave him, Mr. Franklin's boyish grin slid right off his face. "We'll take good care of her, I promise."

Isaac nodded, patting his rifle reassuringly as Mr. Franklin climbed in beside him.

"You better," Frank said, and without looking her in the eye, he added, "Goodbye, Po."

"Goodbye, Frank." The words were just as difficult as she imagined.

The buggy lurched forward. Frank raised his hand in farewell, standing there in the dim lamp-lit shadows of early morning. Legs twitching, she had a sudden inclination to jump out and run after him. Maybe he was right to be worried, and maybe she was being unrealistic.

Good Christian women didn't leave home and hearth when life turned sour. The great Psalmist himself said, *"The Lord is nigh unto them that are of a broken heart; and saveth such as be of a contrite spirit."*

They rounded a corner and she couldn't see Frank anymore. She sat back in the padded seat and let out a sigh. Funny how Bible verses still lectured her when she had no faith left to back them. If she was anything, it wasn't contrite. She had neither asked for nor wanted this life God had thrust upon her. He could go be nigh unto someone else and leave her be for all she cared.

"Don't you worry, ma'am," Isaac said loudly over his shoulder. "The road's pretty smooth and well-traveled. I ain't seen no trouble on it for a long time."

She nodded, though she knew he couldn't see her.

Mr. Franklin turned around partway in his seat. "Tell us if you need anything at all, Mrs. McAllister. It's my job to carry out Beau's orders, and he's ordered me to bring his son a teacher. Dead or alive."

Portia's eyes widened, and Mr. Franklin laughed.

"I'm joking! Take a rest if you'd like. It's fairly comfortable back there."

After a mile or so, she discovered he was right. The wide hood surrounding her seat felt like a firm pillow when she rested her head on it. But before she shut her eyes, she pulled Jake's old shirt from her bag, balled it up, and wedged it under her cheek. It didn't take long for her to fall asleep.

Portia awoke to her backside bumping about on the seat. Sunlight flashed on her face through the budding trees on the roadside. She sat up just as the world tipped violently, throwing her against the side of the carriage. Crying out in shock and the pain that followed, she dove for her bag, figuring she was dead already if robbers had struck. But she wasn't about to go down without a fight. She needed Frank's pistol and fumbled about until her fingers closed around the grip.

The gun hadn't cleared the bag's opening when an iron-strong hand clamped her wrist. She screamed.

Chapter Two

"It's all right," Mr. Franklin said, eyeing the pistol in Portia's hand. "Just a broken wheel, darlin', that's all."

Her heart pounded hard against her ribcage as though it might burst free any moment and run away. She closed her eyes, took a couple deep breaths, and looked up at him. Still gripping her forearm in his strong hand, he flicked his eyes between her face and the gun until she let it slide back onto the other belongings in her bag.

"I'm sorry," she said, rubbing the spot on her arm he had just released. Red marks the shape of his fingers formed on her skin. "I fell asleep. Where are we?"

"Just a mile or so from Lebanon." He held out his hand. "Let me help you out of there so we can get this wheel changed."

Her feet hit the ground. Up ahead, the horses shifted nervously. Issac held one of them by the bridle and patted its neck, speaking softly to calm the animal.

He hollered over his shoulder, "You all right, Mrs. McAllister?"

Thankfully her heart decided to retain its position and slowed a bit. "Yes, I'm fine. How long will we be stuck?"

"Won't take long at all, ma'am. I'll get that wheel changed lickety-split."

Mr. Franklin led her off the side of the road where tall cedars shaded a large gray rock. He gestured for her to have a seat. She brushed off dry evergreen needles and sat, but her sore backside made her regret that decision. Mr. Franklin smiled. With hardly a foot between them, she fought the urge to scoot away from him.

Isaac pulled out a homemade jack from under her seat. He placed it under the buggy's rear axle, ratcheting the handle until the broken wheel spun freely about an inch off the ground.

She glanced at Mr. Franklin, wondering why he wasn't helping with the effort. Instead, he opened a pocket knife and started whittling a small piece of cedar. The wood's pleasant perfume overpowered the scents of damp earth and wagon grease. He kept staring at her as he worked. She could have sworn he scooted closer.

"So Mr. Franklin…" She abruptly stood, brushing stray needles off her skirt. "Are you kin to the Stanford family?"

His eyes lingered on her for a moment. Shrugging, he turned his attention to the wheel repair in progress. "Just a distant relation, but half of Wilson County could be considered distant relations. Me and Beau, see — we were neighbors, spent summers runnin' around together. My folks had gone down to Chattanooga to look at some land down there and left me with the Stanfords. They were thinking of moving, and I didn't want to go. Didn't want to leave Beau and Ezra — that's his pa — behind. They

25

were like second family to me. Anyway, we got word that they'd had an accident on their way back. The wagon rolled off a ledge. Killed 'em both."

"Oh… I'm sorry."

He let his whittling rest on his lap. "It's all right. I was seven, maybe eight. Ezra raised me and Beau together after that, and I've been part of the family ever since. So what about your folks? Any of 'em still around?"

"Not really, no…"

"And your husband? What was his name?"

"Jake."

"I don't recall him, but Beau and I were on the Federal side."

"Oh…" Her mouth went dry. She had assumed they were Confederate. Just a year ago, they were enemies — Jake's enemies. "I didn't know that."

"Yeah, well, our affiliation didn't earn us much fanfare when we returned. You always lived in Brentwood?"

"Yes."

"I've not been through there since before Franklin got blown to hell. Oh, pardon my language, ma'am."

"It's all right."

"Anyway, I reckon that was one awful fight. We were lucky enough to not be involved in that one. Beau and I were both wounded in Allatoona. We healed up enough to get transferred to Smith's regiment for patrol duty along the Cumberland. Nothin' but a muddy mess, but at least we didn't get shot again. So, what happened to Jake?"

"He died in Nashville. I think he might have fought in Franklin, as well."

"Might have took a shot at me a time or two. Who knows?" He grinned and winked, snapping the blade of his pocket knife against his thigh to close it.

"Please don't make light of such matters, Mr. Franklin." She paced away so he couldn't see her chin quivering.

"I'm sorry. Didn't mean to upset you." His footsteps drew closer. She thought he might touch her. The thought made her cringe.

Isaac clapped twice and motioned for them to come along. "All done. Ready to go on?"

"Yes," Portia answered and hurried to the now-fixed and level wagon.

Harry tossed his unfinished whittling creation to the ground. He helped her into the wagon, and she couldn't help but notice the melancholy turn to his features.

With a numb bottom and stiff neck, Portia wondered how much longer it would be before they arrived. The sun had ascended toward its summit. She blinked the sleep from her eyes and took in her surroundings. Along the dusty road, the countryside told its sad story with overgrown fencerows, empty pastures, and abandoned plantations. Wind whistled past her ears, its tone so sorrowful it sounded as if the land itself wept from the wounds of man's folly.

Pulling her locket from under her collar, she rubbed the tarnished silver between thumb and forefinger. Her thoughts drifted back to the day Jake presented it to her. That February afternoon had been one of the happiest days of her life.

"It's beautiful, Jake!"

The silver plated locket was oval-shaped, engraved with the initial *M* for McAllister. The chain was long and delicate. Not expensive, yet she knew Jake would have had to sacrifice something to buy it. They'd barely made any money from the previous harvest. Soybean and corn prices had bottomed out since the start of the war, and what was left had been taken by the army.

"Open it," Jake had said with the same sideways smile he'd had since they were children.

She'd done as he said, and found a miniature portrait from the photo they had taken on their wedding day. "You sold your daddy's musket, didn't you?"

Jake had nodded. "I traded it to Mrs. Overton. Besides, that old gun don't matter. All that matters is you and my sweet baby girl."

He'd leaned over and kissed their newborn on the forehead. Abigail had entered the world only a few hours before — a wriggly, pink bundle now swaddled in a soft knitted blanket and sleeping peacefully. Little brown ringlets of hair covered her head. Jake had whipped out his pocket knife and Portia had yanked up the baby, holding her tight to her breast.

"Calm down, mama." Jake had chuckled. "There's just one thing missing from your gift."

He'd uncovered Abigail's head and, very carefully, cut off one of the longest ringlets on the nape of her neck. Portia had smiled and nuzzled her daughter's sweet-smelling head as she watched Jake's rugged fingers tie a tiny piece of narrow pink ribbon around the silky lock of hair. He placed Abby's hair inside the locket and closed it.

Portia had held her long hair out of the way, while he fastened the clasp behind her neck.

Jake had draped an arm around her and rubbed their daughter's angelic soft cheek.

"Thank you, Jake. I love you," she'd whispered as she rested her head on his shoulder.

"Love you too, Po. You, me, and our baby girl — we're a family now! How about that?"

She'd spied a glimmer of tears in his eyes, which he quickly blinked away. How her heart had swelled as she witnessed her tough-as-nails husband soften up like warm butter. She'd handed Abby to him, and he'd looked scared to death, like she might break.

"You still all right back there?" Mr. Franklin asked, pulling her from the beautiful memory and back to the uncertainty of her present circumstances.

She hoped he hadn't heard her sniffing. "Yes, I'm fine. How much farther?"

"Not long now." He draped his elbow over the seat and smiled. "We're nearing the town up ahead. You been to Lebanon before?"

"No."

"It's a real fine town, prettier before the war, but there's still some nice architecture to admire."

She took the hint and sat up in her seat. They were traveling along a tree-lined street. On her left, a stately white mansion with tall, wide columns came into view.

"That's the Caruthers house," Mr. Franklin said. "He was one of the founders of Cumberland University and governor of Tennessee for a while until the war ended."

"Where is the university?"

"It was over there off Spring Street. Got burned up in the war. It's where Beau's father-in-law taught law until he died. Claire — that's Beau's late wife — wanted their son to go there when he got old enough. I think they're still having classes around here somewhere."

They entered the town square — a busy, spacious place with people moving in all directions on horseback, in wagons, and on foot. Two men unloaded large panes of glass at a store with boarded up windows. Scaffolds holding painters and carpenters crisscrossed other storefronts. Saws chewed through wood and hammers pounded nails. The song of reconstruction, Portia concluded, had become the nation's bitter anthem.

"We're taking you the long way around," he said, "so you can see more of the town. I hope you don't mind."

"No, not at all."

She shifted her weight to ease her aching backside.

Mr. Franklin pointed to one landmark after another. "There's the Presbyterian Church over there, and that's Odd Fellows Hall, where the Yanks cornered John Hunt Morgan's cavalry."

"Almost got him too," Isaac added with a chuckle, "but he got away just in the knick."

"So, you were freed and hired after the war?"

"Oh, no, ma'am. We've always been free. Mr. Stanford's grandfather saw to that."

Isaac slowed the horses and turned onto another street. Children's laughter cut across the road. Smiling, Portia sat up straight to see them at play. A little black boy sprinted in front of the horses, with three white boys in hot pursuit.

Isaac yanked the reins and yelled, "Whoa!" and managed to stop the horses before they trampled the children.

The black boy skirted up a tall sycamore, and the others ran up against the tree trunk, whacking it with sticks, and laughing while they chanted, *The greatest old Nigger that ever I did see, Looked like a sick monkey up a sour apple tree.*

Portia stood and started to climb out of the buggy. Those boys needed their ears twisted plumb off; no child deserved such teasing, but Mr. Franklin extended his arm in front of her and said, "Wait."

Isaac jumped out and ran right at them, waving his rifle, but pointed it toward the sky.

"Get out of here, now. I said, get!" The pursuers started to scatter, but Isaac did get in a kick to the last one's backside before he could vanish, squealing in terror, back into town with his friends.

"Come on down, Jim," Isaac said. "They're gone. They ain't gonna bother you no more today."

The poor child trembled so much, young sycamore blossoms rained upon the ground below.

"Come on," Isaac soothed. "Where's your daddy?"

"I don't know, sir. Mama says he musta run off."

"Well, you get on back to your mama, you hear? Don't come back here by yourself."

"Yes, sir," he said, hanging from the safety of a sturdy limb then dropped to the ground; his bare feet hit the leafy carpet with a soft crunch. He took off through the trees, heading in the opposite direction of his enemies, much to Portia's relief.

Isaac climbed back into the buggy while Portia settled against her seat. He turned to Mr. Franklin. "He said his daddy ran off. Where do you think he went?"

"Clarence? Hard to say. Maybe he's just looking for work. Fannie ought to take Jim to Kentucky. Ain't that where their people went?"

"I think so. Woman's got a head harder than a chestnut. I'll have Bessie talk to her." Isaac removed his hat and swiped the sweat from his forehead. "Sorry, Mrs. McAllister. I'm afraid your tour's not goin' so well."

"I'm fine," she said, staring back toward town. No more troublemakers in sight. "I'm just glad no one was hurt."

"You and me both."

"Well, no sense sitting here all day." Mr. Franklin gestured down the road. "Right down here, about half a mile, is the Stanford farm."

They continued down the road until they turned onto a narrow dirt drive lined by white fences with chipped paint. Wild blackberries and poison ivy clogged sections of the fence. Portia recalled how fastidious Jake was with their fencerows before the war claimed his life.

The drive wound along pastures dotted with a few horses and cows. To their right, wintered crop fields waited to be plowed. Portia spotted a green roof in the distance, and as the carriage climbed one last hill, a house came into view. They pulled up to a large, two-story home with white siding and a porch that spanned the entire front of the house. The siding needed a fresh coat of paint, but it still presented an admirable first impression.

Isaac dismounted and grabbed Portia's bag.

Mr. Franklin offered his hand and helped her down. "I'll go tell Beau you're here."

Stiff-legged, she followed Isaac to the porch steps. She noticed movement at a window on the second floor. Someone of small stature peered down at her. She tried to get a better look at the child — surely it was her new charge — but he saw her looking and let the curtain fall. She wondered what he was thinking at that moment. Was he frightened, excited, or perhaps angry that another woman was here instead of his mother? She figured she'd know soon enough.

While Isaac removed her trunk and bags from the buggy and set them on the porch, she breathed in the unfamiliar scents — horses, wagon grease, and what might be fried chicken. Her stomach grumbled in anticipation.

Isaac opened the door. "Ready?"

"Yes," she answered, sounding more confident than she felt. "I'm ready."

He removed his hat, stood to one side and gestured for her to pass over the threshold. Portia stared into the shadowed interior. This unfamiliar place and all the uncertainty within would be home. At least for a while. *Ready?* No, not by a long shot. But she reminded herself, it had to become her refuge. For sanity's sake, she alone had to make it work.

She took a deep breath and stepped inside.

Chapter Three

Beau Stanford had just placed his best saddle on the rack when Harry strode into the stable. He favored his bad leg again, though he tried to hide it. He'd be injecting his preferred remedy soon.

"Back already?" Beau rolled his aching shoulder to loosen the tension. Eyeing the brown paper package under his friend's arm, he felt the throbbing temptation in his old wound. Numbing the pain would only be a temporary solution, he reminded himself.

"Obviously. And Mrs. McAllister's here safe and sound as you instructed. But she might not be quite what you expected."

"How so?"

"Why don't you go meet her yourself?" He gestured toward the new filly, who gnawed the top of the stable door, leaving ugly ruts in the weathered wood. "How'd she ride?"

Beau slapped too much Neatsfoot on the seat and wiped the excess oil from the leather. He couldn't afford to ruin his good saddle. Setting his supplies on the workbench, he pointed at their latest acquisition. "What do *you* think?"

The filly shifted her weight from one leg to the other and swung her head from side to side as if lost in her own little world.

Harry draped an elbow over an empty stall door. "She'll be fine in a few days, Beau. Turn her out and let her graze for a while."

"You bring me a half-crazed horse that can't trot to save her life, and you think she'll be fine? I wouldn't trust her under Scout. How the hell do you expect us *not* to lose money on her?"

Harry shook his head. "Nonsense! She'll make a stage horse or a mail runner. She gallops fine. We can take her to market in a few weeks."

"We need brood mares, not mail runners." Beau pinched the bridge of his nose. "I swear; I gave you one job, one damned job…"

"Beau, look," Harry said, flicking his thumb across a bridle hanging nearby. His voice turned somber. "It's gonna take time to get the business going again. You know that. We need money now, and don't forget we sold those two saddle horses within a month."

"Fine," Beau conceded, "but they barely brought in enough to buy this crazy thing."

Beau flipped the saddle around on the rack and oiled the other side, wishing Harry still took things seriously like he did before that bullet took a chunk out of his leg and before morphine addled his mind. The man could whittle down the most tight-fisted farmers and bring back some fine stock. Being neither brother nor kin, Harry really had no vested interest in the business besides loyalty. Yet he had put his all into it, even more so than Beau, to be honest. Now they were lucky if he did a half-assed job at anything. Beau could only imagine Harry's acquiring process, which likely involved him buying the horse sight unseen and gallivanting around at the nearest saloon the rest of the day.

"There's a filly over in Lockport I'm going to look at on Monday," Harry said in that soothing tone he employed when trying to win people over. "A thoroughbred. She'll be a good one if we're lucky."

"I doubt it."

"Damn it, Beau, I can't up and shit a brood mare!"

"No, but you can sure talk shit."

Harry balled up his fist and punched the stall door. The filly reared and whinnied.

Beau's pa, Ezra, hollered from the stable entrance, "What's goin' on in here?"

"Nothin'," Harry grumbled and hurried out in angry retreat.

Ezra stared after him. "What was *that* all about?"

"See what he brought us?" Beau angled his head toward the new filly.

Ezra sidled up to the stall. The filly ceased her door-chewing and belched. It smelled like rotten hay.

"Good Lord above," he said, waving his hand in front of his nose. "Her teeth are worn down to near nubs." He rubbed her nose, and she tried to nip him. Luckily the old

36

man's reflexes were still quick, so his fingers remained unscathed. "She'd be a waste of a bullet. What was that boy thinking?"

"He doesn't think. That's the problem." Beau looked down the long corridor of the stable at all the vacant stalls. General Reynolds had raided Wilson County and had taken most of their horses while he and Harry were off fighting. "If you and Isaac hadn't hid Scout and the mules, we wouldn't have had any stock left. But Scout can't make foals by himself. We need some good brood mares. Some *sane* ones."

"I'll put her out to graze. She might bring us somethin' after she calms down a bit."

Beau removed his hat and wiped sweat from his brow. Grateful as Beau was for Pa and Isaac's perseverance, the current problem remained, demanding attention like a botfly on a cow's ass.

Ezra flipped through mail he had tucked under his arm. "Hmm."

"What?"

"It's a bill," he grumbled. "Taxes overdue."

Beau wasn't surprised. "Let me see."

Ezra handed him the bill, and his eyes fell on the dollar figure.

"Shit."

"Watch your language, Beauregard. Can't have you and Harry cursing every other breath with a new lady living here."

Wincing at the number of digits in the *Amount Due* section, Beau crammed the bill in his vest pocket.

"What else we got?"

Ezra opened another envelope. "It's a letter from Claire's uncle."

"Oliver?"

The old man took his glasses from his shirt pocket, put them on his nose, and held the letter at arm's length. "Looks like he's heading back from Philadelphia in a couple of weeks. He's bringing Lydia."

"She was always a sweet little girl." Beau recalled some of the letters he'd received from her since Claire's death. *My dearest Beau... not a day passes that does not carry with it the memories I have of you...*

"She ain't so little no more," he said with a smile. "She's a young woman now. And you ain't so old yourself."

"Not that again." With his thumb, Beau instinctively touched the golden band on his left ring finger.

"They've got money and lots of it."

Here we go. Gold sparkled in Ezra's eyes, or was that the thrill of matchmaking? Either way, Beau didn't like it. He frowned and plopped his hat back on his head.

"Now don't give me that look, son. It's been two years. You need to find somebody. Give Jonathan a mama."

"He had a mama. And we're fine." He hated the way his voice broke every time someone forced him to talk about Claire, so he made his retreat into Scout's stall. The sixteen-year-old stallion was the most level-headed Morgan he'd ever owned. He nuzzled his master as soon as he saw the brush in Beau's hand.

Ezra followed, thumbs tucked behind his overall straps. "You're not fine, Beauregard. You need a lady to run things around here. Harry and Isaac are back with the new teacher, right?"

"I reckon so." He brushed Scout's neck with soft, gentle strokes.

"Portia, wasn't it? Portia McAllister?"

"You'd know better than me. I didn't want to hire her in the first place. It's bad enough she's a Rebel's widow, but Harry says she's not what we expected. Is she blind or deaf or missing a leg or what?"

"Heck if I know, son. I ain't met her yet, either. All I've seen is her letter."

"And according to that letter, her husband worked as an overseer."

"Part-time assistant to an overseer."

"Same difference."

"Don't matter what *he* was. *She's* a former schoolteacher. And you know Claire wanted this for Jonny until he's old enough for the university. I ain't gonna be responsible for her coming back to haunt us for not abiding by her wishes."

"Yeah, well when Claire was here, we had the money for such things. Now, it's all we can do to keep food on the table and the few farm hands we got. With the measly pensions me and Harry get, it's a wonder we can even do that. And now some Rebel woman who may or may not have some sort of deformity will be teaching my son and running my house. What are we supposed to pay her with? Praise?"

"I can't help it if she's the only one who replied."

Beau huffed as he picked prickly burrs from Scout's mane. "Does she know Jonny's mute?"

"He's not mute. He'll come around with the right encouragement."

"Still doesn't solve the problem of how we're gonna pay her."

"If she's so desperate that she's not got any kin or neighbors to stay with, she'll probably be grateful for the room and board alone. Let's give her a chance, at least. We've got room, and we'll still be hospitable, no matter how bare our cupboards are."

"I swear, if this is another one of your matchmaking schemes..."

"It's not, so shut your trap."

Beau heaved a long, tired sigh. "Guess I better head to the house and welcome the crippled up gal like a good host should."

Ezra shook a finger at him, but a spark of amusement flickered in the old man's eye. "You be civil, Beauregard. I can still turn you over my knee if I have to."

Beau chuckled. Despite their arguments, he was thankful Pa was still around. He couldn't imagine life without him.

Ezra smacked Beau's good shoulder. "I'll take the filly out in a little while. Just don't scare the poor widow off."

After Ezra left, the filly pranced around her stall like she stood on burning coals. Beau shook his head and rubbed Scout's velvety nose. Gray hair grew around the old horse's muzzle, reminding Beau of his own silver-specked sideburns.

"I guess that makes two of us," he said.

Thirty-four. Not so old and not so young. By no means beyond marrying age, but every time he even courted the idea, his throat constricted and made breathing a chore. It wasn't that he wanted to be alone. It was just easier that way. With no wife, he had less to lose.

Scout loved a good belly brushing, so Beau flipped over a pail and sat. In the stillness of musty air and horse breath, and with each gentle brush stroke, his thoughts drifted to Claire and the last time they rode Scout together. God, she had felt good against him in the saddle.

Just the day before in Nashville, he and Harry had enlisted. With their departure looming over them like some nightmarish bogeyman, Beau had wanted to treat Claire and Jonny to a picnic. Just a normal day down at Barton Creek with promises of ham and biscuits and a little trout fishing. Jonny had ridden beside them on his pony, chatting happily about something — Beau couldn't remember what exactly — he had been too busy studying the sweet innocence of his son's face. He had those big bright eyes and long lashes, framed by that coppery-blond hair. So much like his mama.

Claire's laughter had tinkled all around them as they skipped rocks. She had masked her worry well enough for Jonny, but Beau had seen it clearly in every long look and lingering touch as they ate lunch on the bank. She contained her emotions like the good Southern lady she was trained to be until they were safe behind their bedroom door.

He had held her as she cried.

"Don't go, please."

"Somebody's gotta look after Harry. He'll get himself killed."

"But what about you? Who will look after you?"

41

"I'll be fine. The war can't last much longer. I'll be home before you miss me."

"I'm so afraid, Beau."

"Then let me love you tonight like only a husband can love his wife. Let's forget there's a war. Let's forget there's anyone but us for a while."

It was the last time they'd shared their bed. He promised her he'd be back, and he kept his promise. He just never thought it would be Claire instead of him. Had two years really passed already?

Two mockingbirds interrupted the silence with annoying squawks, sparring to win a mate outside the window of the stall. Beau led Scout outside and headed toward the paddock. He glanced at the chicken coop where their only rooster mounted a hen. A strange tomcat slunk across the drive on the prowl for female barn cats. Spring had sprung, and life was heeding nature's call.

Once the rooster had done the deed, he flew to the top of the coop to resume his nonstop crowing. *Awfully proud of yourself, huh?* Beau let Scout loose in the paddock, picked up a rock, and hurled it at the coop. It banged off the roof, sending the rooster flying into a squawking, feather-shedding fit.

"Better." He climbed the hill toward the house and the new teacher. How he would manage to pay the woman and keep the farm going, he had no idea. Sniffing the air, he caught the scent of beef stew and cornbread — the one saving grace of the day.

He topped the hill and stopped. There she was, ten yards away, walking across the porch and into the house with Isaac. He caught a glimpse of smooth white skin, brown hair, a slim figure. Not a damn thing wrong with her as far as he could tell. Young, pretty, and single — the perfect candidate for a new wife.

"Damn it, Pa."

Chapter Four

"Welcome to the** Stanford house, Mrs. McAllister," Isaac said, sweeping his hat in front of them.

Portia's footsteps sounded hollow on the polished wood floor. Gazing up at the high ceiling framed with white-painted trim, she felt like Jack venturing into the giant's lair. More furnishings filled the entry hall itself than she had in her entire home. Yet there were bare spaces here and there, indicated by dark rectangles on the floor and plastered walls. Things sold for much-needed cash or chopped up for firewood, perhaps. A portrait of a light-haired woman, a dark-haired man, and a small boy hung on the wall to her left. She shivered, feeling like an intruder trespassing on sacred ground.

A black woman stepped out of an adjoining room. "I suppose you're Mrs. McAllister."

The coolness in her dark eyes matched the tone of her voice and sent goose pimples across Portia's skin. "Yes, and you are…?"

The woman didn't answer. She just stood there, wiping her hands on a flour-dusted apron. Her head was wrapped in a red kerchief, and she wore a necklace made with colorful beads of varying shapes. A pale, diagonal scar ran from her brow, skipped her eye, and came to an end on her cheek. She swept a disapproving gaze over Portia and tucked her arms behind her back.

"Bessie," Isaac said. "This is my wife, Bessie."

Below her faded calico housedress, Bessie's bare, brown feet stepped closer.

Portia offered the warmest smile she could muster. "It's... a pleasure to meet you."

"Mm-hmm."

This woman obviously didn't want her here, and no wonder — how could a freed black woman welcome a Confederate's widow? Would it help to explain that she and Jake never owned any slaves? She guessed not from the way Bessie regarded her like an annoying piece of meat between her teeth that needed to be removed.

"Guess I'd better show you around," she said then turned on her heel and walked into the room from which she had emerged.

Portia glanced at Isaac. He shook his head like he wasn't surprised with his wife's attitude and gestured for her to follow Bessie. So Portia hurried after her.

"This here's the parlor," Bessie narrated and headed through another door from that room. Portia noted a few pieces of nice furniture that looked good for lounging on a Sunday afternoon.

"And this is the dining room." Bessie circumnavigated a long oak table that could seat at least ten or twelve people. She stopped at a swinging door on the other side of the table, pushed it open, and held it there. "Kitchen's in here. Watch your step."

Portia gritted her teeth, walked past Bessie, and stepped down into a spacious kitchen. Bricks lined the floor and walls. She sucked in a breath, scanning the space in amazement.

Bessie stepped down into the room and let the door swing shut behind her. "This used to be separate from the house, but Mrs. Stanford didn't like that. So, Beau had it expanded and attached to the main house. Had those big windows put in, too."

The whole room must have been as big as Portia's kitchen and front room combined. But it felt lighter and airier than the previous rooms. Tall windows and an open back door let in fresh air and the midday light. A big worktable topped with a thick oak slab took center stage. And… was that a water pump over the basin? She walked over to it and touched the cool metal handle just to be sure it was real.

"Ain't you seen a water pump before?" Bessie asked.

"Yes," Portia said, circling around to take in the rest of the space. "Just not inside."

In the corner near the back door sat a smaller dining table with a centerpiece of pink phlox. The petite blooms and needle-shaped foliage draped over the sides of a small jar and skimmed the table's surface.

"You came just in time for supper. We're having beef stew." Bessie walked around to the other side of the work table. A big pot sat on top of the stove. The aroma of beef and potatoes mingled with that of cornbread and fried chicken.

"What can I do to help?" Portia asked, rolling up her sleeves.

"It's all been done. I'm sure you'll want to wash up and change. We'll put you to work soon enough."

She watched the older woman's dark hands as she covered a towel-lined basket of chicken and biscuits, which must have been lunch. Why would Bessie be so cold to her? She and Jake had never owned any slaves. She remembered many nights when Jake had dragged himself in from the fields, covered in dirt, sweat, and blisters.

"A man's not a man if he can't work for his own keep," he'd say when she fussed over him.

Portia thought perhaps she should try harder, engage in more casual chit-chat. "Do you use sweet marjoram in your fried chicken?"

Bessie looked at her quizzically, eyes narrowed into slits.

A blush crept over Portia's cheeks. "That's *my* secret, anyway."

"My recipe's fine like it is." She got bowls from a shelf beneath the work table then stood up straight and nodded toward the door. "Here's your student."

Portia turned to see Isaac there with a young boy. He stared at her with sheepish eyes adorned with long lashes. His hair was the color of an old penny mixed with streaks of corn silk and so straight the ends flipped out over his ears and brow.

Isaac patted the boy on the back and gestured toward Portia. "Mrs. McAllister, this is Jonathan, Mr. Stanford's son. Jonathan, this here's Portia McAllister. She'll be takin' over your lessons."

"Hello, Jonathan." She stepped forward, bending slightly to meet him at eye-level. "I'm glad to meet you."

He tucked his hands behind his back and took a sudden interest in his feet.

"I know I'm a stranger," she said, reverting to her teacher's attitude, "but it's good manners to greet your guests and look them in the eye when they address you."

"My son is mute." The sudden, deep voice behind Jonathan startled Portia so much she nearly jumped from her skin.

Almost afraid to look, she composed herself and lifted her eyes to see a tall man looming over the boy. His steely eyes locked on hers as he removed his hat. He had thick, dark hair, bordering on black, like the Morgans that pulled the carriage in which she had arrived. A stubbly beard shadowed his jaw. She couldn't tell by his frown whether he was simply stern or just plumb angry, but she had the sudden urge to retreat under the weight of his stare.

"Your... son is mute?" She cringed inside — that imposing man was her employer? And why hadn't the letter mentioned the child was mute? None of this had turned out the way she had imagined it.

"Shake the lady's hand," Mr. Stanford ordered.

Jonathan stretched a trembling hand toward her. Portia shook it once gently, and attempted a reassuring smile, though the boy never took his eyes off his boots.

"Mrs. McAllister, this here's Mr. Stanford," Isaac said. Though his softened voice and demeanor suggested a reverence for her new employer, Portia detected a warm familiarity, like a father might have for a son.

"Mr. Stanford." Determined to show some grit and civility in the face of this foreboding man, she forced herself to look him in the eye. "I wasn't aware of your son's condition. I hope you'll forgive my ignorance, and I thank you for this opportunity."

He finally unfastened his glare and turned his back on her. "I hope you will be comfortable here," he said briskly and walked away.

Despite her brave façade, Portia's hands trembled. Heat crawled up her neck, burning a path to her cheeks. She looked to Isaac for reassurance.

He stepped closer and spoke softly. "Never you mind Beau. He's got a lot on his shoulders tryin' to get this farm back to what it used to be. He's out early and back late. You won't be seeing much of him. Come on now. I'll show ya to your room."

Portia followed Isaac and Jonathan back through the dining room, into the entry hall, and up the stairs. A few pictures of various sizes ascended the wall as she climbed. Most were small cartes-de-visite of people who shared a resemblance to the family. Several horses were featured in oil paintings both with and without riders. One studio portrait in particular made her pause. At the left stood a dark-haired man she identified as Mr. Stanford. A blond woman in a silk dress sat on a wingback chair, holding a baby on her lap. Nice as the picture was, something else caught Portia's attention — Mr. Stanford's smile. Besides his hair and stature, the man in the picture didn't match the one she met today. Even in the dull sepia tones of the photograph, his smile lit up the scene.

Quickly glancing over her shoulder as though she had intruded on an intimate secret, she scanned the empty foyer. Mr. Stanford was nowhere to be seen. Good. She hoped to at least get settled in and rested before she came across him again. He wouldn't want to keep a skittish teacher on the payroll.

When they reached the landing, Jonathan sped off to a room just ahead and disappeared behind the door. Considering its placement, she figured it must be the room from which he had watched her arrival. A wide hall stretched along the length of the house. Like downstairs, a dark rectangle shaded the floorboards of the landing as though a large rug had once been there.

Isaac headed right, so she followed. A few narrow rugs had apparently survived the great purging and padded the floor under her feet.

Stopping at the first room to the right, Isaac opened the door and carried her bag inside. "Here's your room, Mrs. McAllister. I'll bring your chest up shortly."

"Thank you." She lingered in the hallway, uncertain what to say next.

He lit a lamp for her and left it on the dresser. Then he came back out, hands tucked in his pockets. In a hushed tone, he said, "I wanna apologize for Bessie. She's not one to warm to new folk easy, especially since Mrs. Stanford passed. She took it real hard. Claire was like a daughter to her... and me. I hope you understand. She's a good woman, and she'll come around."

Portia nodded, hoping Isaac's prediction would be right. "What about Jonathan? Has he always been mute? Is he deaf as well?"

Isaac shook his head. "Oh, no. He hears just fine. He used to talk a blue streak until Beau came home after Claire died and half lost his mind. Said some awful things to Jonny and all of us. Didn't mean none of it. He was just grievin', you see. But Jonny went quiet after that."

Portia touched her locket. "That's... terrible. Poor Jonathan."

"I bet you'll get him talkin' again. It'll just take some time. I'll leave ya to get cleaned up for supper. If ya need anything, give a holler." He headed down the stairs.

Portia entered the room. A dark cherry four-poster took up most of the right side and a matching dresser stood on the opposite wall to her left. Lace curtains on the tall window billowed in the breeze and let in the afternoon sun, which danced on the floor in pretty patterns of golden light. Under the window sat a small rectangular table adorned with a diamond-shaped crocheted doily. Like the table in the kitchen, a small jar of flowers made a pretty springtime centerpiece — snowdrops this time with delicate white blooms — some unopened like white teardrops and others like silky fingers reaching for something below.

Portia pulled back the curtain and peered onto the front lawn below. There was still enough daylight to see Mr. Stanford standing under a giant oak next to an older gentleman. He pointed at the older man and then the house and appeared none too happy. Was he angry about her apparent lack of knowledge? She had half a mind to open the window and yell, *"How was I supposed to know your son is mute when no one told me until today?"*

And what kind of father was he, saying hurtful things that drove his son to silence? Surely he didn't blame Jonathan for Mrs. Stanford's death.

Mr. Stanford flicked his gaze upward, hooking her with those sharp eyes. She gasped and dropped the curtain, giving the wall a reserved, but frustrated kick from her boot. This timidity wouldn't do at all, not with her living and working there all day, every day, for the unforeseeable future. Back before she lost everyone she loved, she would have prayed for courage in a situation like this. But she and God weren't on speaking terms.

Not yet, anyway.

Chapter Five

Portia took a deep breath and expelled it in a long, dreary sigh. She had to do something productive and stop letting her nerves get the best of her. The carry bag sat on the bed atop a star-patterned quilt. She opened it and removed Frank's Smith & Wesson loaded belt pistol, stowing it in the bottom drawer of the dresser under extra sheets and coverlets.

Then she removed Jake's tintype from the bag and placed it on top of the dresser where a large lace doily covered the center. Jake's stern face stared back at her. He had it taken in Nashville right after he could no longer deny the call to conscription. The newly issued Confederate jacket fit him well, though it was secondhand, the butternut dye faded to dull beige. He stood from the seat, hugging her and Abby tight before the blinding camera flash had left their eyes.

"This war can't last much longer, Po. There aren't enough men left to put up a decent fight." His laughter was as light as ever, his hazel eyes dancing with mirth. His smile was as warm as the hopeful sun on that February morning two

years ago. Yet beneath his brave exterior, she felt the fear quivering in his rigid muscles and shuddered in his embrace.

If she'd known that was the last time she'd see him alive, she would have grabbed his starched lapels and dragged him back home.

Nothing but naïve farm boys, all of them, but unlike the days following Sumter, these conscripts no longer believed they could turn the tide of war with misplaced ideals and bravado. By that time, everyone had grown weary of constant hunger and the ever-growing lists of dead men. These soldiers shared a common, and less patriotic, goal — to evade death and come back home. Muted cheers and quartets with their tired renditions of "Dixie" faded into Portia's memory.

On second thought… she stored the picture in the top drawer. She couldn't become a slave to the memories again. It gave her enough comfort to know his picture was there, safe and sound.

She took off her coat and gloves and draped them over the chair. The aroma of supper from downstairs smelled heavenly, so the rest of the unpacking could wait. A ceramic pitcher filled with fresh water and a matching basin stood next to the dresser. She washed her face and hands and rearranged her hair. A few stubborn strands refused to stay put, so she tucked them behind her ears. She started toward the door but hesitated. Her brown woolen dress was appropriate for travel, but surely not for dinner in such a fine dining room.

Quickly, she searched through the few things she brought in the trunk. Spying her Sunday dress of pale yellow muslin, she took it out but decided against changing. If she kept Mr. Stanford waiting, it could make a bad impression. From their earlier meeting, she didn't want to incur any more of his wrath, especially before she even began teaching his son.

She hung her Sunday dress in a small wardrobe by the dresser and, before she could change her mind again, headed downstairs.

Just short of the dining room door, muffled voices drifted into the foyer. Portia squeezed her eyes shut and felt short of breath, but she hadn't come all this way to cower alone in a guest room. Jake always said she was as sharp as a copperhead's tooth, so she took faith in her late husband's assessment and hoped she could hold her own.

The men were already seated at the table, but they stood when she entered. Uncertain where to sit, she lingered in the doorway until the older gentleman she had seen from the window stepped around the table and offered his hand. She accepted it gratefully.

"Mrs. McAllister, I'm Ezra Stanford. I think you met my son, Beau," he said and gestured toward Mr. Stanford, who nodded but didn't make eye contact. "And you've met Harry Franklin already. He and Beau run the horse business. They've been friends since they were knee-high to a grasshopper."

"Lovely to see you again." Harry bowed with a flourish like a stage actor might do.

"Thank you, sir. It's good to meet you all," she said.

Jonathan stood silently by his chair across the table, regarding her with those sheepish eyes. She smiled at him, but he dropped his gaze to the floor.

Ezra chuckled. "Oh, now, none of this sir stuff, and Mr. This and That. I'm just Ezra, but you can call him Beauregard."

With that, he pointed his fork at his son.

"All right now, Pa." Mr. Stanford stood at the head of the table and looked none too pleased. In the flickering light of the chandelier over the table, she noticed his prominent nose and cheekbones and a dimple in the dead center of his chin.

Harry scooted out a chair next to his and gestured to Portia, so she took the cue and sat. He smiled at her like a barn cat who had caught the first mouse of spring, and she couldn't help but feel uneasy. He could have been looking for someone to court or merely enjoyed a good flirtation, but either way, Portia wasn't ready for or interested in any such dalliance.

"Beau hates his proper name," Ezra continued as he lowered himself to his chair. "I had to name him since his mama died right after his birth, and I always liked the name Beauregard. He was one of my favorite horses."

He chuckled again, while Harry laughed and slapped the table. Mr. Stanford, or Beauregard, glanced at his father and cracked the slightest hint of a smile as he shook his head. Portia felt more at ease after Ezra's warm welcome and was thankful to not be underdressed, after all. The younger men were wearing shirts and pants stained with a hard day's work on a farm, while Ezra wore a pair of canvas overalls splattered with white paint. A thick gray beard framed his round face and matched the ring of gray hair growing around his head and above his ears.

"Hope you'll excuse my paintin' clothes," Ezra said as though he'd read her mind. "Fences don't paint themselves, and I was too hungry to change."

Bessie brought in the food and dished out bowls of what must have been beef stew, considering the tantalizing aroma, followed by steaming hot cornbread. Portia's fingers twitched, longing to dig in, but she lowered her head as Ezra said grace. The stew itself was more soup than substance, but still delicious nonetheless. They ate in silence for a while until Portia realized she'd emptied her entire bowl before anyone else had even eaten half.

"You want mine?" Harry asked, scooting his bowl close to hers.

"Oh, no thank you."

"At least have more cornbread." He took a piece from the towel-covered iron skillet and put it on her plate.

Even though everyone's eyes were on her, she couldn't let that steaming piece of heaven get cold.

"Thank you," she said then took a bite, closing her eyes partway as she enjoyed the satisfying pleasures of the warm, lard-laden bread.

"How long has it been since you had a decent meal?" Harry asked quietly.

Swallowing another bite, she blushed and ducked her head, putting the rest of the piece back on the plate. She must look like some starving waif to these men.

"No, you eat up," Harry said, leaning closer. "You won't go hungry here. I promise."

She lifted her eyes enough to see Mr. Stanford looking at her over his glass of water, but she couldn't read his expression well enough to know if he pitied her or thought she belonged in a pig sty.

Bessie came around again with seconds and refilled Portia's bowl.

"Maybe I ought to just set the pot in front of this girl," she said and returned to the kitchen.

Ezra leaned back in his seat and rubbed his round belly. "Keep eatin' like that, young lady, and you'll look like me!"

Portia tried to smile as she picked up her spoon. Across the table, Jonathan had hardly eaten a bite. He slumped in his chair, pushing a potato around in his bowl.

"So, Mrs. McAllister, or can I call you Portia?" Harry asked, and Portia nodded her acceptance. "How long have you taught school?"

Clearing her throat, she wiped her mouth and sat up straight, determined to look as professional as she could, considering her ravenous appetite. "I earned my teacher's certificate right after I finished school myself, and I taught in Brentwood up until my daughter's birth, so about six years."

Mr. Stanford tapped his fingers on the table and fixed her in his steady gaze. "Pa never mentioned that you had a child. Where is she? Back home with your family?"

She remembered then that she had mentioned being a widow, but had not written about Abby in her acceptance letter. The pain had been too fresh then to put it to paper.

"I lost her," Portia said, trying hard as she could to steady her voice. "Typhoid, about eight months ago."

Biting her lip, she focused on the spoon marks on the ceramic of her empty bowl. Before now, she had never had to say it out loud. Everyone in Brentwood knew when someone died. It was newsworthy fodder for conversation. She couldn't even walk the streets without the pitiful glances, the murmurings, and empty condolences.

"I'm sorry to hear that," Mr. Stanford said. The gentle tone of his voice surprised her. The other men followed suit. "According to your letter, your husband worked as assistant overseer at Travellers Rest. Is that right?"

And so the interrogation begins. "Yes. He assisted the overseer occasionally during planting and harvest."

"I imagine he was handy with a whip."

"Beau..." Ezra's harsh whisper made Portia flinch.

Mr. Stanford ignored him. "How *did* he treat the slaves he supervised, Mrs. McAllister?"

"Jake didn't believe in such abuse. In fact, he—"

"And how would you know how he performed his work? Were you there with him?"

"Beauregard, that's enough!" Ezra said.

Mr. Stanford held a silencing hand toward him and kept her fixed in his cold glare. "It's my right to know my employee's background. Were you with your husband while he worked?"

"No."

"Then how do you know he didn't apply a whip to the back of John Overton's slaves?"

"Because I knew my husband, sir!" Her voice had risen to a near shout, so she took a deep breath and tempered her words. "Jake did not employ a whip, and if he did, it doesn't matter now. He'd dead."

"Where did he fall?"

She studied his face for a moment, wondering if he was asking only so he could gloat about a Rebel's death. "Jake died in Nashville."

"My condolences, then." Mr. Stanford wiped his mouth.

Could it be that Mr. Stanford, or perhaps Mr. Franklin, had shot the bullet that had ended Jake's life? The accusations festered on her tongue, but she didn't want to keep feeding this confrontation.

"I lost my wife while I was gone," he said. "I guess we've all got to move on now, with no judgments."

"Yes, sir," she agreed. "I think that's wise."

She risked a glance at him; his wary gray eyes were trained on her like he expected her to bolt or rise further to her late husband's defense. She would do neither.

"I have to admit, Mrs. McAllister, you're younger than we, or at least *I* expected. It seems odd for a young lady such as yourself to leave her home and family behind so readily."

"Beau, I think you've said enough." Ezra's voice carried a distinct warning edge, the same one her daddy had used while winding a belt around his fist. Portia shivered.

Mr. Stanford shot his father a look that silenced him. She clenched the napkin covering her lap and tried to make sense of this exchange before she said something wrong. Considering this house's Union allegiance, she could understand some animosity. But what would her age have to do with anything? How could he find her in fault for some assumed dishonesty? Though she longed to retreat upstairs to the comfort of silence, she knew he wouldn't release her from the shackles of his cold eyes until she answered him.

She quickly decided her best defense was the truth. "My family is gone, sir, except for my late husband's brother and his wife. But they are expecting a third child soon and can't afford another mouth to feed. I can teach your son and handle whatever tasks you require of me."

"No parents, siblings, or cousins?"

The accusing tone of his questioning didn't sit well with her, and *she* wasn't prepared to be the subject of an impromptu trial. Didn't he want a teacher for his son? Didn't he read her letter and then hire her? She bore Mr. Stanford's steely glare and met it with her own unflinching gaze.

"No," she said, "no cousins nearby, and none that I care to associate with. My older brother Rudy died when he was twelve. Fell on an axe. My younger brother Samuel ran off to Louisiana right before I married, and I've not heard from him since. My parents burned to death in their home shortly after I married. So no, sir, I have no relatives who can take me in and none I want to burden with the task. I'm here so I can work for my own keep and move on."

"I see. Pardon my bluntness, but it appears you've already moved on." He glanced pointedly at her brown woolen dress, which despite its modest style, didn't keep her from feeling naked under his judgment.

Her guts churned, threatening to toss up everything she'd just eaten. She found her voice somewhere in the pounding rhythm of her heart. "Sir, if you're referring to my lack of mourning clothes, it is both a financial and a personal decision on my part with no bearing on how well I can perform my duties."

"That has yet to be seen, now doesn't it?"

Ezra slapped the table, his pudgy cheeks reddening over his white whiskers. "Beauregard! You do not speak to a lady like that. I raised you better."

Mr. Stanford smirked, looking from Portia to Ezra. "Yes, and you raised me to have a good bit of sense, too. Did you think I wouldn't figure it out?"

Figure what out? Portia shared the same confusion written on Harry, Ezra, and Jonathan's faces.

"Son, I don't know what's gotten into you, but you owe the lady an apology," Ezra said.

Brow slanting at a skeptical angle, Mr. Stanford recaptured her with his glare. "My apologies, Mrs. McAllister. Assuming you're a God-fearing woman, you can join us for church service in the morning. We leave at eight-thirty."

It sounded more like a command than an invitation, but she simply nodded. Isaac had mentioned that he'd half-lost his mind after he returned from the war. Maybe he hadn't recovered all of it yet.

Jonathan cleared his throat.

Mr. Stanford didn't look at his son but gestured to the door. "Go to bed," he snapped.

She freed her gaze as the boy jumped from his seat. "Jonathan, I hope you are looking forward to our studies as much as I am. We'll start Monday at eight o'clock sharp."

He nodded and darted out in a flash.

The night's tensions and persistent exhaustion left Portia drained. The prospect of being alone in her new room was more appealing with every breath. "I'm afraid I need to retire as well, gentlemen. Please excuse me."

Harry and Ezra stood as she got to her feet. Mr. Stanford only followed her with his eyes. Though Harry tried, he couldn't reach her chair before she scooted it back and escaped the confines of the dining room.

Skirt fisted in both hands, she had made it to the second step when Harry's voice caught her off guard. "Portia, a moment if you would?"

She wanted to pretend she didn't hear him, but knew it would be rude, so she stopped and looked over her shoulder at him.

"I'd like to apologize for Beau's behavior." Stepping closer, he set one hand on the banister and planted the other on his hip. In a quieter voice, he added, "He's been a different man since we came home. Can't please him no matter what we do, but I for one am pleased you've joined us. I'd be happy to introduce you to the other ladies at church tomorrow and perhaps escort you around the town when you have a free afternoon?"

"That's very kind of you, Mr. Franklin."

"Harry."

"Yes, Harry. I'll take your offer into consideration. Now, if you'll excuse me."

"Of course." Harry stepped back and swiped a lock of sandy brown hair from his brow. "Good night, Portia."

She gave him a nod and continued upstairs, certain she'd become the object of unwanted attention. It was also clearly obvious that she had made an unfavorable impression on her employer, though she couldn't fathom how. He couldn't possibly blame her for not knowing about his son's muteness, since no one mentioned it before today. Nor could her husband's occupation have come as a surprise. All her credentials were sent along with her letter of application — her teaching certificate and the letter of recommendation from a former instructor. Surely he had examined them. Trying to find some clue to his cold reception, she replayed the dinner conversation in her mind until she reached the landing.

Then again, both Isaac and Harry had referenced his state of mind. Perhaps his behavior *did* stem from that.

Across the hall to her left, Jonathan's coppery head peeked out at her. She offered him a smile and said, "Goodnight, Jonathan." But he closed the door and, as she expected, didn't answer.

Once in her room, Portia readied herself for bed. She'd made a mistake coming there. All she wanted was some satisfying work to occupy her grief-weary mind, not an employer who couldn't stand her presence or a student who feared being in the same room with her.

Remaining at home, heartbreaking as it was, at least she *belonged* among all those familiar things, even the painful memories. Here, she was a foreigner in a foreign land with no guide to show her how to interact with the natives. Navigating these new waters was much more terrifying than she had imagined it would be, but she wasn't ready to turn tail and run just yet. She had to give it a chance, to know she'd fought the good fight before she surrendered to failure.

She changed into her nightclothes, carried a lamp to the night stand, and settled onto the mattress. Light illuminated her family Bible there on the table's edge. The curved-up corners of the leather cover beckoned to be handled once more. Swallowing hard, she reached for it, but... every time she'd tried to read it over these last months, words that once provided food for her very soul had become empty and useless.

Still it was the one familiar thing in this land of uncertainty. She picked it up, laid the big volume on her lap, and turned right to Ecclesiastes. A few more flips of the delicate pages led to a passage she could recite in her sleep. She read aloud, softly, as her fingers traced the words.

"To every thing there is a season, and a time to every purpose under the heaven:

A time to be born, and a time to die; a time to plant, and a time to pluck up that which is planted;

A time to kill, and a time to heal; a time to break down, and a time to build up;

A time to weep, and a time to laugh; a time to mourn, and a time to dance;

A time to cast away stones, and a time to gather stones together; a time to embrace, and a time to refrain from embracing;

A time to get, and a time to lose; a time to keep, and a time to cast away;

A time to rend, and a time to sew; a time to keep silence, and a time to speak;

A time to love, and a time to hate; a time of war, and a time of peace."

Just as she figured, the words didn't bring solace or any grand purposes of a higher plan. They simply stated the obvious, though she appreciated the poetic arrangement. Closing the Bible with a quiet sigh, she returned it to the nightstand. She extinguished the lamp and settled on her side, pulling the quilt snugly up to her chin. Outside, wind whistled through the trees, while shadows of their branches danced on the moonlit lace curtains. For just a moment before closing her eyes, she imagined Jake's arm around her and snuggled into his imaginary embrace.

Chapter Six

Sunday morning brought clear blue skies and a crisp breeze. A slight chill lingered in the house. Breakfast was a quiet affair, with only Beau, Jonny, and Ezra at the dining room table. Beau was used to Harry skipping breakfast, especially on Sundays, but he wondered about Portia until he found her eating in the kitchen while Bessie made coffee.

Maybe he had her figured all wrong, but Ezra, on the other hand... the old man had been trying to find him a wife for a good year. Perhaps in Portia he'd found a young lady desperate for a husband and a fortune and hoped she'd stick. Pity for her if that was the case — she would get neither, especially the latter.

When church time came around, Beau settled into the driver's seat of the carriage, while Ezra climbed in to sit beside him. Jonny hopped in the back seat. Beau pulled out his pocket watch and stared at the house. Harry and Portia should have been out by now. They were helping Bessie gather food for an after-church picnic. How long could that take?

"Impatient, are we?" Ezra asked.

"No."

The old man looked back at Jonny. "Do you like Mrs. McAllister?"

Jonny shrugged.

"What about you, Beauregard?" Ezra puffed his pipe and remained as straight-faced as a politician.

He'd have to play the diplomatic part on this one for now. "I haven't known her long enough to decide one way or another."

"She's gonna do just fine," Ezra said through a puff of smoke. "And you better mind your manners from now on when she's around."

Beau pulled at his shirt collar. "I'll mind my manners when I'm certain your conscience is clear."

"Never been clearer, son. You know, the war's over. You gotta stop distrustin' everyone and everything. That little lady in there has taken a big risk comin' here to live with strangers. The least we can do is show her some common courtesy. Say, why don't you and Jonny go fishin' this afternoon?"

"I'm tired." He wasn't really lying, but it was more than lack of sleep. He'd never forget all those things he said to Jonny, how he'd screamed like a madman and drove his son to muteness. He couldn't bear to sit on the creek bank, staring at the child he had created with Claire, with the silence between them screaming the ugly truth. Jonny hated him, and probably always would.

Ezra blew a sigh that ruffled his mustache. "We're all tired, son."

Harry walked out carrying a basket in one hand and a blanket in the other. He laughed, and Portia responded with a shy smile. She wore a yellow dress with a flowered print. A white bonnet haloed her head, and she held a Bible in her ungloved hands.

Ezra leaned closer to Beau and whispered, "Looks like Harry's making her feel welcome."

"Good," Beau answered. He raised his voice toward the latecomers. "I'm glad you could finally join us, Mrs. McAllister."

She looked him in the eye and gave a curt nod. "Thank you, Mr. Stanford."

Beau's eyes widened a bit. He had expected her to be more unsettled after last night, especially if she was a co-conspirator in Pa's matchmaking plan. He had certainly done his best to ruffle her feathers. Either she was a good actress or maybe he really was a heartless bastard.

"It's not getting any earlier. Let's go," he snapped.

"Keep your pants on, Beau," Harry said as he placed the picnic supplies in the carriage. He helped Portia to her seat beside Jonny, and his hand lingered on hers a little longer than necessary before he climbed in next to her. Beau rolled his eyes. Did Harry realize he was flirting with his mail-order bride?

Harry answered him with a wink. No woman was safe from his flirtations. Of course, in this situation, Beau couldn't have cared less. He faced forward again and snapped the reins.

They pulled up to the church a few minutes later. Carriages lined the street, emptying their burdens of Lebanon's townsfolk. Women and children filed into the bright white Presbyterian church with the newly rebuilt steeple. Of all the town's structures, this one came first on the list of repairs after the war.

Men congregated in groups of twos and threes on the sidewalk, chatting before the church bells sent them to their seats. Like every Sunday since Beau's return, most of them cast bitter glances his way and turned their backs toward him. They'd never forgive him for joining the Federals. But he couldn't have lived with himself had he not. If he and his family had to forever endure the town's disdain, then so be it, though resurrecting his business would be even more difficult without their support.

Harry jumped out and helped Portia down. He offered his arm, and she took it lightly before they strolled inside the church together. Beau watched them until they disappeared into the darkness beyond the doorway.

Ezra climbed out with Jonny at his heels and turned back to Beau. "Still glad Harry's making her feel welcome?"

"Couldn't be happier."

Beau flicked the reins and drove the carriage behind the church to park. At least he had answered honestly. If Harry and Portia took up together, he'd be happy for them. Harry had been single for long enough and needed a decent woman to straighten him out, not to mention a relationship between the two would prove she wasn't conspiring with Ezra.

When Beau stepped through the church doors, Mrs. Murphy was warming up the organ with the dulcet chords of "*Holy, Holy, Holy, Lord God Almighty.*" Portia and Harry were already standing in place at the traditional Stanford bench — right side, third row from the front. Jonny and Ezra filed in beside them. The place was packed — a sea of black for those still in mourning, with a little color thrown in by those who were more fortunate.

Some visitors occupied the old widows' bench on the second row. The little hunchbacks squeezed in by Ezra, mumbling and grumbling about being ousted from their favorite roost and having to sit beside those *"Yankees."* The only space left for Beau was on the aisle end beside Portia. He considered turning back to endure the service while standing beside the door, but Ezra spotted him and waved for him to come sit.

He could either squeeze in beside this young woman he wasn't quite sure about or risk a slew of stares from the rubbernecked congregation all morning. He chose the former, and with hat in hand, stepped in beside Portia. She glanced up at him. He acknowledged her with a quick nod before she averted her eyes. Her cheeks were rosy, and she gripped her Bible with trembling hands. Maybe he really had ruffled her feathers. Why did he suddenly feel so guilty about it?

From the pulpit, the pastor sang with his throaty bellow, waving his hymnal along with the organ music. The congregation joined in.

"Holy, holy, holy, Lord God almighty
Early in the morning, our song shall rise to thee!"

71

Beau's eyes drifted back to Portia and took in a few more details. Not bad-looking, certainly. The yellow print dress she wore was probably her best gown, but she had taken good care of it. Strands of honey-brown hair had escaped her bonnet to lie on the nape of her neck. She couldn't be much taller than Jonny. The top of her head barely reached his shoulder.

"Holy, holy, holy, merciful and mighty
God in three persons, blessed Trinity!"

He felt the stares before he found their source. Sure enough, the town gossips, young and old, had honed in. Soon as he turned his head toward them, they looked away. Portia was about to be the talk of the town — a young widow living without a chaperone in the Stanford home. So scandalous! He pinched his lips together so he wouldn't laugh. Even the war hadn't silenced these busybodies.

The preacher hollered, "Page 152 — Nearer My God to Thee!"

Mrs. Murphy's round jowls shook as she sang from her organ bench. Beau mouthed the words, but he never really sang. He couldn't hear over the women crowing to his left anyway. He stopped moving his mouth and listened to Portia singing.

"Though like the wanderer,
The sun goes down,
Darkness be over me,"

Her eyes were closed, and though her singing voice wasn't perfect, it was pleasant and soft. Maybe an octave lower than Claire's used to be.

"My rest a stone;

Yet in my dreams I'd be
Nearer my God, to thee!"

Tears escaped from the corners of her eyes by the time the song ended, drawing him ever closer to the conclusion that he was indeed the heartless one, not Portia. Beau fumbled for his handkerchief, but Harry found his first. Portia took the cloth and dabbed her eyes. Beau started to ask her if she was all right, but Harry wrapped one arm lightly around her shoulders and whispered the question instead. She sniffed and nodded.

Adjusting the shirt collar that suddenly seemed too tight, Beau forced himself to focus on the pulpit.

Once the hymns were sung, the service dragged on for an eternity. The preacher bellowed his usual fire and brimstone while a few stray, "Amens," arose from the congregation. Portia stared at her lap most of the time and fiddled with her gloves, nodding and glancing up as Harry whispered to her. Ezra's head drooped down to his chest, while Jonny had fallen fast asleep on his arm by the time the preacher started losing his voice. An onerous snore from the old man finally stalled the sermon.

The preacher snapped his Bible closed on the pulpit. "Well, now," he said, dabbing the sweat from his brow and smacking his fleshy lips, "let's all be dismissed for dinner on the grounds."

With Beau bottlecapping the row, he had to go first, so he stepped into the aisle and stood aside to let the others out. Harry, with his hand flitting over the small of Portia's back, led her toward the doors. Ezra and Jonny ambled out, both of them yawning and rubbing their eyes.

He tried to follow right behind them, but the town gossips, led by Mrs. Peabody, crowded in front of him. He hoped Harry could at least keep Portia out of their talons long enough for them to settle apart from the crowd and have a peaceful meal.

The preacher slapped him on the back before he could make his escape. "Brother Stanford, what's all this about a young lady coming to your home? Should I assume…?"

"No, you shouldn't." At the preacher's taken-aback look, Beau added, "We've just hired her on as a housekeeper and tutor for Jonny. She's a war widow from Brentwood and had nowhere else to turn."

That last part was a stretch, but he figured God didn't mind a little stretching when the moment called for it so long as the basic truth remained intact.

"I see, I see. Confederate or Federal?"

Beau crossed his arms. When would the time come that such distinctions weren't needed? "Confederate," he admitted, hating the feel of that word on his tongue.

The preacher slapped Beau on the back again, this time hard enough to make him wheeze. "Glad to see your Christian charity extended even unto thine enemy. You Stanfords have always done good in the sight of God, no matter what other folks say about it. Why, where would Harry Franklin and them Negroes of yours be without y'all? Speakin' of… looks like Harry might have taken a shine to her."

One more backslap, and he elbowed past Beau and out the door. Nothing moved that man faster than the prospects of cold chicken, molasses, and hoecakes. With his back stinging from the repeated assaults, Beau continued down the aisle and over the threshold, ignoring a few people who scowled at him on the way out. He couldn't let Portia face all those biddies alone. *Not alone, of course. Harry's taking care of her.* The thought didn't bring him any comfort. He wasn't sure why, except that Harry's intentions weren't always good, especially with women.

Rounding the side of the church, he groaned. Mrs. Peabody and the rest of the gossip flock had swarmed around Portia. They ushered her off under a cedar tree for further pecking. Harry, Ezra, and Jonny were setting up the picnic. He started to step in and save her, but she smiled and chatted with them and didn't seem too flustered. More hair had fallen onto the graceful line of her neck. She twirled a lock of it around her finger and glanced at him. He nodded in return.

Harry sauntered over with a conspiratorial look on his face. "Why didn't you tell me that Lydia is coming back?"

Beau pulled his gaze from the women. "What?"

"Lydia Clemons is coming back from Philly, and you didn't tell me. She's got to be what, twenty, twenty-one by now?" Harry slicked his hair down as though Lydia were standing right in front of him.

"I haven't thought much about it since Pa told me. They'll be staying with us until their home is renovated."

"You'd better be thinkin' about it, Beau. Lydia's had her eyes set on you ever since she was a child."

"She's Claire's little cousin, for goodness sake. I can't think of her that way."

"Yeah, well, Claire's not coming back, and you're not getting any younger."

Beau clenched his jaw and bit back words that were not at all appropriate on church property. He managed to strain a more neutral statement through his gritted teeth. "I really don't want to talk about this right now."

"Come on, man, think about it. Why would they come back at all, if not for you? Oliver owns half of Philly already. It's not like they have to come back here to *this* mess. I'd bet my bottom dollar they're coming back because of *you*."

"Nonsense. They've got roots here, that's all."

Beau scuffed up some grass with his boot. Harry's notion had to be way off. His memories of Lydia consisted of pink ribbons and curly blond hair, skipping around Paradise Plantation back in its heyday. He could hardly imagine her as a woman now, especially one interested in marrying *him*. Then again, she had written him several letters since his return. *I'll forever cherish those days when you taught me to ride. They were the happiest of my life…*

Harry shrugged. "I guess we'll see then, won't we? It'll be fun having old Oliver back in town. He always had the best smokes."

"We've got a lot of work to do," Beau said. "I'm not exactly looking forward to entertaining house guests."

"Portia can help with that, right?"

Beau craned his neck to check on her. She wasn't smiling anymore, but crossed her arms and fiddled with her dress collar. The ladies had her cornered against the cedar's trunk, all of them gesturing and nodding passionately among themselves.

Harry shook his head. "I'll go save her."

"No, let me."

76

Beau hurried past Harry before he could respond. Why he felt compelled to play Sir Knight, he didn't know, except he didn't want to talk about Lydia's imminent arrival anymore. And he *had* hired Portia, after all, or at least given his consent for Ezra to hire her, so the least he could do was keep her out of harm's way.

He reached the circle of vultures in time to hear Mrs. Peabody's scathing remarks. "I'm not sure how you all do it in Brentwood, but around here at least, it's considered proper to wear only black or a very dark gray for at least an entire year to mourn properly. And your daughter's been gone for only eight months? We can lend you something, I'm sure…"

"Oh, yes, yes," the others clucked in response.

Beau started to interrupt, but Portia lifted her chin and addressed them all. "While your concern for my apparel is appreciated, I do not need nor want your charity. Abby was the light of my world. I do her memory no justice to go around wearing darkness. Now if you will excuse me."

She pushed past them and seemed startled to see Beau there.

"Good day, Mrs. Peabody… ladies," he said in the most cordial manner he could muster. "I see you've met my new hire, but I'd rather you not scare her off before she has a chance to get settled."

He offered his arm. She latched onto him quickly.

"It's a shame," he added, looking at Portia, "that some folks are more worried about traditions than Christian hospitality."

The ladies fluttered their fans and looked to be on the verge of fainting while he led Portia away.

"Are you all right?" he asked.

"Yes." Portia exhaled as though relieved. "Thank you… for intervening, Mr. Stanford."

"I'm sorry you had to endure that bunch. They've been ruling the roost around here since before I can remember. They weren't even friendly with Claire for a while after we married. Here she was the daughter of a respected slave-owning family marrying an 'abolitionist'. You'd think the past few years would have tempered them down a bit."

"Yes, one would think so." She laughed softly. Thankfully, she seemed able to recover well under such pressure.

"We have Bessie's chicken to look forward to."

Her stomach answered with a loud rumble.

He had to smile at that. "Hungry?"

"Very."

Harry stood up from the picnic blanket with a concerned pout wrinkling his forehead. "Portia, dear, did those women bother you?"

Her cheeks reddened. "No, I'm fine, thank you."

She didn't even look at Harry's outstretched hand as she settled herself on the blanket. Beau sat across from her by Jonny. She straightened her skirt and helped Harry pass around the plates. They leisurely ate their lunch, conversation at a minimum, while Beau kept a discreet eye on Portia and Harry. She didn't seem to be warming up to him at all, actually. He tore a hunk of meat off a chicken leg and chewed slowly, wondering what to make of that.

A chilly wind and light drizzle kicked up leaves and stung Beau's face by the time they reached the house.

Plans to sit and rest on the front porch were ruined, so they all gathered in the parlor. Claire had taken great pains to decorate this room for guests, and Beau thought of her every time he came in here. She'd spent hours sorting through fabric samples until she decided on green brocade for the curtains. She even made him return a brand new settee the same day they bought it because the upholstery color didn't match perfectly. But her fussiness was worth it, because there on the green velvet by the light of a warm fire, they conceived Jonny.

The settee wasn't nearly as lovely with Harry sitting there. Beau sighed quietly and sank into the soft cushiony seat. Portia sat in a chair by the window, her shawl and bonnet placed neatly on the table. She picked up a book and thumbed through it, while the usual discussions began about the week ahead.

Harry said, "I'll head out early tomorrow and check on that filly in Lockport."

"I swear, if you bring back another idiot horse..."

"Don't start on me, Beau."

Ezra cleared his throat and expelled a puff of cherry-scented smoke. "Settle down now, boys. Ain't neither one of you got to paint fences tomorrow, and these old knees are already complainin' about it. So, quit your gripin'."

Portia laughed, and Ezra winked at her. Beau had to admit, it *did* feel lighter with a woman's laughter in the house again, Rebel or not.

Isaac walked in, removed his hat, and took a seat by Ezra.

Beau nodded to him. "Let's get that field over there by your place plowed if it's not too wet tomorrow. We need to get some cotton in the ground."

"All right," Isaac answered. "Ol' Samson is raring to go."

"Good, and we better get on those fencerows too. I'll see if I can do something with the crazy filly." Beau cast a disgruntled look at Harry, who fiddled with a new pocket knife and pretended not to notice.

Resting his elbows on his knees, Isaac rubbed his chin and looked at Beau in all seriousness. "When's the last time ya slept?"

"Why do you ask?"

"Them circles under your eyes is as dark as me, that's why." Isaac turned to Ezra. "He ain't been sleepin', has he?"

"No, not since…"

Beau cleared his throat and flicked his eyes toward Portia, who had been watching them with mild curiosity. Noticing everyone looking at her, she lowered her head back to the book on her lap. They hadn't had any guests since he came home from the war, so they'd fallen into their familiar roles, and Beau hadn't thought twice about it until now. Though in private, Bessie and Isaac were part of the family, they'd been careful over the years to show the public more distance between them. And he couldn't be sure of Portia yet, considering her affiliation.

"Well, Bessie will make ya somethin' that can help," Isaac said with a note of finality.

Beau hid a smile behind his hand. That old bugger always had to get in the last word.

Bessie entered with a tray of coffee and cookies, followed by Jonny. He grabbed a sugar cookie off the plate before she could set it down.

"Jonny, where's your manners, boy?" she chided, but there was no real sting to it.

He put it back on the plate, and with his hands behind his back, flicked his gaze from the cookie up to Bessie. This was Jonny's way of asking nicely, now that he didn't speak.

"Of course, you can have one, honey."

He snatched one up and took a huge bite.

She set the tray on the table beside Portia. Her voice turned as chilly as the wind outside. "Help yourself."

"Um, thank you," Portia said. "Shall I help you serve?"

"No, you best relax until tomorrow. Before the week's out, you'll be prayin' for Sunday to come along again."

Portia lowered her eyes and shifted in her seat. Beau had expected Bessie to be standoffish to their new hire, but her cold reception clearly made Portia uncomfortable. Maybe she had figured out Ezra's matchmaking scheme. She poured coffee and passed it out to the men. She added one lump of sugar to Beau's and handed him the cup.

"Thank you," he said, remembering the days when two sugar cubes in his coffee wasn't a luxury.

Jonny plopped on the floor with his sack of marbles and ate a cookie in two bites. Loosening the drawstring, he poured the marbles on the rug. The colorful glass globes rolled in random directions and plinked softly against one another. They were imported from Germany, a gift from Claire's uncle Oliver before the war began.

Portia closed her book and placed it back on the table. She eased down to the floor beside Jonny.

"What are those?" she asked, as though he would miraculously answer.

He arranged them into a line along one of the grooves in the rug and didn't look up. "Marbles," Ezra said.

"How do you play with them?"

Jonny sat still for a moment, but then picked up the biggest marble and held the clear glass ball between his thumb and forefinger. He glanced at his grandfather.

Ezra narrated. "You take that big one, see — it's called the shooter. And the little ones are your targets. You flick the shooter and see if you can hit the targets."

"Show me."

She kept her attention on Jonny, even when Pa answered for him, and she didn't seem to be feigning interest. Still, Beau couldn't help wondering who she was trying to impress.

On knees and elbows, Jonny leaned close to the floor and closed one eye. With his tongue poking out one side of his mouth, he aimed the shooter by cradling it in the crook of his index finger. He cocked his thumb behind it and let it go. The shooter flew forward across the rug and plinked into a red-painted smaller marble, knocking it out of the rug's groove and onto the wood floor.

Portia caught it before it could roll under the chair. "May I try?"

Jonny shrugged and gave a little nod.

Mimicking Jonny's posture, Portia leaned close to the floor. She even closed one eye and stuck her tongue out. Ezra chuckled. She took her shot, and the shooter hit a blue marble at dead center, sending it flying off the rug, across the floor, and straight into Beau's boot.

Jonny's eyes were bright with excitement. He even bounced up and down on his knees but turned to Ezra again.

"You shoot good, Mrs. McAllister," Ezra said.

"I shoot *well*," Portia corrected.

"Yes, ma'am, very well. Seems I picked the perfect teacher."

"Truly amazing, Portia." Harry nudged Beau. "She's really somethin', huh?"

Cheeks red as beets, she stared down at the marbles and fiddled with her skirt.

Ezra tapped his pipe on the ashtray to empty the ashes. "Hush now, Harry. Poor girl's face gonna burn plumb off. Jonny, why don't you go show her the study? She might want to get ready for tomorrow."

"That's a wonderful idea," Portia said, glancing at Ezra with a grateful smile.

Jonny frowned and picked his marbles up, dropping them one by one into the bag.

"Do what your grandpa tells you, son," Beau said.

Harry sprang from the settee. "Here, let me help you up, darlin'."

Portia took his outstretched hand and got to her feet. "Thank you, Mr. Franklin."

"I told you, call me Harry."

"Of course." Pulling her hand from his, she added, "After you, Jonathan."

She followed Jonny from the room, skirts in her hands, at a quick pace.

"I don't know what else to do." Harry sighed and dropped back onto the settee. "I'm really trying here."

"Maybe a little too hard," Beau mumbled.

"Oh? And how would you go about it, *Mister* Stanford?"

"She's not here for your pleasure, Harry."

"What's that supposed to mean?"

Ezra stopped stuffing his pipe and pointed it at the two of them. "Listen here. I'll not have you upsettin' that poor girl. She's been through hell and back and ain't here to fetch either of your attentions."

"You sure about that?" Beau asked.

Under bushy gray eyebrows, his father's no-nonsense gaze was unrelenting. "It's time you let go of that notion, Beauregard. Portia's innocent, and I didn't bring her here for you. Or are you just too full of yourself to not realize that?"

Shaking his head, Harry crossed his arms and looked away.

"Fine," Beau conceded. "I just thought that…"

"Well, you thought wrong."

"All right, I'll apologize. Sincerely this time." The old man could still lay down the law when he wanted to. Beau got up and made his way to the door. "I still don't know how I'll pay her."

Ezra struck a match against his boot and applied the flame to the cherry-scented leaves. "You know," he said between puffs, "I think she's happy just having a place to stay for now. Give her some time, son. You too, Harry."

Beau nodded and headed to the study.

Portia stood by the shelf that housed the school books. She had stacked some on the desk nearby, and she flipped through one of them. More hair had fallen from her bun like it just couldn't bear to be confined any longer. Honey-brown locks draped down her back and over her shoulders. She seemed enraptured with whatever she was reading. Beau spied part of the title — Tennyson Poems — on the cover.

"I hope you're finding everything you need," he said.

Startled, Portia almost dropped the book, but managed to close it and place it with the others on the desk. "Oh, yes, except I'm not sure where the paper and pencils are."

"Did you try the desk drawers?"

"Yes, but a few drawers are locked. Do you have the key?"

"No, but Bessie might. Just tell her what you need."

"All right." She peered at another shelf. "I don't see any atlases or globes. Would they be somewhere else?"

He moved to stand beside her, wishing he had time and inclination to read so many books. Claire always had her nose in one and could quote Tennyson and Shakespeare in her sleep. Her mind was one of the reasons he'd fallen for her.

"Bessie would probably know that, too," he said. "She handled all that after Claire died. But I don't see why my son would need to know geography. He might never leave Tennessee."

He realized he'd struck a nerve when she stiffened her jaw and stood straight as a fencepost. "I'm not sure how you feel about this, Mr. Stanford, but I believe an education is the most valuable gift you can give a child, apart from love. When a child is lacking in those things, it's a tragedy."

Beau wasn't accustomed to backtalk from his employees, but from the way she jutted her little chin at him, he wasn't sure whether to be irritated or amused. "Are you telling me my son is lacking in education and love?"

"Of course not. I just…"

"Because if you think you can tell that from having been here for barely a day, then you need to think twice. Besides, if I didn't care about my son's education, I wouldn't have hired you, would I?"

She blushed and averted her eyes, placing a trembling hand on the stack of books. "I'm sorry. I didn't mean it to sound that way. Please forgive my forwardness."

There I go again. He had to temper his attitude and meet her on neutral ground. He took another Tennyson volume — Claire's favorite — from the shelf. Flipping to one of her many ribbon bookmarks, he found a familiar poem.

"Claire used to read this to me when we were courting," he said and cleared his throat, hoping it wasn't too late to call a truce.

He read the last stanza.

"If you are not the heiress born,
And I," said he, "the lawful heir,
We two will wed to-morrow morn,
And you shall still be Lady Clare."

Watching for her reaction, he relaxed a bit when Portia smiled brightly. Even her eyes took part in it. "A lady of good taste, I see. And I used to recite this one to Jake:

'*Millions of throats would bawl for civil rights,*
No woman named: therefore I set my face
Against all men, and lived but for mine own.'"

She shook her head, and her smile drooped a little. "He'd laugh and call me a rebel."

"For good reason, I bet."

Her cheeks reddened again.

"Listen, I wanted to apologize for being... less than hospitable. I assumed things that I shouldn't have, and I think it's because I felt guilty."

"Guilty? Why?"

Beau placed the book back on the shelf and raked a hand through his hair. "To be honest, I'm not sure how to pay you. I can barely afford to pay the folks I've got now, and with Jonny's condition, your job will be even more of a challenge."

"I see."

"So, I'll understand if you want to annul this position and call it even."

Exhaling with a sigh, she said, "A mute child can still learn just fine. And with all due respect, Mr. Stanford, I'm not here for the money. You may compensate me when you are able. I'm simply satisfied to have something other than memories to occupy my hands and mind."

"That's what Pa told me. Should have listened."

"If you have any doubt in my loyalty because of my husband's affiliation..."

He held up his hand. "I think it's best not to venture there again. Only time will determine your loyalties here."

Portia ducked her head and nodded.

"Good, then. I expect you to make a scholar out of my boy in return for your room and board."

"I don't think that will be too difficult. Jonathan is a clever young man."

"How can you tell?"

"Once a teacher, always a teacher, Mr. Stanford."

Beau gestured around the study. "Then this place is all yours. If you need more supplies, you're welcome to ask Isaac to take you into town."

"Do you have a buggy I can drive?"

Beau raised an eyebrow. "Yes, however, I'd recommend you have an escort. Times are different now. We have to be careful."

"All right, and thank you. If you'll excuse me, sir, I'll find Bessie and finish preparing for tomorrow's lessons."

"One more thing."

"Yes?"

"You've noticed the scar on Bessie's face?"

Portia shrunk back a little. "I did."

He kept his expression calm. He didn't want to intimidate her again, but he wanted her to see his side of things. "She had gone into town with me and Pa one morning. I was fifteen, sixteen at most. I'd been acting up, being disrespectful — you know how boys are. We had just come out of a store and she smacked my mouth. I deserved it, but one of the local overseers was there on his horse and witnessed it. He struck her across the face with some kind of whip that had metal hooks on the end. Cut her pretty bad. I dragged that man off his horse, knocked him to the ground and kept hitting. It took Bessie and Pa to pull me off him. Perhaps now you can understand my distaste for your husband's former occupation."

She nodded but wouldn't meet his eyes. "I understand." Her voice quivered as though she might cry at any moment. "If it makes any difference, you should know that Jake shared your sentiments. He also paid dearly for it. If you'll excuse me…"

Beau stared after her as she hurried from the room. *What did she mean, paid dearly for it?* This woman was proving to be more perplexing than he imagined.

He pulled out the chair and sat at the desk. Propping himself on his elbow, he rested his chin in his hand. His eyes drifted to the fountain pen resting in its brass stand. He picked it up and traced a finger over the names engraved on it:

Beauregard and Claire Stanford, est. May 17, 1854

Claire had presented it to him when they first married and when she decorated the study. He never liked it much, though he never told her that. It didn't hold ink very well and left black blobs every few words in his correspondence. But he missed the way Claire handled things with such grace and ease. Portia was lucky in a way. At least she could get away from the memories. Beau had no choice but to live under their unpredictable shadows, creeping up on him when he least expected it.

Chapter Seven

The gray cotton dress with the white lace collar hadn't been worn since Portia had taught school before Abby came along. Aside from being slightly crumpled and loose-fitting on her thin frame, it was in good condition. Her cedar chest kept the moths away and it still smelled like her little home. Jake had called her an old school marm when she wore it, and although it did make her feel matronly, the dress had proven comfortable for a long day in a classroom. Now, of course, she had only one student — and a mute one at that. She hoped she could find a way to connect with him despite his silence.

Taking extra care to pin her hair tightly so it wouldn't come loose, she swallowed her doubts and headed downstairs for breakfast. To her surprise, Beau was the only person at the table, and from the bits of egg and half-eaten biscuit on his plate, she could tell he had almost finished with his meal. He looked haggard with dark shadows under his eyes and more wrinkles on his brow than there should be for a new morning. He muttered an indecipherable greeting to her as she entered the dining room.

"Good morning, Mr. Stanford."

She headed for the kitchen, intending to eat in there, but hesitated when he asked, "Sleep well?"

"Yes, and you?"

"I've had better nights."

"Sorry to hear that." She started for the kitchen again.

"Take a seat. Bessie's already got breakfast on the table, as you can see."

He gestured toward a platter containing a few strips of bacon, a nice pile of eggs, and perfectly browned biscuits. A couple jars of preserves and a pitcher of milk rounded out the spread.

"All right." She wondered if he considered her tardy and was upset that she didn't help Bessie in the kitchen. But she figured it was best not to stir the pot and risk further aggravation. She took her seat and added one piece of bacon, a spoonful of eggs, and a biscuit to her plate.

Several moments of strange silence passed, with Beau slowly working his way through another helping of eggs.

Portia wiped her mouth with her napkin and asked, "Where is everyone?"

"Harry's gone to Lockport. I guess Pa and Jonny slept in. I'm usually the first one up. Guess you're an early bird, too."

"Always have been. Farm wife, you know."

That last part incited a heavy feeling in her chest. She turned her attention to her breakfast and nibbled some bacon. At least he didn't think she was late.

Beau cleared his throat. "Right." He paused as though trying to figure out what to say next. "I've been wondering something… when we last spoke, you said your husband paid dearly for his sentiments. What did you mean?"

"Well… I suppose it all began with a lie." She fumbled with her biscuit, breaking it into little pieces. "John Overton was the owner of Travellers Rest. He had slaves, yes, but he was good to everyone who worked for him. He was fond of Jake, too. When men started getting conscripted, Mr. Overton vouched for Jake and claimed him as a full-time overseer, so he could avoid being put into service. The head overseer was Mr. Barrett, but the slaves respected Jake more even though he was there only a few weeks out of the year. Some of them confided in him about Mr. Barrett and his ill treatment of them. Jake was very troubled by it. He knew what my daddy… he didn't believe anyone deserved such abuse. By that time, though, Mr. Overton had fled behind Confederate lines. Jake decided to bring the matter to Mrs. Overton, but she made the mistake of confronting Mr. Barrett. In retaliation, *he* threatened to turn in Jake for avoiding conscription. Jake knew if he didn't enlist willingly, he faced prison, fines we couldn't afford, or worse. He joined up in February of sixty-four. Abby was just six months old. That was the last time we saw him alive."

With a slight nod, he stared at his plate, slowly chewing a bite of biscuit. His worry-creased expression relaxed. He spoke but sounded gentler than before. "I apologize for assuming the worst of your husband."

Another tense pause hung between them and then, "Did you... get to see him... after?"

Her eyes widened as she met his gaze.

"I'm sorry," he said quickly, "I shouldn't have asked such a personal thing."

She swallowed past the lump in her throat. "No, it's all right. I did see him. They brought him home in the back of a wagon. He still looked like himself, but..." Putting the memory into words brought tears to her eyes and a familiar ache to her chest. "...it was as though everything that had been my husband was gone, leaving only an empty shell, if that makes any sense."

"It does make sense." He sat silent for a moment as he rubbed his forehead. "I didn't get to see Claire, just her grave. I don't know if it would have been easier or not to have seen her, but I'll always wonder."

Portia had never expected to share such heavy things with her employer, but she found some comfort in it. She hadn't spoken to anyone about Jake or Abby except Ellen, and as sympathetic as her friend had been, she couldn't truly relate. Mr. Stanford, at the very least, understood the pain of losing a spouse — how lonely and topsy-turvy the world felt afterward. She wanted to respond with something that might comfort him in return, but Ezra and Jonathan came to the table before she had a chance.

"Mornin'." Ezra's joints sounded like popcorn as he eased into his seat. "The hips ain't what they used to be. Why the long faces? Somethin' happen?"

Beau glanced at Portia before turning his attention to Ezra. "No. Just tired."

93

"Bad night again, huh? You know, a bit of laudanum could—"

"No." He glared at the old man.

Jonathan absently helped himself to eggs, eyes flicking between his father and grandfather.

Beau turned to him. "Eat up. You've got lessons to get to."

The boy nodded and plopped the eggs onto his plate, spilling some on the table.

"At least let Bessie fix you something," Ezra pleaded. "You need sleep, son."

"Excuse me, I've got work to do," Beau said as he scooted his chair back and stood. He stuffed the last bite of biscuit in his mouth and strode out.

Ezra frowned. When the front door opened and slammed closed, he leaned toward Portia and spoke quietly. "He's not been sleepin' good, ever since he came home. If he's as cranky as a bear, that's why. Just don't tell him I told you."

Portia nodded and shivered, imagining the horrors Beau must have seen in the war. She thought about Jake like she had a thousand times before — of what he must have seen and felt before he died. But she couldn't let her mind drift to that helpless place again. She picked up her napkin, wiped her face, and cleared her throat. It got Jonathan's attention; he looked up at her with a chipmunk cheek full of food.

"Jonathan, have you done your chores yet?"

He chewed and scrunched his eyes at her as though she had suggested something unseemly.

"You've already done them, then?"

Ezra leaned toward her again and whispered, "Jonny doesn't do a lot of chores. Not since he went mute. Dr. Barton said to go easy on him, let him get lots of rest and maybe he'd relax enough to speak."

"Oh, I see." A protest sat on the tip of her tongue, but she bit it back. She couldn't afford to argue until she understood the situation better. "Then let's get started a bit early. That way we can review what you know already and decide where to go from there." Portia looked at her little pocket watch. "I'll meet you in the study in fifteen minutes."

Jonathan swallowed with a gulp and nodded.

Ezra put his hands on the table in a polite effort to stand and see her out, but Portia waved him back down to his seat.

"No need for that. I can handle my own chair. Enjoy your breakfast."

"Mighty kind of you, ma'am. Enjoy your lessons."

"I'm sure we will," she answered and winked at Jonathan. "Both of us."

The large study occupied the front eastern corner of the house. Thanks to Bessie, Portia now had the key to the desk in her possession. The evening prior, she had rearranged things to her liking — pencils and paper in the top drawer for easy access. A ruler, drawing compass, and abacus lay ready and waiting in the second drawer. She placed a sheet of paper and pencil on the smaller desk that sat in front of the rear window. Scanning the room, she admired the two tall windows that let in ample light for their lessons. If they could be so lucky as to acquire some paints and drawing supplies, she'd be thrilled.

Portia touched the marble bust of Shakespeare perched atop a pedestal. Her fingers lingered on William's cool forehead as she took in the little details of the room. Mementos, curtains, rugs, a brass fountain pen and other treasures filled the space — remnants of a wife and mother who'd put her love into this home. What a shame that the boy's mother had passed away before she could see her dreams for her son fulfilled. She felt a strange connection to this woman she never had the chance to meet, and a sudden wave of doubt washed over her. What if she couldn't give him the education his mother had wanted? She didn't come from a wealthy background. No one in her family had any education beyond a few years of grammar school, and her own training hadn't been extensive, certainly not from a well-regarded university like the late Mrs. Stanford wanted for her son.

Before she could decide whether or not she was up to the task, she noticed Jonathan standing in the doorway, head down, and feet shuffling.

"Good morning," she said. "Ready?"

He shrugged and kept studying his shoes.

"What's your favorite subject?"

Another shrug. Obviously gaining the boy's trust wasn't going to be easy, not to mention encouraging him to speak. She decided, however, to treat him as if he wasn't mute at all. If she could lighten the mood perhaps…

"From the looks of it, I'd say your favorite subject is feet."

He snapped to attention at that, looking at her with his head tilted to one side like a curious pup. A tiny smile flitted across his lips before he looked away again.

At least she'd chipped the armor. "Have a seat please."

Jonathan quickly obeyed, sitting at the small desk. He tapped his fingers to a marching drum rhythm. Portia rubbed her chin. Where to start? The best way to combat a child's illogical fear was to repeatedly expose them to it until the feeling subsided. Clearly, Jonathan was frightened of speaking, perhaps because he expected disapproval. Maybe she could remedy that.

"Jonathan, I want you to recite something your mother taught you. Anything at all."

The boy's face paled beneath his freckles. Fear flashed in his eyes. His poor little fingers froze mid-tap.

Portia turned away from him, hands clasped behind her back, pretending to study the titles on the nearest bookshelf. "Anything at all," she added lightly. "No matter how elementary."

Jonathan fumbled with a pencil, rolling it back and forth.

Portia took the lead with her favorite Longfellow poem. "Tell me not in mournful numbers, life is but an empty dream…"

She paused, waiting.

His deep intake of breath was followed by the sound of a pencil scratching across paper. She turned back toward him with a smile. He focused on his pencil, this time tapping it on the desk like a drum stick. Portia walked over, leaned in, and read what he had written.

You're not my mother.

As though Jonathan had punched her right in the mouth, she recoiled and turned around to face the large desk. Closing her eyes, she breathed deep to keep unwanted tears from spilling. She'd expected him to feel this way from the moment she accepted the position. But why did it hurt so badly? Perhaps her pain still festered too close to the surface for her to overcome his rebellion. *Not my mother* — not anyone's mother — not anymore.

Her jaw trembled, and with both hands flattened onto the surface of the desk, she decided to cancel their studies for today. No, she couldn't, she *wouldn't.* Being a teacher meant accepting every student's faults as well as their strengths. It was her job to help him grow and learn, no matter what.

After one shaky breath, she spoke over her shoulder. "I know I'm not your mother. But she wanted you to be educated, so that's why I'm here. Do you want to go against her wishes, or will you honor her memory instead by cooperating with me?"

No answer.

Figuring this whole exchange was probably a waste of time, she tried starting over. "Tell me not in mournful numbers, life is but an empty dream…"

A few painfully slow seconds passed. Then his pencil scratched across the paper again. She feared what she would find, but forced herself to turn around. Easing over to his desk, she leaned in and read.

For the soul is dead that slumbers, and things are not what they seem.

With a quiet sigh of relief, Portia continued, "Life is real! Life is earnest! And the grave is not its goal…"

Once again applying pencil to paper, he wrote, *Dust thou art, to dust returnest, was not spoken of the soul.*

He'd finally become responsive, even if he wouldn't actually speak. She would have to be content with that for now. "Impressive. You are familiar with Longfellow. Let us see what else you know."

Throughout the morning, Portia quizzed him on arithmetic, science, and history. Apart from struggling a bit with fractions and division, Jonathan proved to be very bright, though their interaction never progressed beyond her verbal questions and his written answers. His mother had taught him well, and Portia hoped Jonathan would open up eventually and show his true personality.

They'd just begun some composition when Bessie stuck her head in the room and announced lunch. Jonathan sprang from the seat and scurried for the door.

Portia spoke up. "Jonathan?"

Bessie grabbed his shirt collar before he could disappear into the hall. "Listen to her, young man. Don't make me fetch a switch."

He turned reluctantly and looked up at Bessie, who stood there with two hands on her hips, waiting, until he finally turned his face toward Portia.

"Be back here promptly at one o'clock, please," she said.

He nodded and disappeared behind Bessie. His running footsteps thudded across the hall to the kitchen.

Bessie shook her head and crossed her arms. "How are the studies goin'?"

"He's a very bright boy," Portia said, deciding not to mention his first written reply. "I... wish he felt comfortable enough to speak to me."

"I ain't seen nobody but the Lord work miracles, and I don't expect you will, either." She turned and started across the hall. "Lunch is gettin' cold."

Portia shivered. The real miracle would be gaining Bessie's trust, but how?

APRIL 17, 1866
Dear Ellen,

I hope this letter finds you all well. It is chilly this evening. Rain is pecking on the windows, obscuring our view of the world beyond. Mr. Stanford is still distrustful of me, I suppose because I am a "Rebel's" wife. We have conversed briefly, and though he may never accept me entirely, we have in common the heartache of losing a spouse. Perhaps that will be enough to nurture his trust in my abilities. I worry that he is not sleeping enough or spending time with his son. Both would do him good.

Jonathan reports to his studies on time, and he does everything I require of him, yet he will not speak no matter how I try to persuade him. I fear if I press him further, what little amicability we have for one another will be destroyed.

What I fail to understand, however, is why he is not expected to do chores. The boy's grandfather says the doctor advised rest in hopes of encouraging him to speak again. I cannot see what good that will do him. Boys his age should be gathering eggs, slopping hogs, cleaning the stables, or weeding the gardens. Perhaps he is truly traumatized from his mother's loss and father's distant demeanor, but I think he is capable of much more responsibility.

Tell me how everyone is faring. I imagine the baby will not be much longer in coming…

Portia awoke to the dim light of sunrise. Sun peeked through the clouds, promising a lovely spring day. She extended her arms and legs in one big, satisfying stretch. Something wriggled against her foot. With a startled yelp, she sprang from the bed and threw back the quilt. A garter snake, about two feet in length, wound itself into a frightened coil.

Hand on her chest and heart thudding against her palm, she closed her eyes and took several deep breaths. Her eyes snapped open when she heard a shuffling sound outside her door, followed by running footsteps heading for the stairs.

"Jonathan."

While not surprising, it still hurt that he would do such a thing. He resented her arrival, as Bessie did, and she doubted that would ever change. The next time she went into town, perhaps she could inquire about another position.

Her heart sank as she looked around for something in which to store her unwanted bedmate. She found a double-lidded knitting basket in the bottom of the wardrobe and emptied the yarn from it. Using one of the knitting needles, she gingerly lifted the snake from the bed to the basket. Once the little reptile was safely inside, she snapped the lid shut, retrieved two books from her bedside table, and placed them on each side of the lid. She and her brothers caught snakes when they were little; she knew what escape artists they could be.

Quickly as she could, she washed, dressed, and put up her hair. Downstairs, the dining room was vacant, though crumb-covered plates and an empty platter occupied the table. Portia carried the basket into the kitchen, where Bessie and Jonathan were eating their breakfast at the small table. The boy's eyes grew bigger the closer she came.

She walked right up to him, holding the basket at an angle. Soon as she lifted the lid, the little serpent's head popped out, and he welcomed them all with a flick of his tiny forked tongue.

"Sweet Jesus!" Bessie pushed away from the table, jumped to her feet and backed toward the door leading outside. "What do you think you're doing, bringing that thing in here? Tryin' to scare me to death?"

Portia shut the lid gently, being careful not to hurt the little snake. She looked directly at Jonathan. "I found it in my bed this morning. Care to explain?"

He flicked his eyes from Bessie to Portia and shook his head frantically.

"Jonny?" Bessie said, with a note of warning in her voice. "Did you put a snake in Mrs. McAllister's bed? You best tell the truth or you'll get a good whippin'."

He glanced at Portia and lowered his eyes to the table. Biting his lip, he finally nodded.

Bessie pointed toward the dining room door. "You get upstairs to your room and don't you come out 'til I tell you!"

"Wait," Portia said, as an idea sprang to mind. Jonathan paused at the threshold. "I think we can come up with something much more productive."

Bessie looked at her with one dark, skeptical brow lifted high.

"It's a nice day out. I say we skip lessons and put this boy to work. He's plenty old enough to carry his weight around here, and I have yet to see him do any chores."

Jonathan's shoulders drooped, and he gave her a look that suggested a good whipping would be the better punishment.

"We don't work him real hard, not since he stopped talking." Pity coated Bessie's words, and she looked at him as though he might soon be on his deathbed.

Nonsense. This 'condition' of his weighed down the whole household. The child was healthy and shouldn't be coddled into idleness that fostered disrespect and mischief. "His arms and legs are completely functional. He doesn't need to talk to be able to work."

With her lips skewed to one side, Bessie regarded him for a moment. "All right. What you got in mind?"

"What's on your chore list for the day?"

"Weedin', prunin', plantin' potatoes and beets…"

"Then we'll help you, won't we, Jonny?"

His breath came out in a dreadful sigh as he stomped toward the back door.

"No, not yet."

He paused, looking puzzled.

Portia handed him the basket. "First you'll return this little fellow to where you found him."

He wrinkled his nose and narrowed his eyes at her but trudged out the door with the basket, heading toward the garden.

"I don't know what's gotten into that boy. He never did this kind of thing when his mama was alive," Bessie said.

"It's understandable. His whole world has changed, and he feels helpless. Putting a snake in my bed is something he can control. At least it wasn't a copperhead."

Bessie looked at her for a moment, her eyes softer than usual. "Maybe you're right about that. What are *you* gonna do all day?"

"I'll be working outside, same as you." She rolled up her sleeves and smiled.

Eyes wide with surprise, Bessie said, "All right, then. Gardenin' shed's right out there. You can start by pruning the rosebushes. I'll clean up the breakfast dishes and be out shortly."

Portia found Jonathan by the shed, now with an empty knitting basket. She gathered pruning shears and some gloves. At the front corner of the house near the parlor, they found the first unruly rosebush. He crossed his arms and scowled the whole time, but he watched closely as she showed him how to cut a few dead and damaged stems.

Then it was his turn, so she handed him the gloves and pruners. He swallowed hard and stared at the bush like it might grab him with its thorny arms and never let go.

"You can do it. See these thin, twiggy stems? Cut those out," she said.

With his tongue poking from the corner of his mouth, he obeyed, holding the pruners awkwardly at first. His confidence grew with every snip.

She knew he would feel satisfaction in a job well done, so she continued to instruct and encourage, using the calm, patient voice she had employed in the schoolroom. "And these here that are crossing each other — cut one of those back. Pinch off the suckers next. Perfect!"

When he finished, he lowered the pruners and stood back, eyeing the rosebush with a "that's not too shabby" frown. Portia helped Jonny prune the other rosebushes next to the porch and the garden. By the time they were done, he had worked up a good sweat and had earned a few battle scars on his arms from the thorns. But he wore a relaxed smile of pure accomplishment.

"Now that the sun's had time to dry the dirt, let's go help Bessie plant the potatoes and beets," Portia said.

When they arrived back at the garden, Bessie was hard at work on evenly spaced potato hills. Portia fetched a hoe and showed Jonny how to dig a nice, straight row. She handed him the hoe, and he did his best. His row looked more like one side of a parenthesis, but it would suffice.

Portia followed along, dropping seeds into the furrow. When he reached the end of the row, he came back behind her, covering the seeds and gently tamping down the dirt with the bottom of the hoe. Finally the last few beet seeds were safely under the soil. Jonathan stood up straight and arched his back to stretch his strained muscles. He brushed the dirt off his hands and scowled.

"What's wrong?" Portia figured he would show her blisters on his palms or a rock in his boot.

"I hate beets."

He said it in such a clear, matter-of-fact voice that no one would have guessed he hadn't spoken in nearly a year. He walked to the shed, put the hoe away, and went back inside the house.

Portia's jaw dropped. "Did you hear that? He hates beets."

"He always has." Bessie stared at the back door and wiped the sweat from her forehead with the back of her hand. "You did it. You got him to speak."

"No, he did it," Portia said, leaning on her hoe. "All he needed was enough work to distract him from keeping his voice to himself."

"If I'd known that, I would have had him workin' from sunup to sundown." She pursed her lips into an impressed smile. "We should tell Beau."

"It might be best to wait a bit, see if Jonathan takes the initiative and speaks to him without prompting. If we put too much pressure on him, he might hold back even more."

"Hmm, maybe you're right."

Mr. Stanford didn't utter more than a few words at dinner. He didn't bring up any more serious matters as he had on her first morning there. Harry was as chatty as he'd been from the start, Ezra just as humorous.

The indifference didn't hurt her so much as she hurt from watching Jonathan trying to catch his father's attention. Now and then his eyes would linger on Beau, and his mouth would twitch as though he wanted so badly to share something with him. She was tempted to tell them about Jonathan breaking his silence, but held her tongue. She had to let him speak on his own terms.

But Beau never looked at him, and Jonathan's hopeful countenance fell. He played with his stew and nibbled some cornbread, reclaiming the silence he had possessed before today's three-word marvel. Beau left the table and went to bed without even a farewell or goodnight.

Certainly indifference was better than the brutality she had suffered at the hands of her own father. Still, her heart ached for Jonathan, and she didn't know how to make it better.

Chapter Eight

The next morning's lessons consisted of biology and botany. Portia gave Jonathan the privilege of picking corresponding books that interested him. He picked five, and three of them were books about horse husbandry. *The Horse: With a Treatise on Draught, The Complete Farrier,* and *On Horsemanship*, an English translation of an ancient Greek historian. Though horse-related books were in abundance, they were not the only choices. Portia had already scanned every title on the shelves.

"What made you pick these three?" Portia asked.

He shrugged and turned his head toward the front window. Toward the horse barn.

"I bet your father read these to you."

With a sad sigh, he nodded and scratched at a spot on the desk top.

She sat down at the big desk. The windows into Jonathan's soul had opened a little more. He loved his father and looked up to him. They *should* be able to connect through all those things fathers and sons did together — reading, hunting, fishing, and the family business. Maybe she could encourage that somehow.

The door opened, and Bessie announced lunch before she could form any solid plans. Jonathan sped out as usual.

"How's things goin' today?" Bessie asked.

"Not bad." Portia closed *The Complete Farrier* and propped her chin on her hand. "Do you know when Mr. Stanford and Jonathan last did something together, just the two of them?"

Bessie lifted one shoulder and shook her head. "There's church, but... no, I don't remember when just the two of them did anything. They used to fish down at Barton Creek all the time, and they'd go ridin' almost every evenin' when the weather was good. Things is different now, and it's a shame."

"That it is." Rubbing the tense muscles in her neck, Portia dared to broach another subject that weighed on her heavily. "May I ask you something?"

"You may."

"My husband, Jake..." She swallowed past the sudden dryness in her throat. "...you know which side he fought for, and—"

"I know what you're askin'," she said, holding her palm out to stop the conversation. "I understand you never owned slaves?"

"That's right."

"Had you the means, would you have?"

Heat filled Portia's cheeks. She fidgeted with the corner of a letter to Ellen she had begun writing that morning. She knew then that the only way to gain Bessie's trust, if she ever could, was to offer complete honesty.

Portia finally answered, her voice timid and shaky, "Jake always believed that men should work for their keep. But if we had been wealthy enough... I don't know. Maybe we would have."

Bessie walked to the bookcase and, finger on her chin, scanned some of the books. She chose one and brought it to where Portia sat, placing it in front of her.

Portia read the title on the cover. "*Narrative of the Life of Frederick Douglass, an American Slave.*" Unsure what else to say, she raised her eyes to Bessie and waited.

The older woman tapped the book with one long, brown finger. "We got this book when Beau was a young man, not much older than Jonny. We read it together, and though Isaac and me was never slaves, Beau finally understood what others had to endure. I've seen it with my own eyes, and I've felt it, too." She pointed to the jagged scar that crossed over her right eye. "I want you to read this, so *you'll* understand."

"I will." Rubbing her fingers along the frayed edges of the cover, Portia swallowed hard and forced herself to speak. "I'd very much like to be friends, if you could find it in your heart to accept me."

"It's *your* heart what matters, and I ain't too sure about it yet. Time will tell. Now, come eat lunch. We got plenty of work to do this evenin'."

When she went to the dining room, only Jonathan sat there, munching hard boiled eggs, salt pork, and collard greens. Bessie had already prepared her a plate at her

110

newly claimed spot at the table, so she sat down across from him.

He glanced up at her then kept eating. Bessie emerged from the kitchen, and Portia asked, "Would you like Jonathan and me to take some lunch to the men?"

"They'd appreciate that, I'm sure."

"All right."

She ate everything on her plate, though greens were admittedly not her favorite thing. When she finished, she took her plate along with Jonathan's to the kitchen. He looked up at her while he packed a basket with food. She could sense excitement from his hasty movements and bright eyes. The boy must have longed to be with his father so much that even the prospect of taking him lunch brought him joy.

"How about we take the long way around so you can show me more of the grounds?" she asked.

He answered with his usual shrug.

With the basket all packed, she slipped the handle over her arm and followed Jonathan out the back door. They crossed the backyard and walked along a path of round stepping stones to a small herb garden. An ornate wrought iron fence surrounded it. Though many of the plants were just barely turning green with new growth, she imagined all the dishes she would concoct with mint, tarragon, and thyme. Her own garden back home had once brought such joy when she tended it.

Jonathan paused along the path and pointed at the garden. "My mama planted those herbs. She liked the lavender best because it smelled good."

Trying not to show too much enthusiasm over his voluntary statement, Portia simply nodded and spoke in a neutral tone. "It's a very relaxing scent. I used to add it to our pillows when we stuffed them with fresh feathers in the spring."

"Mama did that, too."

He leapt from one stepping stone to another through the middle of the herb garden and turned left beside the vegetable garden. Portia breathed in the damp, slightly decayed scent of freshly worked soil. She felt like leaping for joy from hearing the sound of her student's voice but decided the best course of action was to act as though he'd never been mute.

Passing around the side of the house, she spied a root cellar.

"What's this?" she called to Jonathan, who had scampered past it. She hoped his talkative streak hadn't already passed.

He doubled back and smiled. "It's a root cellar. Wanna see?"

"I would love to."

The smell of musty earth, potatoes, and old wood wafted out when he opened the door. She lingered on the bare dirt a few feet behind him. Looking over his shoulder, he gestured to her to come closer.

Portia ducked to stand beside him on the other side of the short doorway. There were barrels of salt pork, jars of dried fruits, smoked meats wrapped in gauze, turnips, and a few chairs. The cellar was far from full, but it held enough to get them through the spring.

"I used to play hide and seek with Mama and Pa," he said while he smiled into the dark interior. "I'd hide in here. They'd look all over the place, hollering for me while I peeked through the cracks in the door. I was too little to know it then, but I think they were just pretending they couldn't find me."

"I bet you're right," she said. "I used to love hide and seek, too. Maybe we can play sometime."

He shrugged. "Maybe."

"But don't think I'll pretend I don't know where you are, now that I know your tricks."

He flashed another smile, followed by a quick laugh, before he skipped on ahead. They continued beyond the cellar where a wagon path lined with tall cedars ran past the garden out to a field and a small house. She could make out the shape of a man and mule plowing in the distance, Isaac perhaps, and figured he and Bessie lived in that little house.

All around her, it seemed the land was waking up from a bad dream — stretching, yawning, and trying to shake itself into normality. And if normal meant that she and Jonathan and Bessie could be friends, all the better.

They reached the front of the house and followed the drive down the hill toward the stable. The large barn, white like the main house, must have been a grand structure at one time. Now its paint was faded and chipped, doors and shutters sagged, and the roof had sections of missing shingles. As they neared the paddock, she caught movement — a man and a horse.

Jonathan ran ahead, climbing to stand on the bottom slat of the paddock fence, arms crossed and draped over the top. Mr. Stanford held a lead rope taut in one hand and a smooth stick about four feet long in the other. He stood still in the middle of the paddock with a pretty chestnut horse on the other end of the line.

He must have been training her. Or trying to, anyway.

The horse was having none of it. She pranced and tossed her head, huffing and blowing the entire time. Occasionally, she kicked at the air behind her and reared, her hooves thudding to the ground in cloud of dust. Mr. Stanford maintained a safe distance, calmly pivoting along as if there wasn't a rowdy horse on the end of the line. He made a sound like, "Shh," over and over again, perhaps to calm her. Portia feared he'd take a whack at the poor animal with that stick, but he kept it pointed to the ground at his side.

Jonathan took no notice of her when she leaned on the fence just a yard away. Clearly enraptured with the training session, he watched every move his father made and how the horse responded. Mr. Stanford focused solely on the horse and paid them no mind.

As if some silent agreement had been reached, the horse stopped her antics and slowed to a trot. Mr. Stanford loosened the rope considerably and held it with a relaxed, open hand, though he didn't let go of the lead.

"See that?" Jonathan whispered.

It startled Portia to see how he had scooted along the fence and now stood right beside her.

"What?" she whispered back.

"That's called float in the rope. When the horse does what you want it to, you let the rope float down like that. If it's doing bad, you tighten the rope until it obeys again."

114

"I see," she said, amazed at such insight from this little boy.

She turned her attention back to Mr. Stanford. He led the horse around the paddock, and the filly walked right beside him like they had always been friends. When the two of them came back around from the far side of the space, Mr. Stanford stopped. The horse stopped along with him. He rubbed the thick mane, the white-striped muzzle, the flicking ears. Strangely, he made little clicking noises every time he touched a different body part on the animal.

It was amazing, this dance between horse and man. Portia suspected she'd seen a glimpse of what he must have been like before the war. Before he came back to a dead wife and a dying business. The haggard tension on his face had melted away. There was a softness to his eyes and voice that soothed and encouraged the filly. A gentleness in his hands as he helped her get accustomed to his touch. Pure peace and serenity surrounded them all, and she felt truly blessed to witness it.

Until Jonathan's foot slipped off the fence slat; he banged his chin and let out a yelp. The spell was broken. The horse reared and whinnied. Man and hat were knocked to the ground in different directions. Mr. Stanford let go of the line, and the horse fled to the opposite end of the paddock. Pushing himself off the ground, he retrieved the wayward hat and brushed his thick, dark hair from his forehead. He slapped the dirt from his pants and strode to the fence where Portia and Jonathan stood. The boy rubbed his chin, but cowered as his father approached.

"Why aren't you in the house, getting your lessons?" Though he directed the question at Jonathan, he glared at Portia.

"We brought you lunch," she said. "Didn't we, Jonathan?"

The poor boy's eyes watered. He pressed his hand to his injured chin and looked frantically between his father and teacher. Portia gave him a nod of encouragement, hoping he would say something, whether to argue his case or to apologize. Anything.

His father's rant continued, "You should have left the basket there in the barn. I can't have you out here distracting me. I'm having a hard time getting this horse to calm down and trot."

Jonathan cast a furtive glance at Portia and sprinted away toward the house.

Deep lines formed crevices on Mr. Stanford's face. So much for peace. He waited until his son was out of earshot then impaled her with those sharp eyes.

"I'm not paying you to stand around and keep me from my work," he snapped.

Heart speeding, fists tightening, it had come down to fight or flee. Portia knew what she ought to do, but she could feel her chin jutting toward him, begging for a challenge.

"You aren't paying me at all, remember?"

He looked shocked for a moment before he resumed his angry-with-everything look. She became certain hers would be the briefest employment on record.

He plopped his hat back on his head. "Listen here, that horse could have kicked Jonny right in the head. It's not safe out here, especially with a filly like that."

Oh, how she wanted to tell him that his son was speaking again, but she had to let Jonathan do that himself. She could still fight on his behalf and try to get his father to take notice of him. "I think he knows a lot more about horses than you give him credit for. Besides, there isn't much in the textbooks he doesn't know already. He might benefit from spending time out here with his father, learning the family business."

"He's still too young."

"Really? And how old were *you* when you first climbed on a horse's back and worked alongside your father?"

He forfeited their staring contest and looked down at the ground, arms crossed. "That's not the point. I don't want him getting hurt."

She suspected as much, and truth be known, she'd have probably been overprotective with Abby had she survived. Would she have listened to reason if she were in *his* shoes? Probably not, but it was always easier to see the truth from the outside looking in.

She ventured one step closer to the fence, softening her voice the way he did to calm the horse. "You can't protect him forever, no matter how much you want to. And ignoring him is doing him more harm than good. He needs you."

He made some sort of growling noise and started to walk away, pausing only long enough to say, "It's your job to teach my son, not to give me advice on how to be a father. I have to get back to work. I expect you to do the same."

Biting her tongue until it hurt, she squeezed out a submissive, "Yes, Mr. Stanford."

"Good."

Closing the conversation with that last word, he approached the horse and picked up the lead rope again. Defeated, if only temporarily, Portia walked back up the hill toward the house feeling slightly unsteady on her feet. Whatever had come over her, she had no idea. It had all happened so quickly. She was lucky he didn't send her packing with the way she had just behaved. So why didn't he? Did some part of him realize she was right?

Jonathan was already in the study when she returned to the house. She took a steadying breath and decided to continue with their botany lesson as though nothing had happened. Should he want to talk about it, she would listen, but she had to leave it up to him.

She had gathered some decent specimens early that morning before the day began, including some poison ivy, which she was careful not to touch with bare hands. Jonathan, however, now sat at his desk, holding the three-leafed section of ivy and turning it this way and that. With her handkerchief, she picked it from his grasp and placed it on the window sill so the light would provide greater detail.

"Remember this: 'Leaflets three, let it be'," Portia said.

"Ugh," he grunted, looking at his hands.

She laughed. "You might get an itchy rash, but it's only temporary. We can rub some potato paste or cold coffee on it if that happens."

They were listing all the ways to identify poison ivy and its cousins while sketching them on paper when Jonathan asked, "Do you think Pa's mad at me?"

"No," she said, thankful he was verbalizing his feelings instead of finding snakes to put in her bed. "He's just scared you might get hurt."

He glanced at her then back down to his desk. "I was scared he'd get hurt too, when he was gone."

"It's normal to worry about the people we love."

"I don't think he loves me anymore."

"Of course he does."

He slumped in his seat. "He never tucks me in or takes me fishing or anything that we used to do. All he does is work."

Images of Portia's own father flashed through her mind — passed out, whisky bottle clutched in his hand like it was the elixir of life. She swallowed hard and gave the boy a gentle one-armed hug, hoping he wouldn't shrink away from her touch.

"Sometimes it's hard for people to talk about how they feel. We just have to be patient with them," she said.

"I guess so."

"You did very well today. I can see I'll have to challenge you further. You're dismissed."

"Yes, ma'am." He was out of his seat and out the door before she could say another word.

She got up from the desk and took a short rest in the padded window seat. Just down the hill, she could see Mr. Stanford and the horse trotting around him. Whether she would still have a job come tomorrow, she didn't know. But Jonathan had finally started talking, even confiding in

119

her, and provided Mr. Stanford let her stay, she might be able to help them connect again. A flock of geese flew overhead, ready to settle down in the warm sunshine of a Tennessee spring.

Portia watched their V formation until they flew out of her line of vision. And she realized another little miracle had occurred.

For a good part of the day, painful memories of Jake and Abby didn't occupy her every waking hour. That's what she had wanted, wasn't it? Yet — and the thought made her uneasy — did that mean she was forgetting them?

Chapter Nine

Every strained muscle in Beau's body paid testament to the grueling day he had endured. Especially his right shoulder. He massaged the old wound, feeling the dips and ridges of skin and muscle fibers that had never quite knitted together properly. It hurt. Constantly. And he really didn't want to be cleaning a stall, but he forced his body into submission. Somehow, the pain kept him grounded in reality, kept him focused on the here and now, at least during his waking hours. Sleep only served to plague him with broken images of pleading eyes, bloodied hands, and Claire lying in a coffin. He'd claw himself out of bed, covered in sweat, and could swear he smelled smoke. Working kept him sane and awake — hurting, but awake.

Hours of trial and error had finally gotten Crazy Girl to trot and stop bolting at every noise. For a few minutes at a time anyway. She was going to take some patience, just like Portia. He laughed to himself. Pa hadn't hired him a potential wife — that much he was certain of now —

he'd hired an opponent. A combative little spitfire that had no qualms about speaking her mind.

He wasn't used to such spirit from a woman. Fillies, yes, but not women. Claire had been no push-over, but her methods were more subtle. She had been the queen of emotional bribery: teary eyes, sweet kisses, and batting eyelashes. She had never failed to melt him into submission to get what she wanted.

But Portia... he wasn't sure about her yet, whether that spirit of hers would prove to be endearing or excruciating.

By the time he finished ruminating over it, he'd cleaned the stall and didn't even remember most of the work. A horse whinnied outside — not one of theirs, so he stepped out of the stall to investigate — and almost collided with a horse slowing from a gallop right there in the barn. He had to grab the stall's door facing to keep from falling.

"What the—?"

"Ain't she a beaut?" Harry said in a drawling shout. "Told ya I'd do right by this one."

Harry slid out of the saddle and stumbled when his feet hit the ground. Beau righted himself from the near miss and threw a nasty scowl at him. He couldn't waste time preaching to that fool. Instead, he decided to pay mind to the more important business at hand.

"Easy girl," he said, rubbing her neck and holding her head steady.

She *was* a nice one at first glance, looked to be a Morgan, with a glossy black-brown coat. Even in the subdued light of the stable, he could see her fit muscle tone and ribcage expanding with steady breaths. Already, she had lowered her head to a relaxed, level angle. Though aware of him and her unfamiliar surroundings, she didn't act overly concerned.

Getting a feel of her withers, he asked, "How much?"

"Fifty."

"Got the bill of sale?"

Harry pulled out a half-crumpled piece of paper from inside his vest. "Want me to record it?"

Beau snatched it from him. "You're in no state to record anything. How much did you take *this* time?"

"Oh come on, Beau, see?" Harry started hopping up and down, rather unsteadily, on his bad leg. "It helps."

Something fell from his vest to the ground. Both of them dove for it, but Beau reached it first. It was a green velvet box, oblong like an eyeglass case, and rubbed bare near the opening. Harry grabbed at it as Beau stood back up, but he missed and fell to his knees. Beau opened the box — and sure enough — there lay the syringe, all broken down and tucked into grooves that fit each piece perfectly. He'd seen the evidence on Harry's arms, but had never actually seen the device in question until now.

"This shit is going to kill you," Beau said, closing the case with a snap.

Harry sat up on the ground, hugging his knees and laughing. "Kill me? Hell, it's the only thing keeping me alive."

Beau jutted the case at him. "I didn't drag your wounded ass out of Allatoona for you to come back home and kill yourself."

"I bring you a filly, and a fine one I might add, and this is the thanks I get?"

"Yes, you're right. Why not down a shot or two of whiskey for your bonus?"

"Not a bad idea!"

Clenching his mouth shut before he said things he would regret, Beau took the reins and led the filly toward the door.

"You know," Harry hollered after him, "a little morph might keep those nightmares of yours at bay."

Beau paused; he didn't look back, but his fist gripped the reins so tight it hurt.

"I hear you sometimes," Harry said as he got to his feet. "I hear you thrashing around, calling Claire's name. The dreams are coming more often, aren't they? How long has it been since you've had a good night's sleep?"

"It's none of your damn business," Beau growled and strode out of the stable with the filly trotting along behind him.

"You better get some rest," Harry yelled. "How you gonna bed Lydia Clemons if you're too tired to get it up?"

Beau silently appealed to God and any other deities that might be listening to help him refrain from beating the shit out of Harry. He wasn't sure what was worse — sleepless nights, Harry's drug-induced stupidity, or knowing Claire's not-so-little cousin would arrive within the week.

Portia unfastened the clothespins on a pair of work pants. For laundry, it couldn't have been a better day. The warm spring breeze made the clothes dance on the line and carried the smell of crisp linens and fresh-cut grass. She dropped the pins in a flour sack pouch that hung between her and Bessie.

The two of them had worked in pleasant silence for the last half hour, until Portia felt Bessie's eyes on her. "What is it?"

"How old was she? Your daughter?"

The mere mention of Abby sent a shiver down Portia's spine. For a split second, it was Christmas all over again. She lay crumpled on the frozen ground between Jake's and Abby's gravestones, numb from cold and praying that God would take her now, please... And then Frank and Ellen were there, standing over her while she thawed by their hearth. They'd saved her from freezing to death. But what they hadn't known — or rather, never brought up — is that she hadn't wanted to be saved.

She finally extracted the answer from the shallow grave of her memory. Her voice shook like her body had on that frozen ground. "She was two."

"I'm sorry. It ain't right, children dyin' before we do."

Portia tilted her head back, eyes closed, letting the sun return her to the perfection of a warm spring afternoon.

"Are you all right?" Bessie asked.

"I'm fine," Portia said, trying to cover her lie with a smile. "Is this all the laundry?"

Though her face bore worried wrinkles, Bessie looked down at the full laundry basket and nodded. "Didn't take long with both of us tending to it."

"Many hands make light work."

"Mm-hmm. If you can go put those away, I'll start supper early. I know them men's gotta be hungry. The things on top are Beau's, the ones on the bottom are Jonny's. Just put 'em on their beds, and they'll put 'em away."

"All right."

Portia, with the basket on her hip, started toward the house with Bessie beside her.

They were about to go inside when Bessie stopped, hand on the door latch. "The Lord blessed us with two healthy sons, Curtis and Virgil, but our first boy was born dead. If you ever need to talk…"

"Thank you." Tears stung Portia's eyes. Bessie's unexpected compassion warmed her heart like the sun warmed the garden's earth, promising new growth. She hoped the seedlings of their friendship would keep growing.

Upstairs, the quiet solitude proved soothing, so Portia took her time. She started with Jonathan's room, though his clothes were on the bottom of the basket. Thankfully, his grandfather had fetched him to ride into town for supplies. She wanted to get a glimpse of the boy's personal space while he wasn't occupying it.

He hadn't made his bed, so she set the basket down and did the job herself. Typical of a boy's room, blocks and toy soldiers — facing off in pretend battle — were strewn across the floor. A book lay upside down and open just beneath the edge of the bed. Portia picked it up, impressed with the boy's reading choice of *The Deerslayer*.

She closed the book, being careful to mark the page with a scrap piece of paper. Smiling, she set it on his bedside table. A lesson on how to properly care for a book's spine was in order for tomorrow.

126

After she tidied Jonathan's room, she headed to Mr. Stanford's quarters at the end of the hall. A large four-post bed took up a good bit of the room. Like Jonathan's, the bed was unmade — with a crumpled quilt and sheet thrown to one side and two pillows lying at odd angles as though someone had blindly thrown them across the mattress.

Portia set the basket on the floor and made the bed. She admired the handiwork of the blue and white star-patterned quilt. Her fingers traced along the perfect stitching on one of the white stars. Had Mrs. Stanford made it?

Starting back around the bed, she noticed a chest at its foot. It was a large, heavy thing, wide as the bed itself. The rounded wooden top yawned open against the footboard. She bent to close it, but the gleam of a brass button caught her eye. She couldn't help herself, and ignoring all good sense, peered into the chest. A dark blue Federal jacket stared back. They were the "enemy," according to Jake — all those who wore this color.

Now on her knees, her fingers lifted the heavy garment out of the chest. It didn't look like an enemy she should fear. Not in this condition, with a ragged hole in the shoulder and a blood stain surrounding it. On the sleeve, a bloody hand had left its mark — she counted four fingers, a thumb, and part of a palm.

Her teeth chattered while a full body shiver ran through her from head to toe. This jacket belonged to a wounded soldier, like so many from both sides she had fed and stitched up when they sought help at her house while the war had raged on. But this jacket didn't belong to just any soldier — it belonged to Mr. Stanford.

And it was *his* voice that brought her scrambling back to her feet. "What the hell do you think you're doing?"

Chapter Ten

Portia dropped the jacket. It fell into the chest with a whoosh. "I-I'm sorry."

The pain on his face — like he'd just heard the news of his wife's death all over again — cut her to the bone. He averted his eyes as though he couldn't bear to gaze at the contents of the chest.

"You have no business prying into my things." He didn't raise his voice, but his cold, deliberate tone speared her heart with guilt.

Scooting away from the chest, she planted her hands on a solid piece of furniture behind her and pushed herself to her feet. "I didn't mean to look, I—"

"Give me the key."

"The… key?"

"Are you deaf as well as a thief?" Anger climbed the rungs of every word he spoke. "I said, give me the key!"

"I don't have a key," she yelled back, her own anger rising to meet his. "It was open when I came in to deliver your laundry. I started to close it, but I saw the jacket, and

— I'm sorry. I shouldn't have looked inside. But I did *not* open it."

"Just go." He threw his command at her and stepped aside, holding the door open.

She hurried out with her empty clothes basket banging against the door frame. He didn't look at her. She reached the stairs, and his door slammed shut. The floor itself rattled as did the pictures on the stairwell wall. Her insides felt like they'd been taken out and thrown back in no particular order.

Dear God, what have I done?

Supper preparations weren't going well. Portia burned her fingers when she tried to take the cornbread from the oven with no mitt. She knocked over an open jar of green beans, filling the kitchen with the sharp smell of vinegar.

Hands and knees on the floor cleaning up the mess, Bessie joined her and asked, "Are you all right? I know you ain't worked in *this* kitchen for long, but I'd have thought you'd got cookin' down pat."

"It's not that."

"You tired?"

"Yes. Well, no, not exactly."

"Sick?" Bessie picked up the last stray bean, staring at Portia like she had seen something hideous.

Portia stood and wiped her brow with her sleeve. "No... I... saw something I shouldn't have."

"What did you see?" Bessie held to the countertop to pull herself up.

"I saw Mr. Stanford's army jacket."

"Oh, dear Lord — how'd you see that? Ain't nobody seen it since he came home."

"I put the laundry in his room like you asked and decided to make his bed. When I came around the footboard, the chest was open... and there it was."

"But you didn't—"

"I did."

"And?" Bessie stood still as a pointer hound who'd found a flock of quail.

"He caught me."

"Sweet Jesus." She dabbed her forehead with the corner of her apron. "What did he say?"

Replaying their brief but tense encounter brought tears to Portia's eyes. "He said I had no business prying into *his* business and accused me of taking a key and told me to leave his room. So I apologized and came down here."

Bessie retrieved the cornbread from the oven before it burned. She plunked the pan on the work table and jabbed a knife into it. "Did you take the key?"

"What key?"

"The one to the chest. When Beau came home from the war, we thought he might have to be sent off to one of them places for lunatics. He raved and cussed and carried on so much, it scared us. I know he was just grievin' for his wife, but it was bad. Real bad. One day, he locked himself up in that room and didn't come out for a week. We was all scared he was gonna do somethin' to himself, but I kept putting food outside the door every mornin' and it would be gone by evenin'. He finally came out, and he'd calmed down. More like the Beau we all knew before, but

131

he warned all of us to never touch that chest. I reckon he put all his war memories in there and some of Claire's things too and locked 'em out of sight so he could go on with his life."

The weight of this revelation hit Portia hard. Tears dripped from her eyes. She had trespassed into his most painful memories. He could have dismissed her easily. Probably should have.

"I should leave," she said. "I should pack my things and go… somewhere."

Bessie handed her a kitchen towel. "No, you dry them eyes and get a hold of yourself. If he really thought you was guilty, he'd have thrown you out then and there. Both of you's got a lot of pain to work through. It'll just take time. Now, let's get supper done."

When they finished preparing the meal, Portia helped Bessie set the table and serve the food. Mr. Stanford never made eye contact, and everyone but Ezra stayed quiet. Harry winked at her and patted the empty chair beside him, but she pretended not to notice. She couldn't bear to join them in the dining room, so she took her meal with Bessie and Isaac in the kitchen.

Later, after dishes were cleaned and put away, Portia retreated to her room. Thankful to have a pillow to muffle the sound, she wept until exhaustion took over. She woke to a pretty pink sunrise brightening her window and a rooster announcing the new day. Though tempted to run away and never show her face there again, she had a job to do. Reluctantly, she got up and dressed, determined to soldier on.

How could she ever face him again without feeling like she had trampled on his heart?

Portia took her breakfast in the study with the excuse of needing to prepare the day's lessons early. Mr. Stanford wasn't in the dining room when she passed through, but she didn't want to take any chances. A little distance might help emotions settle enough so everyone could be comfortable in the same room again.

Jonathan came in at ten till eight, nodding to her with a muffled, "Good morning."

He took his seat, licked his pencil lead, and wrote his name on the blank sheet of paper on the desk. Blinking those long eyelashes of his, he looked at her and patiently waited. The thought she had been pondering all morning stopped ricocheting from bad idea to good idea now that she had a more willing student.

"Jonny, I want to indulge your interest in the horse business," she said, deciding to call him by his nickname.

His face brightened momentarily but quickly turned fearful. "Won't Pa be mad?"

"Not if we don't get in his way. There's more than one way to learn about something, so let's be clever about it."

They reviewed some of the horse journals from their prior lessons. Portia assigned him an essay on native forage suitable for horses. Jonny grumbled about it, having had his heart set on a full day outdoors. Though she was adamant he finish before they ventured out, she sat at the large desk, smiling, watching his tongue poking from the

133

side of his mouth in concentration while his pencil scratched across the paper. She'd never been so thankful for a grumbling student before.

After lunch, carefully avoiding the barn, they spent a half hour observing the horses in the pasture.

Jonny pointed at one of them. "See that Morgan? That's Pa's horse, Scout."

"He's a fine horse."

The boy nodded and added, "And that's a new filly Pa just bought."

"I wonder if they get along."

Face scrunched in thought, Jonny put his feet on the bottom fence slat and draped his elbows over the top. "Well, see how he's bobbing his head up and down. I think that's how they say hello to each other."

"Oh, and she just did the same. I suppose she's saying hello back. So, now they're touching noses. Is that like kissing?"

Jonny smiled. "Maybe. At least they like each other. They'd have to like each other to make babies."

"I'm pretty sure that's a necessary factor." Portia stifled a laugh, hoping a detailed lesson on reproduction wouldn't be requested.

"He's a good ridin' horse, too."

"I'll take your word for it."

Looking rather incredulously at her, he asked, "Don't you know how to ride?"

"Not that well. My daddy had a work horse I used to ride when I was little, but he got drunk one day and traded it for an old drippy milk cow. Jake and I never had any horses either, just some mules. The first time I tried to ride one, a snake spooked it, and I fell off. I hurt my backside and my pride too much to try again."

He laughed, but his smiling face soon turned solemn. "I haven't ridden for a while, either. Pa won't let me go out by myself, and everyone's too busy to ride with me."

Portia watched the horses graze happily beside each other and contemplated her next move. *If only his father could hear him right now.* With Jonny confiding in her like this, she had to keep him interested. That really meant only one thing, and the thought made her stomach do a somersault. She'd have to take up riding.

It's worth it. It'll do Jonny good, but... She had to seal her fate with a verbal promise before she could change her mind. "Tell you what. If you concentrate on your lessons and mind your manners for the next couple of days, and if your father approves, I'll go riding with you this weekend."

If his jaw had been unhinged, it would have fallen right off. "Promise?"

"Yes, that is, if you can find me a gentle horse to ride."

"The geldings are real gentle. You'll be fine on one of those."

She scrunched her face in mock seriousness. "Good, because I'm putting my life in your hands."

"I'll keep you safe. Promise."

That afternoon, Portia caught Isaac at lunch and asked him to hitch up a horse and cart. She had decided to go into town with Jonny to see if they could trade a few eggs for art supplies. With the weather growing warmer by the day, she wanted to take advantage of it and have a few drawing lessons outside.

With Jonny seated beside her, she lifted the reins. "Ready?"

Jonny nodded excitedly. Poor boy was thrilled just to have some companionship. She hadn't heard any mention of friends and wondered if he had anyone his own age to play with. If not, she would have to remedy that. Children needed playmates. How she would broach the subject with his overprotective but distant father, she had no idea.

She was about to snap the reins when Harry came running up the drive, arms waving in the air. "Whoa! Hold up!"

"What's wrong?" she asked as he reached the wagon.

He panted to catch his breath as he answered, "What's wrong… is that you didn't… ask me to come along."

Had Mr. Stanford asked Harry to come along? He did recommend she be escorted into town. Or maybe Harry had other intentions. She groaned quietly.

"Did you need something in town?" she asked, hoping to dissuade him with her independent spirit. "I can pick it up for you."

"My dear lady, I'd be remiss to pass up an opportunity to escort you." His smile nearly blinded her, and she tried not to cringe at the wink that followed. "Scoot over and leave the driving to me."

Apparently, her independent spirit could not sway Harry Franklin from intruding on her plans. Tempted to snap the reins and drive off, leaving him in a cloud of dust, she remembered what her mama always said. *"No matter how poor one is, it doesn't excuse bad manners."*

Reluctantly, she scooted closer to Jonny and handed the reins to Harry as he jumped in. She looked to Jonny for support on her right. He shrugged. No help there. She kept quiet between the grown man and the young one, while Harry pointed out this and that along the way. He kept leaning too close when he spoke and kept brushing her arm with his. The unwanted contact distracted her too much to pay any mind to the tour.

They arrived in town as Harry said something about him and Beau not being able to borrow more money. How could she respond to *that*? Before she had a chance to say anything, two rough-looking men near a hitching post started laughing. She noticed Jonny's eyes growing wide at their conversation.

"You gotta be kiddin' me."

"Naw, sir. That feller in Lockport said they had a nigger strung up last night. Reckon they barbequed him, too."

Portia's thoughts immediately turned to Bessie and Isaac. If things had come to that in Lockport, just a few miles away, it could easily be the same here.

"Ain't no niggers gonna be safe out after dark. Shoulda known they had it comin'." He scratched at his bushy red beard and turned his head toward them. With a nod of recognition, he threw his hand up in greeting. "Mornin', Harry. Is this the girl you been talkin' about?"

Harry's jaw tightened, but he smiled back, eyes shifting from the man to Portia. "Randal, this is Portia McAllister. Portia, Randal Stevens."

"Pretty little thang, ain't she?" Randal said to his companion as his gaze wandered over her.

She shivered in disgust, but patted Jonny's back to reassure him. The poor boy stared at his boots and gripped his knees with white-knuckled fingers.

"Well now, we've got lots of errands to run, and I'm sure you do, too. Good day," Harry said.

Randal lifted his hat in farewell, revealing his greasy, mostly bald head. The two men mounted their horses and rode off in different directions.

"It's all right," she whispered to Jonny. "They're gone now."

He nodded and hopped out. Portia picked up the egg basket, and Harry helped her from the cart. He kept her hand in his a little too tightly, rubbing her knuckles with his thumb.

"Don't worry about all that," he said. "I think they came home from the war with shrapnel in their heads."

He tried to laugh it off, but Randal's gritty voice still polluted the pleasant spring air. "...*Is this the girl you been talkin' about?*"

Anger carried a hot blush up her cheeks. She jerked her hand from his. "From the sounds of it, you're well acquainted with them, Mr. Franklin."

"No, not since we were boys. They joined up with the Rebels and ain't been right since. Besides, news carries fast, and everyone knows about you. They just want to get a rise out of you."

Sincerity poured from his sparkling blue eyes. She decided to give him the benefit of the doubt, but there was still the matter of what those horrid men were discussing.

She looked to see where Jonny went — he stood several feet away, gazing at some tin soldiers in a store window. Keeping her voice down, she turned her attention back to Harry. "What about Bessie and Isaac?"

"Probably just a rumor. They'll be fine. But you ought to let me escort you to town at all times... just in case."

He took advantage of her close proximity and slid an arm around her shoulders, drawing her close. Though other women might welcome such a gesture, guilt clawed at her conscience and burned her cheeks, as though Jake could come around the corner at any time and catch them in the act.

Hugging her basket of eggs, she stepped away from him, shrugging one shoulder to release his hold. "If you'll excuse me, I have some shopping to do."

His frown didn't go unnoticed.

April 20, 1866
Dear Ellen,

These two weeks have flown by, but they have brought a few blessings. Jonny is talking to me more every day, and to Bessie some, though he will still not speak to his father or anyone else. We were able to trade a few eggs for heavy drawing paper, charcoal pencils, and a used leather portfolio. I'm looking forward to sketching again, though I am most assuredly not looking forward to riding. I promised Jonny, however, so I must keep my word. It will help him to spend time with someone.

Mr. Stanford possesses a gift for training horses. I watched him perform this act, and it was like watching a different man. His cold nature had departed, and I saw the warm, unburdened man he must have been before the war. I only wish he would spend time with his son. I'm not certain as to why they have grown apart, but I want to help them reunite if I can. Doing that may prove more difficult than turning water to wine. Mr. Stanford and I haven't spoken since I stumbled upon his open chest and army jacket. At the very least, I am encouraged that Bessie seems to have warmed to me. Knowing I'm not viewed as an enemy will make my time here more pleasant.

However, even as I write this, I shudder to think of the hatred she and Isaac could come up against. Mr. Franklin and I were in town earlier today and we heard of a dreadful lynching in a nearby town. I fear for their safety, though he assured me it was likely a rumor. Mr. Franklin seems rather fond of me, but I cannot fathom entertaining such thoughts. I know what you're thinking, Ellen, but I'm not ready for a courtship with anyone yet.

I've just finished a book Bessie gave me about a freed slave named Frederick Douglass. He was born into slavery, barely knew his mother, and suspected his owner had fathered him. This poor man was so abused, he was thankful to be sent to a "negro-breaker" because there he would at least be fed. Poor and abused as Sam and I were, we were never hungry for very long, and we had the choice to leave.

What hurt me most is that Mr. Douglass was denied the right to an education. He took it upon himself to learn to read and write, and even those endeavors were risky. If I ever get the chance to teach a black child, I will do so in a heartbeat...

Chapter Eleven

Portia lay in her bed the next morning, half-awake, watching the sun's pink light brighten her window. It was Saturday, so there were no lessons, and Bessie had told her to sleep in if she wished. She felt a tad guilty leaving Bessie to prepare breakfast, but the bed felt particularly comfortable this morning. Sighing in contentment, she pulled the quilt up to her chin and let the downy softness of the pillow and mattress caress her back to sleep. Just a few more minutes. Surely no one would mind...

A soft rap sounded on her door. Portia groaned and sat up. Bessie must have needed her help sooner than later.

"Just a minute," she called. After a short yawn and stretch, she got up and cracked opened the door. "I'm sorry, I'll get dressed and... Jonny?"

He stood there, smiling and bouncing up and down on his toes. After glancing over his shoulder, probably to make sure no one else could hear, he whispered, "We're going riding today, remember? That is, if you still want to."

Lowering his head, he bit his lip and shuffled his feet. Though she had halfway hoped he would forget about their deal, she couldn't say no to him now. Not when he looked so excited and eager. She liked this side of Jonny and wanted to encourage him to stay that way for a while, even if he wasn't taking full advantage of his voice.

"Of course I still want to."

His face brightened like the sun that had just popped over the horizon. "Can we go after breakfast?"

"I'll have to see if Bessie needs some help with chores first. Then we can."

"Oh," he said, and his face clouded over a bit. "That'll be fine. I can get the horses ready while you're doing that."

"You should wait for me to go with you."

"Grandpa's going out with me."

"You… spoke to him?" She tried not to sound too eager, but couldn't help the upbeat lilt in her tone.

Digging the toe of his boot into the floorboards, he whispered, "I wrote him a note."

"I see." Her voice deflated a bit. "And have you gotten your father's permission?" The last thing she needed was another confrontation with Mr. Stanford. She still hadn't spoken directly to him since the army jacket incident and had taken all her meals either in the kitchen or study. He hadn't questioned her absence, either. An invisible wall of tension existed between them that neither dared to cross.

"Yes, ma'am," Jonny said, nodding assuredly. "Grandpa asked him. See you outside."

Portia swallowed her last bite of biscuit and gooseberry jam then wiped her mouth with her napkin. She rose from the kitchen table and carried her dishes to the basin, where Bessie was busy scrubbing.

"Are you sure you don't need help this morning?" she asked again.

Bessie chuckled. "You'll do more good out there with Jonny than in here with me. You really that scared of ridin'?"

"No…" She pulled at the cuffs on her sleeves. "Yes, a little."

"He ain't lyin' when he says those saddle horses are gentle. You'll be fine. But we did get word that the Clemonses will be here this coming Tuesday, so I'll need your help this afternoon and tomorrow."

"All right, we can cancel lessons and I'll help with whatever you need."

"It's been a long time," Bessie said, wringing her hands, "since we've had company around here." At Portia's smile, she added quickly, "Except for you, of course."

"Of course," Portia said with a chuckle. "But why all the worry?"

"They've been city folks for a long time. Rich, too. I don't know if what we got will be good enough."

"If you're talking about our cooking, think about it this way. They might be looking forward to some good Southern food after all that fancy Northern fare."

Bessie's face brightened, and she abandoned the hand-wringing. "I never thought about it that way. Maybe you're right. I'll get a list ready of things we need to do. Now you go on out and have a nice ride with Jonny."

Gentle proved to be an understatement for the saddle horse Portia rode. The animal plodded along at a snail's pace, while Jonny had to keep slowing Jack, his pony, to let them catch up. Soft kicks to the horse's sides and flicking the reins helped for about five seconds. The gelding wasn't much taller than Jack — maybe fourteen hands if she were to make a generous guess. At least if she fell off, she wouldn't hurt much more than her pride. Not at this speed.

Jonny led them past one of the plowed fields and along a well-worn trail through the woods. Flowing water mixed with birdsong played a soothing melody as the trail descended. They stopped at a sparkling creek that wove its way along mossy green rocks. Upstream, the water crashed into the foamy white mist of a miniature waterfall. Portia breathed in the fresh forest air, closing her eyes to savor the moment.

"That's Barton Creek," Jonny said. "We used to picnic down here all the time. Upstream a ways, there's good fishing."

He fell quiet and his face looked somber while he scratched Jack's mane.

"What's wrong?" Portia asked.

"I was just wondering… do you miss your husband and little girl?"

Her chest tightened at the mention of Jake and Abby, but Jonny needed someone to talk to now that he'd found his voice, so she had to open up to him. "Yes, every single day. I think of them from the moment I wake to the moment I go to bed."

Jonny's shoulders rose and fell with a heavy breath.

She could guess who was on his mind, so she ventured the question. "What was your mama like?"

"She was real pretty and kind to everyone." He slid off his saddle, dug into his pocket, and pulled out a sugar cube. It must have been risky for him to swipe, since sugar was in such short supply. Jack gobbled it up greedily, while Jonny rubbed his ears. "She helped look after some of the sick kids and older folks in town when Pa went off to war. Then she got sick, too."

Trying not to be overcome with emotion, Portia blinked back tears and slid out of the saddle, none too gracefully. At least she landed on her feet, though her legs felt like mush. "You must miss her a lot."

He nodded, resting his forehead on Jack's nose. "Pa never talks about her, but Grandpa does. I cry sometimes. Does that make me a baby?"

"No, not at all. Crying is as natural as laughing. It makes us feel better."

Though tempted to give him a hug, she decided it might make him feel more ashamed. She had to keep building their connection instead of tearing it down. Sunlight danced on the creek and sparked an idea. She walked to the water's edge, bent down, and picked up a smooth, flat stone. Standing again, she held it just right, flung her arm outward, and let it loose. The rock skipped merrily across the water, coming to rest on the opposite bank.

"Wow!" Jonny said, running up to stand beside her. "You know how to skip rocks?"

She laughed. "I grew up with two brothers. I didn't have much of a choice. By the way, now that we know each other a little better, you may call me Po if you wish — that was the nickname my brothers gave me and it stuck."

"You know something?" Jonny squatted down and inspected a few rocks before he settled on one.

"What?"

"I like you, Po," he said matter-of-factly, and flung his rock out over the water. It skipped along and landed right on hers. "How about a contest — best two out of three wins?"

Feeling lighter than she had in months, she put her hands on her hips and said, "I thought you'd never ask."

Portia read the to-do list over lunch. Guest rooms would have to be prepared, since the Clemons family would be staying in the Stanford home for an undetermined time until their own home was renovated. They'd have to re-stuff some pillows, and Portia wrote next to that, *Add a few sprigs of lavender.* Dusting, sweeping, and window cleaning could be done that afternoon. Tablecloths and napkins needed pressing, meals needed planning. Someone would have to shop for dry goods, candles, and other necessities.

Sleeves rolled up and apron on, Portia was ready for battle. She tackled the dusting and sweeping. Bessie cleaned the guest room windows, took all the rugs out back and slung them over the clothesline for a good beating. Every surface shone from their efforts by the time they were done. During supper, Portia sat with Bessie in the kitchen and started planning meals. Excited voices carried from the next room, with several mentions of Lydia Clemons.

"She must be quite a sight," Portia said.

"You'd think the Lord himself was arriving on the back of a donkey colt," Bessie said, rolling her eyes and laughing. "Everybody thinks she's going to be the next Mrs. Stanford. I hate to tell 'em this, but Beau ain't gonna take to that idea."

Portia felt strange about eavesdropping, but she couldn't keep herself from listening in on the conversation in the dining room. Besides Jonny, the only one *not* talking about the incoming guests was Mr. Stanford. Every now and then, she'd hear him give a one word answer or some general statement, but he certainly didn't sound as enthusiastic as the other men.

Maybe Bessie was right and he didn't have any intentions of marrying Miss Clemons. She realized that her employer's decision about marriage would naturally affect her situation. If he chose to remarry, his new wife would likely want to take Jonny's education into her own hands. But if he didn't marry Miss Clemons, Portia would still have a job and be able to stay with Jonny for a while longer.

For a moment, she pictured Beau Stanford in the paddock, training his new filly. She remembered the peaceful light in his eyes and the way his strong hands moved so expertly along with the horse. Warmth crept up her neck, so she quickly stood, went to the basin, and started washing dishes before Bessie could see her blush.

Mr. Stanford wasn't in the dining room for breakfast on Sunday morning.

Portia brought in coffee from the kitchen. As casually as she could, she asked Ezra about him.

The old man took a sip of the steaming brew and wiped his mustache with the back of his hand. "He had a bad night."

"Oh."

She poured Harry's coffee and felt his eyes boring into her.

"Thanks, darlin'." His hand shook as he took a drink. He set the cup down and focused on his plate. "We better hurry or we'll be late for church."

After the service, they returned to the house for lunch. Mr. Stanford still didn't make an appearance. April showers pitter-pattered outside, triggering contagious yawns. Jonny fell asleep on the parlor rug with his marbles lying in wait under his fingers.

Ezra woke him and led him upstairs for a nap. Portia followed, pausing at the top of the stairs to look down the hall at Mr. Stanford's closed door.

Once settled on her own bed, she tossed and turned, unable to sleep. Surrendering to the mid-day insomnia, she sat at the little table by the window and tried to read from the book of Longfellow poems. Rain pattered on the window panes. The words jumbled into nonsensical language. Her thoughts drifted down the hall and toward her employer. Her heart ached for him; being faced with the prospect of marriage again must be hard to accept, especially when he still wore his wedding ring and the sting of his late wife's death hadn't lessened.

Would he mind if she checked in on him? All he could do was tell her to go away — then she would at least know he was alive. She set the book down and started to get up, then sat back down. She'd already intruded once into his personal space. He might tell her to leave and never come back if she did it again.

No, she had to have courage right now — part of her job was to help care for everyone here, and she couldn't live with herself if he lay in there sick or… worse, with no one knowing. Everyone else might be afraid of intruding on him, but it was better he yell at her than Jonny. Harry, Ezra, and even Bessie, acted as though nothing was amiss, but the strange quiet that had settled over them had completely *un*settled her.

Before she could change her mind again, she stood and went straight out into the hallway, walked quietly but quickly to his closed door, and rested her ear upon it. She heard nothing, and no one stirred from the other rooms.

She closed her eyes and lifted her hand to knock, but hesitated. *What am I waiting for? Surely he wouldn't send me away for being compassionate?*

With three quiet raps on his door, she stepped back, and waited.

Nothing.

She knocked again, a little louder.

Still nothing.

Cheeks burning from the blush this decision brought, she knew she had no other choice. She had to try the door. If it was locked, she'd just have to give up and return to her room and hope he emerged eventually. If it was unlocked, she'd have a quick look and make sure he was in one piece.

Deep breaths. She turned the knob and slowly eased open his door.

"Mr. Stan—" She closed her mouth when she saw him sprawled across the bed.

Was he...? Soft snores from his partially open mouth flooded her with relief. He lay atop the quilt on his back with one arm resting above his head and one folded over his stomach. Not dead, thank God. From the looks of it, he simply needed this deep sleep. She was about to close the door when her eyes drifted to his bare chest and lingered on his tanned skin, the soft-looking curled hair, the firm muscles of his abdomen. He wore loose gray cotton trousers, and one leg was bent, supported by one large bare foot. His other foot hung off the side of the bed.

Her eyes widened, and she quickly but quietly shut the door. She stood there breathing hard with her hand on the knob. She had just gawked at her employer without his knowledge. Her *half-naked* employer. If someone had thrown bacon on her cheeks at that moment, it would have sizzled.

Portia let go of the door knob and stepped back. He was all right. He hadn't woken up and exploded in anger. No one had to know, and she could rest easy knowing he was fine. She turned around and came two inches from colliding with Bessie. She clapped a hand over her mouth to contain a scream.

"Calm down, Mrs. McAllister," Bessie whispered. "You're gonna scare everybody. I was just bringing him some coffee. He told me to wake him up at four o'clock. I talked him into drinking some of my sleep tea this mornin' when you all went to church, and he's been asleep ever since." She held a steaming cup of coffee in one hand and rapped hard on his door with the other.

At a groggy-sounding, "Come in," she started to turn the knob but turned to Portia first, winked, and whispered, "He *is* a fine-looking man. Can't blame a young woman for havin' a peek."

Bessie opened the door, and Portia caught a glimpse of Beau sitting on the edge of the bed, running a hand through his tousled dark hair. She fled down the stairs and out to the porch before her face caught the house on fire.

Chapter Twelve

On **Monday morning,** the entire household stirred before sunrise. The men dug into breakfast as soon as Portia and Bessie got it on the table. Portia poured Mr. Stanford's coffee. He looked much more rested than he had since she arrived — the circles under his eyes were lighter, his face clean shaven. She caught the soapy tallow scent of William's Yankee Shaving Soap. Jake had used it religiously; she used to run her fingers over his smooth jaw right after he shaved and would kiss him to take advantage of his not-so-prickly affections.

Beau took a sip from his cup and caught her looking at him. A smile tugged at one corner of his mouth.

"Sugar?" She peeled her eyes away from him to focus on the few white cubes in the pretty porcelain dish.

"One, please."

Quickly as she could so no one saw her hand shaking, she plucked up a sugar cube with the little silver tongs and plopped it in his cup. Coffee splashed onto the table from the sugar's sudden dive.

"Is something wrong?" His voice held an undercurrent of laughter.

Portia's eyes widened. "No, nothing at all. Sorry," she muttered and escaped into the kitchen. Ezra's throaty laugh followed her until the door swung shut behind her. Bessie looked up from getting the biscuits off the pan and onto the plate and pursed her lips together, holding back a laugh.

Setting the sugar down on the counter, Portia exhaled loudly and put a hand on her hip. "What?"

"I've seen that look before, mm-hmm, sure have."

What look? Dear Lord, is it that obvious? "He knows, doesn't he?"

"Maybe he does, maybe he don't." Bessie chuckled and carried the biscuits into the dining room.

Portia dipped a kitchen towel in the water basin and dabbed her cheeks. The only way she would be able forget that image of him sprawled on his bed was to dive headfirst into chores and not stop until bedtime.

So that's what she did.

Portia leaned on her elbows at the kitchen table that night, having devoured her dinner of boiled eggs, green beans, and salt pork. Her eyelids grew heavy, as did her head, which bobbed as sleep tried to claim her. She and Bessie were both exhausted after a day spent cleaning, shopping, weeding the garden and flower beds, and stuffing pillows. The good thing was, she hadn't thought about her half-clothed employer all day… until now. Hopefully, a good night's sleep would take care of that.

The men had all gathered in the sitting room, enjoying a bit of whiskey — whether in celebration or resignation of the Clemons imminent arrival, she didn't know. But it would give her a chance to retreat to her room without gawking at anyone.

"Get some sleep. You earned it today," Bessie said.

She smiled in gratitude. Hearing praise from Bessie was a welcome surprise. She yawned and started to stand from her chair.

"Wait a minute. Let me doctor them blisters first."

"You don't have to do that. I've had blisters a plenty."

"Come on, let me see 'em," Bessie said firmly while she opened a small tin can of salve.

Portia did as she was told and held her hands out palms up, while Bessie applied the pungent-smelling, greasy mixture to the red blisters. A clean white bandage came next, wrapped snugly around her right hand. After a slight burning sensation, the salve provided a cool tingle to her raw skin.

"How do you make that?" Portia asked.

"A little cedar sap, some alder bark, and slippery elm, among other things." Bessie tilted her head and grinned — clearly unwilling to share her complete secret recipe.

"Well, thank you. It's feeling better already. Perhaps I can learn a thing or two from you about salves and teas."

"Perhaps."

"I'll see you in the morning."

Body weary and head full of jumbled thoughts, she left the kitchen, already imagining the downy comfort of her pillow. She passed through the dining room, headed for the stairs... and walked straight into a solid wall of a man.

"Oh!" Bouncing off him, she steadied herself and looked up into deep-set eyes that were just as startled as hers.

"Sorry," Mr. Stanford said. "Let me just—"

He stepped left, and she stepped right, blocking each other's path.

"Sorry," Portia said.

She stepped left, and he stepped right. Blocked again.

His mouth stretched into a wide smile. "If you're trying to dance with me, just say so."

"No, I wasn't... I mean... um..."

Slapping his thighs, he broke into laughter — rich, hearty, and completely unexpected. Hard as she tried, she couldn't hold it in. The two of them laughed like they hadn't done it in a million years. Heads started peeking out at them from the sitting room, slowly retreating as their guffawing subsided.

Mr. Stanford wiped his eyes. "I think I needed that."

"Me too," she admitted, trying uselessly to tuck her wayward hair behind her ears.

He nodded toward her bandaged hand. "Are you hurt?"

"Just blisters." She held it up and wiggled her fingers. "Battle wounds for a hard day's work. Bessie's salve is working wonders though."

"She's really good with medicine. Shame she couldn't be a doctor. By the way, thank you for your help around here. Bessie tells me you've lightened her load quite a bit."

"That's my job, right?"

"Right, but I reckon it needs sayin' now and then." He looked away and scratched his jaw. "Truth is I'm not ready for tomorrow."

"We have everything ready for them," Portia said, trying to sound reassuring.

"No, it's not that. It's the reason they might be coming. I'm not ready for it."

"Oh. I see." She swallowed hard and crossed her arms, feeling a sudden chill. Her sleepy mind hadn't picked up on the obvious: he wasn't ready for re-marriage. Racking her brain for the right words, she settled on the only thing she could think of. "Do not worry about tomorrow, for tomorrow will worry about itself."

"Each day has enough trouble of its own."

His eyes drifted back to hers, and his lips curved into a soft smile. He looked much more pleasant with a smile on his face. Handsome even.

"Matthew 6:34." She couldn't break the lifelong habit of quoting scriptures. Not everyone appreciated the talent. Before Jake and Abby died, she spouted them right and left to grieving widows back in Brentwood. Oftentimes, they didn't appreciate the sentiment, and soon enough, she understood exactly how they felt. Even after everything she'd been through, old habits proved hard to break.

Her employer, however, didn't seem offended. He took a step closer and looked more relaxed than ever. "I never could memorize scripture like that. Claire could, and I probably should have appreciated it more. It's good to know you're a woman of faith, Mrs. McAllister."

She shrugged and shook her head. "I don't know about that, Mr. Stanford. Like so many things these days, faith seems to be in short supply."

"Maybe you'll find it here." He turned toward the stairs but stopped and faced her again. "Since you'll be here awhile, you might as well call me Beau."

"Only if you call me Po."

His brow knitted together, and he went completely still for a moment, as though her nickname came as a shock. Shaking his head slightly, he rubbed his forehead until his features relaxed again.

"Po and Beau," he said with a soft chuckle. "Now, isn't that something? Goodnight, Po."

He lightly grasped her fingers with his and gave a gentle squeeze. Then he climbed the stairs, crossed the landing, and disappeared around the corner. She heard his door click shut and glanced at her hand — the one he'd touched. It was a completely innocent gesture, so why did it feel like some un-scalable wall had fallen, and an undiscovered territory lay before her?

Beau watched the birth of Tuesday morning from the front porch. Orange and magenta clouds streaked the horizon. The obnoxious rooster had taken his place atop the chicken coop, crowing like his racket alone could draw the sun into the sky.

"Today might be a good day for chicken dumplings," Beau said, hoping that would silence the ill-tempered fowl. No such luck.

He hadn't slept a wink all night. The days and weeks ahead held too much uncertainty to let him close his eyes and stall his racing mind. Why couldn't things be simple anymore? He heard the first stirrings of life from inside the house and wondered if Portia was awake. *It might be nice to sit here and talk to her for a while.*

Last night, when they had laughed together, all his tensions had melted away, if only for a little while. She had certainly earned her keep, even if he couldn't pay her yet. Those blisters on her hands proved she didn't mind hard work and that she was willing to sacrifice her comfort to do what needed doing. Claire, busy as she used to be, never wore the blisters and calluses of a working woman. He had loved that about her — that soft femininity — and felt proud that he could provide her with such a life.

But Portia was a different woman. Jonny seemed to have taken to her, though he still wouldn't say a word, not that he had heard, anyway. Was it possible he spoke to her in private? The thought stirred up a mess of emotions he didn't want to sort through. Not today.

The door creaked open, and Harry stepped softly out to the porch. He froze when he saw Beau sitting there on the stoop.

"What are you selling this time?" Beau stared at the bundle of lavender fabric under his arm.

He flashed his innocent smile and rotated the stolen goods around his side until they were partially hidden. "Selling? I'm not—"

"Give me the key."

Harry's face went deadpan as he dug the key from his vest. He flipped it at Beau, who caught it in his fist.

158

"The dress, too."

He must have decided the dress wasn't as flightworthy as the key, so he took one step toward Beau and thrust it at him. Beau took it, and Harry stepped back to his original caught-red-handed spot. Turning away from Harry and back toward the yard, Beau let his eyes linger on the lavender dress his wife once wore. His fingers caressed the delicate fabric, and he imagined her warm body beneath it when they waltzed together. He'd already sold or traded many of Claire's dresses and jewelry to make ends meet, but he'd held on to a few items like this — locked them away to keep them safe and out of his sight. So he thought.

"Look, Beau, I'm sorry. We need the money."

"No. *You* need the money. I don't care how you get your damn morphine, but you will not touch Claire's things again. Is that understood?"

"But I can't—"

"Stop talking!" Beau's voice roared across the yard. The rooster went silent in mid-crow. He rubbed his eyes and groaned. "Stop making excuses or get your ass out of here."

The air hanging between them felt thick and foreign before Harry conceded with, "Yes, Lord Stanford." He didn't try to hide his limp as he walked past Beau and across the yard toward the barn.

Beau returned the dress to the chest in his room. He had to force his fingers to relinquish the soft fabric. Tucking it beneath his bloodied jacket and the tear-stained letter telling him of her death, he closed his eyes and shut the lid. The lock's tumbler clicked into place as he turned the key. Once that was done, he put it in his pocket. For

one long, lonely minute, he allowed himself to cry —
quietly of course, so no one could notice him surrendering
to emotion. He couldn't pay bills with emotion. Only hard
work could do that. He splashed his face with water at his
basin, scrubbed it dry with a towel, and went straight for
the barn.

Come mid-morning, he was trimming the newest
filly's hooves. Harry occupied the next stall, doing the
same with Crazy Girl. And it wasn't going so well, much
to Beau's amusement and satisfaction.

"Ow!" That was the third "ow" of the morning.

"What now?"

"She bit my ass!"

Beau laughed. "She's *your* girl, Harry. Be a good daddy
now."

"Ha, ha, you're hilarious."

"Just tie her head tighter and steer clear of those teeth."

Ezra hollered from outside, "Looks like we've got
company!"

Beau let the horse's foot down gently, and with one
hand on his aching back, he stood up straight and hollered
back, "Be right there!"

Leaving the stable, he squinted into the sunlight and
peered down the drive. A coach and two large carriages
full of luggage rolled along toward the house. He pulled
out his handkerchief and wiped his face and hands.
Probably should have taken the time to wash up before
they got there, but it was too late now.

Ezra gave him a one-armed bear hug. "Excited?"

"I can hardly contain my joy."

"Be nice, Beauregard."

The closer their company came, the harder it became to breathe. He didn't really know how to feel. Never once had he considered remarriage in the two years since Claire had passed, but that possibility now rolled up their drive on four expensive wheels. Worse yet, he couldn't deny the obvious. He'd be marrying for money, if he married her at all, and knowing that made him feel like a whore.

Harry joined them, rubbing his horse-bitten backside. "Here comes the bride…"

"Shut up." Beau popped him on the shoulder with his fist.

"Ow! Damn, you tryin' to cripple me all over again?"

"Watch your language," Ezra reprimanded. "Let's go greet 'em."

Climbing the hill toward the house, Beau's feet could have been made of lead, they felt so heavy. He spotted Jonny, Bessie, and Portia coming out the front door. His eyes met Po's. She smiled and nodded at him in assurance, much like she'd do with a student, he imagined. Smiling back, he did feel a mite calmer and ready to face the new arrivals.

He recognized their black driver, Tipp, husband to Bessie's niece. Beau recalled rainy days spent at Bessie and Isaac's house trying to beat Tipp at checkers. Never could. His old friend lifted a hand in greeting and smiled as though he was thinking the exact same thing.

When the coach came to a stop in front of the house, Tipp climbed down and opened the door. A blonde angel swathed in royal blue satin and white lace set her dainty feet on the ground. Beau's eyes traveled past the fawn-leather gloved hand, up the ivory-skinned arm and matching full bosom. His breath stalled. He could have been looking at Claire come back to life, the resemblance was so close. But it wasn't Claire. It was her little cousin, Lydia Clemons, all grown up, and Beau was the first to receive her stunning smile.

"Whoa," Harry whispered in his ear. "She'll have you before the night's over."

Next to exit the coach was a well-dressed man with tufted gray hair and a perfectly trimmed gray beard. Two older women clad in drab traveling dresses followed.

"Oliver!" Ezra hollered, offering his hand. "I hope y'all had a good trip down."

"We did, thank you," Oliver answered and granted him a handshake. He repeated the gesture with Beau. "So good to see you again, though it pained my heart to hear of Claire's passing. She was a fine woman."

"She thought a lot of you, as well," Beau said.

Having his wife's family there again woke a strange mixture of feelings. First was the resemblance that tugged at his heart and made him miss Claire all the more. But seeing the Clemons family also brought flashes of days past — happy times with barbeques, dances, and Claire's sweet laughter.

Oliver smiled morosely and put a hand on his daughter's back. "I'm sure you remember Lydia."

"Of course," Beau said, doing his best not to stammer and stare. She removed one glove and offered her hand. He took her soft, warm fingers in his, and kissed her smooth knuckles. "But I remember a little girl with that name, not a lovely young woman."

"You don't say." Lydia's gloved hand settled on her chest in feigned shock, but her blue eyes were bright and playful. "And I remember a man who once called me Lily-doodle and taught me how to ride."

"I hope you haven't forgotten how."

"I'll have you know, good sir, that I am an accomplished equestrian thanks to you. Aren't I, Daddy?"

"Yes, yes," Oliver said, choosing a cigar from a box Tipp had just opened for him. "Let's not prattle on about it. We've had a long trip."

Tipp struck a match and held the flame to the end of the tightly rolled Cuban figurado. Oliver puffed on it until he expelled a nice cloud of tobacco smoke and waved Tipp off. He clomped up the stairs past Portia and Bessie and entered the house. Apparently he'd had enough of the reunion.

Lydia waved a hand and rolled her eyes. "Never mind Daddy. He's even more cantankerous than before we moved to Philly. Isn't that right, Mama?"

Her mother, Polly, nodded slowly in agreement. She reminded Beau of a wilted flower with her drooped shoulders and short, stocky build. Her hair was tucked neatly under a brown silk bonnet, but her features were so forlorn, it looked like her face could slide off at any minute.

"Polly, I trust you are well," Beau said, hoping a warm welcome might add some light to her dark expression.

No such luck.

He had a hard time hearing her meek voice, but he thought she said, "The ride has aggravated my rheumatism, I'm afraid. I do hope you have a room ready for me to take a rest."

"Um…" Beau glanced at Portia, who nodded. "Yes, yes we do."

Polly's older sister, Amelie, was the last to step out of the coach. Petite and silver-haired, the spinster looked around like she'd never seen the place before, even though she had once called Lebanon home. Beau had always thought fondly of Amelie Hamilton. Claire had spent a great deal of time with her as a girl, and it was Amelie who had introduced him to Claire.

"Good to see you again, Amelie," Beau said.

She reached up and pinched his cheek. "You're too skinny. Did you and Claire build a new house?"

Beau took her cool, limp hand and patted it. "No… don't you remember coming here to visit before you went to Philadelphia?"

"Where is she? I want to see her and give her a few things." She leaned in close like she wanted to whisper, but her volume never changed. "She was always my favorite niece."

Eyebrows raised, he looked to Lydia, who mouthed, "She's going senile." Then she added aloud, "She still owns the Hamilton Estate. A few of her loyal people stayed on to maintain it in her absence. We hope they have it ready for her to reoccupy it soon." She ended that last remark with an annoyed glance at her frail aunt.

"Ah, I see," Beau said. "Claire missed her and all of you when you moved to Philly."

"And we missed you all, too. I cried for weeks after I heard about her passing." Lydia had acquired a clipped Northern accent with only a slight trace of a Southern drawl. She dabbed her eyes with a lacy handkerchief. "I have such sweet memories of my cousin. But you can imagine my relief to know that you came home safely."

She settled her hands on his chest, while her bosom brushed against his shirt. Before his excitement became embarrassingly obvious, he took a step away from Claire's lookalike and motioned for Jonathan to come down from the porch.

"You remember Jonathan? Come here, son."

Jonny came close and offered a shaky hand to Lydia. She took it in hers and patted it lovingly, while he stared down at his wriggling boots.

"My goodness, he's grown! He looks so much like his mother, God rest her soul."

Harry cleared his throat loudly and nudged Beau.

"And you remember Harry, I'm sure," Beau grumbled.

Head tilted to one side, she batted her eyes at his friend. "How could I forget that old charmer?"

"Miss Clemons, what a pleasure to see you again." Harry took a deep bow, kissed her hand, and employed an Adonis-like smile.

She snatched her hand from him and giggled. "Your charms no longer affect me, Mr. Franklin. Beau, did you know that Harry used to bribe me with little gifts, like oranges and hair ribbons? He'd go on and on about how he would wait for me to be grown up so he could marry me, but the next time I'd see him, he'd have another young lady on his arm."

Harry grinned and winked, eliciting more giggles from Lydia.

"Nothing surprises me about Harry," Beau said. "Oh, you remember Bessie. She and Isaac stayed on throughout the war, though their boys have since moved up north. We lost a few more of our hired hands, but I've got some temporaries here for the season. And we've just hired on Portia McAllister as Jonny's tutor." He gestured toward her and added, "She's been a big help around here this week."

Lydia lifted her head toward the porch. With one eyebrow arched, she scanned Portia from head to foot. Beau's muscles tensed, his senses on alert like the final seconds before the first shot of a battle. Before now, he hadn't given any thought about how a potential bride might react to a young widow living in his house. To his relief, Lydia waved the white flag with a smile that could rival the sun.

"A pleasure to meet you, Mrs. McAllister," she said, sashaying toward her, gown rustling across the ground. "I am *so* relieved to have another young lady to converse with. My mother and aunt are pleasant enough, but they get tired of me going on and on about the latest fashions and socials. I'm sure we will get along splendidly."

"I'm sure," Portia said.

She smiled back, all right, but her eyes told another story — one of uncertainty and maybe even... jealousy?

Chapter Thirteen

Had anyone told Portia that this woman's feet never touched the earth, she would have believed it. Lydia Clemons reminded her of a peacock strutting around the barnyard in all its glory. No one could deny her beauty, and it didn't take much to see that she'd been denied nothing in life.

Having turned her attention back to Beau and the other men, Lydia floated away, leaving Portia to notice the rest of the party. With the Clemons family came five black servants — three men that drove the coach and carriages, along with a woman and child. The woman ran onto the porch and hugged Bessie tightly. Young and pretty, she had skin a shade lighter than Bessie's. Her gray cotton dress and matching bonnet were plain but well-made. A little girl hid behind her skirts.

"Mrs. McAllister, this is Lucy Jenkins," Bessie said. "She's my niece. My sister was owned by the Clemonses until she passed on several years ago, and Lucy's stayed on with them. Been up in Philadelphia this whole time, haven't you?"

Lucy nodded and smiled. "Ain't nobody up there can make fried chicken like yours, Aunt Bessie. My mouth's waterin' just thinkin' about it."

"You're in for a nice surprise, then."

Lucy reached behind her, tugging at the little girl's sleeve. "Sallie Mae, come here, child. Say hello to your great-aunt."

The girl stepped partway from behind Lucy and waved her fingers at Bessie, who bent down to get a better look at her.

"Bless my soul, is this Sallie Mae?" Bessie patted the little girl's head, which was covered with braids tipped with beads of different colors. "You was just a baby last time I saw you, girl. Time sure does fly. Lucy, this is Portia McAllister. She's tutorin' Jonny and helpin' out around here."

Lucy curtsied. "A pleasure to meet you, ma'am."

"Likewise," Portia said.

Bessie pointed toward the carriages. "Tipp there is Lucy's husband, and the other two are Saul and Joseph. They work for Miss Amelie."

The three women, along with Sallie, who retreated behind Lucy's skirts again, turned their attention to the grand reunion of Stanfords and Clemonses. Portia tried not to look at Beau, but it wouldn't matter if she did. His eyes had never left the beautiful peacock dressed in royal blue.

He woke from her spell long enough to turn to the rest of the party. "Saul, how about you and Tipp start unloading the luggage? Bessie can show you the rooms we have prepared. We have plenty of storage space upstairs and in the attic."

"Oh, Beau, I have something for you," Lydia said excitedly. She pulled him toward one of the horses they had hitched to the last carriage. "Do you like her?"

Beau shook his head in confusion.

"She's yours, a Standardbred from the line of the great Hambletonian himself."

Eyes wide, he stroked the horse's neck. "I don't know what to say."

The stunning specimen of a horse was charcoal gray with a jet black mane and tail and well-muscled with a shiny coat. *A very lavish gift, but probably not beyond means for this family.*

"Don't say anything," Lydia said, slipping her arm through his. "Just put her out there with Scout and enjoy her. We had Tipp buy her at a sale in Nashville before we arrived. I'm glad she turned out so well. You still have Scout, don't you?"

"Yes."

"Wonderful! I used to be terrified of him. Do you remember?"

Beau laughed. "What I remember is you squealing with terror when I rode past you. Claire accused me of doing it on purpose. She was right."

Having heard quite enough of this reunion, Portia went inside with Bessie, Lucy, and Sallie Mae. She didn't like the way her cheeks had flamed and how images of her own feast or fast life had flipped through her mind in an instant comparison with the life Miss Clemons must have led. Jealousy was something she had rarely entertained, and she didn't want to be its host. She dove right into lunch preparations, glad to have something to keep her occupied for a while.

After serving the guests, Portia ate her lunch standing at the work counter in the kitchen. The constant chatter from the dining room and Lydia's high-pitched laughter blended with the conversation from Bessie's family reunion and gave her a headache.

"Y'all gotta be careful now." Bessie's happy voice had deepened into a serious warning tone. "They found Clarence over near Cainsville, hanging from a hickory tree. Burned so bad Fannie could hardly recognize him. Don't none of you go out alone, you hear me? Take Isaac or Harry along and make sure one of you's got a gun."

Portia paused mid-bite, her appetite giving way to a knot of fear in her gut.

"What about Fannie and Jim?" Lucy asked. "They all right?"

"Yes, they're fine. Isaac took 'em up to Kentucky. He oughta be back tomorrow."

Lucy blinked back tears and hugged Sallie Mae close. "You and Uncle Isaac's all we got, Aunt Bessie. If somethin' happened…"

Bessie reached across the small table and took Lucy's hand. "Don't you worry. Isaac's got Deputy Bandy with him. He don't like seein' this kind of violence, no matter white or black."

Portia abandoned the rest of her lunch and helped serve coffee and cookies to everyone in the parlor. Mr. Clemons had new toys for Jonathan, who laid belly-down on the parlor floor playing with each one in turn. Miss

Clemons sat across from Beau at a table by the window. Her girlish giggles punctuated their conversation.

Harry took his cup and saucer from Portia and brushed his thumb over hers. "Thank you, darlin'."

She saw a note of concern in his eyes.

"You all right?" he added quietly.

"I'm fine, thank you."

Harry caught her wrist lightly and scooted to the edge of the settee. Drawing her down toward him, he whispered, "How about you and me go for a walk in a little while? You know, get some fresh air and all."

Tempted to take him up on the offer, she decided she would feel guilty about taking Harry away from the guests. Being alone for a while would suit her mood better anyway.

"Thank you," she said, gently slipping from his grasp. "I'll probably have a rest upstairs instead. Maybe another time."

Harry sighed and scooted back in the seat. He plunged a cookie in his coffee then crammed it in his mouth, staring straight ahead. She felt a little guilty turning him down when he tried so hard to gain her attention, but… she hurried back to the kitchen before she could change her mind.

Portia took on the task of cleaning the dishes so Bessie could continue reminiscing with Lucy and Tipp. Sallie Mae fell asleep on her mother's lap. As wonderful as these reunions were, Portia couldn't help the nagging feeling of being an outsider. And why had she taken such a sudden and terrible dislike of Miss Clemons? Maybe some fresh air *would* be nice.

By the time she climbed the stairs to her room, Portia had decided to take a walk, after all. The Clemons ladies were all napping in their rooms, while the men remained in the parlor enjoying those smelly cigars. She retrieved her shawl, came back downstairs, and slipped outside. Following the path she and Jonny had taken the other day, she strolled down to Barton Creek. Pulling her shawl tighter around her, she shivered in the chilly breeze, but it felt good on her face and eased her throbbing headache. Up above, rain clouds hung heavy in the sky. They began to release their burden drop by drop, and she watched each one hit the creek's surface, making gentle ripples before they joined the current.

Backing up to a tall cedar at the edge of the bank, she leaned against its wide, ragged-barked trunk. A few minutes passed as she let her mind drift along over the rough rocks of her memories. She had just remembered that she needed to answer Ellen's latest letter when something crunched the fallen evergreen needles behind and to the right of her cedar refuge.

She groaned. Harry must have spied her leaving the house. Not feeling up to his company, she considered slipping away on the opposite side of the tree when she saw Beau's familiar hat and his broad shoulders beneath an oilskin duster.

He stopped down by the bank and didn't seem to notice her presence. Portia watched him rub his right shoulder while he stared out across the creek. A prickly sensation of awkwardness traveled down her spine. Was he there looking for her? Or did he just need some fresh air, too? Either way, she could think of nothing to talk about — nothing she ought to share with her employer, anyway.

She pushed herself slowly away from the tree and took a quiet step away from him.

"Didn't mean to intrude," he said.

Too late.

"You didn't intrude," she replied, trying to still the quiver in her voice. His presence stirred up a longing she couldn't afford to have. "I mean… it's only intruding if you know what you'll find when you get there."

Beau chuckled. "I guess you're right. I thought you were upstairs napping, like the other ladies. Just needed a little air. Stuffy in there. You?"

"Same here." Portia abandoned her escape plan and returned to her post against the cedar. "Guess it's all the cooking — heated up the house."

"Yes, I guess that's it." He tossed a smile over his shoulder. "She's pretty, isn't she?"

"Probably the most beautiful horse I've ever seen."

He shook his head, laughing. "You know who I mean."

Of course she did, and she smiled in return. She couldn't help it. He'd left the door wide open for a little verbal jab at his soon-to-be wife.

"Then yes, she's probably the most beautiful *woman* I've ever seen."

His smile faded, and he shifted his weight from one boot to the other. "So much like Claire."

"Really?"

"In looks, anyway. She's different though."

"How so?"

173

"Just… different."

"That's to be expected, considering she *is* a different woman."

He nodded. "At least they all seemed pleased with lunch. Probably not as much as they're used to eating, but you and Bessie did good with what we have."

"Thank you."

Still looking over the water, Beau took on his even-toned employer's voice. "I'd like you to join us in the dining room for supper from now on."

"I thought perhaps you'd rather have the uninterrupted time with your guests."

"You thought wrong. Besides, Jonny would feel more comfortable with you there. And Lydia asked about you. She would like a woman closer to her age to talk to at supper."

"I see." She could feel her breaths coming more rapidly, her face heating up. "I don't think I'd have much to add to the conversation."

Beau turned to face her fully. "I'm not asking."

His tone was unquestionably authoritative, but his eyes held a certain pleading, a sense of need. No matter how much she wanted to scream, *"Forget it! I'd rather pull my hair out than try to entertain that peacock of a woman,"* she couldn't deny him this request disguised as an order.

"All right. I'll join you for supper, though…" She looked down at her dress and rubbed a hand along the worn fabric. "I don't have much in the way of dinner dresses."

"I think you look fine without all that fancy garb." He stepped closer, stopping just beyond arm's reach. His eyes lingered on her face then dipped lower, quickly rising again to meet her gaze as though he had to force his attention to the proper place.

Her cheeks burned so hot she wanted to dunk her head in the creek.

Beau focused on his boots, cleared his throat and tightened his coat around himself. "Better get inside before you catch a chill."

He walked past the tree and out of her sight. Instead of wrapping her shawl tighter, she took it off, stepped to the creek, and dipped a corner of the crocheted material in the chilly water. She dabbed the coolness on her face and exhaled the breath she'd been holding. When he'd looked at her that way, she couldn't help picturing his hands — those rugged, gentle fingers of his — pulling her close, touching her bare skin. And he was concerned with her taking a chill?

She patted her cheeks with the wet cloth again and silently repented. *Sorry Lord, if you're listening, but taking a chill is the last thing on my mind.*

175

Chapter Fourteen

Beau waited in the parlor with everyone else, dressed in his Sunday best, which felt odd for a Tuesday night. Even Pa was in fine feather in a clean, pressed shirt. He'd slicked down what was left of his gray hair, and he'd trimmed his beard. He rarely brought it up over the years, but Beau wondered why Pa never remarried. The only thing he'd ever say was that he had married the perfect woman once, so why bother trying again? He'd always been a good man that any lady would have been lucky to have, but now with Claire gone, Beau understood Pa's decision. So why did Pa keep insisting his son get remarried? Was it possible he regretted never having done so himself, that the years of sleeping alone had been harder than he ever let on?

He realized Portia was missing from their little pre-dinner gathering. She must have been helping in the kitchen. Maybe he'd been too harsh when he told her to join them for supper. Like most women, she worried about the adequacy of her clothing. Beau couldn't care less about such things, so long as folks took time to be clean and presentable, and she'd managed that just fine. The last thing he wanted to do was to make her feel awkward or embarrassed.

Lydia would be making her appearance soon for supper. He couldn't believe how much she resembled Claire. Still, thoughts of marriage, even to his late-wife's lookalike, tensed his muscles until they hurt. He rotated his shoulder to lessen the ache and poured a shot of whiskey.

Ezra pointed his pipe at him. "A little early for that, ain't it, Beauregard?"

"Not at all." Beau downed the whiskey and let out a breath as it blazed a trail down his throat.

"She sure did turn out to be a pretty young lady," Ezra said, waggling his bushy eyebrows as he took a puff of his pipe.

"I'd say," Harry agreed. He sat by Oliver on the settee, dressed in his own finery, bowtie included. He lit one of Oliver's cigars and massaged his leg. The morning's work had taken a toll on both of their old wounds.

Oliver draped an elbow over the back of his seat and expelled a thick cloud of smoke. "I thought our door knocker would be worn down to a nub, she had so many suitors calling in Philly." He looked pointedly at Beau. "I often had the unpleasant duty of turning them away. She refused most of them, and entertained a few others for only a brief moment. None of them fit her expectations."

Beau downed another shot.

Lydia finally made her entrance, to the sound of Harry's appreciative whistle, dressed to the nines in a gown of green brocade. Pinned up high, her blond hair bounced with a bouquet of perfectly formed curls. A string of pearls grazed the edge of her cleavage and complemented her ivory skin. Matching earrings swayed gently from her ears. Besides the curls, no trace remained of the little girl he remembered in this stunning woman.

"My apologies for keeping you waiting, Beau. Lucy had a terrible time finding my jewelry. The box got lost among some of the other things."

"You're forgiven." He held out his arm, and she slid hers into the crook of his elbow. "You look lovely."

"Why, thank you. You look quite handsome yourself."

The way she smiled and tossed her head, yet another reminder of Claire, made Beau's heart skip a beat. Lydia hugged his arm so tightly he could feel the warm pillow of her breast. He snapped to his senses and led her into the dining room.

After helping Lydia get seated, he glanced around the room. Still no sign of Portia. Once Polly and Amelie were settled, he took his seat and drummed his fingers on his knees, trying to pay attention to something Lydia was saying about art.

"…said I rivaled Delacroix. Now I don't know about that, but I brought some with me…"

Beau heard stirring from the kitchen. Portia entered with Bessie and Lucy to serve the meal.

Moving stiffly, Portia avoided eye contact while she sat a plate of sliced bread and butter on the table's center. She walked around to the sideboard and retrieved a butter knife.

"Excuse me," she said and reached between Oliver and Polly to place the knife on the breadboard.

Beau didn't know why she had been worried about her choice of attire. She looked just fine in a crisp clean white cotton dress with green vertical stripes. It fit her nicely and accentuated her slender figure. She'd braided her hair and coiled into a bun at the nape of her neck. No jewelry except for her wedding ring and a tarnished silver necklace and locket. Simple, yes, but pretty nonetheless.

She met his gaze. He smiled and gave a little nod, hoping that would be enough to encourage her to stay.

Oliver tucked his napkin neatly into his collar. "I sure have missed Bessie's cooking. Is that her fried chicken I smell?"

"Oh, you do go on, sir!" Bessie said with a chuckle. "Eat up now. Plenty more where that came from."

Bessie returned to the kitchen, while Lucy stood quietly by the sideboard in the corner closest to Oliver and Polly. Portia came back around the table. As she crossed behind his chair, Beau sighed into his water glass, sure she was heading back into the kitchen. Instead, she took the empty space between Harry and Jonny, who jumped up and helped her get seated.

"Thank you, Jonathan," she said, smiling at him. Portia focused on her napkin as she spread it across her lap.

Jonny smiled and grabbed a piece of bread. Harry whispered something to her, at which she blushed. Beau set his glass down with a thump. She seemed to be warming up to Harry. Perfectly natural, he reasoned with himself — single man, widow woman — why not? But she'd only been there a couple weeks. Harry shouldn't pressure her into courtship so soon.

Lydia, to Beau's right, smiled sweetly. "I'm so glad you could join us, Mrs. McAllister. Your dress is... charming. Stripes never go out of style. If I am correct, that particular gown would be a forties design, would it not?"

"I believe so, since it belonged to my late mother," Portia answered, though her tone was tense and uncertain.

"*My* mother will tell you I have quite the eye for fashion, and have a collection of gowns from every decade of the century, and even a few from the century prior."

"She does," Polly said, turning toward her daughter. She sat between Lydia and Oliver, blinking her sad eyes as she nodded.

Aunt Amelie sat hunched in her chair beside Ezra at the other end of the table and stared him down. "Did you take my curtains?"

Eyes wide, Ezra leaned away from her and shook his head. "No, ma'am. I can't remember the last time I touched a curtain." Half-grinning, he shook his head and looked at Beau.

"Crazy old bat," Oliver muttered. "She'll be back at her place soon, and those niggers of hers can deal with her nonsense. I've listened to it for six years."

Beau cleared his throat, about to warn Oliver to hold his tongue around a lady, senile or not. But Amelie scratched at an invisible spot on her plate and didn't seem to have heard a thing. No sense raising a fuss if she didn't take offense.

"Daddy, honestly," Lydia chided then leaned toward Beau. Her peppermint-scented breath warmed his cheek. "She's mostly deaf, poor thing. Not at all the formidable lady she once was." Earrings swinging beneath her delicate ears, she quickly turned back to Portia. "Do you read Godey's Lady's Book? I can't keep myself from perusing them, though some of the fashions are so outlandish."

"I have seen a few issues," Portia said while she absently touched one of her own unpierced earlobes.

Oliver downed his water in three gulps. "Not that again." He held his glass up and shook it. Lucy immediately came over with a water jug and gave him a refill. Taking another sip, he smacked his lips as though testing the water's quality, and set the glass down. "She could wallpaper an entire house with the pages from that silly magazine."

Lydia dismissed her father's comment with a flick of her hand. "I'd be happy to let you borrow mine and perhaps we could even purchase new materials and piece together a new gown or two. I'm trying to better myself at sewing, since our economy is dreadful."

"As if she needs to save money," Oliver said with a huff.

"If I can spare the time," Portia said, flicking her gaze to Oliver while she shifted in her seat. "Jonathan's education is my priority."

"Well, of course! I wouldn't want to separate him from his schooling."

"Best leave the discussions of economics and schooling to the men, my dear," Oliver said. "Besides, our dinner is getting cold. I'd hate to waste it. Who wants to bless the meal?"

"I will," Ezra said.

The meal was blessed, and everyone dug in. The dinner party spoke only a few words until seconds came around. Beau listened to the other men discuss politics and economics. The women talked about local gossip and charitable affairs. Portia, God love her, politely participated, but she clearly had no interest in all the babble. He appreciated her trying anyway. She attempted to engage Jonny in conversation now and then, but he only nodded or shrugged in response.

Beau let the talk buzz around the room while everyone enjoyed dessert. He answered whenever necessary. In his head, he wrangled more practical matters, like estimating how much money he might get from Crazy Girl if he got her calmed down enough to sell. He wanted to give Portia her dues before she felt like a slave. Oliver might treat *his* help like they were less than human, but that wasn't how it worked here. Before he could come up with a dollar figure, Oliver slapped the table in the middle of one of his political tirades, reminding Beau just how abrasive he could be.

"By the grace of God, I managed not to lose everything in Philly, and then I come back here and get taxed to death. Soon they'll be taxing the air we breathe, mark my words!"

Harry adjusted his bowtie and laughed. "The only way to pay for our mess is with taxes, unless you want to jump out there with a hammer yourself."

Lydia giggled, and Harry threw her a wink before digging into a second helping of apple pie.

Clearly not amused, Oliver wagged a finger at the ceiling like he reprimanded God himself. "I have been inconvenienced, I tell you. We are lucky to not have had to pay to reclaim our property. I only managed that because I left here before the damn war started and declared my loyalty to the Yankees. We had to in order to live among them. But now look, I'm out fifty dollars a week to fix the damage done, when I had perfectly good Negroes at my service before this travesty of justice."

"We lost people, too," Beau said, smirking. "You aren't the only one... suffering."

Unperturbed by Beau's sarcasm, Oliver propped his elbows on the table and thrust his shrewd gaze at everyone as he spoke. "Can you believe one of them had the nerve to have a letter dictated and sent to me, demanding wages for time served, and the balance for the injustice he was entitled to? Regular satirist, that one. Or rather his Yankee translator. Son of a..." Oliver sat back and pounded his fist on the table. Dishes rattled. "I know for a fact that Negro couldn't read when he ran off. He was too lazy to do much but eat me out of house and home. Why would he bother to learn to read or write?"

He has some nerve, spewing that filth here at my table. Beau yanked his napkin from his collar and threw it onto his plate. "Maybe he knew a lot more than you think he did."

"Damn Yankees couldn't leave well enough alone. They're hell bent on making this a colored nation, and you can see what's come of it." Oliver pointed his fork at Portia. "That poor woman's husband would still be here, and so would my niece if it weren't for them."

Beau glanced at Portia, who clenched her locket and stared down at her uneaten food. Under the table, he gripped his knees so hard it hurt. Had the ladies not been present, he would have said exactly what he thought of Oliver Clemons.

"Daddy, please," Lydia protested with a pretty pout. "Let's not ruin the evening for everyone with such depressing talk. Think about our friends back in Philadelphia who were nothing but hospitable to us."

"I'm speaking truth, young lady. We *had* to consort with them to survive." He glared at Beau. "We didn't throw our lots in willingly like some people here."

Beau looked away, and it took every ounce of willpower he had to hold his tongue. Harry wasn't so censored and muttered, "Bullshit," under his breath.

Ezra shook his head at Harry and smiled at Oliver, but he had that fire in his eyes that used to put the fear of God into Beau before a good whipping. He struck the tabletop with the butt of his pie fork, drawing everyone's attention. No one even so much as twitched, as they waited for Ezra Stanford to have his say.

He let his gaze meander from one captive audience member to the next. "I wouldn't complain so much if I was you. I mean, look at that jacket of yours. That'd pay for ten hired men's wages for a month, and look at me — my suspenders are so threadbare, I'm about to lose my drawers." He pulled out his suspenders and snapped them against his belly, prompting a giggle from Lydia, but no one else made a sound. Ezra's voice took on the authoritative tone he'd handed down to his son. "I think we're all capable of being civil at the dinner table, aren't we?"

Oliver slowly wiped the corners of his sneering lips, tucked his napkin back into his shirt, and picked up his fork. Beau breathed a little easier when he turned his glare from Ezra back to his dinner plate.

One by one, the rest of them finished dessert. He'd lost his appetite by then, but Beau was grateful for Ezra's attempt to lighten the mood. Without him there, things would have likely gotten out of hand.

With a wary glance at her father, Lydia tried to divert Portia's attention back to their end of the table. "Mother and I want to start an organization here to help widows and orphans. We did something similar in Philadelphia, but this is our home town, you see, so we feel even more obliged."

Aunt Amelie cupped her ear toward Lydia and yelled, "Who died?"

Lydia sighed and closed her eyes briefly before continuing, "Would you be interested in helping us sew garments or knit socks? Anything at all would be of great service."

"Indeed," Polly said, smiling indulgently at her daughter.

"I'll do what I can," Portia answered. "But like I said earlier, my teaching must take precedence."

"Teaching is such an admirable profession, if you have the patience for it. But I'm sure you're much more agreeable than the governesses I had. Hampton's finishing school did much more for me than those strict old disciplinarians."

"A fine education is a blessing and privilege."

"I agree, and new schools are opening everywhere, even for the colored children. The Freedmen's Bureau is seeing to that."

Oliver belted out a sarcastic laugh. "Don't get me started on the Freedmen's Bureau. Giving land and literacy to Negroes who don't even know what to do with it."

Bessie entered from the kitchen. She wore a deep frown but cleared the plates along with Lucy, who showed no emotion whatsoever. God only knew why she and Tipp stayed on with Oliver. He probably had them under contract, with the threat of impossible fines, imprisonment, or worse if they broke it. He'd heard talk of such shady activities before, but had hoped they were rumors.

Beau opened his mouth to suggest the women retreat to the parlor so they wouldn't hear the foul language he was about to throw at his late wife's uncle. But then he saw Portia's face. *Oh, dear Lord.*

Cheeks fiery red, she sat ramrod straight in her chair and glared right at the old fool. "If any child wants to learn to read, it is his or her right and should be encouraged."

Oliver yanked his napkin from his collar, swiped his mouth with it, and tossed it on the table. An amused smile puckered his thin lips and creased around his eyes, but Beau could see the fury behind his mask.

"Mrs. McAllister, did your late husband ever own any Negroes?"

"No."

"I see. If you had, then you might understand the weight of my words. Why, we have a little colored child in our midst." He pointed toward the kitchen, where Sallie Mae peeked around the doorway. She quickly darted out of sight. "Perhaps you will feel the impulse to teach her a thing or two while she is here, and then you will see how futile your efforts will be."

"Perhaps I will take you up on that challenge." She flattened her hands on the table like she might launch herself at Oliver and claw his eyes out. Her chest heaved and nostrils flared. Not taking her eyes off the old bastard, she turned her head slightly and said, "It's getting late, Jonny. You should go to bed."

The poor boy looked scared to death, but damn, Portia sure could put up a fight. Beau cupped Jonny's shoulder and gave it a gentle squeeze. "Go on now, get upstairs."

He nodded, shot out of his chair, and fled the room.

Beau would have loved to do the same, but instead, he rubbed the throbbing pain in his temple and abruptly stood. "I think the ladies should convene in the parlor while we take our conversation to the study."

Lydia nodded emphatically. "Great idea."

Portia was up and gone before Harry could help with her chair, but he took off after her. Beau heard the front door open and slam shut, and it took everything he had to keep from following them. He wanted to reassure her that Oliver Clemons would be here no longer than necessary, and he hoped to God she wouldn't let the bastard drive her away. Harry was probably saying as much. He should have been grateful, but as the man of the house, it was Beau's job to protect her. But he had to stay there and play host, if nothing else, so he could keep an eye on Oliver. He would have to apologize to her when he got the chance.

Lydia, Polly, and Amelie headed to the parlor.

"Women never know when to keep quiet," Oliver said, grasping his lapels like he'd conquered an army.

Beau waited until Pa left the room before he stopped Oliver at the doorway. "I'd like to have a word with you, please."

"I'm listening." The older man pulled a cigar from his pocket and struck a match on the door facing.

Standing half a head taller than his ass of a houseguest, Beau closed the gap until mere inches separated them. He held the stubborn old man's gaze with one just as commanding. "I've always tolerated you because you're Claire's uncle, but this is my house. I will not have my decisions questioned, or my employees disrespected. Is that understood?"

"Perfectly." Oliver puffed on the cigar and grinned around it. "But you know why we came back. Lydia hasn't shut up about you since we left. So *I* expect that our return won't leave her disappointed. Besides, this little farm of yours could use some financing, couldn't it?"

Beau didn't answer. True — he needed money, and Lydia probably had one hell of a dowry. He had to do the right thing for his family and make certain they would have food on the table and a roof over their heads. If marrying Lydia meant he could do that, then he had to consider it. But goddammit, he wasn't about to let Oliver or anyone else force him into marriage. If Lydia really had marrying on her mind, he had to get to know her as the woman she had become before he made any decisions. Oliver he couldn't care less about, but he didn't want to hurt Lydia. She might be spoiled and materialistic, but she didn't seem to have inherited her father's nastiness. Besides, Claire had been crazy about her, so Beau had to play this right.

Calling forfeit to the stand-off for now, he stepped back and gestured toward the study.

"Smart man," Oliver said through a cloud of acrid tobacco smoke. "Let's go have a shot or two. I'm in the mood for some libation."

In the study, Pa perched on the chair by the fire, stuffing his pipe. Beau poured their drinks and passed them around, while Oliver plopped down on the settee and raised his glass.

Oliver toasted the occasion, eyeing Beau expectantly. "Here's to a strong and united country and a bright new future!"

"A bright new future," Ezra muttered.

Beau downed his shot, hoping the whiskey would numb his pounding headache. Lydia's laughter rang out from the next room. He poured another one and in hindsight, realized he should have followed Portia outside instead of letting Harry chase after her. She was probably out there now, all wrapped up in his arms. Beau stared at the window but couldn't see anything in the darkness on the other side. The only thing he knew was that he didn't like the notion of Portia and Harry together. Not at all.

Chapter Fifteen

Portia stood at the far right end of the porch, one arm wrapped around the freshly painted corner post, the other hand gripping the top of the porch railing as though she needed anchoring to keep her from flying into a blind rage. Stars twinkled in the indigo sky, and a gentle breeze ruffled her dress. Her hair had already started to escape, and now rogue strands of it whipped about her ears and neck. Leaning her head against the corner post, she breathed in cool April air scented with daffodils and horses.

She'd come there to get away from the toll grief had taken on her but had never expected to be barraged with different emotions that were equally as strong. How could she handle this job if she was always in a state of such constant turmoil? She had to calm down and focus on her work. Beau, Ezra, and the rest of the family were good people. They were the only ones she should concern herself with, not that hateful old pig of a man.

Harry had followed, much to her dismay, and now he stood beside her, telling her something about how Oliver had been one of the wealthiest slave-owners in Wilson County.

"He's just upset that his old way of life is gone," Harry said. He rested his hand on hers softly, but she didn't recoil from his touch this time. "I'd guess two, three weeks at the most, and they'll be out of here. Beau and Oliver never did see eye to eye, but Claire always tried to get along with him. Her folks died young, so she wanted to cling to what family she had left. I guess you can understand that."

Portia nodded. Harry squeezed her hand gently, staring at her like he thought she might break into a thousand pieces at any moment.

She looked out over the starlit yard. "It must be hard on Beau, trying to be hospitable to his wife's family without her here."

"It is," Harry agreed, moving in a little closer. He picked up her hand and brought it to his lips, applying a warm, gentle kiss to her knuckles. "I'm sorry you had to witness all that."

"Thank you." She wanted to pull away and go to bed so she could fall into the blessed oblivion of sleep. But much as she didn't want to admit it, Harry's presence and touch were comforting. At least he cared enough to apologize. Beau was still in there smoking and drinking, maybe even making wedding plans. Surely he was smitten with the beautiful Lydia Clemons. What man wouldn't be, especially if he thought she wanted him?

Harry let go of her hand and slid an arm around her shoulders, drawing her close. "It's hard being people like you and me, not much more than poor relations and no real power to change anything. The only way to survive is to show 'em we can stand on our own two feet."

Portia lowered her head, turning it away from him, and squeezed her eyes shut. She shouldn't be out there alone with Harry. She shouldn't want to lean into his strong arm and the warmth of his chest. She shouldn't be trembling with the need for his gentle voice in her ear, someone to whisper away the shroud of loneliness she had worn for so long — especially when she didn't really feel anything for him where it counted. And especially when she pictured herself in Beau's arms instead.

Growing closer to Harry felt a little like standing on the edge of a snake pit. If she took another step, she could be bitten. It had never been that way with Jake. Maybe her emotions were out of control, making her more scared than a woman in her position ought to be, but she couldn't take any risks in becoming attached to anyone… not yet.

Shrugging from his embrace, she took two steps away — just out of reach — and said, "Thank you for your kindness. I'm tired, so I'll retire for the evening. Goodnight, Harry."

"Goodnight, Portia."

The disappointment in his voice made her wince. She swallowed past the lump in her throat, went back inside, up to her room, and shut herself away from the world.

April 27, 1866
Dear Ellen,

Oliver Clemons is an insufferable fool. He had the nerve to say black children didn't deserve to be educated. He even challenged me to teach Sallie Mae. If the occasion arises, then mark my words, I will do just that. Lydia's pointless chatter is almost as intolerable as her father's hatefulness, but at least it's harmless. I think Mr. Stanford confronted Mr. Clemons after that first horrid display, because he's been quiet over supper ever since. I should probably thank him, but I'm not sure how or if it's proper to do so.

To show my gratitude, I am putting extra effort into my work. Jonny and I are having lunch and drawing lessons by the creek when the weather allows. He's not as interested in art as I hoped, but he confides his troubles and dreams with me, and I'd not trade that for anything.

Lucy and Bessie are taking on most of the housework themselves, but I'm pitching in when I can. The gladiolas and daffodils are in full bloom, so I arranged a centerpiece for the dining room table. It seemed to brighten everyone's spirits, even Mr. Stanford's. He remarked that the table hadn't looked that nice in a long time. He smiles more often now, though I'm sure Miss Clemons is responsible for the change in his demeanor. No matter the cause, he seems happier, so I'm happy for him. I hope his good spirits will lead him to pay more attention to Jonny.

In the evenings, I am joining the other ladies in the parlor to knit blankets and socks for Miss Clemons' charity. I think she is really sincere about it, though she is planning monthly brunches and socials for their 'meetings'. So long as the items go to a good cause, I don't concern myself with what she does. My priority is Jonny's education. He is such a bright and sweet boy...

Saturday arrived with a bright blue sky and not a cloud to be seen. Jonny escorted Portia on another riding lesson, which led them along a trail that looped around the property. They ended up at the top of a hill, surrounded by tall cedars. Portia could see the entire town from there. She started to comment on the gorgeous view when high-pitched giggles drew her attention back to the base of the hill. Through the papery tree trunks, she caught glimpses of Lydia's yellow silk dress atop her horse. Beau's hat bobbed in and out of view beside her.

"Let's go," Jonny said, mouth puckered and eyes narrowed at the two riders below. He kicked Jack with more force than usual, and the pony took off at a fast trot down another path that wouldn't intersect his father and Lydia.

Portia kicked her snail of a horse into something like a trot and followed after him. She wished she could reassure him that everything would work out as it should, but how could she? Uncertainty still hovered all around her, making the future clear as mud.

Before she could coax the horse more than a few yards, something wet dripped on her cheek. She wiped it away. Thick, gooey liquid the color of molasses coated her fingertips. Flies buzzed around her face. She shooed them with a sweep of her hand, but a smell wafted in — the odor of decay, blood, and burned flesh.

The horse lowered its head to graze on whatever grew beneath the tree. Every bit of moisture evaporated from her mouth, and though her mind screamed, *"Don't look, don't look!"* her eyes drifted upward toward the treetops, where a pair of feet spun in a lazy circle over her head.

They were bare and attached to a dead man. Another drop of blood hit her forehead.

She screamed. Her horse reared, and she fell backward, trying to grab hold of the reins, the saddle, the horse's tail, but she caught only air. The ground met her back, knocking the wind from her lungs. Her horse galloped down the trail, passing Jonathan. He turned his pony around to come see about her.

Worry shrouded his face; he slid off his pony and rushed to her side. Pushing herself up on her elbows, she waved at him to get back. She tried to tell him to stop, but she wheezed instead.

Jonny hit his knees. "Are you hurt?"

Portia shook her head. Her eyes flicked toward the body above them. Before she could stop him, he looked up. A second later, he twisted away from her, fell on all fours and wretched. Beau and Lydia galloped up the trail, bringing their horses to a stop ten feet away. Without noticing the corpse, Beau flew off the saddle and ran straight to Jonny.

Falling to his knees mid-run, he slid the last few inches to his son and put his hand on his back. "What happened?"

Beau pulled out his handkerchief as Jonny coughed up the last of his stomach's contents. He wiped Jonny's mouth and helped him up to his knees. In a rustle of silk and petticoats, Lydia caught up with him.

"Jonny — what happened?" she asked in a breathy, shocked whisper. "Mrs. McAllister?"

Portia pushed herself to a sitting position and pointed upward. Beau and Lydia both turned their eyes to the hideous sight in the tree. Lydia let loose a banshee's scream, both her arms making an X in front of her as though the dead man might fall to the ground and come after her.

Beau took another look at the body. Then he helped Jonny to his feet. Arm around his shoulders, he led him away toward their horses and to his blonde houseguest. "Lydia? Lydia, look at me. It's just a dummy. Probably soaked in pig's blood."

The breeze picked up. Portia dared a look at the corpse as it swung lazily back and forth on its creaking rope. Suppressing a gag, she finally noticed the crudely stitched seams down the legs, sewn-together toes, and farther up, the stuffed head adorned with only a stitched mouth curved upward in a taunting smile. She tore her eyes from it and focused on Beau.

He ran his hands up and down Lydia's arms, speaking in the calm, soothing tones he'd used with the spooked filly. "Take Jonny to the house. Send Isaac out here. Understand?"

Her pretty head gave a quick nod; she put her arm around Jonny's shoulders and led him to Jack. "Follow me, Jonny, all right? Don't look back."

Once the two of them set off down the trail, Beau hurried to Portia. He held out his hand and helped her to her feet. "Are you hurt?"

"No, just had the wind knocked out of me. I'll be fine."

He held her hand for a few seconds. When he released it, her eyes released the tears she'd been holding back. She pulled out her handkerchief and wiped her cheeks, refusing to look at the ugliness she had discovered.

"Why, Beau? Why would anyone…?"

"I don't know, but I intend to find out."

Crickets chirped and tree frogs answered the nocturnal roll call as midnight closed in. Sitting on the front porch steps, Beau waited for Harry. Like most Saturday nights, his closest friend was out late doing God knows what. The lantern flickered softly beside him, its wick turned as low as possible so as not to attract attention. He rested the side of his head against the porch railing but jerked awake at the sound of horse hooves on the drive. A few minutes later, Harry staggered toward him. Beau turned the dial on the lantern to raise the wick; light flared out to illuminate Harry's unsteady feet.

Wearing a grin fit for a possum, he slid to a sudden stop about three feet from the porch. "You waitin' up for me now? Am I in trouble, Pa?" The words wobbled from his drunken mouth.

Without a sound, Beau got up and carried the lantern to the cart he left in the drive. He reached for the man-shaped lump lying in the back, picked up the corner of a thick horse blanket, and threw it back. The bloody effigy they'd found earlier that day smiled back with its nightmarish stitched mouth.

Harry stumbled back, waving his nose and coughing. "Shit, did you kill somebody?"

"No, but I'm about to if you don't tell me why this dummy was hanging in a tree on the riding trail."

"I don't know nothin' about that nasty thing. Why you askin' me?"

"Because when Isaac and I cut it down, we found this on it." He held out a blood-dampened, wrinkled note.

Harry came close, snatched it out of Beau's hand, and retreated as far as he could. Holding the paper at arm's length into the lantern light, he squinted at the messy handwriting, eyes growing wider as the seconds passed. He dropped the note and smacked his forehead, fingers forking through his unruly hair.

"I... look, I'll talk to 'em. Tell 'em I need more time. I've been savin' up some money—"

"Who is it, Harry? Who's got you cornered this time?"

His Adam's apple bobbed up and down, and he shook his head. "I can't say."

"Pack your things and get the hell out of here."

"What? Where am I gonna go? Nobody around here gives a whit about us 'Yankees', and if I leave town without paying... they'll do worse than that, and they won't stop with me. They'll get their money however they have to."

"I swear to God, if Jonny or anyone else gets hurt, you'll wish it was you in that tree."

"I know, and I swear I'll pay 'em. If I had a little cash to start with, that would settle them down some."

Beau removed his hat and waved it at Harry to keep from knocking his teeth out. "Do you have any idea how much trouble you've gathered since we came back? No wonder the folks in this town have no respect for me or you. They see you stumbling around drunk and on morphine when you ought to be working 'til your fingers bleed like the rest of us."

"We could sell that fancy horse Lydia brought you."

"No one in Tennessee would give us what she's worth. We've talked to Deputy Bandy. He's lent me a couple men to patrol the place. Only trouble is, I've got to compensate them for their trouble. The little bit I had saved for Portia's pay now has to go to them. So no, Harry — you're not selling my stock, and you won't pilfer through the house this time either. This one's on you."

Eyes wild and scared as a deer in a hunter's sights, Harry nodded. "I'll put my calves up for sale on Market Day. They'll bring enough."

"And until then?"

"I'll sell the flintlock."

Muddled as Harry's mind was, Beau never thought he'd let go of the only thing he had left of his father. The house he'd grown up in had sold for lumber long ago, the land long since parceled out. He'd kept very few mementos of his dead parents, and most of those he'd already sold for one reason or another. But that pistol he'd kept shut away in a special case he'd handcrafted himself. It was the sole resident of a shelf above the head of Harry's bed. He never spoke of his folks, but Harry's memories were tied up in that Revolutionary War artifact passed down through generations of Franklin men.

Beau looked at the dummy in the cart and spat on the ground. "You should keep it."

"What do you expect me to do, then? I ain't got anything else." Harry sounded sober and helpless, his voice sharp with desperation. "I've never had anything much to my name, so what's one gun?"

Underneath the self-pity, Harry's shame came through loud and clear. Most folks would have thrown him out a long time ago. But blood or not, they were brothers. Beau didn't abandon him on the battlefield, and his conscience wouldn't let him abandon him now. He'd provide a roof over his head, but he had to make Harry face his own problems and deal with them.

"Fine, do it tomorrow. Now, get your ass in the house and sleep it off."

Harry scowled— probably feeling more sorry he'd been caught than for what he did — and walked to the house. Quietly, he climbed up the steps and went inside. The note skittered across the drive in the midnight breeze. Beau caught it with his boot, dug his heel into it and tried to smash it from existence. But the proverbial threats were already planted in his mind.

To Mr. Franklin: The rich rules over the poor, and the borrower is the slave of the lender. Slaves who won't repay their debts are no good to their masters. You have one week.

He got in the driver's seat of the cart and hauled the thing into the fallow field he couldn't afford to sow and set it on fire. Flames danced, eating through the fabric and crackling the hay stuffing. Smoke curled ever upward, polluting a perfect night sky sprinkled with silver stars.

Hands in his pockets, he stared blindly at the inferno. His conscience slumped under the Atlas-sized burden of protecting his family. He wouldn't sleep again tonight.

Church service the next morning was more circus than sermon with the Clemons family back in town. In a way, Portia was glad to have the gossipmongers off her back and swarming around Lydia instead. Yet a twinge of envy gnawed at her, especially with Beau standing at Lydia's side, graciously accepting the town's approval. Everyone expected the two would soon be engaged.

It shouldn't have bothered her in the least, but… the crowd and chatter were too suffocating. The weather wasn't great — with chilly air and drizzling rain — but anywhere was better than inside. And though Beau had assured them over breakfast that everyone would be safe, the prior day's incident still plagued her senses. Portia made her exit around the crowd and waited outside near the carriage. Someone touched her shoulder from behind, and she jumped.

"Sorry to startle you," Harry said. "You all right?"

"I'm fine. Just a little crowded in there."

"With the richest family in Lebanon back in town, it's no wonder. You're really pretty today."

"Thank you." Why did Harry's compliments always make her want to wrinkle her nose? He'd been nothing but kind to her, handsome to boot. Any other woman in her position would have probably welcomed the attention.

"Say, why don't we take a walk around the square while we're waiting for the excitement to die down?" He offered his arm and winked.

Portia glanced toward the church, still crowded with spectators dying to get a glimpse of Lebanon's most-talked-about couple. "Sure, why not?"

Harry led her across the square, down a sidewalk by the general store, and around the corner down a narrow alley. They ended up at a little bridge over Barton Creek where it ran through town. Portia looked over the rail, catching flashes of minnows as they schooled together in the shallows. She sucked in a breath when Harry touched her cheek.

He gently lifted her chin and turned her head toward him. "Beau's lucky. He managed to snag two wealthy, beautiful women."

She arched one eyebrow. If he had meant to brighten her spirits, he sure picked a strange choice of words. Averting her eyes from Harry's heartfelt expression, she turned her head, but he guided her back until she faced him again.

"But I'm luckier," he said, cupping her cheek and moving in until they were just a breath apart. "I found *you.*"

Just as his lips brushed hers, she heard someone running toward them.

Portia pulled back, putting a hand on Harry's chest to ensure some distance. "We have to go."

Before he could say anything, Jonny came into sight. He threw up a hand in greeting, and relief flooded through her veins, competing with her confusing guilt for hurting Harry again. She wished she knew how she felt about him so she wouldn't be the cause of such pain in his eyes. But she didn't.

They reached the front of the church as the crowd dispersed. Beau helped Lydia into the Clemons's fine coach. He looked up just as Portia and Harry were about to pass by him on the way to the less-fine buggy. He caught her in his steady gaze as he watched their progression. Goose pimples pricked across her skin, followed by a strange ache in her chest.

Tamp it down; don't raise eyebrows. She forced herself to look straight ahead and let Harry help her into the buggy, where Jonny and Ezra had already claimed the front seat. She took one last look over her shoulder to see Beau climbing in beside Lydia. Gritting her teeth, she let Harry hold her hand while Ezra flicked the reins. She would *not* allow her heart to go where it had no business going.

Back at the house, after lunch, everyone gathered in the parlor. Harry sat beside Portia on the settee, chatting with Ezra and Oliver, who acted like an almost-civil gentleman, except for the occasional obnoxious quip. Harry kept his arm draped across the top of the seat; his fingers brushed her shoulder now and then, but Portia resisted the urge to flee. She couldn't bear his hurt puppy-dog expression again today. His attempts at courtship were not mean-spirited, but all this flirtation and mixed emotion had taken her to a new and awkward territory. She would have to figure out what to say to him before she confronted him one way or another.

Amelie nodded off by the fire, emanating gentle snores from her drooped head. Polly sat in the window seat and worked on an embroidery sampler, glancing at Lydia and Beau. The couple sat in the corner, laughing about some story from the past.

Harry's wandering hand found a piece of her fallen hair and wound it around his finger. Ezra's bushy eyebrows lifted, and he cleared his throat.

Portia sat up enough to untangle herself and addressed Polly. "Mrs. Clemons, do you miss Philadelphia?"

Polly looked up with her hound dog eyes and sighed. "I always had something to occupy my time there. Socials and opera, that sort of thing. And our son Charles and his wife had our first grandchild and are expecting another."

"That's wonderful."

"Charles runs the business there now. I suppose it will take some time to reacquaint ourselves to the slower pace here." She turned her sad eyes to her daughter. "Lydia has always wished to return, and we want to see her happy and settled."

To be uprooted for the sake of a daughter's wishes seemed like an unnecessary sacrifice. Yet, from her short time as a mother, Portia understood how one's world could revolve around a child. She regarded the couple in question.

Lydia reached across the little table and took Beau's hands in hers. "The sun is coming out — it looks like a fine afternoon for a ride. What do you say?"

Beau glanced out the window. "I suppose, but there'll be mud."

Lydia waved her hand at him. "That's what my plain riding habits are for. Lucy!" At the servant's appearance, she added, "Can you fetch my gray riding habit? And the black boots? Not the high heeled ones, though. I'd rather not get stuck in the mud, though I'm sure Beau would rescue me."

With that last bit, she winked at him. Portia squirmed in her seat as Lydia turned her way.

"Do you ride, Mrs. McAllister?"

"Not much, but I've been getting some fine lessons."
She smiled down at Jonny, where he played with his
marbles on the rug. He didn't look at her, but the corners
of his mouth turned up for a brief moment.

"Pity. I have two plain riding habits, and you are
welcome to borrow one." She touched the edge of her
dress right above her ample cleavage and added, "Though
it would have to be taken in, especially in the chest. Now,
if you'll excuse me, I'll go change."

"I'll be waiting." Beau said.

The nerve of that... Anger burned her cheeks, while she
slumped to hide her lacking assets.

He turned to Portia. "You all right?"

She forced herself to regain her straight posture. "I'm
fine, why do you ask?"

Something flashed in his eyes that made her feel less
ashamed, maybe even pretty, before he hid it with a
neutral smile. "How are the lessons going?"

"Fine, except for the gelding I've been riding."

Beau sat forward, brow creased in concern. "What's
wrong with him?"

"Forgive my bluntness, but riding that horse is like
pouring cold molasses from a jar."

"Really?" Beau chuckled but looked relieved. "He's the
gentlest one we have. But I think I know why he's being
so hesitant."

Warmth climbed her neck and gathered in her cheeks,
but she sat on the edge of her seat, ready for the challenge.
"Why is that?"

"My son can hardly keep his eyes open at supper. The
poor horse is afraid you'll work him to death."

Amelie snorted herself awake. "Who's Beth?"

Beau's hearty laughter filled the room, while Ezra cackled and slapped his knee. Portia found herself laughing along, too. Everyone else looked at them like they were crazy, except for Oliver, who sneered at them through his cigar smoke.

Clearing her throat, she said primly, "I promise to be gentle."

Beau's warm smile thawed the awkward atmosphere, and she wanted to bask in it a little longer. But this sort of familiarity could raise a few eyebrows if they weren't careful. As if he realized this too, Beau resumed his straight-faced expression when Lydia came back downstairs and fetched him moments later.

The mood turned awkward again as soon as they left, and she didn't want to be subjected to Oliver's scrutiny, so Portia excused herself and headed upstairs to her room. Through the window, she watched Beau and Lydia, walking arm in arm toward the stable. Spoiled and materialistic she might be, but what man *wouldn't* want her? Not only was she beautiful, but the money she would bring to their union must be especially tempting to a man struggling to make ends meet.

Portia pulled herself from the view and opened the top dresser drawer. She picked up Jake's tintype. When they were married, money wasn't a concern, though they'd never had much of it. They grew and made most of what they needed. All that changed when the first shot at Sumter was fired. With everything in short supply, taken at will to feed both invading armies, money became the only sure ticket to survival.

With nothing to her name, Portia realized how undesirable she must be, especially for a man like Beau. Her mouth twitched as she stared down at Jake's pretend stern face. She never had cause to compare herself to anyone before. Jake had been her one and only, and she had been his. They were going to grow old together and watch their grandchildren scamper across the yard from the comfort of their front porch rocking chairs. That dream now lay scattered in her memories like the dust of a summer draught.

She hugged Jake's picture to her chest and whispered, "I miss you."

Chapter Sixteen

Monday morning flew by as Portia and Jonny studied the metaphors behind Shakespeare's plays. She hadn't planned on going into such in-depth topics, but Jonny kept proving to be the brightest student she had ever encountered. The challenge of challenging *him* made her eager to wake up and start each school day. It felt beyond good to look forward to a new day for a change.

Of course, now that he had let down his guard, he proved to be a typical boy who'd rather go fishing or riding than sit in a classroom. After some moaning and groaning on Jonny's part, he perked up when they turned to Hamlet.

"What metaphors do you hear in this one?" Portia asked before quoting what might be Hamlet's most famous lines.

"To be, or not to be; that is the question:
Whether 'tis nobler in the mind to suffer
The slings and arrows of outrageous fortune,
Or to take arms against a sea of troubles,
And, by opposing, end them."

Chin in hand, he pondered this awhile and then answered tentatively, his voice halting as he composed the right words. "I think the metaphor is war or fighting... Hamlet's upset with all the troubles in his life — that's the sea... The slings and arrows are him being hurt by all of it... and he can't decide whether he ought to just live with it or fight back."

"Very good. Can you come up with your own metaphors in a short paragraph?"

He shrugged, turning wistful eyes to the sunny day outside the window. With a long sigh, he picked up his pencil and chewed on the tip of his tongue as he wrote. After a few stops, starts, and scratching out discarded words in place of better ones, he slid the paper toward Portia.

She read it silently. *Pa saw how the chains of slavery held people like animals. Their sadness speared his heart and hurt him real bad. He hoped the chains would be loosened without fighting, but he saw it wasn't meant to be. So he picked up his gun and fought against injustice.*

Portia's lip quivered as she laid the paper back on the desk. For years, she'd been amazed by the insight of children, but this was almost more than her heart could bear. Despite Beau's distant behavior, Jonny's admiration and respect for his father was undeniable. His understanding of why his father went to war, even if Beau's real intentions weren't so pure, made her question everything. Why did Jake fight for the Confederates when he didn't like how slaves were treated? Why would Beau consider marriage to a former slave owner? What point in her own life did she stop thinking like a child — seeing the good in people, seeing a clear division between right and wrong? She had to dab her eyes to keep the tears from falling.

Jonny touched her hand. "Po? Did I write something bad?"

"No, sweet boy. You wrote something beautiful."

A rustle near the door drew her attention. Sallie Mae disappeared behind the doorframe as soon as Portia spotted her.

"Sallie Mae," Portia said as gently as possible, "would you like to come in?"

Her little head appeared in the doorway again, eyes wide and uncertain. She nodded.

"Come in. Have a seat."

She did as requested and perched on the window seat. Her bare brown feet dangled a few inches from the ground. She hugged a cloth doll under her chin and smiled, revealing a gap where two front teeth had been.

"How old are you, Sallie Mae?"

"Eight."

"We were just doing a little reading and writing. Would you like to join in?"

Sallie Mae sighed down at her doll. "I can't read much, ma'am."

"I see. You're welcome to sit and listen in, if you'd like."

"I'd like that, if I ain't in the way too much." She lifted her head, and Portia immediately recognized the look in her bright, eager eyes. Here sat a child who craved knowledge, one who would, if given the chance, take what she learned and do great things with it.

Portia laughed and gestured around the study. "You won't be in the way in this big old room." Sallie Mae giggled at that, and Portia added, "Would you *like* to learn to read?"

The little girl nodded emphatically, and of course, the challenge posed so cruelly by Oliver Clemons came to the forefront of Portia's mind. More importantly, though, she would be teaching a child to read, opening up a whole new world for her.

Lucy stepped in the room, keeping her voice quiet but harsh. "Sallie Mae! What you doin' in here, child? Get back in the kitchen!"

"Yes, mama." She scooted off the window seat and ran out behind her mother.

"I'm terrible sorry, ma'am," Lucy said, sounding exasperated. "She won't bother you no more."

Portia stood and came closer to Lucy, noticing a purplish welt under the young woman's eye. *Best not to mention it now.* She pretended not to notice and kept her voice light and joyful. "She's no bother at all. Actually, I was wondering how you would feel about letting her sit in on Jonathan's lessons for an hour or so each day?"

Lucy shook her head. "No, ma'am, I couldn't have you teachin' her like that, not interruptin' Mr. Stanford's son and all."

"She wants to learn to read, and I'd love the opportunity to teach her. But I won't proceed unless I have yours and Mr. Stanford's permission."

Crossing her arms, Lucy bit her lip and sighed. "She knows her letters, ma'am, and can read a little. But Tipp and me, we can't read much more than she can. I'd love her to do better than that, but I don't want nobody gettin' upset about it."

"I understand. But while you're here, it could be the perfect opportunity to keep her occupied. And…" she added, winking at Jonathan behind her, "Jonny's getting plumb bored listening to me prattle on all day. He could use another schoolmate to keep him company."

Playing an actor worthy of a Shakespeare comedy, Jonny nodded, let out a dramatic sigh, and slapped his hand to his forehead.

Lucy laughed a little. "All right, ma'am. You can teach my girl if you want and if it's all right with Mr. Stanford. But if she bothers you at all, just send her back to me."

"I will do my best," Portia said.

Sallie Mae poked her head around the doorframe, her pretty dark eyes looking expectantly up at her mother. Lucy hugged her daughter to her side. "Thank you, Mrs. McAllister, for your kindness."

Reclaiming her seat by Jonathan's desk, she could hardly wait for lunchtime. Not for the food, but to find Beau and ask him to agree to her plan. She hoped he'd see the good in it and not be swayed by Oliver's remarks. Lucy and Sallie Mae weren't slaves anymore, so they should be able to learn if they so desired.

Still, the chance of her idea being rejected shadowed her optimism. But as the noon-time hour closed in, she thought of the huge hurdle she had already crossed just by coming there in the first place. Asking for permission to teach a child to read should be as easy as finding the roast pig at a barbeque.

"That was exhilarating!" Lydia craned her head straight up to look at Beau where he stood precariously on the rafters. She was breathless with rosy cheeks and locks of blond hair escaping from beneath her riding hat. Her mount — the gorgeous new Standardbred she'd gifted him — pranced along the earthen stable floor, foaming at the bit and glistening with sweat. She had just taken a solo ride through the fields, and from the looks of it, a wild ride at that.

Beau hammered one last nail into the intersection of crisscrossed boards. He hung the hammer on his belt and carefully lowered himself to the ladder. He really didn't like heights — it made him queasy and slightly dizzy, especially if he looked down. But the sagging door frame needed shoring up, and that meant he had to play monkey for a while. It also meant he had to make the most of this lumber, since he'd run up his tab at the mill. He quickly learned that asking for any sort of financial assistance meant one of two responses. There was the polite, *"I'm sorry, Beau, I can't loan you any more…"* but more often it involved the word *Yankee* and curses he hadn't known existed until he joined the army.

He had to sell something. Shoot, he'd sell that highbred horse Lydia sat upon if he knew anyone with enough money to buy it. He couldn't stomach that big a loss on such a fine animal. Not yet — not until he had no other choice. But harvest time was a long few months away.

Finally reaching solid ground, he walked to the pretty filly and rubbed her neck. "You really should have let her cool down more."

"Oh, she'll be fine," Lydia said. "She's young enough to handle it."

"Overheating *any* horse is asking for trouble." Her flippant attitude bit into Beau's good sense. No matter how much a horse was worth, he'd always cared for them well. Lydia might have been used to throwing money away, but she'd have to do better if she wanted to share his company.

"Sorry." She held out her hand, and he helped her dismount from the sidesaddle. Lydia dabbed her forehead with her handkerchief.

Beau removed the horse's saddle. "She'll need some water."

"Is that lunch I smell? I better go change."

Before she could turn and flee, Beau caught her arm in his firm grip. Lydia snapped her head around, eyes wide. He let her go and pointed to one of the buckets of water he had drawn that morning.

"Not before you water your horse," he said.

"Me? I… yes, of course." She held her head high and marched over to the bucket. She bent and picked it up with one hand, but let it clunk back down with a slosh. Lips pursed, she picked it up with both hands and held it in front of her, arms extended to their limit. Her lovely face strained with the effort as she waddled to the horse. Water splashed onto her blue velvet riding habit with each step.

214

Finally, she reached the horse and set the bucket in front of her. The filly drank greedily, while Lydia looked down with disgust at her dress and dabbed at the invisible water spots with her handkerchief.

"Better," Beau said.

Lydia looked up with a sigh. "I suppose you think I'm spoiled and lazy."

"You've never needed to work like that. I can't call someone lazy unless they refuse to work when they need to."

Her relieved smile brightened up the dim barn. "I'm willing to get my hands dirty, if you're willing to teach me."

She stepped up close to him, caught his hand, and entwined her fingers with his. Head held back so she could look him in the eyes, her voice took on a sultry tone. "Will you teach me?"

Beau found it hard to swallow past the sudden dryness in his throat. "That depends."

"I love it here, Beau. The air is so fresh." She closed her eyes and inhaled deeply.

"If you like the smell of fresh manure, it is."

Her eyes popped open while she giggled and pressed herself against his chest, still holding his hand hostage between them. "Oh, you know what I mean. Philadelphia was nice, but I was so homesick there."

"At least you avoided all the ugliness here. You probably had all kinds of things to do and a number of suitors vying for your hand."

She blasted him with that smiling, head tilted to one side gesture, reminiscent of her late cousin. With Claire, it usually meant she was about to ask him for something, and with that look, she usually got what she wanted.

"You're right," Lydia said. "There were many young men who called, but there were none that I wanted."

Beau shifted his feet, knowing what was coming, but not sure how he felt about it. "Out of all those men in the city, there must have been one fella or two you took a shine to."

Her eyelashes fluttered as she gave a little shrug. "Don't get me wrong. I could have chosen one and had a good life there, but none of them fit my expectations."

"What expectations?"

She pressed her bosom against his chest. He couldn't help but look at the dark canyon of her cleavage and the voluptuous hills beckoning to be explored. "Beau, I loved my cousin dearly, but I envied her every day I saw her with you. All I could think was that she had found her prince charming. And I knew that I wanted what she had."

Breathing became difficult; his throat was so tight. He turned his head and coughed before looking back at her. "I'm afraid you'll be disappointed. I'm not half the saint you thought I was. You were a child with a child's dreams."

"I'm not a child now," she said, her voice more somber, more mature than he expected. "I understand why my cousin loved you. You're strong, kind, honest. I know how much she wanted to give you more children."

A heavy pain squeezed his chest. He closed his eyes and swallowed hard. He and Claire dreamed of a house full of little ones, but they'd only been blessed with Jonny, whom they loved dearly of course, but...

Lydia unwound her fingers from his, reached up, and cupped his face with both hands. "I've never met anyone that compared to you. If you would have me, we could bring this farm back to life, and I could give you the big family you always wanted."

Beau didn't know how to respond. He never imagined she would be so forward with him. On one hand, she just declared her love for him and all but proposed marriage, and on the other, he didn't know if he could ever open his heart again to allow such a thing.

Tiptoeing, she pressed her lips to his — their soft warmth melted the last of his resolve. Excitement buzzed through every nerve ending as he slid his hands around Lydia's waist, feeling the corset that hugged her sensuous figure. She sighed and parted her lips further, deepening the kiss. Her fingers swirled through the hair at the nape of his neck.

She smelled like gardenias. Like Claire. Memories flooded his mind of their last night together. These sensations brought it all back. *Her* lips and *her* sighs and the glorious feel of slipping inside her, moving together, completely lost in each other's arms.

Footsteps just outside pulled him back into reality and away from Lydia, whose lips were still parted and red from their kiss.

Portia stood there, frozen, eyes shifting between him and Lydia. "I'm sorry, I didn't mean to… um… intrude."

As though her muscles suddenly thawed from the shock of catching her employer in a passionate embrace, she gathered her skirts in her fists, spun around, and high-tailed it toward the house.

"Po, wait!" Beau came to his senses, extracted himself from Lydia's arms, and ran after her.

He finally caught up to her, but she kept walking, head down and determined to escape. "No, it was a bad time — I didn't mean to intrude. I can speak with you later."

Beau grabbed her arm, and she stopped but wouldn't look at him. He let go, not knowing exactly why he was chasing her or stopping her for that matter, except he felt the need to reassure her that she didn't have to be afraid of coming to him for anything.

He spit out the only thing he could think of. "It's not intruding if you don't know what you'll find when you get there, right?"

Portia finally met his gaze, a flicker of expectation in her eyes. Beau felt like he ought to explain or apologize or... something, but Lydia caught up with them.

She linked one arm in his, effectively staking her claim, and glared at Portia.

"Perhaps we could speak privately about the matter," Portia whispered.

Lydia let out an exasperated breath. "Well, if it's so important as to leave your student to come find Beau, you might as well say what you wanted to say and get it over with."

Beau raised an eyebrow toward the blonde on his arm, who stood there tapping her riding boot impatiently. What happened to that sweet, vulnerable woman he had just kissed? An uneasy feeling settled in the pit of his stomach.

With a sidelong, and irritated, glance at Lydia, Portia's voice was cool, but steady. "I have spoken with Lucy, and she has given her blessing for me to teach Sallie Mae for an hour each day. I wanted to ask your permission as well."

"What of Jonathan's lessons?" Lydia asked.

"She will sit in on them, nothing more. And as he's working on his assignments, I would like to teach her to read, for she would very much like to do so."

So, she's taking Oliver up on his challenge. That's my girl. Beau's mouth twitched, tempted to offer her a proud smile. But he wondered if she'd thought about the consequences.

"I know you want to help her, but I don't think it's a good idea," he said. Disappointment clouded her eyes and wounded his sensibilities. But he had to make sure she remained safe while she lived under his roof. "We should probably let her family handle that, Po. Teaching a black child could be risky, if word got out."

To Beau's surprise, Lydia said, "You know what, Beau — I think you should let her teach Sallie Mae."

He and Portia both uttered a simultaneous, "What?"

Smiling a little brighter than the situation called for, Lydia added, "Really, it's a charitable idea, considering she's not being paid for the extra work. And if... Po... is willing to take it upon herself, then why not? Poor Jonathan is still mute, but perhaps she'll have better luck with my maid's child."

Beau winced. Lydia's challenge, though veiled, was a challenge nonetheless, and she had slighted Portia's abilities to teach his son. How could he deny her the chance to take it on now? He could tell by the stubborn set of her chin, red cheeks, and flashing eyes that she would teach the girl to spite the devil, if nothing else.

"Fine," he conceded, since these two strong-willed women had effectively usurped his power in this situation. Still, he couldn't ignore the edgy wariness tickling his senses. "Just keep it quiet. No one in town needs to know right now. And no more than an hour a day. All right?"

Portia's face relaxed into a tight smile. "Understood. And thank you."

She headed up the hill and entered the house, as Beau and Lydia took their time along the same path. Lydia lessened her death grip on his arm, allowing blood to flow again to his tingling fingers.

"Well now, isn't she something," she said.

It wasn't a question, but he answered anyway. "Yes, she is."

He felt Lydia flinch but pretended not to notice. Her jealousy was unwarranted, and he knew better than to keep poking a mad horse. Still, seeing her get all riled up over that tiny spitfire of a teacher made him smile. Yep, Portia McAllister sure was something all right.

Chapter Seventeen

Portia stole a bit of time for herself between the end of lessons and the start of supper. Bessie had soup on the stove already, and Lucy had the laundry on the line, so she wasn't needed and wouldn't likely be missed. With a notebook and charcoal pencil in hand, she headed to the creek. She needed solitude, just a little while to sort out her thoughts and to forget what she'd witnessed at the barn. That hungry look in Beau's eyes, the way he held Lydia with such burning desire… *Stop it! Just walk.*

The late afternoon sun danced on the creek, making it look like liquid gold. Portia settled beneath the cedar tree where she and Jonny had skipped rocks and where she and Beau had taken refuge from the rain a few days before. Propping the sketch pad on her knees, she looked for a subject to draw. About ten yards away on the other side of the creek sat an old icehouse. A little wooden bridge spanned the creek in front of it.

She began to sketch the little structure with its arched stone set back into the creek bank. Ivy grew from above and drooped lazily in front of the door. Dark green moss carpeted the walls. Her pencil recreated the pointed outlines of the ivy leaves, the tall cedars on the bank, a squirrel on a stump nibbling his lunch. With the gentle bubbling of the creek and the melodic birdsong above, and with nothing but her and her notebook, she felt truly at peace.

Footsteps approached, and Portia turned to see Ezra strolling down the hill.

"'Ey there, sorry if I'm interruptin' you. I didn't think anybody was here."

"It's all right. It's your land, after all."

"Mind if I sit with you a spell?"

Though she had hoped to have some quiet time to herself, she didn't mind Ezra being there all that much. She gestured for him to have a seat. Holding his pipe with one hand, the old man lowered himself cautiously to the ground. He rested his back on the tree with his legs sprawled out in front of him.

"Nice here by the creek," he mumbled through his mustache.

"Yes, it is," Portia agreed.

"I come down here often just to sit and listen. It's calm and peaceful-like." He took two puffs from his pipe. Cherry scented smoke mingled with the damp, mossy air. "You know, it's been nice having a young lady here again."

"Miss Clemons is quite comely."

Ezra chuckled and smoke billowed toward the sky. "I meant you."

"Oh… well, thank you." She smiled, but her cheeks didn't catch fire like they usually did when someone said such a personal thing.

"Seems you and Jonny are gettin' on good."

"He's such a bright and sweet boy. I'm fortunate to be his teacher."

"He's started talkin' to you, hasn't he?"

Uncertain whether he'd be upset with her for keeping the news to herself, she nodded slowly, watching for his reaction.

"I thought so. He almost spoke to *me* this mornin', made a little peep then snapped his mouth shut. I told him to start talkin' to me when he was ready, that I ain't gonna rush him. But I don't blame you for not telling Beauregard."

"You don't?"

He shook his head. "Naw. It's up to him and Jonny to work things out. They're both as stubborn as can be, but I know it'll happen." A quiet pause hung between them, filled only with the gentle bubbling of the creek water before he spoke again. "I hear you're gonna teach Sallie Mae to read."

"I am."

"I'm proud of ya. Takes guts to do what you did, to stand up for others who ain't treated right."

She set her notebook and pencil down on a dry patch of cedar needles. "I don't know about that. It just felt like the right thing to do. Every child deserves an education."

He took another puff and grinned, looking at her through the corner of his eye. "Beauregard is impressed. He didn't think you'd be quite so forthright."

She scrunched her face. "I'm... sorry?"

Ezra slapped his knee and laughed. "You ain't got nothin' to be sorry for. Beau needs a few more straight-talkers around here." He pointed down at her notebook. "That's a real good drawin'."

"Thank you."

"I was quite the finger painter when I was a boy."

"And quite the fence painter now, I hear."

"An artist's gotta move up in the world, I reckon."

He winked, and Portia laughed, feeling relaxed enough to resume her sketch. A few tranquil minutes passed with Ezra puffing his pipe and the creek bubbling over mossy stones. Above them, a mockingbird sang a stolen chickadee melody from his invisible perch in the tree.

Ezra finally broke the silence. "So what about *you*, Po?"

"What *about* me?"

"I reckon it's been hard comin' here to live with folks you don't know. Must have been hard losin' your family like you did. So... are you all right?"

"I'm fine." Her mouth twitched, and she had to focus on something — anything else — to keep from choking up. She stared out at the icehouse and at the ivy swaying in the breeze.

"If you ever need to talk, I'm never too far away." Ezra drew in his knees and shifted his body as if he was about to get up. But she realized she didn't want him to. His presence added as much comfort as a warm hug.

She took a deep breath and decided to let a few memories loose. "Jake was a farmer."

The old man settled back onto the mossy earth and rested against the tree trunk again.

"He grew corn, soybeans, wheat — whatever the soil would take."

"Honest profession, farmin'." Ezra refilled his pipe from the can in his bib pocket.

Portia rubbed her hand along the velvety moss between them. "He never was that good of a farmer. His brother Frank shared the land with him. He was better at it. Jake would have rather been hunting or fishing than plowing a field."

"We'd have got along good," he said with a quiet chuckle. "I hate farmin'."

She had to laugh at that, and discovered she really liked Ezra. He reminded her of her own daddy, before he became a drunken monster.

Portia drew her knees to her chest and rested her elbows on them. "Jake was a good man and a good father. He never should have left."

"That seems to be a pretty common sentiment nowadays." Ezra took his pipe from his mouth to rest it against one knee. "I didn't think Beauregard was gonna come back to us either, and when he did... well, he ain't been the same man since."

"It must have been hard raising him on your own."

"It was. Hadn't been for Bessie, he might have starved to death. Lucky for Beau, her youngest boy Curtis was born just a few months before. And Isaac was a real big help when Harry came to live with us. Them boys was a handful." He grinned as though remembering some of their adolescent capers. "Tell me about your folks. I knew a few people from Brentwood back in the day."

"They were Sullivans — Charles and Iris." She waited for any sign of recognition on his face, but his expression didn't change. She wiped her palms on her skirt, and her heart raced, uncertain how much she should reveal about them. "Daddy was a good carpenter. I think every home in Brentwood had a piece of his furniture. But he stopped working and turned to the bottle when my older brother died. Nothing was the same after that."

He took a long draw from his pipe, lowered it from his mouth, and let the smoke out slowly. The gentle warmth in his eyes eased her spirit. "Ain't right for a man to mistreat his family. I reckon everyone handles grief different, like you and Beau and Jonny. But you know somethin'? I still believe in the good Lord, and I think he brought you here for a reason."

"Do you? And why's that?" She tried to keep the sarcasm out of her voice but failed miserably. God's reasons didn't seem to serve any purpose but to take whatever He wanted when He wanted it.

Ezra's mustache curved upward like a fuzzy gray caterpillar arching its back. "I guess we'll just have to wait and see."

After supper, everyone settled in the parlor as a spring storm raged outside. It didn't faze Aunt Amelie, who nodded off not five minutes after she sat down. Beside her sat Polly, hunkered over some knitting. Lydia was upstairs somewhere, as was Jonny. Oliver lit a cigar as he, Pa, and Harry discussed politics or some such thing.

Beau was in no mood for it, so he sipped some whiskey and tuned out their conversation. What had politics done but tear the country apart, leaving honest working folks like himself broke while filling the pockets of opportunists like Oliver? His foundry in Philadelphia supplied the steel for railroads — those same railroads and locomotives the Rebels had destroyed.

He threw back the rest of his whiskey, savoring the burn. A good distraction is what he needed — some pleasant conversation to take his mind off his finances, or a friendly verbal sparring.

Portia sat a couple yards away.

An open book lay on her lap, but she wasn't looking at it. She stared out the window, lost in her own thoughts. He let his eyes linger on her — watched the lightning flicker in her eyes, and the way she tucked her thick hair behind her ear only to have it escape again a moment later. He wanted to ask her what was on her mind when Lydia came in, carrying a large framed portrait. Tipp followed behind at a respectful distance and waited near the door. Beau gave him a friendly nod in greeting, and Tipp returned the gesture. He'd have to snag him for a checkers game soon.

"I have something for you," Lydia said, smiling and wiggling like an excited puppy.

"Oh?" Beau glanced at Portia — who didn't seem to have acknowledged this interruption — and put on a smile for Lydia.

Lydia flipped the frame around and waited expectantly. It was a church, or maybe a school, with a tall steeple. White birches or fence posts surrounded it. What looked like a cemetery — or were those stepping stones? — sat in the foreground.

"Well, what do you think?"

He strummed his fingers on his glass and put on an expression that he hoped said, *I'm impressed*. "It's... really nice. Did you...?"

"Yes." More excited wiggling. "I painted it while at Hampton's. It's the St. Peter's church in Philadelphia. A wonderfully historic old building. Where can we hang it?"

"Uh..." Beau scanned the room. Plenty of bare spots to choose from, since they had sold so much to make ends meet. "I guess anywhere's fine."

"How about over the mantle?" she suggested and waited for Beau's nod of approval. "Tipp, would you mind?"

Tipp answered with, "Yes, Miss Clemons," and came over. He took a footstool and set it in front of the mantle. Luckily a nail still stuck out on the wall from whatever had been hanging there before. Lydia handed him the painting, and he started to step on the stool, but Oliver cleared his throat loudly.

"Take your boots off, boy. You'll ruin the upholstery."

"Yes, sir," Tipp said in an even tone and did as commanded, but a mixture of humiliation and anger emanated from his eyes.

Still slaves as far as Oliver's concerned.

Once the picture deed was done, Tipp strode from the room.

Oliver chewed on his cigar and looked right at Portia. "You can never civilize a nigger."

Portia snapped her book shut, got up, and walked out without a word. Glaring at the hateful asshole, Beau went after her into the foyer. But she had already made it halfway up the stairs when Lydia grabbed his shirt sleeve.

"Beau, wait." She pulled him around and away from the parlor's door; her pretty face was grief-stricken. "I apologize for Daddy. You know how he is — but he's got a good heart, really. If he's upset Portia, I'll talk to him and get him to apologize."

"I won't hold my breath." He glanced up the stairs; no Portia, just the click of a shutting door.

A huge streak of lightning and clap of thunder rattled the house. Lydia flinched; her shaking hands rested on his chest. "Trust me. I know my daddy. He'll listen to me."

"I've had enough of your daddy tonight."

"I know. I hate that he soured the evening. Claire kept such a beautiful home here that I simply wanted to help restore it to its former glory."

"It'll take more than one painting to do that."

Her hands migrated from his chest to his waist. Beau's jaw clenched; damn it — why did her touch have to feel so good?

"Let me take care of it, then. Let me buy what's needed to refurnish this place."

"It's my job to provide for this home, not yours." He narrowed his eyes and removed her hands from his waist, keeping hold of her wrists so she couldn't touch him into submission. Either she was naïve to a man's pride or she had already assumed the role of his wife. Neither of those options sat well with him, even though the latter choice would ensure they'd never want for anything again.

"I know, but I want to do it. For you, and for my cousin's memory." She wriggled from the trap of his hands like a clever escape artist. Gripping his forearms, she pulled her body right up to his and guided his hands around her waist.

"Lydia…"

"Please, Beau, let me do this," she whispered. Then her lips were on his, and he was caught in her spell — the world spun out of control to the tune of her tongue flicking against his.

His arms tightened around her. Her breasts molded hot and soft against his chest. Her body trembled with excitement under all the trappings of dress and corset. Telling her no wasn't possible now. But with eyes shut tight and lips locked into the deepest kiss he'd had in a very long time, he wasn't picturing himself with Lydia.

Or Claire.

It was Portia he pictured, and he had no power to stop it. The funny thing was, he didn't want to.

Chapter Eighteen

Dear Ellen,

The morning has brought us a warm day and a cloudless sky. I've opened all the study windows, and oh my! Sweet honeysuckle-scented breezes are refreshing the air in this house. There is the occasional fly, but even their buzzing is a welcome sign of spring in full bloom.

Sallie Mae is soaking up knowledge like a little seedling. She finished one primer already. She writes quite well, so I assigned her the task of writing verses from Psalms. I think I'll collect her work and make her something special with it, because I don't know how long I'll have the privilege of tutoring her. I must make every moment count. At the rate she is learning, I expect her to be doing figures right along with Jonathan by month's end. They get along so well one might think they were brother and sister but for their different skin colors.

Mr. Clemons has moved back into his own home to supervise renovations that are nearly complete. Everyone's spirits are lighter with him gone, and I don't care to ever lay eyes on him again, he's such a hateful man. Amelie is back in her home being cared for by devoted former slaves. I do hope she fares well. I worry that her mind is too far gone for her own good. I wish I could say that Miss Clemons and her mother had gone as well, but they have remained here for now. I suspect they view me as competition for Mr. Stanford's affections. They are wrong, and I want no part of such manufactured ideas.

I will remain forever grateful for Mr. Stanford allowing me to teach Sallie Mae. He can be quite reasonable and kind when he chooses to be, though Jonny is still not speaking to him, nor is Mr. Stanford encouraging him. I do believe he is genuinely regretful over that disgusting effigy we stumbled upon. Two lawmen now patrol the property several times a day, though I can sense Mr. Stanford's unease about the situation. He is already overburdened from work and lack of sleep. ~~In regards to sleep, I neglected to tell you that I saw him~~

You must be thrilled to have your mama there with the little one coming so soon. Did she bring any of those Irish ginger ales? I'd so love to drink one again. Please give her my love and write to me as soon as you can when the baby comes…

Portia finished the letter and sealed it. She smiled at Sallie Mae and Jonny. They were working diligently on their assignments. Such a peaceful morning. She settled back in the chair and let the warm breeze caress her face.

Harry came bursting in like the place was on fire. "Get ready! Let's go!"

Portia sprang from her seat as a dozen terrible scenarios swam through her mind. Pencils, paper, and who knew what else went flying. "What's wrong?"

Harry doubled over laughing.

Hands on her hips, she narrowed her eyes and admonished him. "I see nothing funny about scaring people half to death, Mr. Franklin."

"It's Harry, remember?"

She answered with a glare she hoped would wipe the mischief from his face.

It worked. His clownish smile fell into a contrite frown. "I'm sorry. Anyway, it's Market Day, so close those books and let's go!"

She opened her mouth to protest when Jonny yelled, "Woohoo!" and took off with Sallie Mae right on his heels. "I'll buy you some candy," he said as they ran out the door.

"Honestly!" Portia said, gesturing after them. "I don't see the need to cancel lessons just for a jaunt in town."

That boyish grin returned as Harry sidled over to her in a checked shirt with rolled-up sleeves. He slipped an arm around her shoulders; she did her best to not shrink away.

"Po, honey, you've been working too hard. Let me take you out for a good time, show you around town."

"You already did that."

"Not on Market Day I didn't. Maybe you can even find you a little trinket or something."

"I have no money for such things."

"Well, I do." He patted his pocket, which jingled in return, and held out his arm. "Shall we?"

Harry hadn't officially asked for her courtship, but he sure acted as though the two of them were headed for the altar. She had to be honest with him and couldn't put it off anymore. Taking a deep breath, she decided it was now or never.

"Listen, Harry. I appreciate how very kind and hospitable you've been to me, but... I'm not ready for... an association beyond friendship. I hope you understand."

Harry's jovial expression sank into seriousness. His shoulders drooped as he put his hands in his pockets and studied the rug at his feet. "That's fine. I just thought that..."

"You're a good man," she said and stepped closer, until he looked up at her again. Hurt filled his eyes, along with... anger? She guessed she couldn't blame him. "I'm sorry."

He shrugged and blew a breath through his tight lips. "Don't be. I shouldn't have assumed anything. We'll still be friends, right? And maybe, someday..."

"Maybe," she answered.

"Then let's go to Market Day as friends and nothing more." He jingled the change in his pockets again. "Will you at least let me buy you some treats when we get there?"

"I don't know..."

"Trust me, you'll want to try 'em."

"All right. I am a bit hungry."

Market Day in Lebanon surely was a grand event. Carriages lined the sides of every street. Harry found an empty space on Spring Street and parked the buggy. Beau, Jonny, Lydia, and Ezra rode in a separate conveyance. Portia didn't see them anywhere. She wished Sallie Mae

234

had been able to go, but her heart swelled a bit knowing Jonny intended to buy her some candy.

But her mind didn't linger on their whereabouts. The festivities around them overwhelmed all her senses.

People on foot wound between horses, mules, and cattle of every color and breed, many of them up for sale or trade. Music played from somewhere. Banjo, French harp, and fiddle battled it out for the best melody, depending on which way she turned her head. Merchant stands occupied every corner with cries of, "Come one, come all!" and, "Get it while it's hot!" And the smells — oh, the smells! Portia's mouth watered as Harry helped her out of the carriage. Popcorn, caramels, fried goodies — their aromas coated the air and tempted her nose, and she found herself actually pulling Harry's arm to get to the food faster.

He laughed. "Told ya you'd like Market Day."

They bought some treats and strolled past fluffy white lambs kept in a temporary pen.

"I have my calves up for sale. Let's hope they sell," Harry said.

She stuffed her mouth with some kind of fried cake sprinkled with sugar. "Mmm hmm."

Harry limped to the next merchant stand.

She swallowed down her cake and asked, "Are you all right?"

He turned around, flashing his usual boyish smile, but his cheeks had grown pale and sweat dampened his forehead. She could tell he tried to hide his limp as he walked back to her.

"Try this." He handed her a dark bottle of something.

"What is it?"

"Sarsaparilla."

"I don't partake."

"It's so gentle a baby could drink it from a tit."

Portia's cheeks grew hot.

"Sorry. Slip of the tongue. I'm distracted by a certain pretty lady."

She attempted a smile and took a sip. Not bad — cool with a licorice taste, but guilt diluted her enjoyment of it.

Harry scrubbed a shaky hand across his forehead. "I've got to run an errand. Why don't you do a little shop-gazing on your own, and I'll meet up with you later."

"I can do that. Are you sure you're…?"

He had already taken off, limping across the street and into the crowd. Not having any prior experience with rejecting men, she couldn't say whether she had handled it well or not. He didn't scream or shout or burst into tears, so hopefully she hadn't hurt him too much. She sipped her drink and strolled down a sidewalk toward the general store.

She stepped inside. Shoppers packed the store, browsing the coffee, fabric, flour, and all manner of merchandise. Weaving her way along the aisles, she eyed the goods as she passed. With no spending money, she wasn't tempted to buy anything, so she lingered on nothing in particular.

Circling her way back toward the front of the store, she spied Beau perusing some jewelry and other baubles at a glass merchandise case. The man behind the counter was young, probably in his teens. He placed a few brooches and rings on a swatch of velvet when Portia came up beside Beau.

"Those are pretty," she said.

A flash of surprise registered on his face, but then he smiled. "Which one do you like best?"

"Um…"

The shopkeeper held up a pretty bronze charm with a white cameo of a woman in the center. It hung from a gauzy lavender ribbon.

"It's the Greek goddess Athena," the young man said. "And it would look lovely on your missus here."

Portia's eyes flicked from him to Beau. "But I'm not—"

"A woman to flaunt fine jewelry," Beau added with a mischievous grin. "But you really should let me spoil you from time to time, my dear."

The shopkeeper nodded like he was truly an expert on the subject. "Oh, I see — your wife is a modest woman. That's a commendable trait, but I can assure you that many a fine Christian lady has adorned her neck with this very necklace."

"See?" Beau gestured at him and winked at Portia.

What is this crazy man doing? Embarrassment burned her cheeks. She had half a mind to clear up the confusion there and then so no one could label her a charlatan. But she had to admit, this little role-play was fun.

She forced a sweet smile. "That's very kind of you… darling, but our money would be better spent on those less fortunate." Slipping her arm through Beau's, she pulled him away, adding, "Thank you, though," to the young fellow, who looked quite discouraged.

Once they stood near the door and out of earshot, she whispered, "Why did you do that?"

"Do what?" There was that naughty boy smile again — it did look good on him, though she knew better than to think such things.

She couldn't hold back a laugh. "You don't play ignorant very well, you know."

"All right, all right. It just seemed to fit the mood, that's all. I can't afford it right now anyway, so might as well have some fun. Besides, it wasn't all a lie."

She raised an eyebrow. "Which part?"

"The part where I said you should be spoiled."

"What? I don't... I mean..." Was that smoke coming off her face?

"You deserve it. Jonny's really taken to you. Heck, even Sallie Mae loves you."

She studied the floor, not sure how to respond to such a compliment, when she realized she still had her arm tucked into Beau's. He covered her hand with his, where it rested on his sleeve.

"You've got nothing to be embarrassed about," he said. The deep smoothness of his gentle words calmed her nerves and cooled her cheeks.

She raised her head and really examined his eyes for the first time. They were actually hazel, a mixture of brown, green, and gray, but most of all, they were kind and honest. And they made her feel alive, *he* made her feel...

Pulling away, she tried to reroute the direction of this conversation. "So why were you looking at jewelry in the first place? Where's everyone else?"

"Jonny went with Pa to look for some candy. Lydia's with her mama at the milliner or some such place." He averted his gaze, squinting into the sunlight. "I thought... I might need something soon, provided I can come up with the money."

"Oh." Swallowing hard, she felt like such a fool. Lydia, of course — he would need an engagement ring.

"You rode with Harry, right? Where did he wander off to?"

She shrugged. "Said he had to run an errand."

"I guess he bought you that drink."

"Yes." She looked down at the bottle, having forgotten she still had it.

His usual scowl returned. "Maybe you should..."

"Maybe I should what?"

"Maybe you should let Harry court you."

All the air left Portia's lungs. The change took her by surprise — one minute she was laughing with Beau, lost in his eyes even, and the next, he was pushing her into Harry's arms. Harry, whom she'd just rejected. She wasn't sure why it hurt, except that she'd grown to enjoy Beau's company, to actually *like* him. Had she gone too far? Said too much?

She pushed past him and out the door, intending to walk the two miles back to the house, to be alone with her thoughts and sort things out. But a wave of screaming echoed from her left. Folks ran in all directions. One man had a bag, and... was that a gun?

He leapt onto a horse and kicked it furiously. It reared up and whinnied. Then its front hooves hit the ground, and it broke into a run. From the corner of her eye, Portia spotted Jonny — right there in the street — in the path of the fleeing man on horseback. Her sarsaparilla bottle fell with a clunk on the sidewalk. All the blood drained from her head in one swift rush, leaving her sick and dizzy like dreams she had of falling.

Move!

Skirts in hand, she sprinted to Jonny and flung herself at him, knocking them both to the ground, while the horse bore down like a thundering brown tempest. She held Jonny tight against her chest, using her body as a shield.

Beau's shout came out of nowhere. "Whoa, back, back!"

Portia dared a look over her shoulder just in time to see him waving his arms, sweeping them forward as though shooing the horse away. Mere inches from them, the horse changed directions and veered left.

A gunshot exploded overhead. The horse thundered past. Wind ruffled Portia's dress and hair. Dust pummeled her face. She rose to her knees, scared to look, but Jonny was fine. Trembling all over, but fine.

"Are you hurt?" she asked, quickly looking him over. A crushed bag of candy seemed to be the only casualty.

Jonny shook his head.

Portia stumbled to her feet and turned around. "Thank you, B—"

Beau lay sprawled on the dirt. He didn't move. Blood trickled down his temple.

She dropped to the ground and shook him. No response. "Beau? Oh God, someone help us! Please!"

Chapter Nineteen

*T*his dream was *a familiar one. There was the smoke for one thing — suffocating, thick smoke — that burned his eyes and made him cough. He thought the onslaught was over, but he lay very still, just in case. His ears rang so much he had to rely on his body and eyes for clues. The ground didn't tremble anymore. Bullets weren't cutting streaks through the smoke.*

Time to go. He clawed his way up to level ground and stumbled into a run. The Rebels had never broken their line, but the aftermath was nothing to celebrate. Within a few yards, his path became an obstacle course of shrapnel and parts of men. After all these months, he still gagged at the sight, but he made his way through them. His feet slipped on blood and entrails, but he regained his balance and kept running.

Weak fingers brushed his ankles, and men moaned, "Help me please," but he couldn't. God knows he wanted to, but he had to keep going, he had to find Harry.

Stupid fool jumped out of the trench soon as the first shot rang out. Was he trying to get himself killed?

"Harry!" he screamed, aware that it might draw a sniper's attention, but his voice was so hoarse, he doubted anyone farther than a few yards could hear him.

"Here." A weak plea floated through the smoke.

As soon as Harry came into focus, Beau could see his mangled leg. It looked like a bear had torn off a chunk of Harry's thigh for lunch, leaving behind shredded muscle, skin, and uniform. Blood flowed from the wound, soaking into the trampled grass. He'd be lucky to keep that leg if he survived.

"Come on," Beau said, dropping to one knee as he slipped his rifle strap over his shoulder. "I'll carry you."

"No," Harry shook his head. His voice was raspy, his face paler than hardtack. "Leave me."

"I'm not leaving you."

Beau started to slide an arm under Harry's back so he could pick him up, but Harry shoved him away.

"No! Get out of here. Save yourself, Beau, go!"

"I'm not going anywhere without you."

Harry tried to push him away and to kick him with his good leg. Beau took the weak blows, and being careful to keep Harry's injured leg facing away from him, he lifted him from the ground and stumbled to his feet.

"I said leave me." Harry sobbed against Beau's chest. Tears left pale streaks through the dirt and blood on his cheeks. "Leave me here, just leave me."

"I didn't... come all this way... to leave my brother... here to die."

Beau couldn't catch his breath. Constant fatigue and hunger had weakened him more than he'd realized. He wanted to run but only managed a slow jog as he wove his way through body after body. At every step, his feet hit uneven ground, blown off

242

hats, abandoned guns, and severed body parts. Ahead at the fort, their company waited. Some of their brothers in arms ran to meet them. He could reach them... just a few more yards... Harry still wept against his chest, and he felt like a full sack of feed in Beau's arms.

"We're going to make it," Beau panted, driven on by the men hollering, "Come on, hurry!"

Twenty yards from safety, a loud pop followed by lancing pain cut through his right shoulder. He pitched forward. Harry landed just out of his reach. More gunshots — fire exchanged on both sides, right above their heads. Beau couldn't move his right arm — it was pinned beneath his body. He lifted his head and tasted blood.

Harry's trembling hand reached for him, and Beau reached back...

Smoke billowed in, blinding him, but unlike the other dreams, a voice drifted through the swirling cloud. "Po? Where is Po?"

It was desperate and full of pain, that voice, and he felt it welling up inside him, felt his own lips forming the words, "Po? Where are you, Po?"

Dr. Barton emerged from Beau's room to the expectant stares of everyone in the hallway. "Bullet just grazed him. The horse probably knocked him unconscious, but he's waking up and asking for someone named Po?"

Lydia, who had started forward, stopped short. "Are you... sure?"

243

"Quite — he's repeated it over and over. If this Po person goes in and talks to him, it might help him come around fully. By the way, whoever stitched him up did a fine job."

Portia looked to Ezra for permission to enter. "May I?"

"Go on in," he said. "We'll wait out here."

She hugged Jonny against her side, happy to see the relief on his face. Stepping past a fuming Lydia, Portia opened Beau's door and entered his room.

Beau smiled. *Not a dream.* Portia shut the door quietly and walked to his bedside. Talk about a sight for sore eyes — literally. His vision blurred with each throbbing pain in his head. But he still noticed the blush on her cheeks. He scratched his bare chest, not entirely ashamed of letting her see him so exposed.

"You're awake," she said. The relief in her red, puffy eyes surprised him. How long had he been out? Was he worse off than he felt?

"Po." He tried to sit up.

She held him down. "Lie still, now, or you'll start bleeding again."

Slowly, he lifted his fingers to find bandages wrapped all the way around his head. "Jonny?"

"He's fine."

"And you?"

She nodded. "You're worried about *me*? You're the one who was shot."

"You been crying for me?" He touched her face, brushing his thumb over the smooth skin on her cheek. He hadn't noticed her freckles until now.

"No." She pulled up a chair and swiped at her cheeks. "How are you feeling?"

Pain still pounded an insistent drum in his head. "I've felt worse. Where's everyone?"

"Outside in the hall."

"Lydia?"

She exhaled and rolled her eyes. "She fainted when she saw the blood. Had to lie on the sofa while Harry and Ezra found Dr. Barton. She's fine now."

"Figured as much." Lydia didn't seem the type to handle body fluids with any measure of grace. Yet her absence didn't upset him. He wanted to spend a little time with the woman who had saved his son's life.

"The bullet only grazed you, so we brought you back here, and I stitched you up."

"You can do that?"

"Of course." He must have looked surprised, so she continued, "I've been sewing my whole life. Stitching up wounds isn't much different, just messier." Her face wrinkled up in an adorable grimace.

It hurt, but Beau couldn't help but laugh. "So I'm your test subject?"

"Lucky for you, no. During the war, men from both sides found their way to my door, asking for help from me and Ellen. Some had minor wounds that needed stitching. Others were starving. I did what I could, but..."

"But what?"

She fiddled with the handkerchief on her lap. "There's always a cost."

"Tell me. What happened?"

"Typhoid." Fresh tears dripped from her eyes as she twisted the handkerchief into a tight rope. "A Rebel came to the house sick — a boy both Jake and I knew. He was so young, I took pity on him. His folks were gone, and he had no one else. I let him have a bite to eat. I gave him some of Jake's clothes and washed the filth from his. Not a week later, Abby took ill. I should have turned him away. She'd still be here. My baby would still be here."

She buried her face in her hands. Wracking sobs shook her body. Beau sat up, steadying himself as the room wobbled. He leaned out over the edge of the bed and took her in his arms. Gently, he stroked her half-fallen hair. Things like money and marriage seemed trivial now; his heart ached for Po. On one level, he understood her pain. He'd lost Claire, but to lose Jonny, too? He'd have probably put a bullet in his head.

"Shh. It's not your fault. It's nobody's fault. You did what you could, like any good woman would. And you put yourself in harm's way for my son. I can't thank you enough for that."

After a little while, her crying subsided and her body relaxed, but she remained in his arms and rested her head on his shoulder. Beau closed his eyes, glad that he could offer her solace.

"Beau," she said, her voice muffled against his bare skin. "What was it like? The fighting, I mean. What was it like out there?"

His jaw tightened as he released her and sat up again. "I don't think you need to hear about all that now."

"What are a few more tears in the sea I've already shed?"

Elbows resting on his knees, he hung his aching head. He'd never spoken about the specifics to anyone, not even Harry, though they'd lived through the same hell together.

"I want to know," she said, her voice quaking. "I heard the cannons and gunfire, and I heard stories from the men who sought our help. But Jake never talked about it in his letters, and I never got the chance to ask him face to face. My mind sculpts images of what he must have seen and felt, but I can't sort truth from fiction. It haunts me, not knowing, and I fear I might lose the courage to ask about it again."

A war raged inside him, but courage won the battle. Po's husband fought and died out there, so she deserved to know the truth of how things really were. Or at least what he could remember of it. He swallowed hard and forced himself to speak.

He scratched the stubble on his jaw, focusing on the rug and her little feet. "No one thought the war would amount to much when it started. We enlisted and went through training, learned about formation, how to use cover fire, things like that. It was all orders and marching, forming columns and dressing the line. We got to know each other, and we learned to hate the enemy."

Portia let out a soft groan. He looked up to see if he'd said too much. Her fingers curled around the ends of the armrests with white-knuckled tension, and she averted her eyes. But she hadn't moved, and she didn't ask him to stop, so he continued.

"Once the real fighting began, everything changed. One minute you're cuttin' up with your friends, and the next minute you're watching them get blown apart. And you forget all the strategy, you forget the reasons you're there in the first place. All you want to do is stay alive. You want to get back home. Nobody's your enemy — not in the smoke and blood and sweat. It's life or death, shoot and don't think. Just get back home."

She turned to him again, tears budding from the corners of her eyes. Without a word, she reached for his hand and took it in both of hers. When she nodded for him to continue, his muscles relaxed; her strength gave him the courage to keep talking.

"And when it's all over, if you're not dead or wounded, you have to bury the bodies. You have to bury your friends. And God... some of them were just boys, Po. Little boys who would never get back home."

He didn't realize he was crying until she moved from the chair to sit on the bed beside him. Without hesitation, she gathered him in her arms. Resting his forehead on her shoulder, he wept as quietly as he could and dried it up with a few sniffs. Someone would be in any minute to ask about him. They didn't have much time.

He lifted his head and cupped her cheek in his palm. She shivered as he searched her eyes. They matched her hair — honey-brown and beautiful. "Do you hate me?"

"No," she whispered. Tentatively, she touched the bandage on his head. "I can't hate you. You saved my life."

Beau drew her closer, feeling her sweet, warm breath on his chin. He had to kiss her, just once...

The door opened. "Any change? Oh..." Pa stood there, half shocked, half grinning.

Beau broke away from Portia, sitting up straight on the edge of the bed. Jonny ran in and threw his arms around him. He held his son while Lydia peered over Pa's shoulder, glaring daggers at them.

Chapter Twenty

MAY 8, 1866
Dear Ellen,

*I **didn't aim** to write you two days in a row, but I had to share this news with you. Yesterday, at Market Day, we had a wonderful time, ~~except that Harry~~ A wretched incident occurred when a ~~robber~~ criminal tried to flee on horseback and headed straight at Jonny. I threw myself on him, ~~knowing~~ dreading our departure from this earth in that manner. Mr. Stanford intervened, waving his arms and shooing the animal aside. But that man, whoever he was, shot ~~Beau~~ Mr. Stanford.*

He's fine. By God's grace the bullet only grazed him. I stitched his wound. When he woke we spoke at length about the war and the things he saw because I had longed to hear them from Jake's mouth, but — What happened next, I don't know how or why, but we came so close to ~~ki~~ being more intimate than an employer and employee should be. What ails me most is that Miss Clemons might have witnessed it. To my knowledge, I have never been viewed as a woman of loose morals, but now I dread facing anyone.

It's already well past sunrise, and no one is stirring. The events yesterday must have taken their toll on everyone, though I've been up for a good while. Lessons will be late, later still for I must help Bessie prepare brunch for Miss Clemons and her acquaintances. It's one of their charity meetings, I believe, though the few things I've knitted still sit unused in the parlor. Should they not be taken today, I will deliver them to the preacher. He should know who would benefit most from them.

I hope to hear news of a healthy babe from you. What will you name — Sorry, I hear the family stirring in the hall. Please write soon...

As Portia helped Bessie cut sandwiches into fancy shapes, tension boiled over. Ellen wasn't there, and writing it in a letter wasn't the same as a good old-fashioned talk. She and Bessie were alone in the kitchen. She had to spill her secret.

"I almost kissed Beau," she blurted out as quietly as possible. "Or rather, he almost kissed me..."

The look on the older woman's face — something between bewilderment and disbelief — had Portia's cheeks sizzling and her hands trembling. She grimaced at what should have been a plate of egg salad sandwich triangles. Hopefully the ladies wouldn't mind abstract shapes.

Portia set the knife down before she turned the sandwiches into hash. She went on to tell her about their heart-wrenching conversation and how Lydia and Ezra had seen everything.

"How do you feel about him?" Bessie asked, her even voice masking any tell-tale emotions.

"I... owe him my gratitude. He did save my life, after all."

"And you saved his son. He won't forget that. And neither will I."

Her kind words made Portia smile a little. They weren't the best of friends, not like she and Ellen. But a pleasant warmth had formed between them that was finally melting the ice like a spring thaw.

Bessie wiped her hands on her apron and leaned on the counter. "I've been around awhile and know these things don't make sense sometimes. I think you care about him, and he cares about you, too."

"What about Miss Clemons?"

"Oh, he's noticed her, all right. Ain't no doubt about that. She's a pretty belle and rich to boot."

"That answers my question, then."

"Not until they say I do. Besides, I helped raise Beauregard Stanford right alongside my own boys, and I raised him better than that."

Better than what? To trust his common sense and marry someone who could provide everything he needs? Portia shook her head to clear it. At least Beau and Jonny were all right. That was all that mattered. He left early with Harry that morning to look at a new horse, grabbing a biscuit and barely looking at her on the way out. Things would be awkward now because of her weakness. If Miss Clemons became Mrs. Stanford, Portia wasn't likely to have a job much longer. It broke her heart all over again, thinking about leaving the children she had come to love.

Once the sandwiches — Bessie's pretty ones and Portia's not-so-pretty ones — were prepared, she headed to the study, happy to see the children already there and working hard on their assignments. Sallie Mae had written more verses from Psalms, and Portia planned to surprise her by binding them into her own little booklet. Hunkered over her paper, she bit her little tongue as she concentrated, just like Jonny. He even helped her with spelling now and then and showed her the correct way to write troublesome letters, like S and Z.

A knock at the front door drew her attention to the foyer. Lydia glided from the parlor and opened it. Excited chatter and laughter echoed through the house. Portia headed to the study door, intending to close it and drown out the noise.

She had her hand on the doorknob when one of the ladies asked Lydia, "Have you set a date?"

"Not yet."

"But he's asked you?"

"Not yet, but he will."

"How do you know?"

Lydia's eyes cut to the study door, where Portia stood frozen. "Because I always get what I want, one way or another."

Portia shut the door and, closing her eyes, rested her forehead on it. Awkward wasn't the right word for her situation. The whole thing had become one giant mess. She had half a mind to run upstairs, throw a few of her things in a bag, and go back home.

Then Sallie Mae burst into laughter. Portia turned around to see Jonny with a piece of paper in front of his face. He had cut two eye holes and had drawn whiskers and two buck teeth to make it look like a silly squirrel. He wiggled in his seat and chittered at Sallie Mae. She quaked all over with delighted giggles.

No, not yet. Portia couldn't leave these children. Not until she had to. Hand covering her mouth, she smiled and laughed quietly then cleared her throat. Jonny slapped the squirrel mask down on his desk and both of them immediately snapped to attention. At least she had them trained well.

Leaning her ear close to the door briefly, she couldn't hear the ladies in the foyer anymore. They must have migrated to the parlor to enjoy their sandwiches and tea.

"The weather is too nice to stay inside all day," she said, opening the study door. "How about a round of hide-and-seek?"

The children looked at each other, wide-eyed.

"You're gonna play too, Po?" Jonny asked.

"Of course. Hide-and-seek's my favorite game."

He and Sallie Mae bolted from their seats and flew out the open door in a flurry of excited squeals. Lessons could wait.

They got the horse for a steal — the poor old man in Cainsville looked like he hadn't eaten well in months. He offered to trade the Morgan stallion, which had fared much better than his owner from grazing on the lush spring grasses, for half a dozen chickens and two hams. How he'd acquired such a fine horse in the first place... well, Beau didn't ponder on that. He had enough to think about, not the least of which was Portia and how close he'd come to kissing her. He should have regretted it, but he had a hard time convincing himself of that.

But the old man said something as they left that weighed harder on Beau's conscience.

"If you got coloreds, you best keep an eye on 'em."

"We know about Clarence. Is there more trouble?"

"There's been more talk around here. That's all I can say."

And he'd hobbled back into his shack before they could question him further.

Beau had expected there to be backlash of some kind. You can't have a war that robs the country of thousands of good men and expect things to return to normal overnight. There was a reason he slept with a loaded rifle by his bed and now had two hired men patrolling the property every night.

Darkness fell before he and Harry returned, with Beau ponying the new stallion by a loose rope alongside him. Would have been sooner if Harry hadn't needed to stop and give himself a shot of morphine. The shakes and cold sweats were coming sooner between each dose.

"You should just quit," Beau said when they arrived at the stable. "Be a man and deal with the pain."

"Easy for you to say."

"This shoulder of mine hurts every damn day, and I got shot in the head yesterday. What's easy about that?"

Beau gritted his teeth and took his time removing the saddle and bridle from Scout. It wouldn't take much for him to pummel some sense into Harry. Easy? Hell, no. Morphine would be easy. For a while, anyway. He took it himself after getting shot while saving Harry's ass. Or rather, had it given to him. Field doctoring consisted of little more than sawing off appendages or injecting something to keep you quiet.

When he learned of Claire's death, he vowed never to touch the stuff again.

But his shoulder reminded him of that vow when he lifted the saddle from Scout's back and set it on the rack. He winced and rubbed at the old wound.

Once he'd gotten Scout settled, Beau led the new horse into a vacant stall and removed his bridle. Luckily, he seemed to be just as even-toned and unflappable as Scout. Never spooked once the whole way from Cainsville. This one had promise — four white socks up to his knees, a splash of white on his belly and face, and a fine stance.

Harry had already taken care of his horse, and now he sat unusually quiet on a stool and chewed the end of a piece of hay. "Randal said they caught the robber — poor fella didn't even get a buck," he said, breaking the silence.

"Why the hell are you meeting up with Randal? It wouldn't surprise me if he robbed the bank himself."

"I know he ain't the most likable character, but... well... he's cheaper than what they got in Nashville."

Beau huffed a laugh while he bent over, horse leg propped on his knee, and picked debris from one of the stallion's hooves. "So *he's* your supplier, huh?"

"Don't worry about it." Harry draped his elbows over the stable door. "Randal said the banker pulled a gun on him first. Fella wasn't too handy with a gun, if you ask me." He ended that last bit with a laugh and a wink.

Beau's head wound throbbed when he put the horse's leg down and stood up straight again. "You wish he'd had better aim?"

Harry rolled his eyes. "God, Beau, take it easy. If you were dead, where would I be, huh? Maybe you should have left me there when my leg got blown half-off. I wouldn't be a problem for you anymore."

Beau plopped his hat back on his head, feeling half guilty for Harry's outlook on life, and half annoyed. He bent to clean out hoof number two. "I saved your life. You could try being grateful for once."

Harry slammed his fist into the stable door. The stallion whinnied and reared, and Beau had to fling himself backward into the corner to avoid the flailing hooves. After a few shushes and gentle pats, the horse calmed down, and Beau quietly exited the stable.

Soon as the bar fell across the door, he whipped around, grabbed Harry by the shirt collar, and crashed him into the opposite wall. Wood rattled, horses whinnied, and Beau prepared to beat the stuffing out of Harry once and for all.

Until he saw his face. Tormented, like he'd never recover from all the pain in his life, no matter what Beau said or did.

"I didn't ask you to save me," Harry said through his clenched teeth. "I'd have been better off dead. Maybe I wanted it that way, did you ever think of that? Maybe that's why I crawled out of that trench too soon."

Beau shook his head. "I don't believe that."

"Of course you don't." Harry lifted a hand and gestured to their surroundings. "Look around you, Beau. You had a reason to come back. You still do — hell, you've even got *two* women wanting you now, and what do I have? A little room under the stairs. Same place I've been since your daddy took me in as your pretend brother. But we all know who the real prince is, don't we?"

Jaw clenched tight enough to crack a walnut, Beau released Harry, letting him slide down the wall to land on his feet. He paced far enough away so that he couldn't choke him. "This jealousy is ridiculous. You've been friend *and* brother to me my whole life. What else do you want? More money? That ain't happenin'. A house of your own? A wife? I can't give you any of that."

"Let me have Portia."

Those words froze Beau on the spot. *"Let me have Portia."* Like she was livestock to barter with. But his statement had carried much more weight than that. Harry knew Beau felt something for her. Giving him his blessing to court her would be a sacrifice on Beau's part. It would prove once and for all that Harry meant more to him than just another mouth to feed.

But he couldn't. Because Portia *also* meant something to him. And he cared about her too much to decide her fate there in a barn without her knowledge. Beau didn't look at him as he headed for the door, but he did say one thing, though he figured it wasn't the answer Harry wanted to hear.

"She's not mine to give."

Chapter Twenty-One

Light spilled from the parlor window, throwing long yellow rectangles across the ground as Beau walked back toward the house. He could see Portia's profile inside, concentrating on a book or maybe knitting. If she ever found out Harry had just tried to buy her from him like a prized mare...

Isaac stood from one of the porch rockers, wringing his hat in his hands. "Beau, could I have a word?"

He was in no mood for interruptions, but the man sounded distraught. "What is it?"

"If you don't mind, could ya come out to the house?" This meant Isaac and Bessie's house, of course, but they didn't ask him to come there unless it was something serious. Was Bessie sick? If she was, Isaac would have already said so.

Worry threaded down Beau's spine, but he nodded. "Let's go."

He followed Isaac for a quarter mile on the smooth-rutted wagon road to a row of clapboard houses. Once slave quarters, most of them now served as temporary living for hired farm hands. And there was Isaac and Bessie's house — larger and better furnished than the others. He and Harry had spent a lot of time there as boys, playing with their sons Curtis and Virgil, learning alongside them. He owed them beyond what he could ever repay for helping Ezra raise him, and he owed them a safe home. All this talk of violence, Clarence's lynching, that dummy in the tree — it rattled him so much his teeth chattered until he gritted them tightly together.

Soon as he stepped in the door, he knew why Isaac had asked him to come. Lucy sat at the kitchen table, while Bessie daubed a poultice of some kind on her cheekbone. Her eye was swollen almost shut. Sallie Mae was curled up on her lap, sound asleep.

Bessie glanced over her shoulder at him. "Sorry to bother you, but…"

"Did Tipp do this?" Beau asked, though he already knew the answer. The Tipp he knew from before the war wouldn't even swat a fly unless he had to.

Lucy lifted her chin, looking defiant. "Tipp ain't never laid a hand on me."

"Oliver." He guessed nothing much had changed.

As though she'd read his mind, Lucy added, "We ain't nothin' but glorified slaves. They got us under contract, all for some made up offense."

"What offense?"

"Does it matter?" she asked with a sarcastic smile. "You shouldn't have asked him out here, Uncle Isaac."

"You can trust Beau," Isaac said firmly. "He ain't never acted like a Clemons."

"I took a switch to him enough to make sure he never did," Bessie added, smiling lovingly at Beau. She turned back to Lucy. "Honey, you can trust him. He's like one of my own boys, and he went off to fight for the right side."

Lucy still regarded him with some skepticism. "We appreciate ya goin' to fight and all, but ain't nothin' changed. We're still in bondage, and when the contract's done, there'll be somethin' else come up. I stole Miss Lydia's dress or Tipp looked at Ms. Polly wrong. If we run and get caught, we're thrown in jail or hung. No trial, no nothin'. No sir, ain't nothin' changed. Unless we can get out of that contract, we're still slaves and always will be."

Beau pulled out a chair. He removed his hat and brushed invisible dust from the rim. "Did you ever try to run when you were in Philadelphia?"

Lucy hugged Sallie Mae closer and rocked from side to side. "He's got eyes everywhere. Owns half the city and a bunch of politicians. We tried once, right after we heard the war was over. Me, Tipp, and Sallie Mae packed our bags, told the boss we was leavin', and hitched a ride. Didn't get a mile down the road until a band of white men surrounded us and pointed guns at our heads. They told us we best be gettin' back home before somethin' bad happened. If we hadn't had Sallie Mae, we might have fought 'em, but… when we went back, the boss said he'd protect us, said he'd give us a nice plot of land once we got back here. All we had to do was sign a paper sayin' we'd work for five years and give him a portion of our crops." Sallie Mae stirred, and Lucy kissed the top of her head. Her eyes met Beau's. "He promised me he wouldn't come at my girl, and he ain't yet."

"Son of a bitch." Beau rested his elbows on his knees, and pointed to her eye. "Tipp know about that?"

"No. And he ain't gonna know about it. He swore he would kill the boss if he hit me again." Lucy took in a shaky breath, and her voice broke. "I know we shouldn't have signed no papers, and we should've found a way to escape. But I was scared for my baby girl, and I wanted Tipp and me to have some land of our own. We ain't never had nothin', and my Tipp's a good man. He deserves it."

"I know he does," Beau said. "Where is he now?"

"He's out workin' on the big house. I can't let him see me like this. You know what would happen if he did somethin' to the boss."

Bessie laid a hand on Beau's shoulder and whispered, "She's got another one on the way."

"Aunt Bessie!" Lucy's harsh whisper roused Sallie Mae slightly before she settled back into sleep.

Bessie turned to her niece and gave her *that look* — the one that silenced Beau into submission as a child. It still worked, apparently, because Lucy surrendered and looked away.

Isaac stood watch at the door, while Bessie pulled up a chair beside Beau. "Tipp don't know it, but the baby might not be his," she said.

Had Beau's hat been Oliver Clemons' neck, he would be choking the life out of him. "What can I do?"

Eyes scanning outside, Isaac said, "Maybe you can talk him into releasing the contract. Trade him back that high bred horse or somethin'. You're the only one around here that's got a chance of making him listen. We've got to get 'em away from that devil."

No question, Beau knew he had to act. These folks were his family, whether he could admit it freely or not. They didn't deserve such treatment. Nobody did.

"I'll go right now," he said.

Lydia answered the door after Beau's third round of knocking. "Beau?" Her blue eyes grew wide, and she blinked as though he might not be real. Fitting, since Beau thought this whole situation felt like one horrible dream after another. "Wh-what are you doing here?"

"I need to speak to your father."

"Oh… really?"

Lydia's presence didn't make him feel any better. She had hosted a small party there at her family's home and had decided not to stay at Beau's house tonight, of all nights. At least she was easy on the eyes in a white silk dressing gown splashed with a pattern of roses. Her blond hair hung in loose waves down her back and over her full breasts.

She stepped aside for him to enter. "Is Lucy any better? Mama said she was sick."

"Bessie's taking care of her. I'm sure she'll recover soon."

She looked and sounded sincere enough. Either she was making excuses for her father's behavior, or she really didn't comprehend the situation. He hoped for the latter, because he didn't want to believe she could be anything like Oliver.

"I do hope it's nothing serious. I would hate for you or Jonathan to become ill," Lydia said.

"We're fine. Sorry if I woke you." Beau shut the door behind him, glancing at his boots to make sure they weren't too filthy to step off the rug onto the newly polished floors. They'd do.

"You didn't. I had just come down for a drink of water before bed." She twirled both sets of fingers through her hair and tilted her head to one side, flashing her winning smile. "But I *was* thinking of you."

"Were you?" Beau removed his hat, trying to smile and play the gentleman, though he felt more like a peasant now than ever before. "Nothing bad, I hope."

"Of course not. My sweetest dreams are of you." She came to him, reached up, and gently touched the stitches on his head. Her fingertips drifted down over his cheek, traced along his neck and lingered on his collarbone. "Daddy's in his study. I'm sure he'll be glad to see you."

He caught her hand and held it in a neutral position, trying to cool the embers her touch ignited before he answered, but his shaky voice betrayed him. "Thank you."

It dawned on him, then — the reason she thought he had come to call. She would be disappointed, but it couldn't be helped. Or would she? How badly did Oliver want his daughter wed? Beau suddenly felt unsteady on his feet, like he'd drunk two shots of whiskey on an empty stomach. He released Lydia's hand before she could tempt him further and strode down the expansive hall to the second door on the left.

No second thoughts. Just knock. The door opened, and Beau took a step back, grimacing from the sudden whoosh of body odor. Grungy-headed Randal stood there, grinning at him with those rotten teeth. What that no good waste of bones was doing there, Beau could only imagine.

"What an unexpected surprise," Oliver said, rising from a chair across the room. "Randal was just leaving."

As if on cue, the nasty visitor brushed past him. "Heard ya got shot. Can't be too careful these days." He whistled at Lydia, who retreated into the nearby sitting room.

"True, and we can't be too careful about who we let into our homes."

Randal's raspy chuckle followed him out the front door until it shut solidly behind him.

"Don't be a stranger. Come on in." Oliver chewed on the end of an unlit cigar and gestured for Beau to take a seat on the interrogation side of his big mahogany desk.

Beau settled into the chair and wrung his hat so hard he thought it might actually produce water. His stomach churned, and a bead of sweat ran down his temple over the wound Portia had so painstakingly sutured. A cuckoo clock hung on the wall above the desk, with a tiny carved woodcutter frozen in time with his axe held high, waiting for the clock to strike ten so he could chop his firewood. Beau still had no idea how he would secure Lucy and Tipp's freedom. Buying it wouldn't be an option. He would have to appeal to Oliver's humanity, if he had any at all.

Instead of taking the captain's seat, Oliver perched on the left front corner of the desk. One expensively shoed foot brushed the Oriental rug, and the other swung lazily back and forth, uncomfortably close to Beau's leg. The tick-tock of the clock filled the awkward silence with a sense of impending doom.

Oliver lit his cigar and peered down from his seat on high. "What brings you here at this time of night?"

No sense beating around the bush about it. "I want to know what you'd take in exchange for releasing Lucy and Tipp from their contracts."

Brief shock registered on the old bastard's face. He scratched at one bushy gray sideburn. Cigar smoke puffed out in spurts as he chuckled. "I should have known this was coming."

"How much do you need?"

"Did you come into a sudden inheritance, my boy?"

"No."

"Then I fail to see how you'd have a leg to stand on in this conversation."

"Tell me how much you'd take, and we can work something out."

"Twenty thousand dollars."

"That's twice what their contracts are worth."

"I'm a businessman, Stanford. Can't stay ahead by breaking even. Besides, taking them off my hands in such short notice would be a great inconvenience. Tipp's the best field hand we have, and Lucy's our only house girl right now. It takes time to find good people. Can you supply me with replacements?"

"No, and I wouldn't, even if I could. The war's over, Oliver. Let them go."

"I have to ask — why them? I have a number of Negroes under contract."

"You know why."

Tick-tock. Tick-tock.

"I don't make deals based on differing ideas of morality, son. You'll have to do better than that."

"I'll trade the Standardbred for them."

"You'd give back my daughter's gift to you? Well now, at least you're starting to sound like a businessman, but I'll have to pass. We bought that horse for a pittance. It wouldn't bring enough."

"Then you can put *me* under contract. I'll give you a portion of everything I earn until their contracts are paid for."

Tick-tock, tick-tock. The minute hand slid ever closer to the Roman numeral twelve.

Oliver slid off his perch and laughed. "You'd really trade your soul for two worthless niggers? I knew you were an unrealistic idealist, but I never thought of you as stupid. Shame my niece isn't alive to talk some sense into you. But then, had you not gone off to fight for the damn Yankees, she might still be here."

"How dare you bring Claire into this, you son of a bitch!"

"Temper, temper. Tell me this — how many times have you tried to borrow money or run a tab since you came home? How many times have you been turned away?"

Too many damn times. Beau couldn't say it out loud, but he didn't have to.

"That's what I thought. You're traitors to the Cause, you and Harry. Left a bad taste in everyone's mouth. They don't get a little pension like you do, and most of them don't have the means to loan you anything. Those who do answer to me."

Tick-tock, tick-tock. The woodcutter shuddered once, as though he couldn't wait to bring down that axe.

"What do you mean?"

"Why do you think I went up north before the war started? Not for my health, certainly. Winters are brutal. I accumulated a great deal of wealth, and I bided my time, made connections. Our economy is in shambles, and my associates and I have ensured its survival. The South is desperate, as is Lebanon, and you'd be amazed how eagerly people will pledge allegiance to those who can feed them."

"You're buying them out."

"I practically own the town. All that's left are a few nobodies and you."

"So all this talk of coming back here to fulfill your daughter's wishes..."

"There's the bright young man I once knew. I wouldn't come back to this hellhole just to secure Lydia's fairy tale prince. The entire South is one big business venture for the taking now. How could I *not* take advantage of it?"

"When did you stop being human, or were you *born* a monster?"

"Oh, come now. Most folks are grateful for my protection."

"What protection?"

"Protection from unfortunate mishaps, untimely demises — whatever you want to call it. From what I hear, Lebanon's become quite the lawless town, more than poor Deputy Bandy can handle. We had that attempted bank-robbing — your stitches can attest to that. Some niggers strung up, too. It'd be a real shame, wouldn't it, if something happened to yours? Or to that little teacher you've taken up with."

Beau's blood turned to fire, burning its way from his gut to his toes, which propelled him out of the chair. This man had a seat reserved at Satan's left hand, and Beau was ready to escort him to it. Randal and those other imbeciles were his lackeys, of course. He had no doubt they were the ones responsible for the lynching and who knows what else. Proving it would be another matter.

He had to force himself to stay rooted to where he stood and hoped his words conveyed how badly he wanted to break the bastard's wrinkled neck. "You lay one finger on my family or Portia, and I swear to God I'll kill you."

Oliver seemed nonplussed and waved his cigar at him in a *calm-down* motion. "Easy now, soldier. This isn't the battlefield. I'm just an old man who wants to maintain the peace and ensure I live in comfort for the few years I have left. So let's strike a deal, shall we? Come up with twenty thousand dollars by Friday, and I'll let Tipp and Lucy go wherever they want."

"That's impossible."

"Then marry my daughter and give me the deed to your property. I'll even forgive Harry his debts."

The blood-soaked dummy swung through Beau's mind. "I should have known."

"He's run up quite a big tab here and elsewhere. I'm not the only one he's got to worry about. But I'll try to call off the other dogs if you and I can come to some agreement. Time's wasting, Stanford."

Tick-tock, tick-tock. Beau knew it would come down to this, no matter how many futile bargains he tried to strike. The worst part was knowing this snake wasn't giving him the choice simply because he wanted to make his daughter happy. He wanted to own him in every way he could. Giving Oliver his land would mean he controlled everything, and Oliver knew Beau was a man who would never break a vow of 'til death do us part. Beau would be his new slave.

"Come now," Oliver said. "She's not repulsive to you, surely. She's young. She'll give you more children, and her dowry will pay off your debts. It's a rather generous offer, don't you think? How badly do you want their freedom? You know, I think I'll go fetch Lucy. Mrs. Clemons and I haven't shared a bed in years. It gets rather lonely at night."

Ambushed, caught in a trap with Oliver on the high ground. Beau's heart danced a drunken jig in his chest, and he felt plumb dizzy. "Give me a few more days…"

"Can't do it. We have to close the deal tonight. Either you agree to find a source for the money by Friday, or you marry Lydia and hand over your deed. Or you do neither, and they remain for me to use as I please. And you forfeit any protection I could provide. The choice is yours."

Beau looked toward the door. Each tick of the clock grew louder, more urgent, pounded in his head, counting down the final seconds...

"Don't worry. She can't hear you. I've made certain this room is completely sound proof. Now, I want you to go out there, put on your best smile, get down on one knee, and propose to my daughter. You'll say nothing to her or to anyone about our deal. You'll get rid of that stubborn little teacher and carry on like before. And soon as you say 'I do', I'll let them go."

Oliver Clemons couldn't be trusted to do anything unless it was in ink, and even then, it was a long shot. But he had no other safeguard left in this battle. Beau was out of ammunition.

"I want your word, on a contract, that you won't lay another hand on Lucy between now and the wedding, and you will not interfere in nor will you threaten the lives of anyone in my household."

Sweat dampened every inch of Beau's skin. He might as well have been standing just outside the gates of hell as he waited for the axe to fall.

"We might make a businessman out of you, after all." Oliver extended his hand. "It's a deal."

Beau swallowed hard, but his mouth was devoid of spit. He stared at Oliver's hand for a few tense seconds before raising his own. They shook. Deal closed. The old man's grip was as strong as the devil's.

"I'll get my lawyer over here first thing in the morning." Oliver mashed the end of his cigar butt into an ashtray. "Be here at eight o'clock sharp."

The cuckoo popped out the door and announced the ten o'clock hour. The woodcutter lifted his axe and brought down jerky mechanical arms to hit the pretend chopping block. Beau flinched.

He walked to the door and opened it. There was no other choice. He had gone into this battle knowing he was outgunned, but hoping this power-hungry tyrant would miraculously have a change of heart and prove to be a decent human being. He had failed.

On the fifth chop, Lydia emerged from the sitting room across the hall and came toward him. Her eyes were wide with expectation, hope, and... love?

Whatever feelings he had for Portia, he had to erase. She was a good teacher. Once he had the money, he would pay her what he owed her and give her more to help her start a life elsewhere. But how could he forget her heart or her spirit? How could he forget how she had saved his son?

He took Lydia's hands and smiled as best he could. Lydia resembled Claire so much, he tried to picture that day long ago when he had asked the question he never thought he would ask another woman.

The woodcutter's axe made one final chop at the stroke of ten.

Beau got down on one knee.

Chapter Twenty-Two

On Wednesday night, Portia picked at her supper, feeling an odd loss of appetite. Beau avoided her gaze, like he'd been avoiding her all day. Their tender moment had caused an awkward ripple in the whole household, and she feared things would never be comfortable between them again.

Ezra and Harry engaged in their own conversation about squirrel hunting. Someone mentioned squirrel brains and scrambled eggs. Polly listened in, sipping her soup with little slurps. Portia grimaced, but the conversation at her end of the table wasn't any better.

Lydia talked non-stop with hardly a breath in between. "Since our home is completely restored, we've planned a lovely gala for Saturday night. You're all invited, even Jonathan and Portia."

Well, isn't that nice? "That's very kind of you," Portia said.

Beau threw a glance at Lydia and stared down at his plate, jaw clenched. He massaged his head where the scar from the bullet wound still healed.

"Don't worry, Beau," she said, nudging his arm. "I won't make you dance… much." She turned to Portia. "Our charity is going to be a huge success. Do you need more yarn?"

"No, thank you."

Lydia touched Beau's hand, rubbing his skin in feather-light circles. "Mama and I bought twenty more skeins yesterday and several bolts of fabric. Those little socks and bonnets you knitted are adorable." She leaned as close to Beau as she could without climbing in his lap. "I can't wait to dress my own babies in such things."

Her fingers massaged his forearm like she kneaded bread. He pinched the bridge of his nose and squeezed his eyes shut. Did his head ache from the wound or from Lydia's mapped-out future plans?

"All you all right?" Portia asked. "I could get you some coffee or a cool cloth, perhaps?"

He shook his head and opened one eye, then the other, training them on her. She sat up straighter and inhaled a quiet gasp as though someone had stepped on her toe during church. Pain — not simply from the wound — emanated from his eyes, and she felt it keenly. So much so that she reached for his face. Her fingers brushed his cheek before she remembered they weren't alone.

Beau scooted away from the table. "Excuse me," he said and left the room without a word.

"Beau, where are you going? Are you ill?" Lydia called, craning her neck toward the dining room door. She fought against her dinner dress until she freed herself from the table and followed after him, giving Portia a chilling glare on her way out.

Everyone's eyes fell on Portia. Was Beau so disgusted with her that he couldn't even stand to stay in the same room? Guilt crawled through her veins. She'd managed to tear up this entire family with one almost-kiss and now this.

Before her cheeks could ignite the tablecloth, she muttered, "I'll just clean up the dishes." She got up and gathered the two abandoned bowls along with her still full one then hurried into the kitchen. To her disappointment, Bessie wasn't there. Neither was Lucy. She poured her soup in the slop bucket and set the dishes in the basin. Come to think of it, she hadn't seen Lucy all day, and Bessie only briefly. She hoped one or both of them weren't ill. Sallie Mae had seemed fine when she joined them for lessons that morning...

Harry interrupted her thoughts when he came through the swinging door. "It would be my pleasure to accompany you to the gala tomorrow night."

"I don't think that's a good idea," she said and at his frown added, "I don't have anything fancy to wear, and I can't dance."

"You look pretty in anything, darlin'. That dress with the green stripes fits you real nice."

"Thanks, but..." Had she not made herself clear in letting him know she didn't want courtship? He must have known what happened between her and Beau, so why would he still want her?

He leaned one elbow casually on the counter. "Just friends, nothing more. Trust me, if you get invited to a Clemons' party, you want to go." He grinned and winked. "More food than you could ever eat."

Her stomach rumbled at the thought. She glanced at the slop bucket, now wishing she hadn't dumped her soup.

Harry chuckled. "Don't worry about Oliver or any of the party-goers either. After a few drinks, they won't care what you're wearing. I won't even ask you to dance. Jonny will be there, too. We can just eat our fill, come home, and sleep it off. What do you say?"

She considered Harry's offer while pumping water into the basin. Beau would be with Lydia for the evening, so she wasn't likely to run into him and stir up a scandal. Plus, Harry talked enough for the both of them, so she wouldn't have to worry about socializing much. And she'd never been one to turn down free food.

"All right. I'll go with you."

He took her hand and kissed it then gave her a wink. "You won't regret it, darlin'. G'Night, Portia."

"Goodnight, Harry."

Once in her room, she hung her dress from a hook on the wardrobe to air it out, trying not to think about the gala or Beau or Harry or anything for that matter. On impulse, she took Jake's picture from the drawer and set it on top of the dresser. It didn't hurt so much to see his image now. She smiled at his stern face, knowing all too well the seriousness was a farce. The laughter in his eyes was unmistakable. She could hear him in her head — Jake, always laughing and joking, playing pranks on his brother — and she laughed quietly as the memories passed.

Maybe she had finally started healing, was finally ready to start living again, but the future was still one blurry mess. She had no idea where she would be in the next five years or even tomorrow.

Hugging Jake's picture to her chest, she closed her eyes, and though she hadn't done it in a long time, she prayed. "Lord, if you're out there and care to hear me at all, could you grant me strength? Help me take things one day at a time."

With Jake's picture gracing the top of the dresser, she changed into her nightclothes and heard a gentle tap on the door. Maybe Jonny had a nightmare or felt ill. Her heart sank at the mere thought of him being sick. She cracked open the door.

"Pardon me," Lydia said, glancing over her shoulder toward the stairs. "May I have a word with you?"

"I suppose," Portia said hesitantly. Lydia paying her a visit at that time of night couldn't be a good thing. But since this wasn't her house, she had to play nice. She opened the door wide, and Lydia sashayed into the room, leaving a trail of gardenia perfume in her wake.

"Would you close the door, please?" The perfectly primped blonde said. "We need to speak in private."

"All right." Portia did as is Lydia requested. With her back against the door, she smiled politely and asked, "What is it?"

Facing the window, Lydia took a deep, shaky breath. "Don't take Beau from me."

"What?" She had heard her clearly, but the statement took her by surprise nonetheless.

"I've been in love with him my whole life." With a tremulous smile, Lydia turned to face her presumed rival. "Don't you see? I loved my cousin Claire dearly. Yet not a day passed that I didn't envy her — the way he looked at her — I wanted that for myself."

Had this conversation been started by someone less… privileged, Portia would have felt more empathy. She tried to keep the irksome tone from her voice but failed. "Sorry if I misunderstood you, but I thought you had claimed him already. He seems plenty attracted to you."

"Of course he is. He asked me to marry him last night."

No… Portia's heart felt like it might sink from her chest, plumb out her feet, and into the floor. But she forced herself to maintain some semblance of pride.

"Attraction is one thing, you see," Lydia continued with an upturned hand, "but how long-lasting can it be if it doesn't come from here?" She patted the top of her full bosom for emphasis.

Feeling a headache coming on, Portia rubbed the brow bone over her left eye. "You're saying what, exactly? That Beau doesn't love you? I don't know what it's like back in Philadelphia, but from what I know of love, it's not something you can force. If you were so concerned about it, why not choose from a suitor in Philadelphia instead of gambling on Beau's affections?"

Lydia drummed her fingers on her collarbone with a quiet *thump, thump, thump*. The tremulous smile disappeared, replaced with a tight-lipped frown. Take off a few years, and Portia would have been looking at a petulant toddler on the verge of a tantrum. Nothing she hadn't dealt with before, but tonight she lacked the patience to contend with such behavior, especially from a twenty-one-year-old socialite. She expected Portia to concede in a heap of groveling humility, to play the part of timid mouse and servant under Her Majesty's rule. Well, the queen was about to be terribly disappointed.

"You did have suitors in Philadelphia, I presume?" Portia prompted, hoping to send the brat stomping from her room in a huff. "I mean, to look at you, one would imagine…"

"Yes, yes, of course I had suitors," Lydia blurted out. "I amassed so many calling cards, I couldn't keep count. Some of those gentlemen, I even courted briefly, but none of them compared to Beau."

"Then we are back to the question of how or why you think I might take him from you. Do I look like someone who has the resources to do such a thing?"

Oh how badly Lydia must have wanted to shout, "No!" to the rooftops. Rather disappointingly, she dropped her hands and lifted her chin, standing perfectly straight, as she'd most likely been taught in that finishing school she attended.

"Your resources have no bearing on this matter." Her clipped words were as haughty as her upturned nose. "We all witnessed how he almost kissed you. He… noticed you long before that. A man like him — upstanding and unselfish — how can he not notice a woman who arrives with so much grief upon her? He feels guilty for leaving Claire here to die alone, so his protective nature is exaggerated when it comes to you."

"Has he told you this?"

"No, but it's obvious. I've known Beau much longer than you have. I can tell how he feels. Beau needs someone who can meet his needs, someone with an undamaged spirit. I know he takes pity on you now, but he'll soon grow weary of your dependence. Normally, I wouldn't confide these things to anyone, but I want you to be aware of what he's like before you act on any… urges."

Deciding the ridiculous exchange had gone on long enough, Portia opened the door with an impatient swish. She forced herself to remain civil, though her tongue longed to throw a few choice words at Madame Peacock. "How kind of you, Miss Clemons, to be concerned for my welfare, but unless you can read Beau's mind, how can you presume to know what he needs or what guilt he bears if he has not shared this with you? And I don't need protecting, nor do I act on any *urges* without careful thought, so your worry is misplaced. Now, it's late, and I'm tired. Unless there's anything else you'd like to discuss…"

Lydia glided toward the door, but instead of leaving, she twirled around and leaned against the door frame. Her pretty face wilted into a well-practiced pout.

"Please," she whispered. "If I lose Beau, I lose everything I've ever dreamed of. I'll have nothing left."

Portia clung to the door to keep herself from slapping some reality into this girl. She couldn't take any more of this nonsense.

Forcing herself to maintain her crumbling composure, she whispered harshly, "You have no idea what it means to have nothing or to lose everything. You cannot fathom the pain of true loss, what it feels like to wake up day after day just to wish you were dead. Furthermore, I don't know how Beau feels about you, me, or anything else, nor do I care. Good night."

Portia shut the door forcefully — some might have called it a slam. Lydia let out a little yelp, retracting her fingers just in time to keep them out of harm's way.

The nerve of that woman! "Don't take Beau from me," Lydia had said. As if Portia were really capable of such a thing. They were engaged, for goodness sakes. Wasn't that confirmation enough? She was too upset to sleep, but made herself settle under the covers, sitting up so she could read. Hopefully, a Longfellow poem or two would drown out the residual whine of Lydia's pleas.

Hours passed until her head finally sank onto the pillow. She stared at the darkened ceiling. Lydia might have been right about a few things, after all. Were Beau's feelings for her really based on the guilt he felt over losing his wife? She had no desire to be a charity case to anyone, especially him.

Her eyes closed on the memory of how Beau had jumped in front of that horse and how he had held her when she cried. Guilt could have accounted for that. But then she recalled their shared laughter, the way his anger had melted away during those moments, and how warm his breath had felt when they had almost kissed. There had to be more to his feelings than that, even if nothing came of it. There had to be, because…

Don't even think the words. Don't even think…

Beau woke to a horrific scream. He flew off the bed and grabbed his rifle. Running into the hall, he blinked the sleep from his eyes. It had come from Portia's room. Jonny poked his head out of his door, eyes wide and fearful. Beau shooed him back into his room as he ran past him down the hall. He didn't think to knock and charged inside.

The sun had halfway risen, and in the rose-gold light, Portia stood there in her nightgown, hair loose and feet bare. Her hands were clapped over her mouth, while she stared at the wardrobe and a dress.

Or what used to be a dress.

It now hung in shreds, like a bobcat took a shine to it and used it as a scratching post.

Without hesitation, he took two strides and wrapped her in his arms. "What happened?"

She trembled and shook her head against his bare chest. "I don't know. I woke up and found my dress… like this. I'm sorry if I scared you."

Beau realized a little too late that everyone had gathered outside her door. Including Lydia, who arched one eyebrow and glared at Portia as though she'd like her to fall dead at his feet.

He let Portia go and stepped back. "We'll find out what happened. Did anyone see or hear anything?"

Pa, Jonny, Lydia, and Polly all shook their heads.

"We should search the rooms and see if there's an intruder. Beau, will you please come with me? I'm so scared," Lydia said.

"I'll look downstairs," Pa said.

Beau spotted the rifle in his hands as the old man eased down the stairs. But his stomach turned somersaults. Had this been some warning from Oliver to ensure he carried out his end of the deal? Or something else entirely — with the rumors of retaliation against coloreds, he couldn't be sure. Portia had been teaching Sallie Mae, after all.

Lydia wrapped her arm around his waist, led him out of the room and down the hall toward the two unused guest rooms and the attic stairs. Beau looked over his shoulder to see Jonny pale-faced and trembling outside Po's room. Po wrapped her arms around Jonny's shoulders. Beau couldn't help a little smile at how wonderful she was with him. Whoever did this to her would pay dearly.

He held his rifle ready. Polly stood against the wall by her room, gray hair hanging in one thick braid over her shoulder. She had a quilt wrapped around her and scratched at a spot on her usually-covered neck. It looked plumb raw. Beau tore his eyes from her peeling skin and searched her room. Nothing except a laudanum bottle on her bedside table.

That explains the itching. He searched Oliver's former room and another he and Claire had planned to use as a new nursery should they have been so lucky. He left Lydia in the hall briefly and climbed the stairs to the attic. Rifle first, he peered through the dusty, dim light, walking around forgotten crates and a few covered furnishings. Nothing.

With Lydia clutching his waist again, they went back down the hall and reached Jonny's room. He wouldn't hesitate to blow the brains out of an intruder lurking near his son. Beau peered under the bed and in the wardrobe.

"Beau, you should see this," Lydia said.

He came to where she leaned over Jonny's bedside table. A pair of scissors rested in her hands, and on their blades... white and green threads just like those on Portia's dress. Beau lowered the rifle and looked at his son there in the hall. Jonny started shaking his head. Tears dripped from his eyes.

Beau took his son's shoulder in a firm grip. "Did you do this?"

His answer consisted of more head shaking and more tears.

"Damn it, Jonny, answer me! I know you can talk. For God's sake, open your mouth and talk!"

Portia pushed his arm away. "Beau, please…"

Jonny broke free and bolted down the stairs. The front door opened and slammed shut again. Portia's bottom lip quivered. She quietly returned to her room and closed the door behind her.

Lydia pulled Beau into the hall. "I think I know what's going on."

He scrubbed a hand over his face. "Really? Enlighten me, then."

"He's rebelling against authority. I saw it a few times at Hampton's. He isn't happy with the current situation, and I hate to say it…" She ran her hands soothingly over his bare chest. "But I don't think Portia's being strict enough with him. The boy needs structure, something beyond what a small town teacher can give."

Beau started to ask what she meant by that when he realized they stood in front of Portia's door. And Lydia hadn't exactly been quiet.

"Come downstairs. "We need to have a talk," he said.

Lydia backed away, wrapping her dressing gown tightly around her, eyes averted from him. "Oh, um, of course."

Beau went downstairs to the study. He poured a shot of whiskey and downed it in one gulp. It hit his empty stomach with a punch that made him groan. Either his son had gone mad or he was about to marry one crazy bitch. Neither of those was a comforting thought.

Lydia sashayed in, dressing gown hanging wide open, and closed the door. Her thin cotton nightgown left little to the imagination. He forced his attention to his desk. A little handwritten book lay there, bound by pink ribbon, with a note on the cover. *To Sallie Mae, one of the best students I've ever had. Remember that you can do anything you put your mind to. Love, Po*

He set the empty shot glass down, closed his eyes, and leaned over the desk. "Did you do it?"

"What?" Lydia walked to him and touched his arm.

He shrugged her off. "Did you destroy Portia's dress?"

She put her hand to her chest and batted her eyelashes. "Why do you think I would do such a thing?"

"Don't play games with me, Lydia." He balled up his fist and slammed it down on the desk. "Tell me the damned truth!"

"I did *not* destroy her dress! I'd wring the neck off a chicken before I'd damage such a vintage garment."

"Then your father did this, or had it done."

"Daddy? Beau, darling, I know you two don't see eye to eye, but he's not that petty."

"Isn't he?"

"What do you mean?"

Questions swirled in her tearful eyes. He swallowed down the temptation to tell her everything. In utter frustration, he snatched up his shot glass and hurled it at the wall. It shattered. Lydia recoiled, taking refuge by a bookshelf.

"I'm sorry," he said, palms down on the desk, head hanging low between his shoulders.

After a moment's hesitation, she approached him cautiously and gently touched his arm. Her voice trembled, barely above a whisper. "You know I would never hurt Jonny. But… is it so hard for you to consider that he might be unhappy with her? Bessie told Lucy about the snake incident."

"What snake incident?"

She sighed. "Lucy and I, we talk now and then. We're so close in age, after all, and I have no sisters." He turned his head and looked at her. She smiled back. "I'm actually quite fond of her. She told me that Jonny put a snake in Portia's bed not long after she arrived. Just a little garter snake, but enough to give her a scare."

"Why didn't Bessie say something to me when it happened?"

"Would you have listened or done anything about it?"

He wanted to defend himself and tell her how wrong she was, but was she? He said nothing as he stood up straight and ran a hand through his hair.

"This is what I mean. You're so worried with everything that you can't see how your son might be capable of such a crime."

"Not Jonny. He loves her… and she loves him."

"Maybe you're right, and I hope you are, because you might soon have a troubled young man to deal with instead of a boy who can be redeemed."

Harry came to mind — God forbid Jonny become another Harry. But Jonny destroying something so special to Po? He couldn't believe it. He wouldn't. Not his boy. He'd raised him right... or had he really raised him at all? Between Claire, Pa, and Bessie, he had never had to worry about Jonny. Then he'd left for war and missed so much of his son's short life. And since his return, with Jonny's complete silence and the long hours trying to turn this place around... how much did he really know about his son? He felt sick.

She turned him to face her and wrapped her arms around his neck. He didn't stop her when she pulled him to her for a kiss. "I'm sorry, Beau. I don't want to add anymore burdens to your conscience. Since Mama and I are moving out today, I'll get dressed. We can discuss things later." Her blue eyes had never shone with such sincerity as her hand slid down to his chest and rested over his thumping heart. "I love you. I want to be the kind of wife Claire was to you, and I will, if you'll open your heart to me."

He said nothing but wrapped his arms around her and rested his chin on her head. Maybe this marriage wouldn't be what he had with Claire, but perhaps it could be better than he expected. But there was still the matter with Jonny and there was Portia. He could see himself comfortably married to Lydia, he could work things out with Jonny, but he wasn't ready to say goodbye to Portia. For her sake, he had to figure out how.

But not yet. He owed her a new dress.

287

Portia dressed quickly. She didn't bother putting up her hair. Hurrying downstairs, she flung open the door and took off at a run. She had one destination in mind, and she didn't stop until she got there.

Sure enough, Jonny was at the creek, still in his long johns. She stopped right at the big cedar tree, leaning on it and trying to catch her breath. He skipped rocks one after another, but it looked more like an assault on the water. An angry shout accompanied every throw. Portia eased down the bank and stopped just beside him.

He glanced her way and kept throwing.

She picked up a stone. "Remember, it's all in the wrist," she said and flung the rock across the creek. It skipped once, twice, three times, before coming to a stop on the opposite bank.

Jonny sank to the ground and cried. Not worrying about the wet, sandy bank, Portia sat beside him and wrapped her arm around his shoulders.

"I didn't do it," he sobbed. "I swear I didn't."

Portia took a deep breath and let it out slowly. "I believe you."

"She wants to send me away," he said between sobs. "I know I'm not supposed to eavesdrop, but I heard her talking to Aunt Polly the other day. She wants Pa to send me away to school. Some military academy. I hate her, Po. I don't want to go. I want to stay home. I want to stay with you."

He melted onto her shoulder, and she gathered him in her arms. "I know, sweet boy. I know."

"I'm sorry about your dress. It looked really pretty on you."

"It's just a dress. Things can always be replaced. It's the people we love who matter more."

She held him, closed her eyes, and tried to burn him into her memory. Chances are, they would have to part. But one thing was for sure. She loved this little boy with all her heart and would fight for him until her last breath if that's what it took.

Chapter Twenty-Three

Saturday came, and the time passed quickly. A mere hour before the gala, Portia had given up on any notion of attending. She had worked in the garden all day, weeding and pruning, doing all she could to take her mind off yesterday's events. Jonny worked alongside her the entire time. He didn't say a word, but she knew without a doubt he was innocent.

Lydia must have staged the whole thing. Worse still was knowing the woman had come into her room as she slept. Mutilating her dress was bad enough, but she could have done worse. Much worse. Thank God she and her mother had left not long after it happened. From her window upstairs, she and Jonny had watched as their things were carted out of the house and into their coaches. Beau had ridden along behind them, and she hadn't seen him since.

Now, as they gathered up their tools, she finally worked up the nerve to ask Jonny, "Has your pa spoken to you about yesterday?"

He shook his head. "No. Do you think he believes me, Po?"

"I don't know," she admitted, "but if he thought you did it, don't you think he would have punished you by now?"

"I guess, maybe," he said with a shrug. "Just wish I knew for sure."

"Well, there's not much we can do about it right now, so try not to worry."

She gave him a quick one-armed hug, wishing for once that Beau would just talk to his son instead of leaving him in a perpetual state of confusion. With dirt under her fingernails and a satisfyingly sore back, she and Jonny headed back toward the house.

Harry met her at the back door. "It's not too late to change your mind, Po. You can swipe one of Lydia's dresses. She's left some here and has so many, she wouldn't notice anyway."

"I'm sorry Mr. Franklin, but I wouldn't wear one of her dresses if you paid me to. Now, if you'll excuse us..."

"It's Harry, remember?"

"Go to the party and enjoy yourself. I'm not in a celebratory mood."

She pushed past him to the kitchen with Jonny right behind her. Bessie was sweeping the floor. No need to make supper tonight.

"Honey, you want some cold chicken or..." She held her upturned hands out as though she longed to help matters but didn't know how.

"No thank you. I'll clean up and have some tea in a little while," Portia said.

"All right. You hungry, Jonny?"

"No, ma'am, thank you."

She saw no one else as they climbed the stairs to their rooms. Beau and Ezra must have already left. Tonight, she'd tuck Jonny in and read with him, maybe from one of his Natty Bumppo books. It might be the last night they'd be together. She had to make the most of it.

In her room, she spied something hanging on her wardrobe. Not her torn dress, but a different one. Lavender chiffon with a luxuriously soft white shawl. A bit wrinkled, but beautiful nonetheless. A note was pinned to it. She removed the paper, and her eyes widened as she read.

This dress was one of Claire's favorites. I kept it in the chest at the foot of my bed. I hope you will accept this as a little compensation of all that I owe you and for the loss of your mother's gown. If you don't want to come tonight or feel uncomfortable wearing it, I understand, but I'd like to see you.

Beau

Portia buried her face in her dirt-caked hands and cried. Indecision played tug-of-war in her heart. On one hand, she had no desire to be anywhere near Lydia again, especially after that blonde peacock mutilated her dress and blamed Jonny for it. On the other hand... Beau had taken *this* dress from his locked-away memories to replace hers. He wouldn't do that for just anyone.

She knew she had to go, no matter how much it would hurt to see him with *her*. Hard as she had tried to deny it, she loved Beau. It didn't make sense, not with all their differences and within the span of a month's time.

But she couldn't doubt it any longer. Beau inspired that same pinched-heart feeling she'd felt for Jake, the kind that left her breathless when he was near and lonely when he wasn't. Just seeing him smile and hearing his laughter chased the darkness from her days. Beau, like Jake before him, was the kind of man she could picture herself growing old with, rocking through their twilight years in the lazy comfort of their front porch.

A spark of hope lightened some of the burden. Whether he loved her in return or not, Portia couldn't imagine how he could still consider marrying Lydia after she had committed such an atrocity — surely he didn't believe Jonny did it.

Swiping away the last of her tears with the back of her hand, she made up her mind. She would go tonight, not out of some misplaced hope that she and Beau would ever be together, but simply because he wanted her there.

The sun sank just below the horizon, leaving its orange and violet tracks at the bottom of a star-sprinkled sky. Isaac turned right off the main road and drove the cart under a wrought iron arch. In the very center hung a varnished cedar sign reading "*Welcome to Paradise*". She assumed this was the name of the plantation.

"Paradise Plantation. Name don't fit the place, if you ask me," Isaac said.

Tall oaks and cedars lined the wide drive toward the house, but several had been reduced to stumps. Victims of the war, most likely. Uneven low-rise stone walls also lined each side of the drive. Gaps appeared here and there, showing her glimpses of bushes and lawn.

Isaac followed her gaze. "Lot of that stone got taken during the war. The house was used as a Confederate officer's headquarters. Lucky weren't no battles close by or it might have been an infirmary. They wouldn't have got *that* mess cleaned up quick, no sirree."

They finally reached the house and rounded the circular drive in front of it. A large rose garden formed the centerpiece of the drive with a bare pedestal among the blooms.

"Used to be some half-neked statue there," Isaac said as he guided the horse carefully beside the other parked carriages and stopped in front of the door.

Portia stared up at the place in amazement. It was the biggest house she'd ever seen or probably ever would see. Huge white columns stretched from the large porch all the way to the roof. Open double doors showered her senses with light, music, and laughter from the party inside.

Isaac asked, "You sure you wanna go in, Po?"

She put a hand on Jonny's back; he stared up at her, waiting. *Time to be brave.* "Yes. We'll be fine. We'll just stay a few minutes. I don't think either of us is prepared for a lengthy gathering, and young men don't need to stay up all hours of the night."

"I hear ya. I'll be waitin' right out here when you're ready to go."

"Thank you, Isaac."

He helped her down, climbed back in, and tipped his hat as the cart pulled away.

Portia squeezed Jonny's hand. "Ready?"

294

He nodded.

"I'm sure your pa will be happy to see you. And don't go too far. I just might want a dance."

Jonny smiled. "I don't really know how to dance, Po."

"Me either, but it's never too late to learn."

They climbed the steps together, passing two colored servants who bowed as she and Jonny crossed the threshold.

"Watch the time up there," she said, pointing to a tall grandfather clock by the wide staircase. "Fifteen minutes, then meet me here at the door."

"Yes, ma'am." Jonny let go of her hand and headed straight toward a buffet on one side of the grand entrance.

Portia stood still for a moment, wrapping the shawl tighter around her shoulders. She was grateful to Beau for offering her this dress. Sad as she was to have had her mother's old one destroyed, she would have been indistinguishable from the servants had she worn it there. The only thing she needed was a pair of gloves, but her ensemble would have to do.

Bessie had arranged her hair into a coil of braids with some curled tendrils caressing her cheeks. The older woman had cried the whole time, saying, "You're so beautiful, honey. Ms. Claire would want you to have this dress, I just know she would."

Portia didn't have the heart to tell her she only planned to stay for a few minutes, just long enough to seek out Beau and let him know she appreciated his gift. Finding him, however, might be more of a challenge than she thought.

Every lamp and chandelier in the place must have been lit. Portia squinted into the golden brightness, which could have rivaled the light behind Heaven's gates. In the midst of the huge foyer was a wide set of red-carpeted stairs. Unoccupied instruments rested on the second story landing — the musicians must have taken an intermission. Party guests took notice of her entrance, whispering and pointing discretely with their fans and glasses.

"Unescorted — how gauche."

"…after his money. Thank God he came to his senses…"

"I've seen that dress. It's… no it couldn't be Claire's…"

Head down and cheeks on fire, she followed Jonny's lead and retreated to the buffet. Neither he nor Beau was anywhere to be seen, unfortunately. Some sort of pink punch filled a large crystal bowl. Ice bobbed happily in the fruity waves. She couldn't remember the last time she'd had an iced drink. Thankful for the treat, she ladled some into a matching crystal cup and kept to the perimeter of the room. She hoped to spot Beau so he could see her in the dress and know she had cared enough to come.

Instead, she caught Harry's eye. His jaw dropped when he saw her, and he held up one finger to the man he spoke with then made his way to her.

"Lo and behold — you came! And look at you, just gorgeous." He leaned close and whispered, "Took my advice, huh?"

Deciding it might be best to keep mum on the dress's origins, she simply smiled and sipped her punch. Harry offered his arm, and not wanting to shun him in front of everyone, she accepted it lightly.

"I'll introduce you to some folks," he said.

He led her around the room, introducing her to Mr. This and Mrs. That. Portia nodded politely, let them take her hand, and offered a word or two. But her mind might as well have been on the moon. What was she thinking by coming, anyway? And what was Beau thinking by asking her? Maybe he felt guilty about her dress and didn't know what else to do. Or had she read his note all wrong?

Her presence surely wouldn't help matters. Lydia had made it crystal, and dangerously, clear that she wouldn't tolerate any competition for Beau's affections. What if she caused some dramatic scene in front of everyone?

"Will you excuse me, please?" she interrupted Harry in the middle of a rather lewd joke. "I would like to take some fresh air."

"Good idea, darlin'. I'll come with you."

"No," she said a bit too quickly and smiled to cover her impatience. "No, you should stay here and enjoy yourself. I'll just be a minute…"

"Oh, I see," Harry said with a wink, then whispered in her ear, "The facilities are out the veranda doors to the right of the flower garden."

"Thank you." She hurried back into the grand hall then turned left. The veranda sat opposite the front entrance. Both sets of doors stood wide open, allowing refreshing breezes to pass through and cool the crowded room.

Outside, Portia stepped onto the wide flagstones and took a deep breath of the crisp, magnolia-sweetened air. Torches were lit along a winding maze of a path through the biggest flower garden she had ever seen. She wished she could see it in the daylight when the muted colors would come to life in vivid splendor. Wrought iron and painted wood furniture occupied the left side. Light from the door and windows spilled along the stone floor, making rectangles in patterns of light and dark. No lamps or torches were lit on the veranda itself. Besides a strolling couple in the garden, the place was unoccupied, giving her the opportunity to sink into the shadows against the wall.

But instead of the house, she backed into something less solid... and warmer.

"It looks good on you."

She pivoted on her heels, crossing from the safety of shadow into the window's light. "Beau! You scared the life out of me."

His eyes twinkled along with his smile. "You look plenty alive to me."

Dressed in a dark suit and bowtie, he looked more gentleman than farmer. Hands in his pockets, he rested his back against the house, the sole of one booted foot casually planted on the white stone wall.

"Where's Lydia?" Her voice sounded as taut as her nerves.

He shrugged. "Upstairs somewhere. Probably changing again. I think she has a new get-up for every round of dancing."

Before she lost the little bit of nerve she had left, she asked, "You know Jonny is innocent, don't you?"

"I *don't* know, but I'm grateful that you don't harbor anger toward him." Fatigue burdened his words as he stared at the ground.

Though it wasn't quite the answer she had hoped for, she wasn't sure what else to say. With so many people in attendance, any slight against Lydia could be easily overheard should someone else happen to step outside.

Rubbing her bare forearms nervously, she broke the awkward silence. "Thank you for the dress. It was quite unexpected."

"I felt the need to replace what you lost." Dropping his foot back to the ground, he pushed off the wall and stepped closer. "I didn't think you'd come tonight."

"I didn't know if I should... or if you... wanted me to."

The musicians must have come back from their intermission, because the flowing, rhythmic sounds of a waltz floated across the veranda.

Beau held out his hand, breaking the border of shadow and light that separated them and revealing the calluses of a hard-working man. "May I have this dance?"

Her heart thumped a warning inside her chest. *You're stepping over a line you shouldn't cross.* But the warm beacon of his eyes caught her in his spell, and she lost all notion of refusing him. Slowly, carefully, as though she were about to touch Briar Rose's spindle, she accepted his hand. His other hand settled on her waist, and he drew her to him, away from the window and prying eyes. They stood like that for one eternal moment, secure in their shadowy refuge. Portia could have soared into the cosmos, had Beau not kept her secure in his arms.

"I don't dance very well," she admitted quietly as she rested her palm on his chest. She could feel his strong muscles and the steady rhythm of his heart.

"It's just a waltz. Simplest dance there is. It's the only one I ever learned, though Claire tried her best to teach me. Her toes paid the price."

"My toes are just as penniless as I am, so let's not spend beyond their means."

"Deal."

Portia smiled, relaxing with their easy banter. Beau led, keeping her hand in his firm but gentle grip. She followed, and they soon fell into the rhythm of sultry strings and piano chords. Glancing down at her feet, she missed her step and landed on Beau's toe.

"Sorry."

"Up here." His soothing, deep voice eased her fears as expertly as he calmed his horses. "Don't look at your feet. Always look ahead or into your partner's eyes."

"All right."

It is *easier this way, looking into your partner's eyes.* And there was no place she'd have rather looked. His deep-set eyes were gray in this light and softened by his serene smile. She could have stared into them until her feet grew numb if time allowed.

As the last notes of the waltz glided out onto the veranda, she burned into her memory the strength in his hand on her waist, the way he smiled and gently guided her back into the step when she lost focus. No matter what happened from this night on, she never wanted to forget the way it felt right then, dancing in Beau Stanford's arms.

The final chords faded into silence. Beau went still, but he held her there against him. She longed to remain in the sanctuary of *him*, man and woman, united body and soul. He let go of her hand and touched her face, trailing his fingers lightly along her jaw. Portia lifted her chin to accept his kiss, but her spirit fell back to earth when his jaw tightened.

He spoke in a ragged whisper. "There's something I need to tell you…"

Harry's voice shattered the illusion. "Po?"

She and Beau parted quickly, but Harry frowned, eyes darting everywhere but never landing on the couple in front of him.

"I thought you might have gotten lost. Can I… escort you back inside?" he asked.

Beau took a step away, back into his section of shadow and leaned against the wall where she found him as though their dance had never happened. Tears burned the corners of her eyes, but she blinked them into submission and took Harry's arm. They went back into the great hall and weaved through the happy couples. Portia couldn't look at their faces and tried to block out their laughter and giddiness and whispered plans of later affections.

She was about to ask Harry if he could help her find Jonny and escort them out when a bell clanged from upstairs. Everyone around them migrated toward the sound. Following the flow of the herd was easier than escaping at the moment, so they gathered with everyone else at the bottom of the stairs. There on the first landing, Oliver Clemons rang a hand bell, with Polly standing demurely beside him.

The clanging died down as Oliver held up his cigar in a benevolent gesture. "I'd like to thank you all for coming tonight to celebrate the rebirth of Paradise Plantation. Sadly, our home will never be back to its former glory, but that pales in comparison to the news I have to share with you now."

Portia's heart skipped a beat. She tightened her grip on Harry's arm.

Oliver gestured to his right, where Lydia appeared and glided toward him. When she stopped at his side, he said, "I'd like to announce the engagement of my daughter, Lydia Clemons, to Mr. Beauregard Stanford."

Tucking the bell under his elbow, he started clapping. Everyone except Portia took the cue and applauded, even Harry, until he looked at her standing there frozen in place. He wrapped an arm around her waist and mumbled something to her, but she didn't take much notice. The applause, the cheers and congratulations pummeled her ears. Her heart beat wildly, urging her to surrender the battle and retreat, but her knees wobbled like soft clay.

"Beau!" Oliver yelled over the din. "There you are. Come on up here, my boy!"

The crowd parted slightly, as Beau made his way from the veranda to the stairs. Lydia wore a powder blue gown with loose pagoda sleeves and smiled ear to ear. She held both hands out, waiting for him to claim her, as Beau ascended the steps. When he reached her, she grabbed his hands and kissed his cheek. Madame Peacock had won her perfect mate. Arm in arm, they started down the stairs.

Beau's face was a blank mask. His eyes drifted across the crowd as they descended toward the waiting guests. Mid-way down the stairs, he paused and caught Portia's gaze. In a split second, she read a multitude of emotions from him. Guilt, shame, and such heavy sadness. Tears stung her eyes, threatening to spill out and confess her loss.

His sudden halt stopped Lydia short. She rebalanced herself and looked at him questioningly. Then she followed his gaze and spied the object of his attention. She lifted one eyebrow and threw Portia a glare as ice cold as the punch.

How can he? How can he possibly marry that woman after what she did to Jonny? Tugging on Harry's arm, Portia whispered, "I want to leave. I have to leave."

"What? I can't hear you." Harry said, leaning in closer. "I said I..."

Beau and Lydia stood just a few feet away. Portia abandoned Harry's arm and tried to cut through the crowd, but they formed a dense army of well-wishers, eager to greet the newly engaged couple. She found herself being nudged forward, as two lines formed — men on Beau's side and women on Lydia's.

The person in front of her stepped to one side, and there she was — face to face with Beau's fiancée. Portia couldn't help but picture the scissors lying on Jonny's bedside table and how triumphant the she-devil looked when she 'discovered' the evidence.

Lydia snatched her hand, squeezed it hard, and drew Portia close enough to whisper venom in her ear. "You thought waltzing in here wearing my dead cousin's dress would change his mind? You must have forgotten... I always get what I want."

Smiling and blushing like any soon-to-be bride, she flung Portia's arm away with a forceful push, already looking to greet the next person in line. But like the snares Jake once set with the saplings on their farm, Portia's hand sprang back, smacking Lydia's face with a resounding *snap!* Horrified gasps rippled through the crowd as Lydia's head whipped to one side and an earring went flying into oblivion.

Portia immediately locked eyes with Beau. He took a step toward her, but Lydia, blond hair disheveled and cheek flaring red, clamped onto his arm.

Expecting to be detained at any moment, Portia elbowed her way through the shocked faces and horrified stares to make her retreat. She wasn't even sure if she was moving toward the exit, with her heart beating a deafening rhythm in her ears and tears clouding her vision. Finally, she spotted Jonny standing just inside a parlor. He peeked out around the doorframe, crying quietly. She reached for his hand, and he took hold. Luckily no one had recovered from the shock of the moment to come after them just yet. Pulling Jonny along with her, they made their escape to Isaac and the waiting cart.

Harry called out, "Wait!" and caught up to them, panting. "Isaac, take Jonny on home. Portia can ride with me."

Isaac looked to Portia as though seeking her approval. She nodded, too upset to care how she got back, so long as she could lie in bed and try to forget this night. Isaac helped Jonny into the cart, while Harry led Portia to another carriage.

She sat quiet, numb even, as Harry took the long way back, driving through the quiet evening streets of Lebanon. The back of her hand stung, so she rubbed at it absently, wondering what Beau thought of her savagery. Worse yet, she couldn't squash her feeling of satisfaction — *oh, how good it felt to smack that blonde peacock* — but oh, how wrong of her to feel that way. When they reached the road leading to the Stanford's place, Harry broke the silence.

"I'm sorry, Po. If you ask me, Beau is a fool, and Lydia's past due for a good beating. She's all fluff and no substance. Good for a poke or two, but not a lifetime commitment. Know what I mean? Her money's attractive, all right, but he can turn this farm around if he'd just give it some time."

She didn't answer — what was there to say, anyway? *What's done is done.*

They pulled up to the house, and he helped her out of the carriage. She started to pull away from him, but he kept hold of her hand.

"I'm tired," she said, avoiding the angry fire in his eyes. "I want to go inside."

"Po, listen to me." He released her hand and captured her upper arms instead, pulling her close. "I know you think he felt something for you, but let's face it. You don't have what he wants. You need someone who understands what it's like to have nothing. Me and you — we could set out on our own and make something of ourselves."

"Harry, I—"

He smashed his lips against hers. She tried to wriggle free, but his fingers became cold, hard shackles. The horse whinnied, and the carriage rattled when he pushed her against it, kissing her wildly. His wet tongue probed her tightly closed lips, digging up things she wished she could scrape from her mind. *"You such a pretty girl."* Whiskey and body odor, her daddy's hands locked around her neck, a shock of pain, bawling her eyes out, trapped under a hundred eighty pounds of dead weight.

Portia jerked her head to the side and broke free of his mouth. "Let me go!" Bringing her hands to his chest, she tried to shove him away, but to no avail.

"Damn it, Po. You still want him, don't you? Even after tonight." The fury in his voice and the beastly glint in his eyes fueled her courage. She would be *no* man's whore, not again.

"I don't know what I want," she screamed, "but I know I don't want *you*!"

With that, she lifted one foot behind her, drew back her knee and brought it full force between his legs. He made a strangled sound and released her. She took off, making it onto the porch as he cupped his crotch with both hands and fell to his knees.

She threw open the door to see Bessie there and let out a startled scream.

"Honey, what's wrong?" The question had barely left her lips before she looked outside over Portia's shoulder, her face contorting with horror. "Dear Lord, what's he done to you?"

She couldn't answer, not with her throat constricted and eyes burning. Fisting her skirts in both hands, she sprinted up the stairs and into her room. Her pillow caught the night's burdens, and she cried until there were no tears left, until she couldn't breathe. She cried alone, like she'd done every day since Jake and Abby died.

Always alone.

Chapter Twenty-Four

Still in the borrowed dress that once belonged to Claire Stanford, Portia sat on the edge of the bed in her darkened room. No more tears, no anything really, except emptiness. Harry, horrible as he acted tonight, was right about one thing. She had nothing Beau wanted. Leaning over, she rested her elbows on her knees and covered her face with both hands. She should have listened to Frank and Ellen, should never have come to Lebanon. She came to escape the pain, not to accumulate more.

There was a soft knock on the door and dim yellow light beneath it. "Portia, honey," Bessie asked gently. "Can I come in?"

Portia got up, went to the door, and opened it. Stepping back, she let Bessie in. The older woman set the lamp down on the bedside table and turned to Portia, arms open wide. Portia accepted her hug, resting her chin on Bessie's shoulder. She smelled like flour and thyme and wood smoke. She smelled like Mama.

"Did Harry hurt you, child?"

Portia shook her head.

"I don't know what's gotten into *him*, but Ezra told me about what happened at the party. Jonny's asleep now. He was pretty upset about it, too. But there's somethin' I want you to know."

"What?" Portia stepped out of Bessie's embrace.

"Honey, Beau ain't marryin' Lydia because he wants to. He's doin' it to buy Lucy, Tipp, and Sallie Mae's freedom."

As Bessie told her the whole story, Portia sank onto the bed, trying to take it all in.

"I know you're hurt, but I know my Beau wouldn't marry that girl unless he had no other choice. We asked him to help, and that must have been the only option he had at the time. That don't make it any better on you, but try not to hate him. He loves you, else he wouldn't have let you anywhere near that dress."

"But... why did he want me there when he knew I would hear the big announcement?"

"I doubt he knew it was gonna be announced in public, probably thought it would be kept quiet. He ought to have known better. Dealin' with Oliver Clemons is like handlin' a rattlesnake. Ain't a question of *if* he'll bite you. It's when." She sat on the bed beside Portia. "I think Beau wanted you there because you make him feel like Claire used to. I can see it every time he looks at you."

Portia glided her hands across the lavender skirt of the dress. "I'll miss you, Bessie."

The older woman broke into tears and wiped her eyes with her apron. "I'll miss you too, honey, I'll miss you too."

Before Bessie left her room, Portia said, "One more thing."

"Yes?"

"Don't tell anyone about Harry and what happened tonight. Emotions were high, and I think he just got carried away."

Bessie frowned but finally nodded and closed the door behind her. Portia changed into her nightgown, hung the beautiful lavender dress on the wardrobe, and lay on her bed admiring it. Ever since Jake died, she'd imagined *him* lying beside her, holding her tight. It was Beau she pictured now, and as much as she wanted to hate him, his sacrifice made her love him even more.

Morning dawned, and Portia got up to greet it. She woke Jonny and told him to get dressed. Ten minutes later, they surprised Bessie in the kitchen.

"My goodness, you two's up early for a Saturday," she said brightly, but Portia could tell her joyful tone was for Jonny's sake.

"It's time for my riding lesson," Portia said. "We thought we would take advantage of the lovely weather and make it a full day." Knowing she couldn't say much with Jonny there, she added, "How are Lucy and Sallie Mae? Any better?"

"They're coming around but will be at our place until the sickness passes."

Portia nodded. Lucy and Sallie Mae were taking refuge for now, maybe until after the wedding. She couldn't blame them. As hard as life had been for her, Portia couldn't imagine what poor Lucy had been through.

Bessie put her hands on her hips as Jonny stuffed a bite of steaming biscuit in his mouth then danced around, fanning his burnt tongue with his hand.

"Serves ya right, bein' all greedy like that." She pumped him a cup of fresh water, which he drank down in three gulps.

"Thanks," he said and wiped his mouth on his sleeve.

Portia smiled at him. "Why don't we take a few biscuits and some jam with us and enjoy breakfast down by the creek?"

"Sounds like a nice day," Bessie said, but her lip quivered before she turned away to fetch their supplies. "You two go and have fun now, you hear?"

"We will, and thank you," Portia said.

She took the small food basket from Bessie and followed Jonny outside. They headed to their favorite spot under the big cedar down by the creek. After they'd eaten their fill, they waded ankle-deep in the cool water. Jonny giggled at the minnows nibbling his toes.

He looked up at her. "Ready for a ride?" His eyes held a bittersweet sadness that tore at Portia's heart.

"Ready as I'll ever be. You're a pretty good riding instructor, you know."

"Thanks, Po. I guess when I'm your age, I won't have anything else to learn."

"Well, I'm not *that* old." She laughed. "But if you never remember anything else I've taught you," she said as they sat on the bank and dried their feet in the warm sunshine, "remember that we never stop being students.

Every day we are granted is an opportunity to learn something new."

"I'll remember. Always," he said.

It was midnight before the party died down, and Beau couldn't remember half of it. The look on Portia's face as she heard the news kept repeating in his mind. He didn't blame her one bit for slapping the daylights out of Lydia — he hadn't heard the words they exchanged, but felt certain they weren't pretty. *Damn Oliver and his spoiled brat daughter.* Beau had promised to go through with the wedding, and Oliver had promised to keep it quiet until then, have a simple ceremony and be done with it. Of course, that part wasn't in the contract.

No doubt Oliver had planned it that way the whole time — to make sure everyone in Lebanon, including Portia, knew that he was marrying Lydia Clemons. A small wedding would never do for his socialite fiancée. His life sentence would be public knowledge from here on out.

Harry and Ezra didn't say a thing over breakfast, didn't even look at him. Both of them gobbled down their food and left without a word to work out in the fields. Beau was glad, because he was in no mood for Ezra's lectures or Harry's bullshit.

Unfortunately, Ezra caught him in the barn as he gathered hammer and nails to repair the shutters.

His pipe bobbed from his mouth as he fussed. "What were you thinking, Beauregard?"

"I'm doing what you wanted me to, that's what."

"I never wanted you to marry someone you don't love."

"Why not? Shit, Pa, look at this place." Hammer in hand, he gestured around them. "It's falling apart. Everything we've worked for, everything *you've* worked for is going to hell and this is the only way I can turn it around. Besides…"

"Besides what?"

"Never mind. I've got work to do." He hated keeping secrets from his own father, but this time, he had to. Word couldn't get out about the contract he had signed, or Oliver might make good on his threats. He couldn't risk anything else happening to his family because of him.

"I guess you know Portia and Jonny are out riding. She loves that boy, Beauregard, and he loves her too. He didn't tear up her dress."

"How do *you* know that? Did he tell you? He sure as hell ain't told me anything."

"Have you given him a chance? You're not even around him long enough to have a conversation should he start talking."

Beau's shoulders tensed so much his wound threw a current of pain down his arm. The hammer fell to the stable floor. He bent down, snatched it up, and brushed by Pa without a word. "I told you I have work to do. I don't have time to argue."

"Fine, but you've broken Po's heart. And there ain't no amount of nails can put it back together." He exhaled a puff of smoke, turned around, and walked back toward the house.

Beau took the ladder down from the hook. Ezra's disappointment hurt more than the constant ache in his shoulder. The old man had no idea how much he longed for things to be different. In another time and place, he might have been able to follow his heart and marry the woman he truly loved. He might have been able to look at and talk to his son without feeling like a complete failure.

Fighting against a knot in his throat, he clambered up the ladder beneath one of the barn's sagging shutters. Staying busy was the only outlet he had to keep from losing his mind again. He pried up one corner of a shutter, started on another, and dropped the crowbar. It landed on the dirt below with a thud.

"Damn it!"

He made his way down the ladder, and his feet had just hit the ground when he heard Portia's frantic call. "Beau!"

Peering in the direction of her voice, he finally saw Jonny leading Jack up the hill, with Portia walking her saddle horse beside him. Jack was limping. *Not good.*

Beau met them halfway. "What happened?"

"Snake. Just a big old rat snake, but it scared Jack, and he threw Jonny," Portia said.

"Are you all right, son?"

Jonny nodded and with a trembling hand, pointed to Jack's right front leg.

"He got his foot stuck in some roots," Portia said, dread filling her words as though she expected the worst.

Beau bent down to take a look. As he feared, it was broken just below the knee. He took the reins and led the pony slowly to the stable and into an empty stall.

Jonny followed and stood in the doorway. His chin quivered. His eyes brimmed with fearful tears. It reminded Beau of the day he had returned from the war, how he had shaken Jonny and screamed those awful things at him before falling to his knees at Claire's grave.

Eyes squeezed tight against the memory, he spoke over his shoulder to Portia. "Take Jonny back to the house. I'll take care of the horses."

Jonny ran in and hugged Jack's neck. He buried his head in the pony's mane and bawled, shoulders jumping with each sob.

Beau stepped out of the stall and gestured for Portia to follow. They walked just outside the barn. Wind whipped some loose strands of hair over her face. She brushed it back but never took her eyes off his.

"You've got to take him back inside," he said.

"He knows what you're going to do. Comfort him, Beau. Explain it to him."

"I can't," he said through clenched teeth. "I can't let him watch me... just take him to the house."

"Stop underestimating him. He understands life and death, but what he doesn't understand is why his father won't talk to him, why you won't tell him you love him, and that you're proud of him."

Beau closed his eyes and scrubbed a hand over his face. "What do you want me to say, Po? That every time I look at him, I think about the day I came home, and it tears me up inside? That I'm marrying his mama's spoiled cousin because I'm too damned broke to do anything else?"

"Yes," she said, her voice rising and fists clenched at her sides. "Yes, all that, and tell him you won't send him away."

"What are you talking about?"

"Jonny heard Lydia and her mother talking about sending him to military school."

"He told you this?"

"Yes, he's been talking to me for some time now."

Deep down he knew all along, but the truth hurt more than he thought it would. His son was talking to a woman he'd only known a short while but not to his own father, who'd held him seconds after he was born.

"I suppose I should be grateful to you, then, but that's ridiculous. He's not going to military school. It's not part of the deal," Beau said.

"Really? What better way to ensure she's got you all to herself?" Her voice broke, though her chest heaved in an effort to stay calm. "I'll leave willingly, right now if you want me to, but promise me you won't let them send him away. He needs you, Beau, now more than ever. Please promise me that."

The gunshot startled them both. Beau ran into the barn and to the open stall, Portia on his heels. Jonny stood over Jack's body, which lay still and quiet on the hay. He cried so hard the gun quaked in his arms.

Beau reached out carefully, snatched the gun, and tossed it into the corner. He engulfed Jonny in his arms. He held his little boy, the only thing he had left of Claire, and cried with him for the first time since she died.

He cradled Jonny's head against his chest. The dam of emotions separating them crumbled, and all the things

315

he'd wanted to tell him for so long came spilling out. "You're not going anywhere, you hear me? This is where you belong, right here with me. I love you, son. I love you more than anything in this world."

Jonny whispered through his tears, "I love you, too, Pa. I'm sorry I shot Jack."

Beau took Jonny's arms and held him out far enough so he could see his face. *He spoke to me. Jonny finally spoke to me.* His voice was the most precious music Beau had ever heard.

Smiling through his tears, Beau hugged Jonny close once more. "You did what had to be done. I'm so proud of you, and I'm sorry for ever leaving you in the first place. I'm sorry I haven't been the daddy you deserve. Will you forgive me?"

Jonny nodded against his chest. "I forgive you, and I'm proud of you, too."

Beau dried both their tears with his shirt sleeve and helped Jonny to his feet. He looked up, but Portia was gone, hopefully not for good. He thanked God for letting her walk into their lives, if only for a little while. He prayed that somehow he could find a way to let her stay before it was too late.

Chapter Twenty-Five

Portia opened the front door, sorrowful that her day with Jonny had to end so soon, but at least she had witnessed a reuniting of father and son. She could leave right now with her broken heart and feel good about that one thing.

She stepped inside to see a bearded man rising from where he sat at the bottom of the stairs. His clothes were baggy, cheeks sunken in, like those poor soldiers who once sought her help. Startled, she backed toward the door, but he smiled… and he looked just like Mama.

Just like Mama!

Portia clapped a hand over her mouth and cautiously approached him. She reached out with one hand to touch those loose brown curls she used to caress to get him to sleep at night during thunderstorms.

He brought her hand to his lips, and kissed her palm. "Po, my God, you're a woman now!"

"Samuel, is it really you?"

"In the flesh." He'd picked up a lazy sort of accent that was difficult to interpret.

"How did you find me?"

"I came back home, and you weren't there. Wasn't nobody there. I saw the graves and I feared something had happened to you. I hurried to Frank and Ellen's place and they told me what happened and where you were."

"Is that right?" She yanked her hand away and slapped him with it.

Eyes wide, he took a step back. "What was that for?"

"For making me think you were dead all these years. No letters, no visits, nothing. Mama and Daddy…"

"I know," he whispered. "I'm so sorry, Po. I did write that one letter."

She raised her hand to slap him again.

He captured her hands in his before she could give him the beating he deserved. "The woman I wrote about in the letter — the Creole woman. Her name was Vivienne, and I married her. When the war started, I joined up with Pemberton's forces in Louisiana and fought at Vicksburg. The Yanks captured me, and I sat in prison for months."

He wasn't lying. He had never looked her in the eye when he lied, like he did now, brown eyes as serious and sad as they had been when the two of them used to hide from Daddy in the cornfields.

"And your… Vivienne?" It was hard to imagine her little brother with a wife.

"Dead. Buried. Long before I could return to her. So, I started back home. I had to work along the way to keep myself fed, else I'd have been back sooner. I'm sorry, Po. Can you find it in your heart to forgive me?"

She stood there looking at him for a moment, at that manly, hairy face. Her little prodigal brother, the only blood kin she had left in this world, had returned.

Throwing her arms around him, she cried happy tears for a change. "I've missed you so much! Don't you ever leave me again."

Laughing, he lifted her off the floor and spun her around. "Just you try to get rid of me, sis. I'll be like a wart on your toe."

Dinner time felt surreal, like a bizarre dream. There was Beau at the head of the table — the man she loved dearly but couldn't have. To his right sat his father Ezra, a man who'd been a better father to her in the short time she'd been here than her own daddy had ever been. To Beau's left was Jonny, whom she loved like her own child. He had scooted his chair as close to his pa as he could, and the two of them whispered and conspired with one another like she imagined they had done before the war. Harry, a man who made her feel uneasy and guilty at the same time, sat across the table from her.

And there was Samuel, whom she thought had been dead all these years, sitting beside her, solid and real, and very much alive.

Samuel's appearance fascinated everyone, even Beau, who set his usual scowl on him. Ezra asked about the battle of Vicksburg, and Samuel went into great detail about it — the destruction, the siege, and near starvation. Portia took her brother's hand as he spoke, moved to tears by his account. She'd always be his big sister, would always want to comfort him, even if she couldn't take away his pain.

Harry held a piece of cornbread, crumbling it into little pieces. His half-angry, half-wounded gaze fell on Portia, but he addressed her brother. "So, Samuel, what's New Orleans like?"

"I think I can answer that…" Samuel finished up his third piece of chicken, licked his fingers, and peeked under the table. "Bet you a nickel I can tell you where you got them shoes you're wearin'." He slid a nickel — which mysteriously appeared in his hand — across the table toward Harry.

Harry glanced down at his feet, looking confused at first, but then he dug inside his vest pocket. Slapping a nickel on the table, he said, "I'm in."

"On your feet," Samuel declared with a victorious grin. "You got 'em on your feet, that's where." He snatched up both nickels and laughed. "That's what New Orleans is like, my friend. You gotta be clever if you want to get a leg up down there."

"I think I'm gonna like you," Harry said and stuffed what was left of his cornbread in his mouth.

After dinner, Portia and Samuel walked arm-in-arm down the wagon path that wound along the back fields. The setting sun painted a lovely orange and red sky on the horizon. Fireflies woke up, greeting each other with green twinkling lights as they rose from the tender new blades of hay and corn.

"Tell me just this one thing," Portia said. "Why did you leave us?"

"I often ask myself that same question. At the time, I thought maybe Daddy would calm down if I wasn't there. Every time he drank, I was the first one to feel his belt across my back. I thought maybe if I was gone, you and Mama would be better off."

"You were wrong."

He stopped walking and asked quietly, "How bad was it, Po?"

Portia couldn't look at him. A tight knot lodged itself in her throat. "It was bad, Sam. He…" She couldn't finish.

Samuel drew her against his chest and held her tight. "I'm sorry. I was still a boy back then and didn't have the mind to think things through. But I shouldn't have left, not without you. What about Mama? Did he hurt her bad, too?"

Portia pulled away and resumed their walk, brushing the tears off her cheeks. The memories were hard to put to words, but he needed to know what they'd lived through. "Mama took the most of it. I got strong enough to fight back and busted a whiskey bottle across his face one night. He didn't dare touch me after that. I stayed to protect her, though. She begged me to marry Jake and get out of there, not that she had to beg, mind you. I'd loved him my whole life."

"I miss that boy. He could shoot a squirrel dead in the eye every time we hunted." His voice grew somber. "Tell me about Abigail."

"She reminded me of you, with those curls and her independent spirit." It felt strange to smile while she talked about Abby. She never thought the day would come. "She was always climbing, dancing, being as silly as she could to get a laugh out of us. I wish you could have seen her."

"I wish I could have, too. The last letter I got from you was about the fire."

"Jake and I hadn't been married very long. I'll never know for sure, but I think Mama did it. She waited until I got out of the house so she could end it once and for all."

"I shoulda come back. I shoulda been here. For you."

"All that matters now is that you're home and safe."

"I'll look after you from now on, Po, like a brother should."

She rested her head on his arm, and he wept as they walked, not bothering to wipe the tears away. They turned around after a little while, and he pulled a French harp from his pocket. The melancholy notes of *Au Claire de la Lune* followed them until they reached their temporary home.

Beau couldn't sleep, not that he'd planned on it. He sat on the edge of his bed, thinking about Portia. She occupied most of his thoughts these days, no matter how hard he tried to redirect his mind. Her brother's miraculous return troubled him — not that he wasn't happy for her, but it made her imminent departure more real. Samuel would probably take her back to Brentwood and take care of her until she found someone else to marry.

Someone else.

Damp-smelling wind whistled through the trees and his window, bringing with it the promise of rain and sending a hot shiver down his spine. The mere thought of Po with another man and how that man would know her as intimately as Beau longed to know her... it tore at him, complicated things more than ever. He got to his feet, strode to his window, and slammed it shut. Standing there with his hands on the sill, he looked over his shoulder when his door creaked open.

"Pa?" Jonny poked his head inside. "I can't sleep."

Beau turned to him and couldn't help a smile. "You either, huh? Want me to read to you?"

"Can I... sleep in here with you?" He held his pillow under one arm, ducking his head as though embarrassed to ask such a thing.

"Sure."

Beau turned down the covers, and Jonny climbed in, settling down on what once was Claire's side of the bed. Beau lay down beside him, covered them both, and kissed Jonny's forehead.

"Goodnight, son."

"Pa?"

"Yes?"

"Would you think I was a baby if we slept back to back? Mama and me used to sleep like that sometimes."

"You're not a baby, and I don't mind."

Beau flipped to his left side and scooted to the middle of the bed, while Jonny did the same on the other side until their backs settled against one another.

"Thanks, Pa."

"You're welcome."

"Pa?"

"Yes?"

"Do you think Jack's in Heaven?"

"I don't know, son, but if God lets animals in, I think Jack would be there."

"Do you think Mama's in Heaven?"

Beau lay silent for a moment, fearing the knot in his throat would betray his voice. He needed to be strong for Jonny, had to be strong for him. His son had been too long without him being there, *really* there like a pa should be.

Finally, he answered, "I have no doubt she's there. Your mama was the kindest, most loving woman in the world."

"Do you love Lydia?"

Jonny's questions were harder to face than being on the front lines of a cavalry. But he had to try. His son deserved to know these things. "No."

"Then why are you marrying her?"

"Because I made a promise so Tipp, Lucy, and your friend Sallie Mae can be free."

"What about Po? Will she have to go away?"

Damn, this is hard. Heaviness settled in his chest, squeezing the air from his lungs, and dampening his eyes. "I don't know yet, but yes, she probably will."

"I wish you could marry Po instead."

"So do I, son. So do I."

Beau didn't know if it was a good idea to admit that much. But there in the darkness of his room, just father and son, it felt good to express some of what he felt for the little woman with nothing to her name who'd walked into their lives and brought him and Jonny back together.

Jonny yawned, wriggled around a bit, and fell asleep. It didn't take Beau long to follow, with his son's small, warm body nestled against him. His thoughts painted pictures of him, Portia, and Jonny, all together, relaxing on the banks of Barton Creek. They rode through the tall, majestic cedars before gazing in awe at a small bundle of joy wrapped in a warm blanket.

He smiled as he drifted into the best sleep he'd had in a long time.

Chapter Twenty-Six

May 16,1866
Dear Ellen,

Wedding preparations are causing a ruckus in the household. Miss Clemons and her mother have been coming every day for one thing or another. First, to discuss new décor that 'signifies our new beginning' she said. Yesterday, they arrived with a seamstress to be fitted for her wedding gown. Of course, they had all the measurements done right there in the entry hall for everyone to see. They've set the date for June 2. The children and I have taken refuge outside for our studies. Thankfully, the weather is pleasant enough.

Sallie Mae is still coming for lessons. Isaac fetches her each morning. I wish she and Lucy hadn't returned to Mr. Clemons so soon, but he insisted. Bessie told me Mr. Stanford is going there every night to make certain Lucy has no new bruises. I hope for her sake that Mr. Clemons will be merciful. I admire Beau for caring so much about her wellbeing.

Samuel (and oh, I am so glad he is here!) joined the men in cutting down trees from a wooded portion of the property. He has befriended the owner of the local sawmill and has negotiated use of the mill to process the lumber for Mr. Stanford. He says he is 'happy as a clam at high tide' to be working in exchange for his food and board. He also says he will ask about more work so he can get a little money saved. Then he and I can return to Brentwood and start over. Last night, however, he was out late with Harry and didn't come home until after I had retired. He whispered, "Night, Po," through my door, and he sounded as if he had been drinking. I hope he will not make this a habit…

The very same day, a letter arrived from Ellen. She'd had her baby. By now he would be a week old. Portia's eyes welled with bittersweet tears as she read.

We named him Jake. I hope you don't mind. His head is covered in red-blond fuzz, the same color as his uncle's hair. He's a hungry little thing and eats round the clock, but he's got rosy cheeks and is getting plumper every day. I'm thankful Mama's here to help. Even Louise is doing what she can, though she can barely handle a broom. She's getting good at changing diapers. I hope you will come visit soon, Po. We miss you something awful…

Nothing could dampen Portia's joy over the news. She would plan a visit soon, her and Samuel. For the first time since she'd arrived in Lebanon, she wanted to go back home, just to see those familiar faces and hear their voices, to kiss the sweet little one that bore her husband's name.

On Thursday morning, during breakfast, Beau tossed his napkin on his plate. He stood up, brushed his hands together, and announced, "Jonny, get the fishing poles. I feel like trout for dinner!"

"Sure, Pa, I'll go right now!" Jonny smiled from ear to ear and tripped over his own two feet. He couldn't get out the door fast enough.

Portia feigned indignation. "And what of our lessons, Mr. Stanford? We are discussing the riveting Magna Carta and its contribution to constitutional law."

Beau laughed. "When we need a good nap, we'll be sure to return and be lulled into sleep."

She turned up her nose and harrumphed. But she couldn't hide the joy on her face.

From the front porch, she watched them leave. Jonny sat on one of the saddle horses, and Beau on Scout, fishing poles bouncing on their shoulders. Lydia came around the side of the house with a gardener just then, pointing at bushes and flower beds and talking a mile a minute. The poor gardener hastily scribbled on a notebook, trying to keep up with her orders.

Before Beau and Jonny got too far, Beau turned back, rode up to the porch and removed his hat. His face — relaxed and happy — reminded Portia of the man she had seen in the photograph on her first day there.

He put his hat to his chest, and with a quick bow of his head, he said, "Thank you, Po, for everything."

After Beau rode off, Lydia tore her ferocious glare from Portia and directed all her wrath on the gardener, yelling, "I don't care if it's not the right climate for delphiniums. You're the plant expert. Figure out how to make them grow!"

Portia hid her smile as she retreated inside. She lived on Beau's words the rest of the day, but she felt sorry for that gardener.

She couldn't help worrying about her brother, though. Harry and Samuel had become quite the pair, working on the farm together, heading into town in the afternoons and playing cards in the evening. Portia wasn't sure how she should feel about that, but at least Harry didn't pursue her anymore, and Samuel seemed happy to have a friend.

Friday after lunch, she sat with Sam on the front porch for a little while. Rain poured down from a juvenile cloud — one of many that provided scattered showers that day. They both rested their heads on the backs of the rockers, enjoying the momentary solitude and soft shushing of the rain.

"Harry says you're in love with Beau," Sam said, shattering their peaceful silence.

Portia stopped rocking, sat up straight, and looked around them. Luckily no one was visible, and hopefully no one was in earshot. "Don't say such things, Sam, not out here in the open like this."

"I've seen you look at him. You used to get all googly eyed over Jake like that when we was youngins."

She gave another quick scan of their surroundings. No one else stirred. She sighed and slumped back into her rocking chair. Just above a whisper, she turned her head toward Sam and asked, "Is it that obvious?"

"Is a frog's ass watertight?"

She chuckled. "Got me. But it doesn't matter what I feel. He's marrying Lydia Clemons."

"Then I oughta wring his neck for you." He actually sounded angry, unusual for the Sam who never took things seriously.

"While the sentiment's flattering, that's not necessary. Besides, he doesn't have a choice in the matter."

"Why not? She got his balls held hostage or something?"

She had to laugh at that one, but she realized she couldn't tell Sam all the details. "It's a long story. Have you found work yet?"

"Ain't much to be had around here, Po. I think we should consider going to Nashville. Should be easier to find a job there. I could put us up in a boarding house until we get enough saved up to find our own place. You could probably find a better teaching job, too, one that actually pays."

"Maybe you're right." Much as she hated to admit it, no matter how much she loved this house and no matter how much she loved Beau, Jonny, Ezra, Bessie, Isaac, and Sallie Mae, she didn't belong there. Their lives were meant to flow along different courses.

She reached across the space between her and her little brother and took his hand. He squeezed hers in return and gave her a reassuring smile. At least she had Sam.

At dinner that night, Beau had somehow managed to avoid Lydia's company and joined them. Samuel and Harry were late to the table, stumbling in while laughing about something. They plopped in their chairs and started digging in.

Portia stared in disbelief. "Samuel Joseph Sullivan! Are you drunk?"

"Not nearly as much as I'd like to be." He scratched his beard and snickered.

Harry chomped down on some potatoes, cheek rounded out like a chipmunk, and grinned at Beau, who looked like he could strangle him then and there.

Samuel tried to take Portia's hand, and she snatched it away. "Look, sis, I ain't had a drink in months. Harry and I are just havin' a little fun."

"You could have been here working, like the rest of us."

He didn't seem fazed by that and gulped down his water. "Guess who I met?"

Portia sighed. "I give up. Who?"

"Aw, you're no fun. I met an Irishman, some fella who wants to teach colored children."

Drunk or not, everyone paused to listen.

Samuel continued, "I told him my sister's a teacher and that she's teachin' a little colored kid."

"Jonny, get upstairs." Beau waited for the boy to leave the room and then slammed his fist on the table. "What kind of a fool are you? You can't talk like that in public — think about your sister, for God's sake!"

Beau's outburst both surprised and flattered Portia. He must have felt *something* for her if he was that worried about her safety.

"I *am* thinkin' about my sister." Sam turned to Portia, looking decidedly sober. "The man says they're lookin' for teachers to work in their new colored school and he's real interested in meetin' you. He says they got a nice one bein' built in Nashville. And they pay good, Po. Better than what you're gettin' here."

With that last jab, he stared right at Beau, who spoke quietly, but firmly. "I've given her all I can. I don't see you doing any better, out getting drunk instead of working like a real man should."

Portia tried to calm her brother by putting a hand on his chest, but Samuel threw his napkin down on his plate and yelled, "A real man would have figured out a way to be with my sister instead of givin' in to a spoiled little bitch!"

Beau stood up so fast he knocked his chair to the floor. He left the room without a word. Ezra shook his head and followed him out.

"How could you?" Portia said to her brother, not caring that Harry was still there, enjoying the show.

"It's the truth and you know it," Sam said, pointing his finger at her face.

"Truth or not, you have no business coming here just to dally around town all day, get drunk, and then disrespect the man who's letting you stay here for free. You haven't changed, Samuel. Not in the least."

She pushed away from the table and headed for the door.

"Come on, sis, I didn't mean it. I just want you to be happy, that's all."

"Really? Well, you have a lousy way of showing it. Enjoy your dinner, both of you. I'm going to bed."

She reached the stairs and heard Harry calling out with feigned innocence, "Night, Po…"

Though she hated herself for thinking it, part of her wished Samuel had never returned.

Portia abandoned any hope of sleeping after lying there watching the moon rise and listening to the crickets sing. She got up, quietly opened her door, and padded barefoot down the hall. First, she checked on Jonny. He lay on his back, arm hanging off the bed, snoring softly. Smiling, she eased his door shut and tiptoed down the stairs.

May had granted them some very agreeable weather, and the nights were splendid — comfortably cool with gentle breezes. Perfect for clearing the mind. And right now her mind dwelled on what Samuel told her about the Irishman. Nashville wasn't more than a rock's throw from there, but it might as well have been a world away.

Silently as she could, she stepped onto the front porch and stopped short. The silhouette of a man sat at the top of the steps. It took her only a moment to realize it was Beau.

He turned and smiled. "Can't sleep either, huh?"

"No."

He patted the space beside him, and she sat, drawing her knees up to her chin and pulling her gown over her legs.

"Samuel was right," he said.

"About what?"

"About me."

She shook her head. "No, he wasn't. You're doing what you think is right."

"Am I? Or am I taking the selfish way out? If I marry her, I'll get Lucy and Tipp freed and..." He hesitated, rubbing the back of his neck. "I'll also get out of debt. I don't know which one of those really matters most to me."

He locked eyes with her. A storm of grief darkened his face, like his honesty could make her hate him forever. Portia wanted so badly to wrap her arms around him, but she hugged her knees instead.

"Then tell me something..." She was afraid to ask, but the question dangled between them like a loose thread. "...would you still have married her if Lucy and Tipp didn't need help?"

Taking a deep breath, he ran a hand through his hair. "No. I admit, when she first arrived, it was tempting — she looked so much like Claire, I couldn't help... you know... looking at her." He glanced at Portia with a shameful smile. "But it didn't take long to see she resembled Claire in looks alone. They both came from money, but Claire was the kindest, most unselfish woman I had ever known. She fit into fine society, but she wasn't bound to it, and she wasn't ruined by it. No, Lydia's nothing like Claire, and she's nothing like you."

Portia swallowed hard and stared up at the moon. "I'll be fine. I've survived this long, haven't I? As long as Jonny's happy, I'll be fine."

"No one's gonna take my son from me. Not over my dead body."

"That's all I need to hear."

He was quiet for a while before he said, "You should take that job in Nashville. No one would be better suited for it, and... you'll be safer there."

"What do you mean?"

Staring into the darkened distance, his eyes flashed and jaw clenched with anger. "I didn't want to worry you, but

334

Oliver threatened to hurt everyone I love if I don't uphold my end of the contract."

"I'm not afraid of that snake."

He turned his head, locking his worried eyes on hers. "You should be. And I'm sorry I'm not man enough to do anything about it." With a heavy sigh, he slumped onto his knees, head hanging low.

His anguish squeezed her chest and brought tears to her eyes. She longed to touch him but didn't know if it would make things better or worse, so she hugged her knees even tighter. "You *are* a good man, Beau Stanford. It's Oliver and the war we have to blame for all this. We're forced to make choices we never had to before. Sam and I will go to Nashville. We'll find work and make a home there. You'll marry Lydia and be happy again. She'll give you more children, and Jonny will grow up to be a fine man. We will survive, Beau."

"You really believe that?"

"I have to."

He reached over and picked up a lock of her hair, running his fingers gently along its length. "I wish…"

Her heart raced — he was so close, just a breath away. "You wish what?"

"That I could have kissed you just once." He slowly let go of her hair and watched it fall over her shoulder.

Her cheeks flamed, hidden only by the dimness of night. She knew kissing Beau Stanford was beyond a bad idea. It could only tear her heart into a million more pieces, but he was everything she admired in a man. Kind, honest… vulnerable. He had no reason to love her. She could bring nothing to their marriage. Yet there he was, confessing his love in the most tender, innocent way he could. For once in her life, she didn't want to weigh and measure every decision in her path. She wanted to follow her heart.

"If no one's watching, then no one can care," she whispered, letting go of her knees until her feet rested on the next step.

Beau drew closer and lifted his hand to her chin, gently tilting it upward. Portia held her breath and closed her eyes as his lips gently met hers. She reached up and caressed his face, needing to feel his skin, his stubble, the strong jaw and square chin she'd come to love so much. The kiss was time-stopping and heartbreaking at the same time, like those she had once read about in fairy tales, like those she had once shared with Jake.

He pulled away, but they held to one another, resting their foreheads together. It was a goodbye kiss, though neither of them had the heart to name it as such. Tears found their familiar paths down Portia's cheeks, and Beau wiped them away with his thumbs.

Finally, he let her go and stood. He held out his hand to help her up, when Harry came bursting out the door.

"Oh God," he cried. "It's Sam. He's... he's not breathing."

Chapter Twenty-Seven

They ran after Harry and to his room beneath the stairs. Samuel lay prone on the floor beside the bed. Portia rushed to him and fell to her knees. His eyes were open, but vacant. Foamy liquid ran from his mouth. His lips were blue.

"What happened to him?" Beau looked at Harry, who stood there shaking all over and biting down on his fist. He didn't answer.

"Sam, Sam, wake up!" Portia shook him. Leaning close to his face, she was still for a moment before moving her ear to his chest. She sat up again, shaking him harder, slapping his cheeks. "No, no, please wake up, please!"

Beau dropped to his knees beside her and checked for a pulse on Sam's neck. Nothing. He confirmed Portia's fears with a shake of his head. She broke down with wracking sobs, and he gathered her in his arms.

Wild-eyed Harry fisted his hair and frantically looked from Beau to Samuel. Then Beau spotted it — the green velvet box, lying open on Harry's bed, and the syringe lying beside it. On Samuel's arm was an innocent-looking red dot and a raised vein trailing from it.

Holding Portia tight as she cried for her dead brother, he looked up at Harry and said, "Get out."

"Beau, I didn't—"

"I said get out!" Beau roared, scaring Portia into silence. "And don't you ever show your face here again."

Harry grabbed the syringe, the box, and a bottle on the dresser and threw them in a bag along with some clothes. He gave Beau one last look over his shoulder — in his eyes a war raged between hatred, betrayal, and shame. Pa and Jonny stood in the doorway. They must have come to see what all the fuss was about. Harry shoved past them, almost knocking Pa over.

The old man clutched the door frame to right himself and finally saw Samuel. "God help us."

The clock struck half past midnight. Pa had taken Jonny to bed not long after it happened and had stayed with Portia until Beau could fetch the undertaker, who was down there now, preparing the body. Beau went to his bedroom and pulled one of Claire's mourning dresses from his chest. He'd rather see Po in anything but this. The dress was well-made, of course, complete with matching veil, gloves, and feathered fan, but all the lace in the world couldn't hide its purpose.

Portia's door was open, so he entered her room. She sat limply at her table. "You're trembling."

He hung the mourning dress on the wardrobe. Then he came to her, knelt on one knee, and took her cold hands in his. He brought them to his mouth and blew warm air across her skin then rubbed vigorously.

"Thank you," she whispered.

"The undertaker is here. He brought a nice coffin and will have everything ready soon."

"But how can we…"

"He owes me. Claire took care of his sick wife before she became ill herself." He composed his breaking voice. "I brought you one of her mourning outfits."

She nodded and drew a shaky breath. Seeing her like this, so broken and sad, wounded him more than any bullet ever could.

"I should have kicked Harry out a long time ago," he said. "I knew he had a problem. I knew it would lead to something like this. I thought it would be him, though, not…"

"Shh, it's not your fault." She pulled her hands from his and wrapped her arms around his neck, holding to him in a cheek to cheek embrace.

Beau held her gently, feeling her warm body trembling beneath her nightgown. He kissed her cheek, tasted her salty tears. She pulled her head back slightly, searching his eyes then pressed her lips to his. He froze for a moment then surrendered, pulling her tightly to him, kissing her as deeply as he could. She sighed and clung to him. He hoped with all his might that she took comfort from his touch. With his arms around her, he stood, bringing them both to their feet. Tangling his fingers in her hair, he cradled the nape of her neck in his palm and closed his eyes. God, he wanted her — all of her, and he needed her more every day. He needed her to be part of his life.

But he couldn't bring her brother back…

Reluctantly withdrawing from their kiss, he kept her in his arms and held her against him. She laid her head against his chest. He rubbed her back, feeling the delicate curve of her spine, the hard angles of her shoulder blades. His eyes flitted around her room, and he knew he couldn't keep holding her like that or they might do something they would both regret.

Then his gaze landed on a picture. He'd never really been in Portia's room long enough to notice anything specific. Those eyes… it must have been her late husband, but those eyes of his — stern, yet innocent — he knew those eyes. The memory had been locked away in his smoke-filled nightmares, hidden under grief.

He had once looked into Jake McAllister's eyes.

He had watched him die.

"Oh God, oh God…" Beau pushed himself away from Portia and stumbled out into the hall. He hit the opposite wall, gasping for breath.

"Beau?" She followed him out and held his arms, trying to steady him. "What's wrong?"

She tried to look him in the eyes, but he couldn't bear to see her questioning face. He couldn't bear to tell her now… her brother's body wasn't even cold yet.

"I-I'm fine. Just a dizzy spell, that's all. I'm sorry I scared you." He righted himself and hugged her gently.

"You need something to eat," she said, and her voice had grown stronger. She was a woman who drew strength from taking care of others. And he loved her even more for that.

He let her take his hand and lead him downstairs to the kitchen. But he didn't know if he could ever look her in the eye again, or if he could ever forgive himself.

Numb. Too numb to cry. Too numb to think. By early morning, Portia looked upon her brother's casket through the patterned strangeness of a black veil. Death had followed her, leaving its calling cards of covered mirrors and frozen clock hands. She awaited the undertaker, who would be returning soon with the hearse to take her and Sam back to Brentwood.

She had penned a letter to Ellen as soon as Sam's body was prepared, though her hand had shaken so much she didn't know if it would be legible.

Sam is dead. I am bringing him home.

It would be delivered by the fastest mail runner Beau could find, he said. Not that it mattered. Her ongoing duty in life was writing news of death. Whether the news reached its destination sooner than later didn't change anything.

She had to take Sam back home. She should have never stayed this long. She should have never come there at all. Sam would still be alive if he hadn't come to find her.

"Can I get you anything, Po?" Ezra sat beside her in the parlor. He wore a black suit and had no pipe in hand, which seemed very out of place, just like she and Sam had been.

"I'm fine. Thank you."

She had sat up the rest of the night with Sam's body. Beau didn't leave her side until the morning's funeral business had to be dealt with. He had held her close on the ottoman and let her cry on his shoulder. His smell — a mixture of leather, horses, and man — had coaxed her to sleep for a few brief naps between her crying episodes.

Bessie kept them fed, persuading Portia to eat even though grief's lead ball had returned to her stomach. The Stanfords had taken good care of her, and for that she would be forever grateful. But her life there had turned into a strange, tangled-up thing that she didn't have the strength to separate and mend.

Jonny sat on her other side, solemn and quiet. Beau's voice could be heard from the foyer, diverting visitors so she could grieve in private. It sounded as if they were leaving tokens of condolences, however, for Beau would end their visits with, "Thank you for the flowers. Mrs. McAllister will appreciate them. She will be very touched to know you thought of her in her time of sorrow."

It was probably bad manners to turn people away, but she didn't care. No one there knew Sam, and they barely knew *her*. She didn't feel like playing hostess to gawkers, even though she couldn't rid herself of Lydia and her father. Oliver sat apart from them, talking to a few of the visitors who did manage to get in.

Lydia, of course, had staked her claim on Beau and clung to his arm in the foyer, dabbing her eyes with a lacy black handkerchief. Soon as the latest visitor left, she made her way into the parlor and, to Portia's surprise, knelt in front of her seat.

"I'm so sorry, Portia," Lydia said, and her eyes were surprisingly red, her cheeks moist, as though she really felt sympathy for her rival. "I can't imagine... look, I know it's not much, but I've convinced Daddy to lend you our best coach so you can have a more comfortable ride back to Brentwood."

"Thank you," Portia whispered, though it felt more like Lydia was trying to get rid of her in style rather than offering a gesture of sympathy.

Jonny stood and gestured for Lydia to take his seat, so she did. "Thank you, Jonny," she said, patting his cheek. Turning back to Portia, she took her hand and squeezed it warmly. Portia raised a grief-swollen eyebrow and stared at the blonde beauty in black. Who was this woman who looked as sincere as a true friend? Surely not Lydia Clemons.

But it *was* Lydia's voice that emerged, soft and heartfelt as though they'd been fond of each other for years. "I know that you and I haven't gotten along as well as I intended, and that's my fault, not yours. But you've been good to Jonny, and he admires you so. Would you consider coming back to continue tutoring him? You will be well compensated, I assure you. We could even purchase you your own property and have a nice home built for you."

"I..." Bewildered, Portia didn't really know how to respond. Too many emotions rattled against one another like glassware in a crate with no padding in between. Changing her mind now could cause it to shatter, and she had to keep herself together.

"It's all right," Lydia said. "You don't have to decide anything now. But there's one more thing I must tell you before you depart. Jonny didn't destroy your mother's dress, nor did I. My mother did."

"Polly? But why…"

"For me. She thought you wanted Beau for yourself and didn't want me to be hurt." Lydia looked toward the foyer, where Beau had just admitted another visitor. "She confessed it to me this morning. She felt dreadful when we learned of your brother's passing and couldn't bear to face you, though I begged her to come. But she was wrong for doing it, no matter her intentions. I hope you will accept my apology on her behalf."

Portia wasn't sure exactly how she should feel about Lydia's revelation but said what she thought was appropriate. "She has my forgiveness." For the first time, she saw a kindred spirit in the woman who would marry the man she loved. "I think, had times been different, we could have been friends."

"Perhaps someday we will." Lydia smiled sadly and released her hand.

At the sound of wagon wheels crunching on the drive outside, Portia stood. Her bags were packed. She just had to retrieve them.

Isaac met her in the doorway. "I'll get them, Po."

"You can carry the chest if you want. I'll get my other things."

"All right."

She hated to be responsible for Isaac's kind, happy face being filled with this much despair. He followed her upstairs, and she could feel Beau's eyes on her as she went, but she didn't look back. Once in her room, she took one last look around. Picking up Jake's picture, she held it against her chest. Had he only come home like he promised, none of this would have happened.

"Are you all right, Po?" Jonny asked from her doorway. He stepped aside as Isaac carried out her chest. His eyes were wide and full of worry. "Can I get you something?"

"No, sweet boy, I'm fine," Portia said, trying to smile but finding it incredibly difficult.

Jonny looked past her, his gaze falling on the bags on her bed. "Po?" he asked, lifting his frightened eyes to meet hers. "Are you… leaving?"

Portia hadn't found the courage to tell him. She swallowed past the sudden lump in her throat. "Yes."

"But not for good, right?"

"I'm afraid so."

"Why?"

"Because… your pa's getting married soon and they will want to find a better tutor for you."

He shook his head as tears rolled down his freckled cheeks. "No! No one's better than you."

She tried to smile again as she caressed his cheek. *Help me, Lord.* "That's very kind of you, Jonny, but you're so clever, I don't think there's anything more I can teach you."

"What about Sallie Mae? What about Lydia — she'll send me to military school! Please, Po, don't go!" He rushed forward and hugged her tightly. "I'm sorry about your brother, but please don't go. Please."

Wrapping her arms around him, she rested her chin on his head as they both wept. "I have to, but listen to me." She pushed him back, holding him at arms' length so she could look him in the eye. "Your pa promised me he would never send you away."

Jonny bit his lip, trying to hold in his tears.

"You believe your pa, don't you?" she asked.

Finally, he nodded, but escaped from her grip to hug her tightly again. "I believe him, but I'll still miss you. Can't you stay, just for a few more days?"

Closing her eyes, she rested her head on his and breathed in his little boy smell — like a clean wet dog that had been rolling in fresh hay. She'd miss that and everything else about him, but she couldn't stay any longer. Losing Sam had been bad enough, but she could never bear seeing Beau and Lydia together as man and wife. She'd have to find a job somewhere and lose herself in work so her heart would stand a chance of mending.

"I can't, Jonny. I'm sorry. I have to take my brother home."

"I know." He stepped back into the hallway, sniffling, but did his best to wear the stern face of a grown man. "Will you write?"

"Of course I will."

"All right, then." He sniffed and wiped his nose on his sleeve. "I'll get your bags, ma'am," he said and marched bravely into the room.

Beau, Pa, and four men from town served as pallbearers and carried Samuel's casket feet first out the front door and into the waiting hearse. Isaac loaded her trunk in the coach. Jonny came down the porch steps carrying her bags. He struggled to haul their weight, but his face wore the mask of a strong young man. Beau started to help him, but stopped short. Jonny wanted to do his part to help Portia, and he wouldn't dare take that privilege from him.

Sorrow washed over Beau in dizzying waves. She was leaving them for good, and even though he'd known this day would come, he didn't want it, and he sure didn't want it to happen under these circumstances. Sam's death and the uprooted memories of Jake would remain an invisible barrier between him and Portia, like the enormous chasm in the west he had heard about.

Lydia clung to him as Portia said her farewells. Pa gave her a tin of pipe tobacco to take back to Frank. He hugged her tight and said, "I'll miss ya, my girl." Bessie couldn't stop crying and held her for a long time before letting her go. Jonny took her hand and shook it, trying hard to be a little man while his jaw trembled and tears clung to his eyelashes. She bent down to his ear, whispered something, to which he nodded, and kissed his cheek. She kissed Sallie Mae and handed her the book of Psalms she had put together for her.

"Thank you, Miss Po," Sallie Mae said. "I'll keep it forever."

Portia smiled and caressed her cheek.

Then it was his turn, but his mouth couldn't form any words, not that he could say much with Lydia there. All he could do was look at her, but he didn't want to remember her like that — dressed in black and grieving. It was his fault her brother died. He should have never saved Harry. What was done was done, and he couldn't change the past.

Her voice sounded so flat, as though all her emotion had soaked into the dry earth. "Thank you for the opportunity to teach your son. I know he'll be fine, won't he?" Beyond her veil, her eyes locked on his, seeking confirmation that he would uphold his promise.

Fighting the lump in his throat, he finally found his voice. "He'll be fine. You don't have to worry about him."

"Good," she said with a nod.

She started to turn toward the coach when he added, "I'm sorry. I never wanted…"

"I know," she said. "Farewell, Mr. Stanford."

Jonny ran to her and gave her one last hug, as did Sallie Mae. Just before she stepped into the coach, Lydia cleared her throat.

"I pray you'll have a safe journey. Please write and let us know when you've arrived." She sounded more mature and sincere than she had ever been. Beau was proud of her for once. Perhaps, as Portia said, they could eventually be happy. Perhaps they *would* survive, but he couldn't help wanting so much more than that.

"Thank you. I will." Portia offered a tired smile, and that was it.

She was gone.

Chapter Twenty-Eight

They gathered together on a blustery Sunday afternoon at Samuel's grave. Portia had him buried close to Jake and Abby. She didn't want him lying next to their daddy, the man who, beyond helping to bring them into this world, had only caused them torment. Samuel's twenty-two years had been nothing but strife. He deserved some peace.

A few neighbors and friends had joined them. Frank and Ellen stood next to Portia, grim and silent, as the preacher read from the Bible. The wind took his voice and slapped them with it.

"There is a time for everything... a time to be born and a time to die... a time to weep and a time to laugh."

When the service was over, Portia took baby Jake from Ellen and bounced him gently on her shoulder. He did indeed resemble his namesake, for which Portia was glad. She had little left to remind her of the past now that the home she and Jake and Abby had shared no longer existed. The land it had occupied was scraped clean, and the frame of a new tobacco barn had been raised in its stead. Beyond that, where her vegetable garden and the cornfield had once been, lay neat rows of tender tobacco shoots.

The builders had stopped working when the small funeral procession arrived. They stood there by the barn across the road in silence, with their hats off and heads lowered. Portia would have to thank them for their show of respect and invite them to Ellen's house for the meal she had prepared.

The preacher, undertaker, and the guests dispersed, each heading to their own conveyances. Isaac left too, having stayed overnight to attend the service with Portia. But before he got in the coach, he took her hand and squeezed it gently.

"We'll all miss ya," he said. "Are you sure you won't change your mind?"

"I'm sure. Thank you for driving me home and for all your kindness."

"You ain't never been no trouble, Po. You take care now, you hear?"

"I will, and same to you."

It was just a short walk, not even half a mile, to Frank and Ellen's house. Before they left the cemetery, she kissed the tips of her fingers, and touched Jake's then Abby's gravestones in turn. She would take flowers there tomorrow. Ellen had the prettiest gladiolas by her front porch.

"I'm so sorry, Po," Ellen said through her tears.

"Thank you. I've missed you all." Louise took her hand, and Portia smiled down at her sweet chubby face. With baby Jake in one arm and little Louise trotting alongside her down the dusty road, she remembered what it was like to have a family. The pain in her chest repeated its old refrain. *For you, it's not meant to be.*

"I know it's not easy to talk about, but where did this Mr. Franklin go?" Ellen asked. "Is the law on his tail?"

"Beau notified them, and they're on the lookout, but they suspect he's miles away by now. And that's fine by me. I don't want to ever lay eyes on Harry Franklin again, or I just might kill him myself."

"I wish you'd stay at our house instead of in town. I mean, it's nice of the hotel giving you free board because of your loss, but..."

"I love you like a sister and Frank like a brother, and I love these babies of yours, but I don't want anyone to feel the need to take care of me. I saw a pamphlet from the Freedman's Bureau at the hotel. They need teachers in Kentucky and Indiana. I'll make my way north."

What surprised her most was the confidence she felt behind those words. Despite her losses, she didn't *want* to curl up and die. She wanted to live, to test her limits and see what she could accomplish. Anywhere but there. Being *there* meant living under grief's unyielding shadow. Though it didn't last, she had tasted the light of happiness in Lebanon. She wanted more of it.

Frank grunted his disapproval. "Po, you're the stubbornest dang woman I've ever met."

She laughed a little. "Jake used to say the exact same thing."

Beau's pocket watch ticked past one-thirty as he lay sleepless on his bed. Silvery light from a crescent moon flickered through the window. He heard his door open and turned his head.

"Lydia? You shouldn't be out this late. Who drove you?"

"No one. I rode here myself. Let me comfort you." She closed the door and walked to his bedside then leaned close to his face. Her warm, mint-scented breath caressed his cheek. She wore that filmy dressing gown that showed enough of her silhouette to rouse him into temptation.

"No... not yet," he protested, but she straddled him, pressed herself against his bare chest. Her kisses left a hot trail down his neck and collarbone, and God he wanted what she offered, but he caught her wrists and gently pushed her aside until she landed beside him on the mattress. "I can't. Not like this."

"You mean not until we're married."

"Yes."

"But even then, I'm afraid your heart will always belong to someone else."

He threw the sheet off him and got out of bed. Standing by the open window, he let the night's cool breeze calm his heated body.

"Why did you ask me to marry you?" she asked with a tremble in her voice. "Was it for my dowry alone?"

"No."

"Then you must care for me in some small measure."

"I do."

"But you want *her*."

He leaned on the window sill. "Why are you here? We're getting married in less than two weeks."

"Because I love you, even if you don't feel the same yet. I think someday you might. And I don't want you to be alone, hurting like you are. Will you let me lay beside you, if nothing else?"

"I can't."

"Why not?"

He looked over his shoulder. Lydia's voluptuous body was as alluring as Venus on his bed.

"You know why," he said with a smile, tearing his eyes away from the temptation.

"What would be so wrong with that? To take comfort in me and forget your sorrows for a while?"

He rested his palms on the window sill again, letting his head fall back with his eyes closed. How easy it would be to accept her offer for tonight. No one would know but he and Lydia, and damn, it had been a really long time. The bulge in his trousers demanded relief, but...

"I'm sorry," he said, his voice ragged and strained. "If we are to be married, I want things done right between us. No more regrets and no resentment. I hope you can understand that."

He heard her slide off the bed and heard her feet softly padding across the floor. Lydia wrapped her arms around him from behind and kissed his bare shoulder blades. Her lips lingered on the scarred ridges of his wound. "I understand, and this is why I have always loved you. You're a good and honest man. No other suitor ever had the integrity you have."

"I'll see you in the morning," he said.

"Goodnight, Beau."

"Goodnight, Lydia."

After she left, he found some less desirable relief and slept for a few fitful hours.

Monday morning, Beau sat on the porch, letting his breakfast settle. He expected Lydia to arrive any minute with another team of wedding preparers. He'd have to make sure he was out of sight, get busy with... anything to keep from thinking about a future without Po in it.

He strode to the barn with the wind nudging at him, threatening to throw him off course. But with every gust, thorns of guilt pricked his conscience. Po deserved compensation. Now, not later, and not from his soon-to-be wife's dowry. She deserved to have some happiness in her life, and he had failed her miserably in that regard. There had to be something he could do for her, to show her his gratitude.

Nashville. Her brother had told her about a potential job there. Some Irishman that had founded a school for blacks. Whether or not the man was still in town, he didn't know, but surely someone would remember him and hopefully know his whereabouts. Maybe Beau could convince the man to travel to Brentwood and meet with Po. She'd make a fine teacher for any school.

He saddled up Scout and rode into town.

Beau approached the general store, where one of the town busybodies tried to intercept him on the sidewalk. "Congratulations, Mr. Stanford. We are on the guest list, I hope. I keep watching for the invitation…"

"Keep watching," he muttered and walked inside. He headed straight to the counter. The young shopkeeper was there again and offered a hopeful smile.

"Come to buy that broach, Mr. Stanford? It'll look good on Miss Clemons."

He must have finally heard the news of the engagement. "No, um…" The boy's name eluded him.

"Theodore."

"Right, Theodore. Actually I'm looking for someone."

"Who?"

"I don't know his name, just heard of him in passing — an Irishman — he was seen at the tavern."

"Hmm." Theodore looked thoughtful as he tossed the broach in the air and caught it a few times. With a sudden smile, he captured the broach in his fist and slapped it down on the counter. "Yes, now I remember! It's McKee. Reverend Joseph McKee. He's been back and forth between here and Nashville, but lucky for you, I think he's in town today. My pa said he ran into 'that Irish fella' near the post office this morning."

"Thank you." Beau fished a few coins from his pocket. He needed more rope, but this news was worth the sacrifice. "You know, I think I'll buy that necklace from you, after all."

355

This whole idea was a long shot. Even if he did find the good reverend, he might offer nothing but a long-winded prayer and a, *"Thanks, but no thanks."* The only thing he could bank on was the man's connection to colored folk. If he had founded a school for colored children, he could use a teacher like Po, and if he didn't need her there, perhaps he would know of another position she could take. And then again, this whole idea might be a waste of a morning.

But he had to try. Portia's departure cut him too deep to carry on like she never existed at all.

He searched the bank, the post office, and tavern, asking about Reverend McKee as he went. Everyone pointed him back to the place he had just left, but they didn't let him escape without mentioning the upcoming nuptials.

To which he answered only with a tip of his hat.

He was about to give up and ride toward Nashville in case the man had traveled back there already. But he tried one last place. Fakes & Taylor Shoes, where he walked in and heard a man haggling at the counter... with a thick Irish accent.

"Come now," he said to Mr. Taylor, "you say you're a man of the Presbyterian faith. As brothers in our dear Lord Jesus Christ, you should charge me a fair price for these boots. I'm a pastor, sir, of modest means."

Beau liked him already. Taylor was one tight-fisted, greedy businessman who no one dared to challenge. Beau cleared his throat. McKee and red-faced Mr. Taylor both looked his way.

"Reverend McKee?"

"Yes?" The man looked to be about Beau's age. He was stick thin and pale with dark shadows under his eyes, but enthusiasm shined through his sickly pallor.

"I'm Beau Stanford. Could I have a word with you, please?"

"I suppose." The reverend abandoned his boots on the counter and strode over to Beau on legs like stilts, offering his hand. "Joseph McKee at your service. It's a pleasure to meet you — I heard you were to be married soon."

"Did you?" Beau said with a chuckle.

"Do you need a man of God to officiate the service?"

"No." Before the reverend could look too offended, Beau added, "Could I buy you a drink at the tavern?"

"I've never been one to turn down a free drink." He waved at an unhappy Mr. Taylor as they headed out the door and said, "While I'm away, perhaps you'll reconsider the price of those boots."

At the tavern, they sat at a small table against the wall. Luckily, the place was nearly empty. While they waited for their drinks and an order of fresh cobbler, Beau took a deep breath and explained the situation — quietly of course — gossips lurked around every corner. He wasn't Catholic, but by God he needed a good confession. He told him everything about Harry, Lucy, and Tipp, the marriage contract, and Portia's untimely departure. McKee rubbed his chin as he listened, brow furrowed and seemingly concerned.

They went silent when the bartender brought their order — beer for Beau and bourbon for McKee.

"I didn't think preachers partook in such strong drink," Beau said.

Reverend McKee laughed. "I'm Irish-born, Mr. Stanford. The Holy Spirit understands our relationship with *these* spirits and blesses it, I'm sure. So long as we practice moderation, mind you."

"Of course. Now that I've confessed my sins and shared a drink with you, do you think you could offer her a position?"

The reverend spoke softly. "Yes. Mrs. McAllister's late brother, God rest his soul, was very forthcoming after a few rounds. I'm only sorry I didn't come to meet her sooner. I've had a great deal of other business to attend to as of late."

Beau slumped over his beer. "I can't speak for her to know whether she still wants the job or not, but I know once she's set her mind on something, she's going to do it to spite the devil. If she accepts the position, you couldn't find a more hard-working employee."

"She sounds like the perfect candidate, and I've no qualms about traveling to Brentwood to interview her myself. But what about you?"

"Me? I'm not worried about me. I just want her to be happy."

"Spoken like a man in love. But you see, we still have the issue of Oliver Clemons. He's got this family held hostage while you're set to become his next slave. I cannot in good conscience leave you with such a fate. So, what if I told you there might be a way out of your predicament?"

Beau sat up straight, doubt and hope warring in his veins. "I don't see how."

"Can you provide something that will turn a quick profit?"

"Even if I could, I've signed a contract. If I don't marry Lydia and hand over the deed, he won't let them go, so no amount of money I could scrounge up will change that. Besides, even if I had something to sell, there's no one around here who could pay me enough to matter."

"I wouldn't count on that, Mr. Stanford. Surely you have something of value — a horse or work of art…"

Staring down at the table top and its circular markings left from years of drink and similar confessions, Beau remembered the horse Lydia gave him. That was the best, and only, bargaining chip he had.

"Have you heard of the great Hambletonian?" he asked.

"Father of all Standardbreds, isn't he?"

"I knew you were a horse man. One of his descendants would be worth quite a bit to the right buyer, wouldn't it?"

"I would imagine so, yes."

"Then I have the goods. Can you find me a buyer?"

"In two shakes of a lamb's tail."

"And then?"

"Can you get away for a while tonight?"

"I can make it happen."

"Good," Reverend McKee said with a wink. "I'll meet you up at the end of your drive at ten o'clock. Bring the horse."

"You seem awful sure of yourself, Reverend."

"I've learned to make the right friends in the right places. Comes in handy when you have angry mobs chasing you, but that's a story for another day."

"Then… I guess it's a deal." Beau held out his hand, and they shook on it.

Quite the irony that the purebred, expensive mare Lydia had given him could be the ticket to her servants' freedom. Still, he dared not get his hopes up. Even if some miracle occurred and he could obtain twenty thousand dollars overnight, he had no guarantee Oliver would let them go. And if he did let them go, and if Beau could call off this wedding, there was no guarantee Portia would want anything to do with him again.

But he had to take the chance.

Chapter Twenty-Nine

Drizzle carried by the relentless wind pricked Beau's face like cold needles. He rode beside McKee, ponying the purebred mare along with Scout. He had no idea where they were headed, until they arrived across town at the entrance to a very familiar estate. McKee turned his horse down the drive.

"This is the Hamilton Estate," Beau said, kicking Scout to a trot to catch up.

"That it is."

They reached the house as Beau said, "*Amelie Hamilton* — my late wife's aunt."

"Small world, eh?"

"She's just an old spinster living alone with her help, and not to sound disrespectful, but the poor old girl is a bit... well... senile."

McKee just laughed as he slid out of the saddle and tied his horse to a hitching post. Beau followed, removing his hat as he climbed the steps to the big front porch. With a huge smile on his face, the reverend knocked on the door and stood there, hands behind his back, rocking on the balls of his feet. Maybe Amelie had a visitor who could help them — or Reverend McKee was out to swindle poor Amelie out of her money, if she had any left. He couldn't imagine the Hamilton fortune sitting for all those years, untouched. Oliver would have surely absorbed it into his own pockets.

And if she did have access to any of her inheritance, Beau had no desire to trick a senile old lady into signing a big fat check for a horse she didn't need and wouldn't realize she was buying. But he decided to hold his tongue for now. Hopefully the Irishman wouldn't disappoint him.

Saul finally opened the door. Standing well over six feet tall and built like an ox, the colored man intimidated everyone at first glance.

Yet he greeted them in his uncharacteristically soft voice, "Come in, please, Mr. Stanford, Reverend McKee." They stepped inside, and he added, "May I take your coats and hats?"

"Certainly," McKee answered, handing him the requested articles. Beau followed suit.

"Here to call on Miss Amelie?"

"Yes, Saul, can you tell her we're here?" McKee said, smiling at Beau.

"Yes, sir. Make yourselves comfortable."

Beau and the reverend took seats in the drawing room. The place was furnished with items from all over the world — French Monet landscapes painted in soft, soothing colors, a nude Donatello sculpture from Italy, with its private parts discreetly covered by a silk handkerchief. Even the furniture was the design of some famous foreign artisan, though Beau couldn't recall the name. Claire's dearest aunt had certainly traveled extensively in her younger years. Pity she probably couldn't remember most of it.

"I don't like this," Beau admitted. "Even if she has the money, she hasn't the mind to know the purpose for it."

"You know, people aren't always what they seem," McKee said.

It wasn't long before Amelie entered the room, holding to Saul's hefty arm. She wore a high-necked white dressing gown and a puffy nightcap over her silver hair. Beau felt even worse, knowing they woke her for a plan he doubted would benefit anyone.

She squinted at her visitors, let go of Saul, and shuffled over to Beau. Pinching his cheek, her voice was frail as she asked, "Did you bring Claire this time? She hasn't called on me in ages."

Beau gave McKee a see-what-I-mean look, but the reverend addressed Amelie. "My dearest Miss Hamilton, Mr. Stanford and I have come to call on you, just the two of us." His voice took on a serious note as he added, "All is well in heaven and earth."

What a strange thing to say. Beau figured it must have been some Irish greeting when Amelie straightened her back, gaining at least two inches in height. She twisted right and left with a crack and pop.

Much to Beau's surprise, she responded to McKee in the no-nonsense drawl of the Southern belle he once knew. "I thought you'd stopped in at this ungodly hour to ask me if you could have your wedding here or some such nonsense."

Looking at the grinning McKee, Beau answered, "No, nothing like that."

"Well, spit it out, then. A woman needs her beauty sleep, even at my age. Saul…"

She held her hand toward the very large man and wiggled her fingers. Saul pulled a cigarette from his shirt pocket and handed it to her. She stuck it between her wrinkled lips, while Saul struck a match on his thumbnail. It blazed to life, and he lit her cigarette.

"Thank you, dear," she said to him. "Now shut that door while I have a visit with these gentlemen."

"Yes, ma'am," Saul said, nodding to Beau and Reverend McKee as he disappeared on the other side of the closing double doors.

Amelie took a long draw from her cigarette, exhaled a hearty cloud of smoke, and had a seat in a high-backed brocade chair embroidered with swans. Her shrewd eyes landed on Beau as though waiting impatiently to hear his story.

He stammered, "I… um… I'm sorry, but I thought…"

"Yes, yes, you thought me a stooped over, senile old woman, standing at the precipice of death. Good. That's what I wanted you to think. If I didn't trust Joe so much, you would still see me that way." She turned to McKee. "Now, what I want to know is why you think I should blow my cover here in front of my nephew-in-law."

"He's in quite the predicament and needs to turn a quick profit," McKee said.

"Is that so? I thought you were right where you wanted to be, marrying my niece's dowry. You can't wait another few days to get your hands on it?"

"No," Beau said, still finding this whole situation unreal. "I don't want any of that. I want to buy Lucy and Tipp's freedom."

He proceeded to tell her everything about the contract, but he left Portia out of it. There was no sense bringing her up if none of this resulted in his freedom to be with her.

Amelie took another puff from her cigarette and nodded. "So, that's how they got you. Life for a life, huh? I've known you a long time, Beauregard Stanford, and I didn't think you would marry that little hussy, but then I heard the news…"

Beau had to smile at the old lady's assessment of Lydia. "Why, Amelie, that's your niece."

"I don't care who she is, if the shoe fits…" She took another long draw from her ever-shrinking cigarette and flicked the ashes into a nearby ashtray. "Look, I love my sister, but she made a real mistake marrying Oliver Clemons, and she knows it."

"So, she knows about…"

"She knows everything. They haven't shared a room in years, but he's never slept alone. She might be stupid, but she's not blind or deaf."

"I see."

"You're a good man for wanting to help them. I've been trying to for years but couldn't without implicating myself. Can't trust those northerners if you're from below the Mason-Dixon Line. And damn, Oliver's got 'em watched like hawks. One step out of his sights and they wouldn't stand a chance."

"I don't understand... how are you and McKee here connected?"

McKee smiled at her like he could be her long lost grandson. "Amelie has funded my abolitionist movement for years. Thanks to her, a great number of black Americans are enjoying their freedom today."

Beau laughed and shook his head. "All this time, Saul and the others..."

"Oh yes, just like Isaac and Bessie. They've always been free. Ever since I inherited this place, that is. Never did cotton to slavery. I hated what Daddy did to our people. Treated them like beasts of burden instead of humans. Not me. And as you can see from Saul and my other boys, if you treat people kindly and allow them the choice, they're much more likely to be loyal. So, how much you need for that pretty horse? I've got a 'buyer' in Nashville who's been funneling my money for years. He'll be *really* interested, I'm sure, though it will take a couple days to arrange it."

"Twenty thousand."

Amelie whistled. "He really put you in a bind, that old devil. The money is no issue. Lucky for you, I didn't put all my assets in Confederate coin. I'll even pay off your debt now that I know you're not an idiot."

Beau laughed. "I'm glad your opinion of me has improved, though I don't know how I'll ever repay you."

"I'm a sixty-six-year-old spinster with a roof over my head and plenty to eat. What the hell else can I spend my fortune on besides helping folks who need it?"

"Point taken, and thank you, Amelie. Now our problem lies in whether Oliver will even accept the trade."

"I wouldn't count on it. But his language is money, so you'll have a leg up there. Pity we can't wait just a few more weeks."

"Why's that?"

McKee shifted in his seat and glanced at Amelie, who gave him a nod. "We have evidence on him. Evidence that we've reported to the authorities in both Washington and Philadelphia."

"What evidence?"

"Mr. Clemons had his hand in all manner of things. Arson for one. Last February, back in Philly, a warehouse owned by Blackburn and company went up in flames like nothing the city had ever seen before. It housed hundreds of barrels of coal-oil. The fire spread all down ninth, Washington, Ellsworth, and Federal, taking with it innocent families as they slept. Dozens died. Little children were found in the streets, burned to a crisp."

"I read about that. Why in God's name would he orchestrate such a thing?"

"Mr. Blackburn won a munitions contract that Oliver wanted for Clemons Ironworks."

Closing his eyes, Beau gritted his teeth, trying to tamp down his loathing for now so he could concentrate on the matter at hand. "What else?"

"Ever hear of an actor named Booth?"

Beau shivered, instinctively touching the back of his head. "You mean as in John Wilkes?"

"The very same. We believe he helped fund that assassination. We followed the paper trail and thought we had something when Booth's diary was found. But several pages were missing. We still have enough on him to get a conviction for other crimes, not necessarily the hanging he deserves."

Amelie crushed her cigarette butt into the ashtray. "And now that a government physician has proven me mentally stable, I'll be able to stand as a witness and get that bastard put away. They could be coming to arrest him at any time. The bad thing is time isn't on *your* side."

Beau stood and paced across the thick Oriental carpet. She was right about time running out with less than two weeks until the wedding. And who knew when Oliver would be arrested. He'd played by the rules so far, kept his end of the bargain, because he didn't have any other strategy. But now he had the money to back his counterattack, and he had the knowledge that Oliver Clemons wouldn't be an issue at all for much longer.

"Then it's time to move," Beau said. "We get Lucy and Tipp away from him, and we don't take 'no' for an answer."

Still, his conscience warred with his heart. Lydia knew nothing about any of this. He'd almost resigned himself to the marriage, and she had proven to be more loving and mature than he ever thought she could be. But she deserved someone who could truly love her, who wasn't forced into marrying her, and that someone wasn't him. Once he'd dealt with Oliver, he would tell her everything and hoped she wouldn't be devastated.

Chapter Thirty

The next two days crawled by, with Lydia's wedding plans going full steam ahead during the day and insufferable dinners at Oliver's table by night. Luckily, all those plans distracted her too much for her to notice the missing horse or his preoccupied mind. Beau longed to tell Ezra and Jonny about his plans, but he couldn't risk word getting out. He 'just happened' to run into Tipp during a visit to Isaac and Bessie's house.

The two of them played a long overdue game of checkers. Lucy, of course, wasn't there. She wasn't allowed to leave the main house until Beau had handed over his freedom for hers. He hated having to tell Tipp what Lucy had lived through, but he did anyway, though he left out the possibility of their unborn child being Oliver's.

"Jesus, I shoulda killed him already," Tipp said, drawing his lips in tight. His brown fingers squeezed themselves into rock-hard fists.

"You know what would happen if you did." Down to three checkers. Beau jumped one of Tipp's ten red ones.

"Maybe so, but damn it, Beau, I ain't much of a man if I can't protect my family." Tipp slammed a fist on the table, rattling the checkerboard and pieces. His chest rose with a deep breath; his tense muscles relaxed as he exhaled. Then he caught Beau's mistake and jumped two more of his checkers in one move.

"But that's what you've done. You've protected them from seeing you hang. Now we have the opportunity to turn things around."

"She should have told me he was beatin' her again. I would have found a way for us to get out."

Beau took his last move, having to choose between two spaces that were both guarded by Tipp's red checkers. "To hell with it." He slid the checker into enemy territory. "She was worried for you and Sallie Mae, and she really wanted you to have the land Oliver promised, though I doubt he had any intention of keeping his word."

"Once we get out of here, we ain't settin' foot in Tennessee again. But you know I'm gonna miss you, Beau. We ain't had near enough time to visit."

"I know, but maybe we can visit you someday wherever you end up."

"I hope so. We'll play more checkers, too. You sure ain't got no better at it." Tipp jumped Beau's last piece and sat back in his chair with a sigh. "You don't have to do this, you know. You can use that money for yourself and marry Miss Lydia. Live happily ever after."

Beau shook his head and stacked a few random checkers. "Hanging might be the better option there."

Tipp finally managed to crack a smile. "I wasn't going to say anything, but yes, I think you're right. Now tell me how you're plannin' on getting' Lucy and Sallie Mae out."

Beau couldn't help smiling as well when he started putting their plan into words. "Well, first we'll need an Irishman and a great many bottles of whiskey..."

Beau didn't sleep a wink at night in his bed, where he kept imagining Lydia lying there wearing even less than she had on the other night. He managed a couple of cat naps in the barn, but then he dreamed of Portia and how good she felt in his arms and how sweet her lips tasted when they kissed. He was in this sleep-deprived state on day three after his visit to Amelie. He heard a rider approaching, and with hay in his hair and stubble on his chin, he sat up and blinked into the sunlight.

"Top o' the mornin' to ya, Mr. Stanford," Reverend McKee called in an Irish brogue as thick as mashed potatoes.

"And to you," Beau said, brushing hay from his pants as he rose to greet the visitor. "So...?"

"It's all here," he said with a wink, patting a leather satchel that hung at his side. "I feel like a bloody leprechaun carrying this much treasure."

He handed the bag to Beau, who tucked it under his arm.

"Tonight, then? Are you sure you can distract Oliver's minions?"

"Aye, and don't worry. I'm as gregarious as any Irishman you've ever come across."

"Actually, you're the first one I've met." Beau laughed, but his mind drifted west, to Brentwood and Portia. What was she doing right now?

"Then it's especially true." His cheery face turned serious. "You're thinkin' about the other lass, aren't you?"

Beau nodded.

"Bring her back here and marry her, then send her to me, because I could still use a good teacher or two."

Beau couldn't help but laugh that time. "If by some miracle she *would* come back, I don't think I'd let her go for anything."

"I understand. Now, I'm off to procure some libations for the night's festivities."

He rode away while Beau flipped through the pile of cash in the bag. More than he'd seen in ages. Certainly more than enough to compensate Oliver for Lucy and Tipp's departure. Yet even if tonight's plan proved a success, he still had little chance of Po coming back to him. Not after everything he had done. At least McKee had promised to offer her a teaching position when all this was over.

Jonny slept soundly in his bed. He held the handkerchief Portia had embroidered with his name. Beau touched the expert stitching and kissed his son's forehead.

Pa caught him before he could get downstairs. "Be careful, Beauregard."

Beau stood there looking at him, uncertain if he should agree or play dumb.

"Isaac told me your plans and why you were gonna marry Lydia. I'm sorry I doubted you, son."

"It's all right, Pa. I've done plenty to make you doubt me. I just hope I can make some of it right."

"You got your Colt, should any trouble arise?"

Beau nodded. It hadn't occurred to him that if everything went completely wrong, it might be the last time he saw Pa and Jonny. Or maybe he just didn't want to think about it.

Pa descended the steps until he landed on the one where Beau stood. He hugged him and whispered, "I'm proud of ya, son, and I love ya. Now go do what ya gotta do. And when it's all done, go fetch Portia and bring her back to us."

"You remember what I told you about Jake? She won't come back, not after everything I've put her through."

"You did the right thing at the time. There was no way for you to know who he was or who she was, and with everything else messing with your mind, it's no wonder you couldn't put two and two together. Don't underestimate her, Beauregard. A woman like Portia don't hold them kind of grudges. And a woman like her don't show up on your doorstep every day. Don't do what I did. Don't let fear of gettin' hurt hold ya back from lovin' again. I love you and Jonny more than anything, but that bed of mine's been a cold and lonely place for too long."

Beau took a deep breath and looked down the stairs at the front door and the unknown future that waited on the other side. "Watch over Jonny for me."

"I will, but you'll be back before mornin'." His words were layered with worry and warning.

"I'll be back," Beau said, and he hoped to God he could keep that promise.

He and Isaac took the buggy out to Paradise Plantation, thankful that Lydia and Polly were at a party in town. He didn't expect them back until at least midnight. In one of the barns close to the big house, light spilled from the open doors and windows, along with a rousing Irish jig on a fiddle. Oliver's hooligans were inside, whooping and hollering. A couple of them had linked arms and danced around in a circle, holding tin mugs with liquid that sloshed out onto the dirt floor.

Beau chuckled. McKee was good. No wonder Amelie had partnered with him.

They drove the buggy around back, parking by the kitchen door. They sat there for a couple of minutes, listening and watching carefully to make sure there were no guards lurking about. A short whistle preceded Tipp's appearance. He jogged toward Beau from the slave quarters. He wasn't allowed in the big house at night, but he'd instructed Lucy to leave the door unlocked. Beau patted the pistol in his holster and nodded to Tipp, who carefully and quietly opened the door. Lucy and Sallie Mae would be waiting on their pallets in the kitchen.

They dared not carry lanterns, so Beau had to stand still a moment for his eyes to adjust to the dim light.

"Lucy," Tipp whispered. "It's time. Let's go."

Squinting toward the cold hearth where the pallets should be, Beau could see only one lump. His doubts flared — the plan was to sneak Lucy and Sallie Mae out to the buggy where Isaac would take them to the designated ally house on the road to Nashville to await Reverend McKee. In the meantime, he would be offering Oliver that wad of cash and trying to sweet-talk him into a peaceful submission. If he refused, Tipp, Lucy, and Sallie Mae would still have enough of a head start to get away.

But something wasn't right. Tipp crept over to Sallie Mae and shook her gently until she woke and sat up, rubbing her eyes.

"Where's your mama?" he whispered.

She looked around sleepily and then shrugged.

Tipp picked her up, along with her doll and a little bag of belongings. He carried her out to the buggy, where he placed her in the back seat and kissed her forehead. Beau followed him.

"Where's Lucy?" Isaac whispered.

"I'm about to find out," Tipp said. He walked back in the house, eyes flashing with murderous anger that would get him killed if he wasn't careful.

Beau kept his hand on the Colt as they crept through the dark house. No one stirred in the great hall or any of the adjoining rooms. They sneaked up the stairs; thankfully the carpet muffled their steps and the creaking wood. They had almost reached the top when they heard a woman screaming.

"Lucy!" Tipp leaped up the final two steps and ran toward the sound.

Shit. Beau pulled his pistol and ran behind him to a door with a tiny sliver of light underneath. A woman — it had to be Lucy — screamed and yelped on the other side, along with a repeating *thwack, thwack.*

Tipp tried the knob then banged on the door. "Lucy!"

She screamed again. "No, Tipp, get out of here! Get Sallie Mae and go!"

"Lucy! I'm coming!" Tipp backed up to the wall and ran toward the door, ramming his shoulder against the thick oak slab. It shuddered but didn't budge.

"Stand back," Beau said. As soon as Tipp stepped aside, Beau lifted his leg and threw all of his body weight into a wood-splintering kick.

The door surrendered, swooshing open to a horrendous sight. Oliver, in a rage, stood over Lucy. She crouched on the floor, her arms crossed over her head in an attempt to shield herself. Oliver was shirtless. Suspender straps hung loose at his sides, flopping as he struck her again and again with a riding crop. Lucy was naked from the waist up. Bloody welts striped her back and arms.

"You don't tell me no, you useless nigger whore!" He kept beating the shit out of her and in his blind fury, didn't seem to notice the interruption.

Oliver raised the riding crop to strike again. Tipp stepped forward and caught it right on the palm of his hand with an agonizing *snap.*

He didn't even flinch.

The madness in Oliver's eyes turned to bewilderment. Tipp wrenched the riding crop from his hand and struck it across the old man's face. Oliver stumbled back. A nasty red welt made a diagonal stripe on his wrinkled cheek.

Tipp roared, "I'll kill you!" and sprang at his prey, knocking Oliver to the floor.

His fist pounded into Oliver's face once, twice, three times.

Beau holstered his pistol. He sped over to Tipp and hooked one arm around his neck. Grabbing the bedpost for leverage, his boots fought for traction on the rug-covered floor. But he might as well have been fighting a damn solid wall of muscles. Grinding his teeth, pain knifed through his wounded shoulder. Finally he managed to pull Tipp off Oliver. Beau dragged him far enough to get between them.

He spread his arms as far as he could in the hopes of keeping them separated. "Tipp, get Lucy out of here! He ain't worth it."

Oliver writhed on the floor, groaning like a dying bear. His hand covered the right side of his face. Beside him lay a couple of tobacco-stained teeth with bloody roots. Beau scanned the area around the bed and rug for more weapons but saw none.

"Tipp, you have to go," Beau said, lowering his voice to the calm, even tone he used on his most stubborn horses. "Don't be like him. You're better than this."

Blood dripped from Tipp's clenched fist. Chest heaving, his upper lip curled over his teeth. He glared down at Oliver as though he could murder him with one blow if Beau gave him the slightest chance. Finally he tore his attention from the beaten old man and focused on Lucy. Rage melted into anguish as he knelt beside her and took her face in his now-gentle hands.

Arms crossed to cover her bare chest, she whispered, "You came for me."

He nodded and wiped her tear-streaked cheeks with his thumbs. "I'll never let nobody hurt you again. Come on. I'm gettin' you and Sallie Mae out of here."

He yanked a quilt or shawl or something from nearby — Beau didn't take his eyes off Oliver to see exactly what — and threw it over Lucy. He helped her to her feet and led her out the door.

Oliver rolled to his knees, held to the footboard of his bed, and stood on shaky legs. Nose swollen and mouth dripping blood, he turned to Beau. "You'll regret this."

"No more than I've regretted ever knowing you in the first place."

Beau pulled the money bag from his coat and threw it down at Oliver's feet. Crisp new dollars flew out, scattering on the floor around them. "Here's your thirty pieces of silver. Enjoy it while you can."

"Where'd you get that?"

"None of your damn business." God, how he wanted to tell him he would likely be rotting in jail very soon, but he bit his tongue and said, "I came here tonight with more than enough money to buy their contracts, hoping we could resolve this in peace. Instead I come here to find you breaking your end of the contract over Lucy's back. We're done, Clemons. You don't own me or anyone else."

From the corner of his eye, Beau caught light glinting through Oliver's window. Coach lights. *Shit, Lydia and Polly.* He'd have to tell her tonight if he could figure out where and how.

Oliver wiped his mouth with his bare hand, smearing blood and spit across his chin. "I don't think you understand…"

"I understand plenty." Beau couldn't resist any longer. "You're a power-hungry bastard and you're gonna be brought to justice any day now. The U.S. government doesn't take kindly to those who conspired with Booth."

"Bullshit," Oliver spat, returning the dangling suspender straps to his bony shoulders.

"They also don't take kindly to arson. I recall hearing about a terrible fire at a warehouse owned by Blackburn and Company in Philly. Last February, wasn't it?"

Oliver's rage-red face turned gray.

"All those barrels of coal oil gone up in flames, incinerating everything within three or four blocks. How many children died? A dozen? Three dozen? Not counting all the men, women, and firemen and those they never found in the ashes. And all because you had a score to settle with Blackburn."

"Who told you this?"

"Doesn't matter. Enjoy your freedom while it lasts." No matter how Lydia would take the news, it felt good to watch the bastard squirm. Beau tipped his hat and turned for the door.

An all-too-familiar *click, click* spun him around.

A gun barrel pointed right at his forehead. Where Oliver had gotten it, Beau had no idea, but he had no time to go for his Colt. Oliver squeezed the trigger. In one fluid move he'd learned on the battlefield, Beau deflected Oliver's arm and locked it tight against his ribs. A shot exploded inches from his chest. He butted his body against

Oliver's and flipped him over his knee. Oliver landed on the floor with a thud. His head bounced once on floorboards, and he cried out like any wounded man would.

Except when he went silent, a shrill scream intercepted the chaos.

"Lydia! No, no, oh God no... Lydia!"

Beau turned around, heart plummeting into his stomach. Polly was hunched over her daughter, screaming her name. The two of them lay in a heap of fine skirts and crumpled packages. Polly pressed her palm to Lydia's chest. Blood soaked into her white silk glove, climbing up the fabric to her fingers, until she could hold back the tide no longer. A stream of blood flowed down Lydia's side to the floor.

"No." Beau hit his knees, slid his arm under her neck.

She blinked up at him, her pretty lips parted, gasping for air. "I... love..."

"You're gonna be fine. Just hang on. Polly, go fetch the doctor. Hurry!"

But she didn't seem to hear him at all. She lifted her laudanum-dulled face to Oliver. "You... shot... my... daughter."

Beau focused on Lydia and cradled her against his chest. He'd never wanted this, never wanted to hurt her. Spoiled yes, but her heart beat true. She was not her father's daughter. Not like him at all.

"Stay with me," he pleaded, cradling her smooth cheek in his hand.

Tears rolled from her eyes. She lifted her trembling hand to his face. "...love you."

Emotion spilled from Polly's eyes as she sat upright. All those years of pent-up heartbreak from whores both willing and forced, innocents killed in his lust for power, loneliness suppressed in bittersweet liquid addiction. She carried it all with her and crawled to her husband. He clawed himself off the floor to his knees just as she reached him.

Polly grabbed his arms and pulled herself up until they were face to face. Her blood-soaked gloves curled into fists, and she beat them into his chest. *Thud, thud, thud, thud.* "Damn you! Why? Why? You never loved us. You never loved *me*!"

Lydia's body trembled. Her hand slid down Beau's face to his chest and lingered over his heart. Blood trickled from the corner of her mouth. She tried to speak, but the words gurgled in her throat. Her eyes spoke volumes, and he understood every question in their blue depths.

"I'm sorry," he said. "I'm so sorry. Claire would be so proud of you." Though the feeling didn't come from the same place hers did, he added, "I do love you, Lydia. I always have."

She smiled. Her hand slid down his chest. Her body went limp, and she died right there in his arms.

Tears burned his eyes, but he would not release them yet. He turned to Oliver. "She's gone, because of you."

The man who had once owned so many regarded his dead daughter with the eyes of a grieving father as his wife screamed and wailed and beat on his chest. Slack-jawed, Oliver's shoulders drooped in surrender.

From downstairs came thundering footsteps. "Oliver Clemons, surrender now! We have a warrant for your arrest!"

Justice had arrived a moment too late.

Awareness sparked in the tyrant's eyes. Before the police could reach them and before Beau could stop him, Oliver swept the gun from the floor and jabbed it to his own temple. He cocked the hammer.

Men with guns emerged from the stairwell into the hall.

Oliver closed his eyes and pulled the trigger.

Chapter Thirty-One

Sun beat down on Portia's back as she tended the graves, pulling weeds, straightening the flowers in the vases and adding fresh water. She appreciated Frank's dedication to keeping the grass cut, but the finer details were left to the women. Ellen helped clean the bird droppings and dust from the gravestones. Baby Jake slept soundly while strapped to her back with a thin cotton sheet. Jimmy and Louise played tag around the shade trees. Their laughter brought a smile to Portia's face while she dug a thistle from the corner of Abby's stone.

"I know Mr. Stanford is engaged to that rich woman," Ellen said, "but you're in love with him, aren't you?"

"Why would you say such a thing?" Portia's cheeks grew sunburn hot, though she'd only been outside for a half hour.

"You wrote about him in every letter."

"What's so strange about that? He was my employer and I was living in his house."

"It's the way you wrote about him with such reverence and empathy. And you sure didn't seem to like his fiancée, either. You know you can be honest with me, Po."

Portia lowered herself to the carpet of grass, staring at Jake's name. Her voice quivered. "How could I be in love with someone else, when my husband and child are still warm in the ground? And how could I love Beau after having known him for so short a time? He's getting married in a week."

"So now it's Beau, and not Mr. Stanford?" Ellen laughed as she settled on the ground under the nearest shade tree, and out of sight of the barn builders across the road. Baby Jake had started fussing, so she took him from his wrap, unbuttoned her dress, and put him to the breast.

"That's... it doesn't matter." Portia wanted to rip handfuls of grass from the ground and throw them at Ellen, but avoided such desecration and slapped the ground instead. "And even if I was, it's not meant to be. I used the money I had left to book passage on the next stagecoach to Kentucky. I'm leaving tomorrow."

"Is that your answer to everything that doesn't go your way? Just run from it?"

"I am doing no such thing. It's not like I have a choice in the matter, and he doesn't either."

"We all have a choice," Ellen said. She held baby Jake to her shoulder and patted his back. He let out a satisfied burp. "He's in love with you, too, isn't he?"

"Arrrgh," Portia groaned, pushing herself to her feet. She walked to her mama's grave and back again. "You are so infuriating, Ellen McAllister!"

"Infuriating or not, you love that man, and he loves you. If there's any chance you can be together, you should take it."

"Well, there's no chance," Portia said, and swiped the air with her hand, hoping to cut this conversation off at the knees.

"Really?" Ellen re-buttoned her dress and returned baby Jake, now full and content, into his wrap. She pointed past Portia to somewhere down the road. "Then tell *him*."

Portia spun around and blinked into the sun. A carriage rattled down the road, drawing closer with every kicked-up cloud of dust from the Morgans hitched to it. She would have recognized those horses, that carriage, and that familiar hat anywhere.

"Beau…" she whispered. "Ellen, how did you know?"

Laughing, Ellen stood and came to her side, putting her arm around Portia's shoulders. "I didn't, but I prayed to God I was right. Besides, I've never seen you look at another man the way you looked at Jake… until now. Talk to him. Give him a chance. I'll be at the house, waiting for you."

Beau pulled the carriage up to the cemetery gate. He met Portia's gaze with one of uncertainty, while a smile hemmed and hawed on his lips.

He climbed out and took off his hat, nodding to Ellen as she passed through the gate. "Ma'am, I'm Beau Stanford. Pleasure to meet you."

"I know who you are," Ellen said, stopping only long enough to flick her pale green eyes between Beau and

Portia. "And you better make this visit worthwhile, or you'll have my husband to contend with."

Ellen marched on down the road toward her house, while Beau scratched his head, looking dumbfounded. Jimmy and Louise caught up with her, casting wary glances at the dark-haired stranger.

"That's Ellen," Portia said. "She's right about her husband. He'd make two of you."

"I hope I don't disappoint her, then." His face lit up with one of those genuine smiles that made her heart flutter.

She knelt by Jake's grave to rearrange the fresh cut gladiolas that didn't need rearranging. "What are you doing here?"

Hat held to his chest in reverence, he knelt beside her. "I have something for you."

Her back went stiff, as did her voice, and she dared not take her eyes off the flowers. "Oh? What is it?"

From the corner of her eye, she could see him removing a piece of paper from the inner pocket of his leather vest. He held it out to her, and glancing at his blank face, she took the folded square. She unfolded it and read the not-too-sloppy handwriting:

Dear Miss Po,

Thank you for teaching me. Me and Mama and Daddy are all rite now, and I can still read real good. I want to be a teacher just like you when I grow up.

Love,

Sallie Mae Jenkins

Tears burned the corners of Portia's eyes. "They're all right? Does that mean — ?"

"They're free. Should be well into Kentucky by now."

Pushing herself to her feet, Portia smoothed her black skirt and went to stand in the shade of the nearest oak. "Thank you for telling me, Mr. Stanford. I'm happy they're safe and sound."

He followed and leaned casually against the tree trunk. "I thought you would be."

She had no idea what to say next. Words tickled her tongue, but her mind couldn't sort them out. She focused on the fresh timbers of the new tobacco barn and the steady *tap, tap* as the men pieced it together with hammers and nails. He'd come all this way to tell her this, but why? He could have sent a letter. Did this mean he had already married Lydia? Or did it mean something else, something she had not let herself imagine?

"I have something else I need to tell you," he said.

So solemn were his words, that she fell against the tree trunk to stay upright. The rough bark snagged her black lace gloves and poked uncomfortably into her back. She tried to look him in the eyes, but couldn't force her gaze past his leather vest. His chest expanded and relaxed with each heavy breath.

"I hope you and Mrs. Stanford will be happy," she blurted, then spring boarded from the tree and hurried toward the gate.

Don't cry, don't let him see you cry. She captured each choking sob before it could escape and swallowed it down.

"Portia, wait." Beau caught her arm.

She tried to pull away, but he held fast.

"I can't!" Her grief came loose, rushing out with each keening word. "Just let me go. Please."

He had her by both arms now, craning his head this way and that to try to meet her eyes. Finally, he gave her a little shake, and she snapped to attention.

"I'm not married," he said. "Lydia's dead."

His hands fell away from her, and he removed his hat again, twisting the brim as he plowed through the horrific story. She tried to catch all the details of how Beau had found Oliver beating Lucy, and how Oliver had tried to kill him but shot Lydia instead. Then he said Oliver turned the gun on himself and something about a pile of money and Amelie Hamilton and an Irishman named McKee.

She squeezed her eyes shut and waved her hands to silence him. "I'm sorry. I didn't quite follow all of that, but… Lydia's dead? And Oliver?"

"Yes," he said in one heavy sigh. "Polly took both of them to be buried back in Philadelphia. I never meant anyone to get hurt, even if Oliver deserved it. But Lydia didn't. I don't know if I can ever forgive myself, but… I want you to come back to us."

Everything around them went silent, as though the earth itself waited to see what would happen next. She glanced at the barn builders — three of them, hammers frozen in mid-air. They quickly focused on their work again and pounded those nails for all they were worth.

She let her eyes find his once more. "I'm leaving by stagecoach tomorrow to find work up north."

Deep worry lines formed familiar streaks across his forehead and around his eyes. "If that's what you want, I won't keep you from it, but will you sit and talk with me awhile? I need you to know something else before you go."

She filled her lungs with wood-scented breath and nodded. He led her back to the shade tree, where they sat upon the cool, thick blanket of grass.

"I was with Jake when he died."

Not in a million years did she expect him to say that.

The world went wobbly. Thank God she had a solid tree to keep her upright. "W-What do you mean you were with Jake?"

"The night Samuel died, I saw his picture in your room, and it all came back. I couldn't bring myself to tell you then, not with Sam..." He closed his eyes and swallowed hard.

She gathered courage from the only place she could — the desire to know the truth. "It's all right. You can tell me now."

After a deep breath, that's what he did. No matter how hard she tried, this time she couldn't look away, and watched every nuance of his features as he told the story. There was no deceit in the way his eyes penetrated the past, how his trembling words picked up every detail and delivered them with regretful determination.

"It was December," he said. "Cold as hell, with freezing rain that stung our faces no matter which way we turned. My and Harry's wounds had mended enough for us to get put back to work, so we were transferred to Major General A.J. Smith's detachment and assigned to patrol the eastern border of the Cumberland River, there on the outskirts of Nashville.

"I heard a shot, followed by a soldier laughing — one of ours but not in our regiment — and he was waving his rifle in the air. He kept saying, 'I got one, I got me a

Rebel!' His buddies were slapping his back, saying they ought to drown him and finish him off.

"I think Jake must have strayed too far. Might have got blinded by the smoke or fear. I'd seen many a man turn tail to flee in the middle of a skirmish. When you're in all that noise and bloodshed, it's easy to run straight into enemy fire." Beau paused, searching her eyes as though he feared she couldn't handle any more.

She nodded for him to go on.

He looked out toward the fields as he continued. "At first I thought, *So he got him a Rebel. So what?* The damn war had taken everything from everybody. What did it matter?"

Portia closed her eyes and winced.

Beau gently touched her face. "Are you all right?"

"Yes," she whispered. "I want to know. I need to know. Please..."

He took a deep breath and let it out slowly. "Harry said we ought to put him out of his misery. I could justify killing men that were hell-bent on killing us, but not somebody who had the misfortune of getting lost. Or maybe he was deserting. Whatever the reason, he didn't deserve to be killed in cold blood.

"I went over to the boys. They were young, maybe eighteen or nineteen at most. I don't think they saw any difference in killing a Rebel or a rabbit.

"I said, 'That's enough.' I grabbed the barrel of the boy's rifle and shoved it against his chest. He got mad, started cursing, tried to pull the gun away from me.

"So I told him, 'You don't get it, do you? Someone out there's waiting for him to come home, just like someone's waiting for you. I don't care what color he's wearing. You don't kill a man just for the hell of it.'

"I made them go with Harry to fetch the medic. That's when I heard him calling, 'Po... where's Po?'

"At the time, I didn't know who or what a Po was, but I felt compelled to go to him. He lay about ten yards away, and when I reached him, I saw the wound on his belly. It was bad. I'd seen many such wounds and sat with many men from our side as they died from wounds like that, but never a Rebel. Not that it made any difference. At death's door, I figure we're all created equal.

"I said, 'What's your name? Maybe I can take a message for you.' His hand was bloody and shaking, but he reached out and grabbed my sleeve. He kept saying, 'Tell Po...'"

Portia gave herself a moment to simply breathe and to let the resurrected memory sink in. He couldn't be lying, not with those details — the bloody streaks she'd seen on Beau's jacket — Jake must have left them there.

Beau shifted, cleared his throat, and kept talking. "I searched through his jacket to see if I could find any identification. No soldier pin, no tag hanging from a string around his neck... I said, 'Can you tell me your name?'

"He just clung to my arm and looked at me with those eyes. His voice was getting weaker, but he kept saying, 'Po, I'm sorry, Po...'

"I pulled back a lapel and saw a scrap of paper pinned there. But it was covered in blood, and the only ink I saw was smudged into a blurry blot. I told him, 'I'm sorry.

Keep breathing. The medic's coming, and you can go home.'

"I could see it in his eyes. He was thinking of home. It meant a different place to each of us, but it meant the same thing no matter who you were. It meant life as it should be, with family, friends, and an honest day's work. It didn't mean we'd never see hardship, but there'd be someone there to ease the burdens, and a place to lay your head at night. Home meant peace.

"Again, I asked him for his name, but his hand went limp. I caught it before it hit the mud and held it. He was looking right at me when he died. It was that very same afternoon when I got word of Claire's death. From then until now, everything from the war has come back in bits and pieces. I dream a lot of it, like being wounded and seeing this strange angelic glow around me."

"Then how can you be sure this memory is real, that it's not just another nightmare?"

"You're right to question it. I don't know what's real and what's not half the time, but I'm sure about this."

She stared at him, unblinking, for several seconds. "I know you believe your memory is valid — I have no doubt of that — but for my own peace of mind, I need something… some little detail you can give me about him that will confirm it."

Beau propped his elbows on his knees and rubbed his upper lip. His eyes flicked along the ground as though a clue might spring up from the dirt itself. Portia couldn't help holding her breath, waiting. As agonizing as losing Jake had been, not knowing how he died still haunted her.

A dove flew from the tree above them, its *coo, coo, coo* brought Beau to attention. "I first noticed his eyes and light red hair — he had a beard to match. He wasn't wearing gray — his coat was light yellow — like a squash, I guess. When he wrapped his fingers around my sleeve..." He looked down at his arm and mimicked the gesture with his own hand. "...I saw the tip of his middle finger was missing."

She let out her breath and held tight to the locket containing her daughter's hair. "He lost it when he was Jonny's age. A stray dog bit it off. It *was* him. You were really there with Jake."

He squeezed his hands together into one white-knuckled ball. "Had I known his identity, I would have made certain he made it back here. All I know is... you were the last thing on his mind when he took his final breath. I'm sorry. If I could have stopped it... if I could have saved him, I would have. I promise you that."

She'd never felt such a tide of relief and gratitude in her life. In his last moments on this earth, Jake hadn't been alone. Beau, who should have been his enemy, had chosen to sit by him and hold his hand until the very end.

"Thank you," she whispered.

The corners of his mouth lifted in a sad smile. She took his hand — the same one he had used to comfort her dying husband. But that gesture didn't do her gratitude justice. Portia got to her knees and threw her arms around his neck.

"Thank you. Thank you, Beau." Her tears came rushing out in waves as he rose to his knees and wrapped her in his arms.

"Come back to me," he said. "Please come back home."

"Yes," she said, hugging him even tighter. "A thousand times yes."

Chapter Thirty-Two

Leaving Brentwood and her former life behind wasn't nearly so difficult this time around. Ellen didn't cry, and Frank didn't argue, but he insisted they stay for lunch. They all sat around the table in Frank and Ellen's kitchen and devoured Ellen's chicken and dumplings.

After lunch, Portia cuddled sleeping baby Jake on her shoulder. Louise climbed onto her lap, holding a book of nursery rhymes. "Can you weed to me, Aunt Po?"

"Of course." She happened to glance at Beau. His loving smile warmed her from cheeks to toes. No doubt he wanted more children, and she prayed she could make his wish come true. Louise opened the book, and Portia started reading:

"Hey diddle, diddle, the cat and the fiddle…"

Frank sat directly across from Beau and plied him with questions. "So this woman you were gonna marry is dead? How you gonna make sure Po's safe?"

"The cow jumped over the moon."

"With Oliver Clemons gone, the whole town is safer. You don't have to worry about that," Beau said, while

Ellen poured coffee for him and Frank. "Thank you, ma'am."

"The little dog laughed to see such sport..."

Frank grunted his acceptance of the first round of interrogation. He propped his elbows on the table and took a sip of coffee. "What about this horse farm of yours? You gonna be able to keep food on the table and clothes on her back?"

"And the dish ran away with the spoon."

Louise giggled and bounced on Portia's knee. "More, pwease!"

Beau chuckled then turned serious again. "Thanks to my late wife's aunt, my debts are paid, so my business has a much better chance to become what it once was. And I promise to do whatever it takes to make Po happy."

Frank stared him down. Beau shifted in his seat but never broke eye contact. As though satisfied with her future husband's sincerity, Frank then turned to Portia. "Is this what you want, Po? Do you think he'll make you happy?"

She reached across the table and took Beau's hand. "Yes. I never thought I could love again, but I was wrong. And today he told me something that made me love him even more." Looking in his eyes, she sought approval for what she was about to say next. He nodded for her to continue. "Beau was with Jake when he died."

Ellen gasped. With one hand over her mouth, she turned her astonished eyes to Frank. He didn't show any surprise, but sat very still while Beau elaborated on the details of that terrible day. By the time he finished, Beau was choked up and stared down at his lap.

Several long, tense seconds passed before Frank finally spoke. "All this time, I'd been thinkin' my little brother died alone. You might have been a no-account Yankee, but I'm grateful you were there for him. If you want to marry Po, I'll give you my blessin'."

The two men shook on it, though Beau winced from Frank's strong grip. They all drove to the hotel in Brentwood to gather Portia's things. When they were ready to depart, Ellen cried happy tears for once.

Portia hugged her tight. "I'll be all right."

"I know, and I can't wait to stand beside you at the wedding. I'm so glad you answered that ad, Po."

"So am I."

Beau helped her into the buggy and accepted another crushing handshake from Frank. Once her belongings were settled in the back, he climbed in the driver's seat.

Frank held baby Jake in one arm and wrapped the other around Ellen's shoulders. "Drive safe," Frank said. "And you better not wait too long to marry her, either."

"I won't." Hand behind his back, Beau flexed his Frank-squeezed fingers.

Portia pressed a handkerchief to her lips to hold back a laugh.

Traveling after dark was risky, especially in a small open carriage. So they spent the night at the same Nashville inn where she and Frank had stayed when she had first traveled to Lebanon. Beau rented two adjoining rooms. They shared a pleasant supper in the dining room.

"I want to court you properly," Beau said as they finished.

She reached for his hands and held them there on the table. "Do you really think that's necessary?"

"Maybe not, but I want to anyway. I want you to be sure about me."

"In that case, why yes, Mr. Stanford. I accept your offer of courtship."

A few other patrons threw disapproving glances at them, but she couldn't have cared less. The two of them weren't new at this, and conventions didn't seem so important anymore. Arm in arm, they climbed the stairs to their rooms. Before he retired to his own bed, she wrapped her arms around his neck and kissed him tenderly. His hands settled on her hips, and he returned her kiss with one just as sweet.

He pulled back slowly, breathing hard. "Would you… let me stay with you for a while?"

Portia's eyes widened. She hadn't meant to break convention *that* much.

"No, no, not like that." He rubbed the back of his neck and smiled apologetically. "I'm not good at this. I just wanted to hold you a little while, if that's all right."

He was so sweet about it, she couldn't resist. "Why don't you come in?"

He followed her inside, and she shut the door behind them.

Keeping the lamp dimly lit, they lay side by side, fully clothed except for shoes, on top of the quilt. Portia spooned up against him as close as she could get.

After a few moments, she sighed contentedly.

"What's wrong?" His warm breath caressed her neck, reminding her of everything she had missed for all those months she'd slept alone.

"Nothing at all," she answered. "In fact, I'd say it's perfect."

He held her tighter, found her hand, and interlaced his fingers with hers. "I'll stay until you fall asleep."

"Then I'll never sleep again." But the lull of a good night's slumber coaxed her into submission. It didn't matter, though, because tonight she could rest easy in the arms of the second man she'd ever loved.

Portia could not have imagined a sweeter reunion the next evening when they finally arrived. Bessie, Jonny, and Ezra ran down the drive, meeting them well before they reached the house. Soon as Beau helped Portia down, everyone immersed her in hugs, laughter, and happy tears. Even Isaac left the mule in the field where he was clearing fencerows and jogged over to welcome her home.

"Told ya she'd come back, son," Ezra said with a belly-wobbling chuckle.

Isaac took care of the horses and carriage, while the rest of them continued on foot toward the house. Jonny held Portia's hand, swinging it back and forth and talking up a storm about everything they would do together over the summer. Bessie walked with her arm in arm on the other side. Beau and Ezra fell behind them, and it all felt so natural. Portia had a real, live family again, and she planned to enjoy every moment with them.

"Oh, honey!" Bessie said as soon as they stepped through the door. "I knew you two were meant to be the moment you set foot in this house."

"Really?" Portia put a hand on her hip and grinned. "From what I remember, you couldn't stand the sight of me."

"Pshaw! I knew you were his match. I think that's one reason I didn't like you at first. It's always hard for a mama to let go of her boy."

Beau hugged her, and she wiped her eyes with her kitchen towel. "Now, Beauregard Stanford, I'm sure you'll be wantin' to set a date right quick, but you better give me time to plan a meal and make a cake."

Beau laughed and took Portia's hand. He kissed her knuckles and winked. "We'll get to that, Bessie, don't you worry. Po and I are gonna have a proper courtship first."

Ezra huffed through his mustache. "Why you gotta bother with all that? I can get the preacher out here tomorrow."

"Hush your mouth!" Bessie snapped him with her kitchen towel. "A wedding needs to be done right. Don't matter if it ain't their first one."

"However long this courtship lasts," Beau intervened, "is up to Portia. But now I better let my future wife get some sleep. We've got a busy day of courtin' ahead of us tomorrow."

Portia yelped when he scooped her off her feet and started up the stairs, carrying her in his arms. "I'm capable of walking, you know."

"You're the most capable woman I've ever met," he said, pausing the climb long enough to give her a quick kiss. "But just once, I'd like to feel useful around you."

Portia buried her face against his neck and giggled.

At breakfast the next morning, Portia had just taken her last bite of bacon when Beau hollered, "Jonny, get the fishing poles, and Bessie, pack us a picnic lunch."

"Yippee!" Jonny leapt from his chair and streaked out the door.

"For heaven's sake, Beau, let her finish breakfast first," Bessie fussed.

"If I'm gonna court this fine lady, there's no time like the present," he said. "Ready, Po?"

She wiped her mouth. "Ready as I'll ever be."

The rest of the day was better than a sweet dream, and she dared not pinch herself just in case she *did* wake up. She, Beau, and Jonny went fishing. They didn't catch a thing, but it was well worth the attempt when Beau slipped on a mossy rock and fell on his backside with a splash. They gave up and had a picnic under their favorite tall cedar by the creek. Portia challenged them both to a rock skipping contest, and she was the decided winner, much to the boys' pretend consternation.

Later, they lay sprawled on their backs in the cool comfort of a cedar glade, watching the clouds drift by and trying to guess their shapes.

"It's a horse," Beau said.

Portia sat up and picked a nearby dandelion that had gone to seed. "That's what you've said the last five times. Jonny?"

Jonny chewed his bottom lip. "Hmm… yep, it's a horse."

'Father and son shared a belly laugh.

"Oh, you men!" She blew the seeds across Beau's face.

He swatted them away, still laughing. Then he reached up, grabbed her, and pulled her down on top of him. She picked a stray dandelion seed out of his hair and basked in the light of his happy hazel eyes. She'd tied her hair back into a single, long braid that lay coiled on his chest. Beau ran his fingers down the length of it, then cupped the back of her head and brought her lips to his for a gentle kiss.

"Eww," Jonny exclaimed.

Portia blushed and rolled off his father; she'd been so caught up in the moment, she'd forgotten all propriety. But Jonny's face showed more joy than disgust. His happiness made this day all the sweeter.

"I've missed my riding instructor," she said and gently flicked his freckled nose. "How about another lesson?"

"Sure!"

They saddled up and set out on the trail. Jonny rode one of the geldings, and she rode the four-legged snail that had been designated as hers. After a mile or so of waiting for her to catch up, Beau offered to let her ride with him on Scout. She didn't argue one bit. They left Snail to graze where he had stalled over a patch of clover.

Beau wrapped one arm around her waist as they kept a leisurely pace under some of the tallest cedars of Lebanon.

They arrived at the top of a hill at sunset. The view was amazing. Below them lay the town, surrounded by rolling hills, with fields laid out in a multi-colored patchwork bordered with trees and fencerows. The setting sun painted a gorgeous backdrop of red, orange, and gold. Jonny rode a short distance away, leaving them with a little privacy.

Beau whispered, "I love you."

Turning toward him in the saddle, Portia circled her arm around his neck. "I love you, too, Mr. Stanford." She met his smiling lips and soared into one of the best kisses of her life.

Resting in the warmth of his arms, she watched a flock of starlings fly over the town. "You know what?"

"What?"

"I think we've courted long enough."

He chuckled and kissed the top of her ear. "Then let's get married."

"I thought you'd never ask."

"I got you something," he said. "It's not a ring, but I think you'll like it. Hold your hair out of the way."

She lifted her braid and pulled it to one side. He retrieved something from his vest pocket, and placed it around her neck. She let her hair fall and looked at her gift. It was the cameo she'd found him admiring that fateful day in the store and the moment she'd realized she was falling in love with him.

"It's beautiful. Thank you, Beau."

He sealed the promise of their future together with another deliciously wonderful kiss. *Who needs an engagement ring when the man you love kisses you like this?*

403

Though it wasn't exactly a surprise, when they shared the news of their official engagement over supper, Jonny, Ezra, and Bessie were over the moon. Talk swirled around the table about cake and a barbeque and when and if they might have a honeymoon. Jonny even asked when there would be a new baby.

Red-cheeked Portia and an amused Beau looked at him, and he shrugged. "What? I've always wanted a brother or sister."

They laughed, and with a discreet move under the table, Beau patted Portia's stomach. "We'll see what we can do about that."

The happy couple ended their perfect day at the door to Portia's room. They leaned against the wall in the hallway, hands locked together between them.

"I was thinking," Beau said with a mischievous grin, "there's no need for a long engagement."

"My thoughts exactly," she agreed, bringing their joined hands to her lips so she could kiss his rugged knuckles. "We've both done this before, so why wait?'

"Let's give it a couple days, so Bessie can make a cake and all that. She'll have my hide if we elope tonight."

"Then let's not give her reason to. I rather like your hide the way it is." Portia released one hand and ran her fingers through his hair. He closed his eyes and sighed as though she'd taken all his cares away in that one simple touch.

"Do you want me to stay tonight?" He captured her hand between his calloused ones. He lifted his hungry eyes to meet hers, throwing her heart into a crazy rhythm.

She drew in a shaky breath. "Yes… but if you do, I'm afraid Ezra will have to fetch the preacher right now."

Beau rested his forehead against hers, breathing hard. "Don't tempt me. Pa's already asleep, but I bet he wouldn't mind me waking him up for that."

He kissed her before she could say anything else. His fingers pressed into her back as though they longed to explore what lay beneath. Portia's fingers hooked into his shirt collar, flirting with the hot skin and course hair on his chest. Before they lost all control, she gripped his shirt and gently pushed him away, holding him at arm's length.

She almost laughed at Beau's pouting face. "Just a couple nights, that's all. The time apart will make it all the better on our wedding night."

He growled but stole a quick kiss then took two steps back. "I'll hold you to that. Goodnight, Po. Love you."

"I love you, too."

She entered her room and closed the door. The taste of Beau's lips still lingered on hers, and she savored it while resting her back against the cool wood. Her things were back in their proper places, at least until she and Beau could share a bed. She walked to the dresser and picked up Jake's picture. Holding it to her chest, she thanked God for second chances.

Settling into bed after extinguishing the lamp, she wiggled into the comfort of her feather mattress with a contented sigh. For the first time in a long time, she hadn't felt the crushing weight of loss. Instead, hope had reignited, allowing her to clearly see a future full of possibilities, with a home and husband... maybe even more children.

Smiling, she drifted into dreams of babies and Jonny graduating from the university and sitting with Beau on the front porch while they watched their grandchildren play. Sometime in the wee hours of the morning, she woke to the sound of her door creaking open.

She sat up and squinted into the darkness, laughing softly. "Beau, can't you wait just a couple of nights?"

Her eyes caught a silvery flash and a man-shaped shadow. A second later, she was knocked flat to her bed and pinned down under a crushing weight. She tried to scream, but a large hand clapped over her mouth, and all she could utter were muffled shrieks. Something sharp pinched her neck. Her eyes adjusted enough in the darkness to identify exactly who her killer would be.

"Sorry to disappoint you, darlin'." Harry Franklin's breath reeked of whiskey and brought with it every childhood memory she had tried to suppress. "But I ain't Beau, and I ain't waitin' for you no more."

Chapter Thirty-Three

Paralyzed with fear, Portia whimpered as Harry lifted his body off her just enough to loosen his belt. He jerked the covers from between them. A rush of cool air jolted her into action. She thrashed her head to one side and let loose the loudest scream she could. But it was brief. Harry's hand smashed down on her mouth, cramming her lips against her teeth. The knife slipped along her skin, leaving a searing hot pain and rendering her silent once more. Did Beau hear her? Did anyone? Or was she meant to die like this — at the hand of the man who killed her brother?

"Shut up!" He yanked her gown up to her hips and started to wriggle out of his pants. "I gave you the chance to be with me proper-like. But no. All you wanted was Beau. You know what? He can have you for all I care, but I'm gonna have you first."

He hooked his fingers into her drawers and ripped them from her body, wedging himself between her legs. She screamed beneath his hand again, the muffled sound mixing with her sobs as hot tears streamed from her eyes.

Oddly enough, she worried less about her own life than she did about Beau — if he woke to find her raped and murdered, he might lose his mind. And Jonny would be without him…

Someone crashed through her door. "Get off her!"

Everything happened in a nightmarish blur of movement. Beau grabbed Harry by the shirt collar and threw him to the floor. Circling around, he positioned himself between Portia and her attacker, crouched and ready. Harry sprang and slashed out with his knife. Beau caught his wrist and rammed him backward into the wall. A picture of Ezra and Beau's mother fell from its hook. Glass shattered onto Harry as he bashed his head into Beau's. Beau stumbled, and Harry tackled, knocking him to the floor.

Wild-eyed Harry strained over Beau, neck tendons bulging. He tried desperately to sink a knife into Beau's chest. Beau clenched Harry's arm with both hands. His arms quaked. The knife inched closer.

Portia had to act now — she would not let Beau die by Harry's hand. Her eyes locked on the bottom dresser drawer.

Frank's pistol.

She flew off the bed and dove for the dresser. Yanking it open, she fumbled inside for the gun, found cool metal, and closed her hand around the grip. She swept it out. On her knees, she turned to face the chaos. Her thumb cocked the hammer, her finger hugged the trigger. Harry broke loose from Beau's grip, recoiled his arm, and brought the knife down in a sudden strike.

In a split second, Frank's terse instruction bolted through her mind: "*Point, aim, fire — don't think, just hold it steady, line up the sights, and pull the trigger.*"

And that's what she did.

The gunshot reverberated through Portia's body. Her ears rang like she was standing inside a clanging church bell. The knife fell from Harry's hand and clattered silently to the floor. Blood bloomed across his shirt.

He lifted his head and looked at Portia. A million unspoken questions swam in his eyes. He toppled off Beau and hit the floor.

Beau flipped to his hands and knees and crawled to Portia. Blood wept from a nasty red gash on his bare chest. "Po — look at me! Are you all right?"

His voice shoved past the ringing in her ears. She tore her sight from the first man she'd ever shot and met Beau's frantic eyes. Trembling, she set the gun down and let him gather her in his arms. From the corner of her eye, she spotted Ezra and Jonny in the doorway.

Jonny didn't need to see this. She waved at them to get back. "No, get out of here. Go!"

But Jonny's attention was focused solely on the window. He pointed and screamed, "Pa — the barn!"

Yellow light flickered across the ceiling. Panic ignited in Beau's veins. Steeling himself for what he was about to see, he scrambled to his feet and peered through the glass. Down the hill, flames engulfed the stable roof. He scooped up Portia's pistol, took off down the hall, and snatched the rifle from his room. He thundered down the stairs with Pa, Jonny, and Portia right behind him.

Gesturing for everyone to stay back, he flung open the door. His stomach churned at the sight of flames licking the night sky. Rifle ready in his left hand and pistol in his right, he flattened himself against the wall and sniffed the air. The house, for now, seemed to be unscathed. Leading with his rifle, he peeked outside to see if Harry acted alone or brought reinforcements. No one else was in sight.

Turning to Po, he cupped her cheek with one hand. "Stay here with Jonny."

She shook her head, crying frantically. "No, Beau, please!"

"For now, you're still my employee, and I'm not asking." He pressed the pistol grip into her hand and closed her fingers around it. "Keep our boy safe. If you have to, run out the back and to Bessie and Isaac's house. Understand?"

Tears still streaming, she nodded reluctantly. It was all he could do to not take her in his arms and tell her it would be all right. But he couldn't spare anymore time. He pulled Portia and Jonny into a quick embrace and raced out the door with Pa. They had to save the horses if they could.

The old man could still run when he needed to and was only a step or two behind Beau when they reached the stable. The fire hadn't engulfed the whole structure yet. It was contained to the roof and left side of the building.

"I'll get Scout, you get Crazy Girl," Beau said.

Pa shrugged out of his night shirt and ripped it down the middle. He tossed one half to Beau. Both men dropped their rifles just inside the door. Pa headed straight for Crazy Girl's stall, while Beau went for Scout. The horses whinnied in terror.

Scout reared. When he landed on all four hooves again, Beau caught his bridle. Flames reflected in his terrified brown eyes. He pulled Scout's head to his, shushing and rubbing his neck before quickly wrapping the piece of Pa's nightshirt around his eyes. Infernal heat curled Beau's eyelashes and scalded his bare skin. A burning timber tumbled into the adjoining stall as Beau led Scout outside. Pa had already gotten Crazy Girl out. She remained surprisingly calm as he unwrapped her head and shooed her into the paddock.

"Come on, boy," Beau encouraged, trying to pull the stubborn stallion through the paddock gate. He'd never acted like this before.

"Walk on now, Scout, walk on," Pa hollered, holding the gate open wide.

Scout tugged against his master, neighing and huffing, locking up his rear legs. This wasn't like him. Under the sweat and ash, hairs prickled on the back of Beau's neck. He ripped the cover off Scout's eyes, but before he could let go of the bridle, the horse jerked his head to one side and reared back. Beau pitched forward.

A gunshot split the smoke-filled air. A bullet whistled by Beau's head. He hit the dirt, bit his lip, and tasted blood. He didn't have time to marvel over how Scout had saved him. The horse galloped down the drive toward the main road, but other hoof beats came from the wagon path behind the house. Riders were gaining on them fast. Harry hadn't been alone, after all.

Lying flat on the ground, Beau waved at Pa, hoping beyond hope that he hadn't been hit. "Get down!" Spotting the rifles they'd left in the barn, he belly crawled to the doorway and grabbed them both. He looked over his shoulder. Pa had followed him from behind the paddock fence, crouching as low as his knees would allow. *Thank God.*

"Give it here, Beauregard." Pa reached through the fence slats.

Beau handed him the rifle butt first. "Take cover."

Beau wanted to run straight to Portia and Jonny, but he knew better. War had schooled him in more than just pain and agony. Running across open ground for the house would make him easy pickings for any shooter. It could also draw unneeded attention to his son and soon-to-be wife, particularly if his conspirators assumed Harry would handle that end of things. Beau clenched his fists. He'd come too close to losing her already. He had to keep a clear head.

I promised Frank I'd keep her safe. I'm a man of my word. He had to trust Portia, had to believe she would survive — she knew how to shoot and would keep both herself and Jonny alive.

He dove behind two rain barrels that sat at the corner of the stable and paddock fence. Pa hunkered down between the fence and the corner of the stable. Everything they'd worked for was burning down behind them. The horses and mules they couldn't save whinnied and screamed, still trapped inside. It strangled his very soul, knowing they were helpless to escape. But he had to deal with the intruders first, or he could lose much more than his horses.

Rifle held ready, Beau peered around a barrel and counted one... two... three riders veering away from them and headed across the front side of the house. Two of them had covered faces, but one hadn't bothered to hide. Beau recognized him right away — Randal. The authorities had arrested him and the others the night of Oliver's suicide, but they didn't have enough evidence to charge them with any crimes. They had bellowed and bawled so much when they were hauled to jail, Beau didn't think they'd cause any more trouble. Not with their lifeline, Oliver, severed for good.

By God he wouldn't make the same mistake of underestimating Randal twice. He took aim, zeroing in on that stringy, greasy hair. His finger hugged the trigger. Until he saw something that sent a river of ice down his spine.

Chapter Thirty-Four

"Stay down!" **Portia** whispered to Jonny. She tried to keep the fear from her voice but did a terrible job of it. The poor boy wept pitifully, tucked under her arm like a frightened chick.

With the pistol barrel, she pulled back the curtain and peered outside, pressing herself against the wall like Beau had done. Light and various shapes moved around but were hard to make out.

At first.

Squinting past the distorted glass into the night, she recognized men on horseback carrying torches. Bandanas covered their faces from the nose down. Dark hoods hid them from the eyes up. They rode toward the giant oak tree in front of the house. Something bounced along the ground behind one of the riders.

"Oh, God, no."

That something was a man.

"What's happening, Po?" Jonny cried. "Is Pa all right?"

"I don't know." Was it Beau, Ezra, Isaac? Fear coiled itself around her insides and squeezed. She wanted to vomit.

Windows shattered in the study. Portia screamed. A torch landed on Jonny's desk. Flames ignited the curtains, climbing up the fabric faster than she thought possible. Either those intruders were trying to flush them out or were simply bent on destroying everything Beau owned. The fire reached the ceiling, crawling across the plaster. Burning pieces of it landed on Shakespeare's bust and her desk, catching fire to her stationery. Smoke clogged the air.

The intense heat melted into her reasoning. They had to get out and quick, but which way? Sweat glued her nightgown to her skin and dripped into her eyes. Jonny's panicked wailing didn't help either.

Portia grabbed his shoulders and gave him a solid shake. He quieted down long enough for her to say, "Jonny, I need you to stay calm. You're the man of this house right now, so we have to work together. Understand?"

Lip still quivering, he nodded and took her hand. She couldn't rush out the front door with everything happening out there, but they had to flee from the fire. *Beau said run out back to Bessie and Isaac's house.* She dragged Jonny along through the kitchen and to the back door. Nothing was burning in there, but it wouldn't take long for the fire to reach it. She took a final glance at her beloved water pump, reached for the door, but hesitated.

Another one of Frank's brisk lessons surfaced in her memory. *Expect the unexpected.* Holding the pistol ready, finger on the trigger, she pushed Jonny behind her and took a deep breath. Then she yanked the door open.

Someone stood there on the other side. Not Beau or Ezra. A large man, face covered, his huge hand reaching toward her. Not thinking twice, she stuck the gun in his face and fired. He toppled backwards and hit the ground with a thud.

Two bullets down. Four to go. Keeping the gun ready, she scanned the backyard and saw nothing moving. She pulled Jonny's hand, but he wouldn't move. He stood frozen, staring at the dead man with huge, frightened eyes.

"It's all right," she said. "Come on. We have to get you to Bessie and Isaac's house."

"What about you, Po?"

Smoke plumed from the barrel of her gun. She had enough bullets to take down the rest of the intruders if she was lucky. "I have to help your pa and grandpa."

"No! I want to go with you. Don't leave me, please!"

"Come on!"

Still transfixed on the dead man, he let her drag him away. Heading toward the wagon road that led to Bessie and Isaac's house, her lungs ached. Fear wedged itself in her throat. She gasped for air. She'd never been to war, knew nothing of strategy. What if she was doing this all wrong? What if she got everyone killed? First Harry, then that man she'd shot in the face. Was it necessary? She could have aimed to wound, not kill.

Oh God, what have I done?

A sudden scream shook her from her doubts. Someone ran along the wagon path. Portia kept her gun pointed and finger hovering over the trigger. She would shoot only if she must, but then she recognized the voice and the anguished cry.

"Isaac!"

Bessie flew past, nightclothes fisted in both hands. The wind caught her nightcap and stole it from her head. She paid no heed to it or to Portia. Her legs pumped as hard and fast as they could. But it was the pure horror in Bessie's voice that threw an icy lasso around Portia's heart.

"Isaac!"

He must have been the man bouncing along the ground behind the horse. They aimed to lynch him. Harry had gone mad from jealousy and drugs and had taken his revenge. Bessie and Isaac's house was no longer an option. Changing course, Portia led Jonny to the side of the house. She spotted the root cellar. No matter what, she had to keep Jonny safe. She led him to the cellar, flung open the door, and pushed him inside.

She gripped his shoulder and bent to look him in the eye. "Listen to me. I want you to hide. Get behind those crates and don't make a sound. Don't come out no matter what you hear, understand?"

Tears drenched his cheeks. "I can help."

"You can help by doing what I say." Pulling him to her in a tight hug, she fought back tears of her own. "I love you, Jonny. Stay here."

Soon as she shut the cellar door, Portia sprang into action. She ran after Bessie, trying to wave her down without yelling and giving away her position. But Bessie had already crossed in front of her, heading into the fray. Portia opened her mouth to scream when a shot exploded into the night. Bessie spun a half turn and fell limply to the ground.

No… Portia skidded to a stop.

She hadn't made it around the house just yet and thought she must be out of sight from the intruders. So she dropped to her hands and knees to close the distance between her and Bessie. She peeked toward the front yard as she cleared the house. The men had a rope around Isaac's neck, and they'd slung the other end around a thick limb in the oak. Another man sheltered behind the wide trunk, firing his rifle toward the burning horse barn. More shots answered, perhaps from Beau and Ezra?

Portia itched to put a bullet in one of the attackers, but she had to get to Bessie first.

They weren't looking her way, so she crawled the remaining few feet to where Bessie lay crumpled on her side. She wasn't moving…

She rolled Bessie to her back. The older woman groaned. Teeth bared, her mouth gaped open in a silent scream. She'd been shot in the shoulder. Warm, sticky blood soaked the top half of her nightgown and coated Portia's palm.

"I'll get you out of here." She wiped the blood from her hand the best she could on her own nightgown and tried to take Bessie's uninjured arm so she could drag her to safety.

"No. Help my Isaac," she begged, swatting at Portia.

Another gunshot. The man with the rifle crumpled to the ground. *Thank God.* Beau or Ezra, hopefully both of them, was still alive.

Isaac already hung off the ground, hands tied behind his back, spinning in mid-air and kicking his legs. He managed to nail one of the men right in the teeth. With a flurry of cursing and blood-spitting, they finally hoisted him over their heads. The intruders' torchlight and the light from the burning house danced across Isaac's face. Clearly in agony, but still alive. The one Isaac kicked held the loose end of the rope, while his companion skirted around the tree to take the fallen man's place. She finally recognized him as that disgusting man who had leered at her when she was in town with Harry. *What was his name? Randal?*

Another gunshot shook the night, with a returning one from the barn.

Portia's jaw clenched tight. She wasn't about to let them take her family without a fight. Squatting as low to the ground as she could, she tried to lock one hand around Bessie's wrist to drag her toward the house.

"No... Isaac," she groaned, pulling back against Portia's attempt.

"We'll help him," Portia said, straining against Bessie's weight and her resistance. "Stop fighting me."

She dug in her heels and pulled for all she was worth. Bessie cried out in pain, but Portia managed to drag her around to the side of the house and out of view.

Four bullets left. Portia had to make them count. She inched to the corner of the house and behind a pink rosebush, its blooms muted to a dull grey there in the shadows. Thorns scratched her arms as she angled her torso just enough to see around the house and aimed the pistol over the top of the foliage.

419

She fired. The rope slid from the limb, Isaac's body hit the ground, and the man who had almost hanged him fell to the dirt. Dead, she hoped.

Three bullets left.

The man with the rifle aimed his gun right at her. She ducked behind the house as the bullet hit the siding. Wood splinters flew; Portia squinted as they struck her face.

Another shot tore through the rosebush. Leaves and petals went flying. Back flattened against the siding, Portia gulped air into her lungs. She tasted rose blossoms mixed with smoke and gunmetal.

Is Beau dead? Is Ezra? Dear God, don't let them find Jonny.

Portia dared a peek around the corner. The rifleman was gone. Isaac was still tied and struggling to free himself on the ground beneath the oak tree. She had to untie him and find Beau and Ezra. She launched herself off the wall and broke into a run.

But an arm clothes-lined her from behind, trapping her in a choking headlock. She dropped her gun. "Well, now lookie here. Harry's been wantin' a piece of you for a long time. He must not have got his wish. Maybe I will, huh?" He squeezed her breast. "You'd like that, wouldn't you?"

The smell of Randal's greasy hair and his violating touch made her cough and gag. She clawed at his arm. "Let me go!"

"Not until I get a little smooch."

His wet lips and tongue slobbered on her cheek. He held a pistol in the hand he had captured her with. She tried to grab it, but he tightened his other arm around her waist and wrenched his gun arm away. He jabbed the barrel beneath her chin.

"Oh I got me a feisty one," he said.

Someone ran up the hill from the horse barn.

"Beau!" Portia screamed.

He glanced at Bessie where she lay nearby and stopped running. "Let her go, Randal!"

"Why? She feels so good. No wonder you want to ride this little filly."

Slowly, Beau inched toward them, his rifle held solid and level against his shoulder. His finger hovered over the trigger. His eyes projected more rage than she'd ever seen before. But Portia felt his fear. He must have wanted so badly to kill Randal, but he was probably afraid he'd shoot her instead.

"You best not shoot, nigger lover," Randal growled. "Might hurt your little sweetie here. Thought you had it all, didn't ya? Always thought you was better than the rest of us, better than Harry, too. He got tired of your shit like we all did. I reckon we're even now. You gonna put that gun down and let me ride off like nothin' happened or your bitch here's gonna die."

From the corner of Portia's eye, she caught a quick movement from Bessie. Portia turned her head away just in time. A shower of dirt hit Randal's eyes. Though she trembled and groaned with the pain, the satisfied light in Bessie's eyes was priceless.

"Argh… shit!" He released Portia and tried to slap away the blinding dirt.

Beau leapt forward, catching Portia's arm as she reached for him. He pulled her behind him and aimed his rifle. But Randal, blinking through muddy tears, shot first. Beau cried out and wobbled backward.

"No!" Portia steadied him. The bullet had struck his arm. Blood poured down his sleeve.

Randal regained his focus and pointed his gun straight at Beau's head. "I'm gonna enjoy this."

Suddenly, he arched his back and let out a horrendous howl. Beau and Portia ducked as the gun fired. He missed.

But Harry didn't.

Randal toppled face first on the ground. The handle of a knife bobbed around where Harry had plunged the blade into Randal's back. Then it went still. Randal was dead.

Clutching his chest, Harry fell to his knees. Beau rushed to his side, and with one hand behind Harry's neck, helped him lie down on the ground. Portia kneeled beside them.

"I'm sorry, Beau," Harry whispered as he locked eyes with Portia. His breath came in shallow gasps. The skin on his face and arms was red and blistered, seared from the fire he must have crawled through to reach them.

"I know." Beau took Harry's hand and held it tight. "You saved my life."

"I owed you that." A weak smile lifted the corners of his mouth. "I couldn't... let my brother... die."

"Harry..." The pain on Beau's face broke Portia's heart. She wept for these brothers who had lived through hell together, though one of them had never recovered.

Harry's head fell to one side. His bright eyes dulled as he breathed his last breath.

Jonny ran out of the darkness and straight toward his father. "Pa!"

Beau caught him in his arms and held him close, crying softly.

Ezra had cut the ropes from Isaac, and the two hurried toward them. Isaac recoiled like he'd been shot himself when he saw Bessie on the ground and broke into a stumbling run to get to his wife.

"You're all right?" Bessie reached for him. He bent down and gently picked her up in his arms.

"I'm fine," he said. "Better than fine. I still got *you.*" He kissed her tenderly.

Isaac carried her away from the house. The rest of them followed. They stood on the wagon path, watching their home and horse barn go down in flames.

As if God felt their loss, the sky opened up with a merciful downpour of rain. It wouldn't be enough to save the house, though there might be a few things left to salvage. Portia held her family close, knowing things could have been so much worse.

They still had each other, and that's all that mattered.

Chapter Thirty-Five

Three months later...

Besides the wind, the weather could not have been nicer for an August wedding at sunset. Holding Ezra's arm, Portia walked down the grassy aisle between the two sides of the small congregation, feeling so blessed by all the people who had come to their aid after the attack. Amelie sat on the front row, no longer hiding behind her senile guise. She had paid their debts and shared her home for them to reside in until theirs was rebuilt. Mrs. Peabody donated the most beautiful wedding gown Portia had ever seen — fine white linen with a v-shaped neckline and loose, lacy sleeves. The train and bodice were adorned with purple silk taffeta ribbons and embroidered white lace. From the look on Beau's face, she might have been an angel fallen from heaven. Anxious joy warmed her cheeks.

Instead of a church wedding, they chose to be married on their own land, in front of the newly-built horse barn. Beau's wounded arm needed time to heal, so with donated lumber and labor, nearly every able-bodied man in town pitched in to help with the construction. They even let Scout and Crazy Girl take shelter in their stables.

The house still wasn't much more than a bare foundation, but they'd managed to recover a few treasures — Jake's picture, Beau's chest, and Portia's beloved water pump. They had buried Harry in the Stanford family cemetery. He might not have been blood kin, but he was still Beau's brother, mistakes and all.

Now they stood before their family and friends and Reverend Joseph McKee. He brushed his overdue-for-a-haircut locks from his eyes and angled his body to face the strong breeze. He cleared his throat and smiled across the yard at the small congregation.

"Dearly beloved, we are gathered here…"

The rooster crowed obnoxiously from atop his roost on the horse barn. A sudden gust shoved him from the timbers in a flurry of feathers and crazed wings. Beau laughed when the silly bird hit the dirt and ran, flapping and squawking in humiliation.

"If he wasn't our only rooster, I'd have fried him up for the reception," Bessie proclaimed.

Portia giggled and winked at her. Poor Bessie had lost a lot of blood, but by God's grace, had survived. Since the main house wasn't finished yet, Mrs. Peabody and a few of the other ladies from town volunteered their services to prepare the meal. After much protesting, Bessie finally gave in. So a big dinner awaited everyone, laid out on a few long tables in the new barn's wide alleyway.

Portia squeezed Ezra's arm, and he gave her one of his curled-up mustache smiles. He wore a nice suit, but at her request, his pipe hung in its place from his mouth, lending cherry-scented familiarity to the day. Ezra Stanford was by far the best daddy she could have ever asked for.

Reverend McKee cleared his throat again, loudly. "We are gathered here for the uniting of two like souls. Who gives this woman to this man?"

"I do," said Ezra, with unmistakable pride in his lifted chin and puffed chest.

Portia handed her bouquet of lilacs and wildflowers to the maid of honor. Ellen took them in one hand and wiped tears with the other. Then she sneezed.

"Bless you," said McKee. "Now, join hands."

They didn't waste time with that part, though Beau's arm still rested in a sling. It had healed well, but his grip wasn't quite what it used to be. Portia didn't mind. His hands still felt so wonderfully warm and strong, and she could easily imagine how they would feel on her bare skin...

"Um..." Jonny spoke up from his place in the front row. "Baby Jake is wet and he smells."

He'd practically begged to hold the baby during the service, which tickled Portia near to death. She looked up at Beau's smiling face, and from the intensity of his gray eyes, she knew he was thinking the exact same thing. She couldn't wait to try for another addition to their family.

Just a few hours. A few lonnnng hours... focus!

"I'll change him," Frank grumbled. He engulfed the baby in his great big hands and carried him to their wagon.

"For the love of our dear Lord in Heaven," McKee said, waving his Bible in the air, then pointed it at Beau. "Beauregard Stanford, do you?"

"Yes, I do," Beau answered, grinning from ear to ear.

"And Portia McAllister, do you?"

"Of course I do," she said.

"Good! Then kiss the lass already and be done with it."

Beau lifted her veil and smiled. "You heard the good reverend, Po."

He kissed her like nobody was watching, and no one had a cross word to say about it. Instead, they cheered.

At the reception, Beau and Portia sat together at the head of the table. Bessie proudly presented the white-frosted wedding cake. She wiped tears from her eyes and laughed as they fed each other. Beau kissed a dollop of icing from Portia's lips.

Reverend McKee sat across from them. Frank sat beside him, dwarfing the Irishman.

"Mrs. Stanford, I hear your brother-in-law lent his Samson's strength to the barn raising," McKee said, pointing his fork toward Frank, who responded with a rare chuckle. "Pity you didn't relocate to Nashville. I could have used a fine teacher like you."

Portia snuggled against Beau's arm. "With all due respect, Reverend, this is our home, and we'd be remiss to leave it behind. Besides, Amelie has offered to fund a new school here. I'll begin teaching in September."

McKee peered down the table at the many guests. He leaned in close and spoke softly, "I must say, I'm not surprised to see this town pull together in your time of need. They've finally remembered God's call to love our neighbors, now that the war is over and Clemons has no power over them. How's your boy dealing with everything?"

"He took it hard at first, but he's a strong young man. He'll be just fine." Beau smiled toward the stable door, where Jonny and the other children caught fireflies.

Isaac and Bessie's sons and their families had come back to stay. Their children played right along Jonny, Jimmy, and little Louise. They were a mix of black and white, but they shared the same innocence as they chased one another, laughing and squealing in delight.

McKee nodded, holding Beau's gaze for a while before digging into his own cake.

"Have you heard from Mrs. Clemons?" McKee asked.

"We received a letter just a few days ago. She handed their property over to the government in exchange for Oliver's crimes. She's grieving, but I'm glad she's back in Philly with her son and grandchild. Hopefully, she can live out the rest of her days in peace."

Portia finished her second piece of cake and wiped her mouth. "What about you, Reverend? Why don't you stay in town for a while longer?"

"No, Mrs. Stanford, God's called me to do his work in Nashville, and the battle is not yet won until every child, no matter their color, has access to proper education. I won't surrender until this body of mine breathes its last breath."

"Thank you for everything," Beau said.

"My pleasure. Now, go and be happy."

Epilogue

Beau strode from the porch to check on the new foal for the fifteenth time. Ezra stopped him at the barn door. "Son, you're gonna make Crazy Girl a nervous wreck, lookin' in on her so much. You've gotta calm down. Bessie would have told us if something's gone wrong."

"But it's been…" Beau pulled out his pocket watch and stared blankly at the Roman numerals. "…a long time. I think I'm gonna be sick."

He leaned on the paddock fence, forehead resting on the top slat, trying to coax his stomach into keeping his breakfast down. Scout snorted and nudged him, blowing warm horsey air across his neck.

Beau raised his head and rubbed Scout's velvety nose. "Thanks, boy. I wish I could be a calm papa like you."

The yearling Crazy Girl had birthed last summer frolicked with the purebred mare Lydia had given him. Amelie had arranged to have her returned. Her first foal had brought them enough money to repay Amelie. Now, she showed signs of her second breeding.

Beau gazed in wonder at the well-paid field hands in the distance, plowing neat rows for tobacco and cotton. He smelled the fresh paint on the house and fences. He listened to the horses running through the tender spring grass in their pasture. Finally, his farm was thriving like it had been before the war.

Jonny rode by on the back of his new Appaloosa. He'd paid for it himself, giving riding lessons to the local children. Quite the young entrepreneur. Though only thirteen, he already matched Beau in height and had become a handsome young man. It wasn't any wonder that most of his students were young ladies.

"Any word, Pa?" Jonny rode up to the fence.

"No, not—"

He jumped when Bessie yelled from the porch, "Beau, Ezra, y'all come here! Come here quick!"

"Oh God, please dear God... let them be all right." Breathless, Beau ran hard as he could to the house, barreled past Bessie, and flew up the stairs.

He met the doctor just outside their bedroom door. "Are they...?"

Dr. Barton chuckled and patted his shoulder. "Just fine. You've got a beautiful little girl."

"Hallelujah!" Beau threw his arms around the doctor and gave him a bear hug. "Thank you, Doc. Jonny! Where's Jonny?"

"Here, Pa," he answered, laughing as he reached the top of the stairs. "I can't believe I have a little sister!"

"I know. Now, see if you can wake your brother from his nap without making him too cranky and bring him here to meet her."

"Yes, sir." Jonny ran down the hall to the nursery.

Ezra climbed the stairs and met Beau on the landing. Though out of breath, the old man smiled from ear to ear. He loved being a grandpa, and Beau thanked God his pa was still around to see the little ones and enjoy them.

Bessie had a tray of tea and cookies ready, so Beau opened the door and let her in. Then he hurried to the bed, where Portia held their new baby girl. Sweat dampened Portia's hair, but she smiled, looking down at the baby with the heart-rending sort of love only a mother can have for her child.

"She's beautiful." Beau settled himself gently on the bed and kissed Portia tenderly. He stroked the baby's feather-soft cheek. She wiggled and cooed and wound him completely around her little finger.

"Yes, she is."

Portia handed their daughter to him. He took her gently and laid her on his lap, in awe of her tiny, perfect features. Jonny walked in, carrying two-year old Sam, who yawned and rubbed his eyes. Ezra chuckled and wiped a tear from his cheek.

"Look, Samuel," Beau said. "You and Jonny have a little sister."

Jonny knelt by the bed so Sam could see her better. Sam pursed his lips and narrowed his eyes, leaning in close, as though he wasn't quite sure what this funny-looking, pink, wrinkled thing was doing on his daddy's lap.

431

Then his face relaxed, and he looked at Beau with a dimpled smile. "What my sisser's name?"

Portia took his chubby hand in hers and touched the tarnished locket on her necklace. "I think we'll call her… Faith."

Beau looked at his beautiful wife, their two sons, and their new daughter, thankful beyond words for their blessings. There in the quiet magic of their room, he and Portia had created miracles. No more running, no more hiding from their troubles. However long God allowed them to be together, they would do more than survive.

They would live.

THE END

If you enjoyed *A Time for Everything*, I would appreciate it if you'd help others enjoy it too!

Recommend it! Please help other readers find this book by recommending it to family, friends, readers' groups, libraries, and discussion boards.

Review it! The best way to support an author is to leave a review. Please take a minute to review *A Time for Everything!*

Other Books by this Author

Beach Pointe Romantic Comedy Series
Mann Cakes
Jesse's List
All Jacked Up

City Meets Country Contemporary Series
Drive Me Crazy
High on You
Sealed With a Kiss
Ace in the Hole

Lover's Landing Novella Series
Too Close to Call by Mysti Parker
At The Next Table by Leanne Davis
Sweet on Love by Christina Butrum
The Long Route by Kiersten Modglin
The Marriage Sham by Marika Ray
Playing For Keeps by Marie Savage

He Said, She Said by Savannah Sloan
Fifty-Fifty by Kelsie Rae

The Tallenmere Fantasy Romance Series
A Ranger's Tale
Serenya's Song
Hearts in Exile
No Place Like Home

Historical
A Time for Everything

The Magic Massage Erotic Series
Sophie & the Cowboy
Sophie & the Socialite
Sophie & the Professor

Contemporary Novella
Chances Are

The Roche Hotel Romantic Comedy Series
The Roche Hotel: Season One
The Roche Hotel: Season Two
The Roche Hotel: Season Three

Connect with the author
Email: mystiparkerbooks@gmail.com
Twitter: @MystiParker
Facebook:
https://www.facebook.com/RomanceforEveryReader/
Website: http://www.mystiparker.com

Sign up for my mailing list: You get a FREE book just by signing up! https://landing.mailerlite.com/webforms/landing/k1j5q6

Follow me on Amazon: You'll be notified every time I release a new book! https://www.amazon.com/Mysti-Parker/e/B0055LOTX8

Join Mysti's Marvelous Mavens on Facebook: You'll find exclusive excerpts, giveaways and more! https://www.facebook.com/groups/675192926016765/

Bonus: Historical Facts

Any historical novel requires a great deal of research. When I set out to discover the facts behind the fiction of this story, I found several interesting events and personalities. These added a living, breathing feel to Beau and Portia's fictional struggles. Let me share some of those with you now to provide a deeper insight into their journey.

The Civil War cost countless American lives, not only on the battlefields, but also on the home front. Thousands of young low-income women, especially those in the South such as Portia, were widowed, left alone to care for children and tend crops. If they weren't on the brink of starvation, they could just as easily become victims of raids, crossfire, or disease. Portia's daughter Abigail, like so many children of the time, succumbed to typhoid fever. The infant mortality rate in those days was already high, but diseases spread by entrenched armies only added to the death toll. Even though death was as common as rain, losing husbands and children still hurt these women to the core. Only by sheer strength of will did they carry on. Many diaries exist today, written by the women who survived such horrors. One of them, *A Woman's Civil War* by Cornelia Peake McDonald, chronicled the life of a Confederate widow who lost a husband and a little daughter as the fighting raged on. Her story inspired Portia's character.

Without a doubt, the horrors of war that Beau and Harry survived fueled the conflict of their story. The Battle of Allatoona Pass, where they were both wounded, while not a major fight, is considered to be one of the bloodiest in the Civil War. According to the Georgia State Parks website, "*Of the 5,301 men engaged in the battle (2,025 Union & 3, 276 Confederates), 1,603 were reported killed, wounded or missing. This 30% casualty rate was one of the highest in the war for the time engaged.*" (http://gastateparks.org) It was the start of John Bell Hood's disastrous Nashville Campaign, ending with the even bloodier Battles of Franklin and Nashville, where Beau's and Jake's stories intersected.

Though it didn't lie in the main path of destruction, even the Stanfords' quiet hometown didn't remain unscathed. The city of Lebanon, like so many small towns in the South, became a battleground when a Union Calvary surprised Confederate Gen. John Hunt Morgan at the Odd Fellows Hall. Luckily for Morgan, he escaped in the nick of time and went on to lead "Morgan's Raid," an over 1000-mile trek through Tennessee, Kentucky, Indiana and ending in Ohio, the farthest north that any uniformed Confederate troops ever invaded (*Harper Encyclopedia of Military Biography,* Castle Books, 1992, 1st Ed).

Thankfully, that ambush didn't leave a lasting mark. But as pretty as Lebanon was (and is), some very ugly truths remained. Slavery, of course, though abolished by the time our story began, was an atrocity that wouldn't soon be forgotten. Real life accounts such as *The Narrative of Frederick Douglas, An American Slave* provide insight into the abuse and neglect those in bondage experienced day in and day out, as we saw in Tipp and Lucy's story. One rather funny account, a letter from former slave Jourdan Anderson to his old master, inspired Oliver's dinner-table rant about the runaway slave who demanded wages for time served (DaytonHistoryBooks.com). The last line of Anderson's letter sums up the sarcasm and wit his former master deserved: *"Say howdy to George Carter, and thank him for taking the pistol from you when you were shooting at me."*

The end of the war didn't mark the end of the African American struggle. While not held in bondage, former slaves were far from sharing the freedoms of white Americans. They were often forced into indentured servitude, like Lucy and Tipp were, as I discovered in an article entitled "Not Free Yet" on PBS.org. Former masters often threatened their former slaves with violence or prison time, going so far as to have them convicted of "crimes" so they would have to work in order to keep from being locked up or paying huge fines. Sometimes they took advantage of their former slaves' illiteracy, promising fair wages and land if they would simply sign their X on the dotted line. In the tumultuous, war-torn South, one couldn't blame these freed men and women for agreeing to remain under contract in exchange for what they hoped was a better situation. Striking out on their own could be deadly in a society that hated and resented them. But once bound by contract, they soon realized they were no better off than before.

Former slaves weren't the only ones who had to rebuild their lives around tremendous obstacles after the war. Veterans like Beau and Harry came home to dead loved ones and plundered properties. If they were lucky enough to not have lost a limb, they could still work, but the South's economy had bottomed out. Keeping the land they once called home sometimes wasn't possible. Wounded men were also more likely to come home addicted to morphine. Some historians argue about the numbers of addicts created by the war, (The Straight Dope.com) but considering how army doctors at the time used opiates to treat everything from wounds to diarrhea, it's probable that a great many soldiers became dependent on morphine. Opiates were also widely used in civilian life. Many high-bred ladies kept a bottle of laudanum in their medicine cabinets to combat menstrual cramps, headaches, and even to achieve the pale complexions that were fashionable in the day, as we can see in Polly's example.

Our story didn't rely solely on characters with addictions and wounds. A few straight-laced, actual historical figures made special appearances to guide our characters along and balance things out a bit. One in particular was an Irish minister named Joseph McGee. His story intrigued me enough to make him instrumental in helping Beau with Lucy and Tipp's escape to freedom. This young, determined man survived bouts of illness, a swordfight (which he won), homelessness, and angry mobs to start a mission for fugitive slaves in Nashville in 1863 and later founded a school for freed slaves. He died a young man of 36, disappointed that his efforts were overshadowed with better-funded schools such as Fisk University. But it was McKee's efforts that helped pave the way for freed slaves in middle Tennessee to receive the education they so rightly deserved. His inclusion as a fundamental character in this story is partly a way to honor his forgotten contributions.

From historical to fantasy, from super sweet to scandalously spicy, Mysti Parker has

Romance for Every Reader's Taste

Made in the USA
San Bernardino, CA
20 April 2020